THE VOICE OF TERROR . . .

"We want you to join us." He moved forward, next to me. "You're free now. You've cut off your ties to their world. You're part of [our] world now. You thought you had to play by [ ] [ ] do what you want." His sharp [ ] "When I saw you that firs[ ] [ ] one of us."

"You don't even know me.[ ]

"I know you. I know everything about you."

It was true. He was right. And as I stood there and looked at him and that strange feeling settled inside me, I knew that the feeling was good.

"Are you in?"

"I'm in," I replied.

He pumped his fist in the air. "Yes. You're a victor now, not a victim. You won't regret this."

PRAISE FOR BENTLEY LITTLE

University

"Bentley Little keeps the high-tension jolts coming. By the time I finished, my nerves were pretty well fried, and I have a pretty high shock level. *University* is unlike anything else in popular horror fiction."—Stephen King

Dominion

"Delivers shock after shock."
—*Science Fiction Chronicle*

FEAR IS ONLY THE BEGINNING

Bentley Little

THE IGNORED

A SIGNET BOOK

SIGNET
Published by the Penguin Group
Penguin Books USA Inc., 375 Hudson Street,
New York, New York 10014, U.S.A.
Penguin Books Ltd, 27 Wrights Lane,
London W8 5TZ, England
Penguin Books Australia Ltd, Ringwood,
Victoria, Australia
Penguin Books Canada Ltd, 10 Alcorn Avenue,
Toronto, Ontario, Canada M4V 3B2
Penguin Books (N.Z.) Ltd, 182–190 Wairau Road,
Auckland 10, New Zealand

Penguin Books Ltd, Registered Offices:
Harmondsworth, Middlesex, England

First Published by Signet, an imprint of Dutton Signet,
a division of Penguin Books USA Inc.

First Printing, June, 1997
10 9 8 7 6 5 4 3 2

Thanks, as always, to my friends and family.

Special thanks to the employees of the City of Costa Mesa with whom I worked from 1987 to 1995: both the friendly intelligent competent professionals I liked, and the small-minded backbiting bureaucratic assholes I hated.

PART ONE

Ordinary Man

ONE

On the day I got the job, we celebrated.

I'd been out of school for nearly four months, and I'd almost given up hope of ever finding employment. I'd graduated from UC Brea in December with a BA in American Studies—not the world's most practical major—and I'd been looking for a job ever since. I'd been told more than once by my professors and my advisor that American Studies was ideal for someone attempting to start a career, that the "interdisciplinary course work" would make me more desirable to prospective employers and more valuable in today's job market than someone with more narrow, specialized knowledge.

That was bullshit.

I'm sure the professors at UC Brea didn't intentionally try to sabotage my life. I'm sure they really did think that a degree in American Studies was as valuable to people in the outside world as it was to them. But the end result of my misdirected education was that no one wanted to hire me. On *Donahue* and *Oprah,* representatives from major corporations said in panel discussions that they were looking for well-rounded individuals, not just business majors but liberal arts majors. But the PR they fed to the public through the media and what really went on were two different things. Business majors were being hired right and left—and I was still working part-time at Sears, selling men's clothing.

It was my own fault, really. I'd never known what I

wanted to do with my life or how I wanted to earn my living. After finishing my General Ed requirements, I'd drifted into American Studies because the department's courses that semester had sounded interesting and fit easily into my work schedule at Sears. I gave no thought whatsoever to my career, to my future, to what I wanted to do after I graduated. I had no goals, no plans; I just sort of took things as they came, and before I knew it, I was out.

Maybe some of that came across in my job interviews. Maybe that's why I hadn't been hired yet.

It certainly didn't show up on my résumé, which was professionally typeset and, if I do say so myself, damned impressive.

I'd seen the notice for this job opening at the Buena Park Public Library. There was a big binder that contained flyers and notices for all sorts of government agencies, public institutions, and private corporations, and I'd been checking it out each Monday, after notices for the coming week were added. The jobs listed at the library seemed to be of a higher quality than those in the want ads of the *Register* or the *Los Angeles Times,* and anything was better than the so-called Career Center at UC Brea.

This position, listed under the heading "Business and Corporations," was for some sort of technical writer, and the requirements looked promisingly nonspecific. No previous experience was necessary, and the only hard-and-fast rule seemed to be that all applicants have a bachelor's degree in Business, Computer Science, English, or Liberal Arts.

American Studies was nearly Liberal Arts, so I wrote down the name of the company and the address, and after driving back to the apartment and leaving a note for Jane on the refrigerator, I drove out to Irvine.

The corporation was a huge faceless building in a block of huge faceless buildings. I walked through the massive lobby and, following the directions of a security guard at the front desk, to the elevator that led to the personnel department. There I was given a form, a clipboard, and a pen, and I sat down in a comfortably padded office chair to fill out my application. I had already decided in my own mind that I would not get this job, but I dutifully filled out the entire application and turned it in.

A week later, I received a notice in the mail informing me that I had been scheduled for an interview on the coming Wednesday at one-thirty.

I didn't want to go, and I told Jane I didn't want to go, but Wednesday morning found me calling in sick to Sears and ironing my one white shirt on a towel on the kitchen table.

I arrived for the interview a half hour early, and after filling out another form, I was given a printed description of the position and led by a personnel assistant down a hall to the conference room where interviews were being conducted. "There's one applicant ahead of you," the assistant told me, nodding toward a closed door. "Have a seat, and they'll be with you shortly."

I waited on a small plastic chair outside the door. I had been advised by the people at the Career Center to always plan ahead what I was going to say in a job interview, to think of all the questions that I might be asked and come up with a prepared answer for each, but hard as I tried, I could think of nothing that might be asked of me. I leaned back, close to the door, and listened carefully, trying to hear what was being asked of my rival inside the room so I could learn from his mistakes. But the door was soundproof and kept in all noise.

So much for planning my answers.

I looked around the hallway. It was nice. Wide, spacious, with lots of light. The tan carpet was clean, the white walls recently painted. A pleasant working environment. A young, well-dressed woman carrying a sheaf of papers in her hand emerged from a doorway down the hall, passing by me without a glance.

I was nervous, and I could feel sweat trickling in

twin rivulets from under my arms down the sides of my body. Thank God I'd worn a suit with a jacket. I glanced down at the paper in my hand. The description of the job's educational requirements was clear—I didn't have to worry about that—but the actual responsibilities of the position were vague, couched in indecipherable bureaucratese, and I realized that I did not really know anything about the job for which I was applying.

The door opened, and a handsome, business-suited man several years my senior strode out. He had a professional demeanor, his hair was short and neatly trimmed, and he carried in his hand a leather portfolio. This was who I was competing against? I suddenly felt ill-prepared, shabby in my appearance and amateurish in my attitude, and I knew with unarguable certainty that I was not going to get the job.

"Mr. Jones?"

I looked up as my name was called.

An older Asian woman was holding the door open. "Would you step in, please?"

I stood, nodded, and followed her into the conference room. She motioned toward three men seated at a long table in the front of the room, and promptly sat down on a chair next to the door.

I walked forward. The men looked forbidding. All three were wearing nearly identical gray suits, and none of them were smiling. The one on the right was the oldest, a heavyset gray-haired man with a severely lined face and thick black-framed glasses, but it was the youngest man, in the center, who appeared to be in charge of the proceedings. He had a pen in his hand, and on the table before him was a stack of applications identical to the one I had submitted. The short man on the left seemed to take no notice of my entrance and was staring disinterestedly out the window of the room.

The middle man stood, smiled, and offered me his hand, which I shook. "Bob?" he said.

I nodded.

"Glad to meet you, I'm Tom Rogers." He motioned for me to sit in the lone chair in front of the table and sat down himself.

I felt a little better. Despite the formality of his attire, Rogers had about him a distinctly informal air, a casually relaxed way of speaking and moving that immediately put me at ease. He was also not that much older than me, and I figured that might be a point in my favor.

Rogers glanced down for a moment at my application and nodded to himself. He smiled up at me. "You certainly look good here. Oh, I almost forgot, this is Joe Kearns from Personnel." He nodded toward the small man staring out the window. "And this is Ted Banks, head of Documentation Standards." The older man nodded brusquely.

Rogers picked up another sheet of paper. Through its translucent back, I could see lines of type. Questions, I assumed.

"Have you written any computer documentation before?" Rogers asked.

I shook my head. "No." I thought it was best to be blunt and to the point. Maybe I'd get extra credit for honesty.

"Are you familiar with SQL and D-Base?"

The questions went on from there, not straying far from those technical lines. I knew right away that I would not get the job—I had never even *heard* most of the computer terms that were being bandied about—but I stuck it out to the end, bravely trying to play up my broad educational background and strong writing skills. Rogers stood, shook my hand, smiled, and said they'd let me know. The other two men, who had remained silent throughout the interview, said nothing. I thanked them for their time, made an effort to nod to each, and left.

My car died on the way home.

It was a bad end to a bad day, and I can't say that I was surprised. It seemed somehow appropriate. So many things had gone so wrong for so long that what would have once sent me into paroxysms of panic now did not even phase me. I just felt tired. I got out of the car and, with the door open and one hand on the steering wheel, pushed it to the side of the street, out of traffic. The car was a piece of crap, had been a piece of crap since the day I'd bought it from a now defunct used-car lot, and part of me was tempted to leave it where it was and walk off. But, as always, what I wanted to do and what I actually did were two different things.

I locked the car and walked across the store to a 7-Eleven to call AAA.

It wouldn't have been so bad, I suppose, if I hadn't been so far away from home, but my car had died in Tustin, a good twenty miles from Brea, and the belligerant Neanderthal who was sent out by AAA to tow my car said that he was authorized to bring my car to any mechanic within a five-mile radius but that anything beyond that would cost me $2.50 a mile.

I didn't have any money, but I had even less patience, and I told him to take my car to the Sears in Brea. I'd charge the tow, charge the auto work, and hitch a ride home from someone.

I got home at the same time as Jane. I gave her a thumbnail sketch of my day, let her know I wasn't in the mood to talk, and spent the rest of the evening lying on the couch silently watching TV.

They called late Friday afternoon.

Jane answered the phone, then called me over. "It's the job!" she whispered.

I took the receiver from her. "Hello?"

"Bob? This is Joe Kearns from Automated Interface. I have some good news for you."

"I got the job?"

"You got the job."

I remembered Tom Rogers, but I didn't know which of my nonspeaking interviewers was Joe Kearns. It didn't matter, though. I'd gotten the job.

"Can you come in Monday?"

"Sure," I said.

"I'll see you then, then. Come on up to Personnel and we'll get the formalities straightened out."

"What time?"

"Eight o'clock."

"Should I wear a suit?"

"White shirt and tie will be fine."

I felt like dancing, like jumping, like screaming into the phone. But I just said, "Thank you, Mr. Kearns."

"We'll see you Monday."

Jane was staring at me expectantly. I hung up the phone, looked at her, and grinned. "I got it," I said.

We celebrated by going to McDonald's. It had been a long time since we'd gone out at all, and even a trip like this seemed a luxury. I pulled into the parking lot and looked over at Jane. I made my voice sound as British and snobbish as I could, given my complete lack of any dramatic talent: "The drive-thru, madam?"

She caught on and looked at me with a superior and slightly disapproving tilt of her head. "Certainly not," she sniffed. "We will dine indoors, in the dining room, like civilized human beings."

We both laughed.

As we walked into McDonald's, I felt good. The air outside was cool, but inside, the restaurant was warm and cozy and smelled deliciously of french fries. We decided to splurge—cholesterol be damned—and we each ordered Big Macs, large fries, large Cokes, and apple pies. We sat on plastic seats in a four-person booth next to a life-sized statue of Ronald McDonald. There was a family in one of the adjoining booths—a mom and dad taking their uniformed young son for a post-Pop Warner treat—and watching them eat over Jane's shoulder made me feel comfortably relaxed.

Jane picked up her Coke and held it out to me, over the middle of the table, motioning for me to do the same. I did, and she tapped her wax paper cup against mine.

She grinned. "Cheers," she said.

TWO

Automated Interface, Inc.

The name of the corporation said nothing and said everything. It was the same sort of nondescriptive doublespeak adopted as a moniker by thousands of other modern businesses, and it indicated to me that the company I was going to work for produced products of no real importance, of no real value, and that although the firm no doubt made a lot of money, it would probably make no difference to the world if it dropped off the face of the planet tomorrow.

It was exactly the sort of place I never thought I'd work, and it depressed me to realize that this was the only place that would have me.

Truth be told, I had never really thought about what sort of job I would eventually hold. I had never planned that far ahead. But I realized now that I was not the sort of person I'd thought I was—or wanted to be. I'd always seen myself as intellectual, imaginative, creative. Artistic, I suppose, although I'd never done anything even remotely artistic in my life. But now that I looked at it, my perception of myself seemed to be based more upon my empathy with literary and cinematic characters than on any qualities I actually possessed.

I pulled into the parking lot, passing an entire row of reserved spaces before finally squeezing my extra-wide Buick into an extra-narrow space between a red Triumph and a white Volvo. I got out of the car, straightened my tie, and for the first time examined the building where I'd be working. It had seemed faceless to me before and still did now. The facade was cement and glass, modern-looking, though not modern enough to grant it a distinctive identity. Despite it's utter lack of character, something about it appealed to me. I thought it looked friendly, almost welcoming, and for the first time since waking up that morning, I felt a small hope flare within me. Maybe this job wouldn't be so bad after all.

Other cars were pulling into the parking lot, power-tied men and power-suited women getting out of their expensively trendy cars and, briefcases swinging, walking briskly into the building.

I followed the flow.

During my initial interview, I had taken notice of only the personnel office and the conference room in which the interview had been conducted. Now I looked carefully around the building's lobby. Here the impression of sterile newness fostered by the building's exterior faded somewhat. I could see a worn path on the burgundy carpet, a layer of dust on the plastic palms and ficuses that flanked the door. Even the high rounded desk in front of the security guard exhibited chips and scuffs on its wood finish.

The other men and women walking through the lobby strode purposefully past the guard, nodding at him on their way to the elevator. I wasn't sure if I should do the same or if I had to check in, so I walked up to the desk.

"Excuse me," I said.

The guard looked at me and through me, not seeming to notice my presence. He nodded to an overweight man with thick horn-rimmed glasses. "Jerry."

"Excuse me," I said again, louder this time.

The guard's eyes focused on my face. "Yes?"

"I'm a new employee. I just got hired, and I'm not sure where I should—"

He motioned toward the elevator with his head. "Take the elevator to Personnel. Third floor."

It was exactly what he had told me last time, when I'd come for the interview, and I was about to say something to that effect, jokingly, but he had already dismissed me in his mind, again looking past me to the other employees entering the lobby.

I thanked him, though he wasn't listening, and walked back to the elevator.

Two women were already waiting for the elevator, one in her early thirties, one in her mid-forties. They were discussing the younger one's lack of sexual interest in her husband. "It's not that I don't love him," the woman said. "But I just don't seem to be able to come with him anymore. I pretend I do—I don't want to hurt his feelings and give him some kind of confidence problem—but I just don't feel it. I usually wait until he's asleep and then do it myself."

"These things go in cycles," the older woman told her. "Your interest'll be back. Don't worry."

"What am I supposed to do until then? Have an affair?"

"Just close your eyes and pretend he's someone else." The woman paused. "Someone bigger."

They both laughed.

I was standing right next to the younger woman, but I was close to both of them, and I could not believe that two strangers were talking like this in front of me. I felt embarrassed, and I kept my eyes on the descending lighted numbers above the elevator door.

A few seconds later, the door opened and the three of us walked in. The younger woman pushed the button for the fifth floor; I pushed the button for the third.

The older woman started talking about her husband's impotence.

I was grateful when the elevator door opened on the third floor, and I quickly stepped out.

There were five people behind the counter in Personnel: two middle-aged men seated at computer terminals; an elderly woman standing in front of a desk, taking a sack lunch out of her purse; another elderly woman sitting at another desk, and a pretty brunette girl about my age standing next to the counter itself.

I looked for Mr. Kearns, and although I didn't remember which interviewer he was, there was no one behind the counter who looked even vaguely familiar. I walked across the floor, stepped in front of the girl. "Hello," I said. "My name's Bob Jones. I—"

She smiled at me. "We've been waiting for you, Mr. Jones."

I'm late, I thought. It's my first day, and I'm late.

But the girl continued to smile, and I realized as she handed me a manila envelope that it was not even eight o'clock yet. How could I be late? They'd probably been waiting for me because I was the only new employee they had today.

· I opened the envelope. Inside was a paperback-sized booklet titled *All Employee Handbook,* several pamphlets, a pen, and a sheaf of forms that I was apparently supposed to fill out.

"There are a few formalities we have to get out of the way before you go upstairs and meet Mr. Banks. You have to fill out a W-4 form, medical, dental, and life insurance applications, a drug-free oath, and additional information for our personnel file that did not appear on your application." The girl walked through a small gate and stepped out from behind the counter. "We also have what we call our Initiation Program for new hires. It's not an official presentation or anything, but there's a video that runs about a half hour and an accompanying survey. You'll find the survey form in the packet I gave you."

I stared at her blankly, and she laughed lightly. "I know that's an awful lot to absorb at once, but don't worry. Right now, we'll just go down to the conference room, and you can relax and watch the video. Afterward, I'll go through all the forms and everything with you. By the way, my name's Lisa." She smiled at me, then caught the eye of one of the elderly women behind the counter and pointed down the hall. The other woman nodded back.

She led me down the same hallway in which I'd sat while waiting for my interview, and I glanced at the closed door to the interview room as we passed by. I still did not understand why I'd been hired. From the questions I'd been asked, I'd gathered that they were looking for someone knowledgeable about, or at least somewhat familiar with, computers. But I had no computer experience at all. Not only did I not know anything about them, I had no interest in knowing anything about them.

Was this all a huge mistake?

We continued down the hall and stopped in front of a closed door. Lisa pushed open the door, and we walked inside. "Have a seat," she said.

The room was empty save for a long conference table, its attendant chairs and a combination television/VCR on a moveable metal stand near the table's head. I pulled out a chair and sat down while Lisa turned on the TV and VCR. She made a show of it, exaggeratedly bending over, obviously aware of the way she filled out her stretch pants, and I could see the outline of her underwear against the material. "Okay," she said. "Take your pen and survey form out of the packet. You're going to need them at the end of the video." She straightened. "I'll be back down the hall at the counter. Just come and get me when you're done, and I'll help you fill out the necessary forms. You can leave the videotape on, but turn off the TV when you leave the room. Do you know how to turn it off?"

"I'll figure it out."

"It's this button here." She pressed a red square at the lower left corner of the console. The television flicked off. She pressed the square again, and the TV snapped back to life. "I'll see you in about half an hour." She pressed a button on the VCR, then walked around the table. She touched my shoulder as she passed by, patted it, and then she was out the door, closing it behind her.

I leaned back in my chair to watch the show, but I could tell after the first few minutes that I was not going to like it. The video was state-of-the-art industrial PR, but though it had the clean look and sophisticated techniques of a modern production, the narration and determinedly cheerful background music reminded me of those leftover educational films from the early 1960s that they'd shown at my grammar school. That depressed me. Nostalgia always depressed me, and I suppose that was why I never liked to think about the past. It wasn't because it reminded me of what once was, but because it reminded me of what could have been. My past had not been that great, but my future was supposed to have been so.

My future was not supposed to be spent watching PR videos at Automated Interface, Inc.

I didn't want to think about it. I refused to let myself think about it. I tried to tune out the sound track and concentrate on the images, but that didn't work, and I found myself getting out of my chair, walking over to the window, and staring down at the parking lot until the video was over. I returned to the table as sound faded to silence and realized that I hadn't paid attention to the survey question instructions at the end of the video, but I looked down at the form and it was pretty self-explanatory. I answered the questions on my own before turning off the TV and VCR, grabbing my packet, and walking back down the hall.

It took another twenty minutes to fill out the additional forms and answer the questions put to me by Lisa. Although I was required to fill out two pages of personal information for my health insurance, she told me that I had my choice of three plans and that the information would be forwarded to the insurance company of my choosing.

"If you have any other problems or questions, over anything at all, you can come to me." She smiled, and there seemed to be more than friendliness in that smile. It had been a while since I'd been available or looking, and maybe I was misreading the signs, but it occurred to me that she was genuinely interested. I thought of the light pat on the shoulder in the conference room, thought of the way she'd bent over in front of the TV. She handed me the insurance brochures, and for the briefest of seconds, our fingers touched. I felt cool skin, lingering a beat too long.

She was definitely flirting.

I noticed for the first time that she was not wearing a bra, that I could see the outline of her nipples against the thin material of her blouse.

My face felt hot, but I tried my best to cover it by smiling, nodding my thanks, and backing smoothly away from the counter. I was flattered but not in the market, and I didn't want to give her the wrong impression.

"Mr. Banks's office is on the fifth floor," Lisa said. "Do you want me to show you where it is?"

I shook my head. "I'll find it. Thanks."

"Okay, but any problems, you give me a yell." She waved at me, smiling.

"I will," I said. "Thanks."

I stood by the elevator, waiting, willing it to hurry, not daring to look back to where I knew Lisa was still standing, watching me. Finally the metal doors slid open, and I stepped inside, pressing the button for the fifth floor.

I waved good-bye as the doors closed.

I had no trouble finding Ted Banks. He was waiting in front of the doors when they opened, and he reached out and shook my hand the second I stepped off the elevator. "Glad to see you again," he said, although he seemed anything but glad. I remembered him now. He'd been the surly older man at my interview, one of the two who'd sat silently through the proceedings. He stopped shaking my hand and smiled at me, but it was a pretend smile and did not reach his eyes. Not that I could see his eyes very clearly behind the thick black-framed glasses. "What do you say we walk over to my office so we can get acquainted?"

"Okay," I said.

"Good."

I followed him to his office. Neither of us spoke along the way, and I found myself wishing that I had taken Lisa up on her offer to accompany me here. I could not see Banks's face, just the back of his head, but he seemed to me to be angry. There was something about the way he carried himself that seemed . . . hostile. I found myself wondering if I'd been hired over his objections. I got the feeling I had.

In his office, he sat behind his desk in a high-backed leather chair and motioned for me to take the seat opposite him. "Okay," he said. "Let's talk."

We talked. Or rather he talked, I listened. He told me about the corporation, about the department, about my job. Automated Interface, he said, was not only an industry leader in the development of commercial business software, it was also a great place to work. It offered a comfortable yet professional working environment and limitless opportunity for advancement for those with ability and ambition. The most important department within the organization, he said, was Documentation Standards, since it was by the clarity of the software documentation that customers tended to judge the user-friendliness of a product. Documentation was in the front lines of both public relations and customer support, and the continued success of the corporation rested in large part with the quality of documentation. In my position, according to Banks, I would be directly affecting, for better or worse, the statue of the department and, by extension, the entire company.

I nodded as Banks spoke, agreeing with him, pretending like I knew what the hell he was talking about even though I had only a vague idea of what was being discussed. Software documentation? User-friendliness? These were not terms with which I was comfortable or familiar. These were phrases I'd heard but had always made an extra effort to avoid. This was someone else's language, not mine.

"Do you have any questions so far?" Banks asked.

I shook my head.

"Good," he said.

But it was anything but good. He continued to talk, and I continued to listen, but . . . how can I describe it? The atmosphere was uncomfortable? There was no rapport between us? We were different types of people? All of these descriptions are correct, but they do not really reflect what I felt in that office. For as we sat there, as we looked at one another, we both realized that we did not like each other—and never would. There is a sort of instantaneous antipathy between people who don't get along, an unspoken recognition acknowledged by both parties, and that was what was happening here. The conversation remained polite, official, and the surface formalities were observed, but there was something else going on as well, and the relationship that was being forged between us was not one of friendship.

If we'd both been ten and on the playground at school, Ted Banks would have been one of the bullies who wanted to beat me up.

"Ron Stewart will be your immediate supervisor," Banks was saying. "Ron is Coordinator of Interoffice Procedures and Phase II Documentation, and you'll be reporting directly to him."

As if on cue, there was a knock on the door. "Come in!" Banks called.

The door opened, and Ron Stewart stepped into the office.

I disliked him on sight.

I don't know why. There was no rational reason. I didn't know the man at all and really had nothing to base my judgment on, but my first impression was strong, very strong, and definitely not favorable.

Stewart walked confidently into the room. He was tall and good-looking, dressed impeccably in a gray business suit, white shirt, and red tie. He strode into the office smiling, offering me his hand, and there was something about his bearing, about the arrogant way he walked, stood, and carried himself, that immediately rubbed me the wrong way. But I put on a smile, stood, shook his hand, and returned his greeting.

"Glad to have you aboard," he said. His voice was brisk, curt, businesslike. His grip was strong and firm. Too firm.

Glad to have you aboard. I'd known before he opened his mouth that he'd say something like that, that he'd use some sports metaphor, that he'd welcome me "aboard," tell me he was glad to have me on the "team."

I nodded politely.

"I'm looking forward to working with you, Jones. From what I've heard, I think you'll be a valuable asset to AII."

From what he'd heard? I watched Stewart as he sat down. What could he have heard?

"I've been talking to Jones about our overall operation," Banks said. "Why don't you tell him a little bit about Interoffice Procedures and Phase II Documentation."

Stewart began talking, repeating an obviously memorized spiel. I listened to him, nodded in the appropriate places, but I found it hard to concentrate on what he was saying. His tone of voice was unrelievedly condescending, as though he was explaining a simple concept to a slow child, and although I allowed no reaction to show on my face, his tone grated on me.

Finally, Stewart stood. "Come on," he said. "I'll take you on a tour of the department."

"Okay," I said.

We took the elevators downstairs, to the fourth floor, walking through the rabbit warren of modular workstations where the Phase II programmers were housed. He introduced me to each: Emery Phillips, Dave DeMotta, Stacy Kerrin, Dan Chan, Kim Thomas, Gary Yamaguchi, Albert Connor, and Pam Greene. They seemed nice enough, most of them, but they were all so involved in their work it was hard to tell. Only Stacy, a short, ultraefficient-looking blond woman, bothered to look up from her terminal when I was introduced. She met my eyes, gave me a brisk nod, shook my hand, then turned away. The rest of them merely nodded distractedly or raised a curt hand in greeting.

"Programmers necessarily have to develop and maintain a high level of concentration," Stewart said. "Don't take it personally if they're not always as talkative as they should be."

"I won't," I said.

"You'll be working closely with the programmers once you become involved in systems documentation. You'll find out they're not as antisocial as they first appear."

We walked out of the programming area and past a series of glass-walled rooms where testing and other peripheral activities were performed. He introduced me to Hope Williams, the department secretary, and Lois and Virginia, the two women from the steno pool we shared with the third floor.

Then it was time to check out my office.

My office.

The word "office" had conjured in my mind the image of a spacious room. Plush carpeting, wood paneling, an oak desk. A window with a view. Bookshelves. Something akin to what Banks had. Instead, I was led into a small, narrow cubicle slightly bigger than my parents' walk-in closet. There were two desks here, ugly metal behemoths that took up almost all available space and were situated side by side, with only walking room between them. Both desks faced a blank wall, a white add-on separated into even segments by thin metal connecting strips running lengthwise from floor to ceiling. Behind them was a row of gray metal filing cabinets.

Seated at the desk nearest the door was an old man with a crown of white hair and the small, hard eyes and belligerent stare of the terminally petty. He glared at me as I stepped into the office.

This was his domain and I was trespassing, and he wanted me to know it.

All the hopes I'd had of coming into an interesting job in a pleasant working environment died finally and forever as I forced myself to nod and smile at the man Stewart introduced to me simply as "Derek."

"Hello," Derek said drily. His features had a cast of blunt ignorance: pug nose, small mouth with jutting lower lip, tiny intolerant eyes. It was a face that showed no patience to members of ethnic groups, other generations, or the opposite sex. He reached across his desk, took my proffered hand, and shook, but it was clear from the expression on his face that I was too young for serious consideration. His palm was cold and clammy, and he immediately sat back down and pretended to ignore me, scribbling something on a piece of paper in front of him.

"We'll give you an hour or so to get settled. Derek here'll show you the ropes, won't you?"

The old man looked up, nodded noncommittally.

"You can go through your desk, keep what you'll need, toss out what you don't want. After break, maybe, I'll drop by and we can start going over your first assignment."

As with Banks, there were several levels at work here. The surface words were standard, noncommittal, but there was an undercurrent in Stewart's delivery that let me know that, however hard I might try, I would never be part of the "team."

"I'll catch you later," Stewart said. Once again, he shook my hand, pressing hard, and then he was gone.

I moved past Derek's desk in the crowded, suddenly silent office and over to my own. I sat down awkwardly in the ancient swivel chair provided me.

This was not working out the way I'd expected. Somewhere in the back of my mind, I guess I'd thought it would be like *How to Succeed in Business Without*

Really Trying. I'd seen the movie on TV when I was little, and while I had never even considered a career in business, that film had glamorized the corporate world for me, instilling within me a vision that not even years of subsequently grittier and more realistic movies had been able to erase entirely.

But the cleanly stylized offices and boardrooms through which Robert Morse sang were a far cry from the cramped and claustrophobic quarters in which I now found myself.

I opened the drawers of my desk, but I didn't know what to clean out. I didn't know enough about my job to know what I would and wouldn't need.

I glanced over at Derek. He smiled at me, but the smile was not quick enough to cover the hard expression that had been in its place a second before.

"New jobs," he said, shaking his head as though sympathetically identifying with a common experience.

"Yeah," I said, not knowing what else to say.

I looked at the top of my desk. Both the metal in box and out box were full, and a selection of books were stacked next to them: *Roget's Thesaurus, Webster's New Collegiate Dictionary, Creating Creative Technical Manuals, Dictionary of Computer Terminology.*

Creating technical manuals? Computer terminology? I felt like a fraud already, even though I hadn't officially started my work. What did I know about this stuff?

I was still not sure of my duties exactly. Lisa had given me a single-page job description, but it was filled with the same vague wording as the one handed to me at the interview. I had a general idea of what was required of me, but the specific tasks I was supposed to perform, the precise requirements of my position had never been spelled out to me, and I felt lost. I thought of asking Derek about it—he was, after all, supposed to be showing me "the ropes"—but when I glanced again in his direction, he was looking too intently and too obviously at a typed sheet of paper, and I knew that he did not want to talk to me.

Following his lead, I removed the stack of papers from my in box and, one by one, began sorting through them. I had no idea what I was looking at, but it didn't seem to matter. Derek said nothing to me, and I continued to look at each page, pretending I knew what I was doing.

It was an hour later when the phone on my desk buzzed twice, although it felt to me as though five hours had passed.

"Mr. Stewart," Derek said, speaking his first words since the enigmatic "New jobs." He nodded toward the phone. "Press star seven."

I picked up the receiver, pressed the asterisk button and the number seven on the console. "Hello?" I said.

"No." Stewart's voice was strong and disapproving. "When you answer the phone, you say, 'Interoffice Procedures and Phase II Documentation. Bob Jones speaking.'"

"Sorry," I said. "No one told me."

"Now you've been told. I don't want to catch you answering the phone incorrectly again."

"Sorry," I said again.

"I may have forgotten to mention it," Stewart said, "but you are entitled to two fifteen-minute breaks and an hour lunch each day. Your breaks will be taken at ten in the morning and three in the afternoon. Your lunch will be from noon until one. Your break may be spent at your desk or in the fourth-floor break room. You may leave the building and spend your lunch wherever you want as long as you return to your desk by one."

"Okay," I said. "Thanks."

The phone clicked in my ear, and I looked down for a moment, panicked. I'd been fiddling with the phone cord, and I thought I might have accidentally cut him off, but my hand was nowhere near the cradle, and I realized that he had simply hung up on me.

I replaced the handset and glanced over at Derek. "Where's the break room?" I asked.

He did not look up. "End of the hall, turn right."

"Thanks," I said, walking past his desk and out the door.

The break room was small, the size of the living room in our apartment. There was a refrigerator and a soft-drink machine against one wall, a dilapidated couch against another, and two mismatched dining room tables in the center. The room smelled of old ladies, of closeted linen and cloying perfume. Underneath, more lightly, I detected a stale scent that was either refrigerated lunches or lingering body odor.

There were three old women seated around the closest table, dressed in too-bright floral blouses, and pantsuits that had been stylish several decades back. One woman, hair dyed years younger than was flattering, sat nibbling on a bear claw, staring into space. The other two drank cups of coffee, idly flipping through well-thumbed copies of *Redbook*. None of the women spoke. They barely looked up at the sound of my footsteps as I entered the room.

What the hell had I gotten myself into here? I suddenly found myself wishing that I'd kept my part-time job at Sears as a backup. I could've quit this job then. We'd been poor with both of us working part-time, but we'd gotten by, and if I'd known it was going to be like this, I would've turned down this position and waited for another.

But I was screwed now, trapped here until I could find something else.

I vowed to start applying elsewhere as soon as possible.

Cokes were fifty cents. I had three quarters in my pocket, and I dropped two of them into the machine, pressed the button. A can of Shasta Cola rolled out. Shasta? The machine sported a Coca-Cola logo.

I shouldn't have been surprised.

Stewart was sitting in my seat when I returned to the

office. He swiveled to face me as I entered the room. "Where have you been?" he asked.

I looked at the clock above the filing cabinets. I'd been gone less than ten minutes. "Break," I said.

He shook his head. "You're not one of those, are you?"

I didn't know what he was talking about.

"You're entitled to a break by law," he said. "But don't abuse the privilege."

I wanted to respond, wanted to remind him that he had called me and told me to take a fifteen-minute break and that I had been gone only seven or eight minutes, but I didn't dare. I nodded. "Okay."

"All right, then."

I waited. He did not get out of my chair but sat there, leaning back, as he looked at a stapled sheaf of papers in his hand. I stood awkwardly in front of my desk. "On January first," he said, "Automated Interface will be coming out with a new software package called PayPer. PayPer is an integrated payroll and personnel information system that will allow users to maintain personal data files on employees as well as process payrolls, calculate state and federal withholding deductions, and incorporate pretax and posttax flexible benefit programs. I want you to write a description of the product for a press release I'm preparing."

Already I felt hopelessly out of my depth, but I nodded in what I hoped was a confident, competent manner.

"I'll leave this overview with you to look at." He leaned forward, placed the sheaf of papers on top of my desk, and stood. "I don't think you'll have any problems, but if you do, just give me a ring. You can turn in the description before you leave today, or even tomorrow morning if you want. That should give you more than enough time to finish the assignment."

I nodded again, flattened against the wall to let him pass as he walked around the side of the desk.

I sat down, looked at the paper he'd left me. I wasn't

sure what he wanted. A description? What did that mean? No stylistic guidelines had been laid out for me, I'd been given no examples of the company's previous press releases; I had not been told "this is what we want" or "this is what we don't want"; I had not been given a length or line limit. I was on my own, and I realized that this was my first test in the new job and that I'd damn well better pass it.

I glanced over at Derek, and this time there was a real smile on his face.

I did not like the way it looked.

I gathered that Stewart was writing a press release, and that I had to write a short description of this PayPer system for him to incorporate into the release. I read the information he gave me, which was basically a detailed description of PayPer written from a technical standpoint, and figured all I had to do was paraphrase and simplify what I'd been given.

Before I knew it, it was twelve, and Derek was putting away his papers and getting ready to go to lunch. In the hallway outside our office, I saw other men and women carrying sack lunches or jingling keys as they walked toward the elevator. I did not want to be stuck eating lunch with Derek, so I let him leave, then gave him a few extra minutes before walking over to the elevator myself.

I hadn't brought a lunch, and I didn't especially feel like hanging around the building for an hour, so I took the elevator to the first floor and walked out to my car. I'd seen a Taco Bell near the freeway on my way in that day, and I figured I'd eat there.

Apparently, a lot of other people from Automated Interface or the other corporations in the area had the same idea as me, because Taco Bell was packed. It was a half hour before I ordered and got my food, and because all of the tables were taken, I was forced to eat in my car. By the time I finished eating, drove back to work, and found a parking place, I knew my hour would be over.

From now on, I decided, I would bring my lunch.

I saw Lisa walking out to her car when I returned, and I waved to her and smiled as I made my way through the parking lot. She stared at me blankly, then looked away. I realized, too late, that her show up there in Personnel had been just that—a show. She had not been flirting with me after all. She had been doing her job. Obviously, she smiled at everyone the way she'd smiled at me, touched everyone the way she'd touched me.

I returned to my office, feeling chastened and humiliated.

I was finished with my description by two, but I still had three hours to kill, so I spent the time going over my copy, trying to make it perfect. I typed the description on the typewriter next to my desk and brought it to Stewart's office around four-thirty. He said nothing as he read it, and no expression crossed his face. He didn't say it was brilliant, didn't say it was a piece of shit, so I assumed it was acceptable.

He placed the page in a drawer. "Next time," he said, "I want you to write on the PC so we can revise your work if necessary. I'm going to have the typewriter taken out of your office."

I was not that familiar with word processors, but I had used one in a communications course in college and was pretty sure I'd be able to pick it up easily, so I nodded. "I would've used it for this," I said, "but no one told me where it was."

He glanced at me. "Sometimes you have to take your own initiative," he said.

I nodded, said nothing.

Jane was making dinner when I came home—spaghetti—and I took off my jacket and tie, threw them on the back of the couch, and walked into the kitchen. It felt weird to me, coming home like this. The apartment was warm and filled with the smell of cooking food, the local news was on TV, and though these were things that happened every day, I felt out of it and slightly disoriented because they were already in progress when I arrived. I hadn't been home when Jane had closed the windows against the late afternoon chill, I hadn't been home when she'd turned on the TV for *Donahue,* I hadn't been home when she'd started dinner, and all of this made me feel like a stranger, an outsider. I guess I'd gotten used to the way things were, to working part-time and hanging around the apartment for a good portion of the day, and this readjustment of my daily life threw me more than I would have expected.

I walked into the kitchen, and Jane turned to me, smiling, still stirring the spaghetti sauce. "How was it?" she asked.

She didn't say, "How was your day, dear?", but the intent was the same and for some reason it rubbed me the wrong way. It was . . . too *Ozzie and Harriet.* I shrugged, sitting down. "Okay." I wanted to say more. I wanted to tell her about Lisa and Banks and Stewart and Derek, about my horrible office and the horrible break room and my horrible job, but her question put me off somehow and I sat silently, staring through the kitchen doorway at the TV in the living room.

I opened up later, during dinner, telling her everything, apologizing for my earlier silence. I was not sure why I'd taken out my frustration on her—I had never done that before—but she took it in stride and was more than understanding.

"First days are always the worst," she said, collecting our plates and carrying them to the sink.

I closed the lid of the parmesan cheese container. "I hope so."

She returned to the table, reached underneath and gave my penis a small squeeze. "Don't worry. I'll cheer you up later," she said.

We watched TV after dinner, our standard lineup of Monday sitcoms, but I told her I had to get to bed early because I had to wake up at six for work, and we walked into the bedroom at ten instead of the usual eleven.

"Do you want to take a shower with me?" she asked as I sat down on the bed.

I shook my head. "I'm not in the mood."

"Too tired?"

I smiled. "Yeah," I said. "I'm too tired."

"Too tired," was our own personal euphemism for oral sex, one that had gotten started when we'd first moved in together. She'd wanted to make love one night, but I wasn't sure I'd be up for it, so I told her I was too tired. I'd closed my eyes, and the next thing I knew, her mouth had been open and ready for business. It had been wonderful, and ever since then the phrase "too tired" had taken on a new meaning for us.

Jane gave me a quick kiss. "I'll be right back, then."

I took off my clothes and crawled into bed. I was excited and already had an erection, but I really did feel tired, and I lay back and closed my eyes, listening to the sound of the water running in the bathroom, and by the time she finished her shower, I was dead asleep.

THREE

Assistant Coordinator of Interoffice Procedures and Phase II Documentation.

Despite the implications of my rather pretentious title, I turned out to be little more than a glorified clerk, typing memos that needed to be typed, proofreading instruction sheets that needed to be proofread, doing the jobs the Coordinator of Interoffice Procedures and Phase II Documentation didn't want to assign to a secretary and didn't want to do himself.

That first assignment was either an aberration, or else I'd failed so miserably at it that Stewart was not willing to risk having me work on a real job again.

I was afraid to ask which.

I tried talking to Derek the first few days, saying hello when I arrived in the morning, good-bye when I left for home, occasionally attempting to start a conversation at other times throughout the day. But all of my efforts were met with the same stony silence, and I soon gave up. Technically, we were office mates, but our relationship was even more impersonal than that. We shared the same work space.

Period.

The depressing thing was that it was not just Derek. No one, it seemed, wanted to speak to me. I did not know why this was. I was new and knew no one, and in an effort to become acquainted with my coworkers, I tried nodding or waving to other employees I passed in the halls, saying "Hi," "Good morning," "How are you?", but more often than not, I was met with blank looks, my greetings ignored. Every so often, someone would wave back, smile slightly, or say hello, but that was the exception rather than the rule, and pretty damn rare.

Among the computer programmers, my presence was barely tolerated. I was not required to deal with them on a regular basis, but several times those first few days I had to go over to their area and either deliver copies of memos or pick up papers to be proof-read, and they made clear their disdain for me by ignoring me and treating me as though I were a slave—an emotionless, personalityless automaton there only to do my professional duty.

Every so often, I would meet one of them in the break room, and I always tried to break the ice and establish some sort of one-on-one relationship, but my attempts invariably failed. I talked twice to Stacy Kerrin, the blond woman, and I gathered from reading between the lines of what she said and what she didn't say that my predecessor had been well-liked within the department. Apparently, he had maintained friendships with many of the programmers outside of work and had seen them on a social basis. She spoke of him fondly, as an equal.

But I was clearly a second-class citizen.

I wanted to feel superior to these people, should have been able to feel superior—they were dorks and nerds, geeks to a man—but I found myself feeling uncomfortably out of place around them and even slightly intimidated. In the real world they might be losers, but here in their world they were the norm and I was the outcast.

I took to spending most of my breaks at my desk, alone.

On Friday, Stewart had assigned me to correct the grammar on an old chapter of the department Standards Manual, and I spent at least an hour trying to get the paper aligned in the printer. I was supposed to have the assignment finished before noon, and I had to wait until all of the pages were printed before leaving, so I was late for lunch.

It was twelve-thirty by the time I xeroxed the chapter, placed a copy on Stewart's desk, and finally went outside.

The two BMWs that had flanked my car this morning were gone, and I pulled out easily. The Buick was almost out of gas, and there was no gas station between here and the freeway, so I decided to try the other direction. I figured I'd find a Shell or a Texaco or something at one of the intersections.

Ten minutes later, I was hopelessly lost.

I'd never really driven through Irvine before. I'd driven past it on my way to San Diego, I'd passed through a corner of it on my way to the beach, but I'd never driven *in* it. I didn't know the city, and as I headed south on Emery, I was amazed by its monochromatic sameness. I drove for miles without encountering a store, gas station, or shopping center of any kind. There was only row upon row of identical two-story tan houses behind a seemingly endless brown brick wall. I passed four stoplights, then turned at the fifth. None of the street names were recognizable to me, and I continued turning, right and left and right and left, hoping to find a gas station, or at least a liquor store where I could ask directions to a gas station, but there was only that brown brick wall, lining both sides of every street. It was like some labyrinthian science fiction city, and I was getting worried because my gas gauge was now definitely on E, but there was also a part of me that found this exciting. I'd never seen anything like it before. Irvine was a planned community, with businesses all in one area, residences in another, farmland in another, and apparently stores and gas stations in another. Something about that appealed to me, and though I was afraid of running out of gas, I also felt strangely comfortable here. The mazelike uniformity of the streets and the buildings fascinated me, and seemed to me somehow wondrous.

Finally I did find an Arco, deceptively disguised in an unobtrusive corner building the same brown brick as the wall, and I got my gas and asked the attendant how to get back to Emery. The directions were surprisingly easy—I hadn't gone as far afield as I thought—and I thanked him, and drove off.

I returned to work feeling lighter and happier for my little noontime jaunt.

I promised myself I'd spend more of my lunch hours exploring Irvine.

The days dragged.

My job was mind-numbingly boring, made even more so by the knowledge that it was completely useless. From what I could tell, Automated Interface would have had absolutely no trouble getting along without me. The corporation could have eliminated my position entirely and no one would have even noticed.

I mentioned this to Jane over dinner one night, and she tried to tell me that, when you got down to it, most jobs were useless. "What about the people who work for companies that make foot deodorant or those magnets that look like sandwiches and Oreo cookies? No one really needs that stuff. Those people's jobs aren't important."

"Yeah, but people buy those things. People want those things."

"People want computer things, too."

"But I don't even make computer things. I don't design, produce, market, or sell—"

"There are people with jobs like yours in every company."

"That doesn't make it okay."

She looked at me. "What do you want to do? Go to Africa and feed starving children? I don't think you're the type."

"I'm not saying that—"

"What are you saying, then?"

I let it drop. I could not seem to articulate what I was

trying to say. I felt useless and unimportant—guilty, I suppose, for taking home a paycheck when I wasn't actually doing or accomplishing anything. It was a strange feeling, and not one I could easily explain to Jane, but it discomfited me and I was not able to ignore it.

Although I did not like my job, I did not hate it enough to quit. In the back of my mind was the idea that this was temporary, something to tide me over until I found the position I really wanted. I told myself this was a transitional phase between school and my real occupation.

But I had no idea what my "real" occupation would be.

One thing I quickly learned was that, in a major corporation, as much time is spent trying to look busy as is spent actually working. The week's worth of assignments I was given each Monday I could have easily completed by Wednesday, but although workers in movies and on TV eagerly complete their assignments in record time and then ask for more work, impressing those higher up on the corporate ladder and elevating themselves through the ranks, it was made clear to me early on that such initiative in real life was not only not encouraged, it was frowned upon. The people surrounding me in the company hierarchy had asses to protect. They had, over the years, worked out what was for them a comfortable ratio of work to nonwork, and if I suddenly started cranking out documentation, it would throw off the productivity curve in the company's labor distribution study. It would make them look bad. It would make my supervisor look bad; it would make his supervisor look bad. What I was expected to do was equal or improve very slightly upon the output of my predecessor. Period. I was supposed to fit into the preexisting niche created for me and conform to its boundaries. The Peter Principle in action.

Which meant that I had a lot of time to kill.

I learned quickly to follow the lead of those around

me, and I discovered many ways to simulate hard work. When Stewart or Banks stopped by the office to check on my progress, there were paper shufflings I could perform, desk straightenings I could do, drawers I could rifle through. I don't know if Derek ever noticed my little act, but if he did, he didn't say anything. I suspected that he did the same thing himself, since he too seemed to suddenly become a lot busier when the supervisor or department head came into the office.

I missed going to school, and I seemed to spend a lot of time thinking about it. I'd had fun in college, and though it had been less than half a year since I graduated, emotionally those days seemed a million miles away. I found that I missed being with people my own age, missed just doing nothing and hanging out. I remembered the time I went with Craig Miller to the Erogenous Zone, an "adult" toy store in a seedy mini-mall close to campus. We'd been carpooling at the time, and Craig suggested that we stop by the shop. I'd never been there, was kind of curious and said okay, and we pulled into the small L-shaped parking lot. The second we walked into the store, ringing the small bell above the door, all three cashiers and several customers turned to look at us. "Craig!" they called out in unison. It reminded me of the TV show *Cheers,* when the patrons of the bar would all cry, "Norm!", and I couldn't help laughing. Craig grinned at me sheepishly, and I remembered thinking, in the words of the song, how nice it was to go to a place where everybody knew your name.

At Automated Interface, no one knew my name.

I was still not sure why I'd been hired, particularly since both Stewart and Banks seemed to despise me. Was I some sort of quota hiree? Did I meet some type of criteria or fit into the right age or ethnic group? I had no idea. I only knew that if the hiring had been up to Banks or Stewart, I would not have gotten the job.

I seldom saw Ted Banks, but when I did, when he

took his occasional tours of the department, he was
rude to me and unnecessarily abrasive. Unprovoked, he
made derogatory comments about my hair, my ties, my
posture, anything he could think of. I had no idea why
he did this, but I tried to ignore it and play it off.

Ron Stewart was a little harder to ignore. He was not
as obvious or crude in his dislike as Banks; he was
even polite to me in a superficial way, but there was
something about him that rubbed me the wrong way.
When he spoke, it was always with a slight trace of
condescension. His words were pleasant enough, but
they were delivered in a manner that made it clear he
felt far superior to me in intellect and position and was
doing me a great favor by talking to me at all.

The annoying thing was that, when talking to him, I
couldn't help feeling that he *was* superior to me, that
he was more intelligent, more interesting, more sophisticated, more everything. The words we spoke were the
friendly words of equals, but the underlying attitudes
that subtly shaped the subtexts of our conversations
told a different story, and I found myself behaving in a
slightly subservient manner, playing the deferential
flunky to his smug overseer, and though I hated myself
for it, I couldn't help it.

I wondered if I was being paranoid. Maybe Banks
and Stewart treated everyone that way.

No. Banks joked with the programmers, was cour-
teous to the secretary and the steno women. Stewart
was friendly to all of the other people under him. He
even indulged in light conversation with Derek.

I was the sole recipient of their hostility.

It was about a month after I'd been hired that I heard
Stewart and Banks talking in the hallway outside of my
office. They were speaking loudly, just outside the
door, as though they wanted to make sure I heard what
they were saying.

I did.

Banks: "How's he working out?"

"He's not a team player." Stewart. "I don't know that he'll ever get with the program."

"We have no room here for slackers."

My first review was not for another two months. They were just trying to provoke me. I knew that, but still I felt angry, and I could not let such accusations go unchallenged. I stood up, strode around my desk and into the hall. "For your information," I said, confronting them, "I have completed every assignment given to me, and I have completed them all on time."

Stewart looked at me mildly. "That's nice, Jones."

"I heard what you said about me—"

Banks smiled indulgently, all innocence. "We weren't talking about you, Jones. What made you think we were talking about you?"

I looked at him.

"And why were you eavesdropping on our private conversation?"

I had no answer for that, no reply that would not sound like an overly defensive rationalization, so I said nothing but retreated, red-faced, back into the office. Derek, at his desk, was grinning.

"Serves you right," he said.

Fuck you, I wanted to say. Eat shit and die.

But I ignored him and uncapped my pen and silently went back to work.

That night, when I got home, Jane said she wanted to go somewhere, do something. We had not really been out of the house since I'd gotten the job, and she was feeling cramped and restless and more than a little housebound. I was, too, to be honest, and we both decided that it would be nice to get out for an evening.

We went to Balboa, and we ate dinner at the Crab Cooker, buying individual bowls of clam chowder and eating them on the bench outside the restaurant, watching and commenting upon the passersby. Afterward, we drove down the peninsula to the pier across from the Fun Zone, parking in the small lot next to the pier itself. This had always been "our" spot. The site of

many a free date during our poorer days, this was
where I had taken Jane on our first night out, and
where we had later made out in the car. Throughout the
first two years of our relationship, when we could not
even afford to go to a movie, we'd come here: walking through the Fun Zone itself; window-shopping in
the surf stores and T-shirt shops; watching the kids
in the arcades; following the boats on the bay; walking out to Ruby's, the hamburger stand at the end of
the pier.

Afterward, after most of the people had gone and the
stores had closed, we usually ended up making love in
the backseat of my Buick.

It seemed strange going through the Fun Zone now.
For the first time, we could afford to buy T-shirts if we
wanted. We could afford to play arcade games. Out of
habit, though, we did neither. We walked, hand in
hand, through the crowds, passing a gang of leather-
jacketed punks lounging against a faded fence near the
broken Ferris wheel, past a booth offering nighttime
harbor cruises. The air was filled with the smell of junk
food—hamburgers, pizza, fries—and under that, more
subtly, the fishy scent of the bay.

We went into a shell shop and Jane decided that
she wanted a sand dollar, so I bought her one. After
that, we took the ferry across the bay to Balboa Island,
strolled for an hour around the island's perimeter,
bought frozen bananas from an ice cream stand, and
took the ferry back.

Returning to the parking lot and the pier, we heard
music and saw a crowd of well-heeled yuppies
standing on the sidewalk in front of a small club. The
neon sign on the wall between the open door and the
darkened windows read STUDIO CAFE, and a makeshift
sandwich marquee said NOW APPEARING: SANDY
OWEN. We stopped for a moment to listen. The music
was amazing—jazz saxophone, alternately bop hot and
smooth cool, played over soaring, shimmering piano—
and was unlike anything I had ever heard. The overall

effect was mesmerizing, and we stood on the sidewalk listening for nearly ten minutes before the press of the crowd compelled us to move on.

Instead of walking back to the car, we continued up the sloping sidewalk to the pier. Ruby's was little more than a square of light against the darkness of the ocean night, and the pier itself was lined with fishermen, dotted with other strolling couples. We passed a group of dark-haired, dark-skinned, dark-clothed high school girls speaking in Spanish, an old man fly-tying on the worn wooden bench, and an overdressed couple leaning against the railing, making out. The music followed us, ebbing and flowing with the breeze, and for some reason it didn't feel like we were in Orange County. It seemed as though we were in some other, better place, a movie version of Southern California, where the air was clean and the people were nice and everything was wonderful.

Ruby's was doing a thriving business, a crowd of would-be diners clustered outside the small building, people eating at the chrome tables inside. Jane and I walked around to the rear of the restaurant and took a spot at the railing between two fishermen. It was black on the ocean, the night deeper and darker than it ever got inland, and I stared into the blackness, seeing only the lone bobbing light of a boat on the water. I put my arm around Jane and turned around to face the shore, leaning my back against the metal railing. Above Newport, the sky was orangish, a dome of illumination from the buildings and the cars that kept the real night away. The sound of the waves was muffled, a distant breaking.

In the movie *Stardust Memories,* there's a scene in which Woody Allen is drinking his Sunday morning coffee and watching his lover, Charlotte Rampling, read the newspaper on the floor. The Louis Armstrong recording of "Stardust" is on the turntable, and Woody says in a voice over that at that moment the sights, the sounds, the smells, everything came together, everything dovetailed perfectly, and at that instant, for a few brief seconds, he was happy.

That was how I felt with Jane, on the pier.

Happy.

We stood there for a while, saying nothing, enjoying the night, enjoying just being together. Along the coast, we could see all the way to Laguna Beach.

"I'd like to live by the beach," Jane said. "I love the sound of the water."

"Which beach?"

"Laguna."

I nodded. It was a pipe dream—there was no way in hell either of us would ever earn enough money to buy beachfront property in Southern California—but it was something to strive for.

Jane shivered, drawing closer to me.

"It's getting cold," I said, putting an arm around her. "You want to head back?"

She shook her head. "Let's just stay here for a while. Like this."

"Okay." I pulled her closer, held her tight, and we stared into the night toward the twinkling lights of Laguna, beckoning to us across the water and the darkness.

FOUR

We were still living in our small apartment near UC Brea, but I wanted to move. We could afford it now, and I didn't want to deal with the constant flood of drunken fraternity boys who paraded down our street on their way to or from this week's keg party. But Jane said she wanted to stay. She liked our apartment, and it was convenient for her since it was close to both the campus and the Little Kiddie Day Care Center, where she worked.

"Besides," she said, "what if you get laid off or something? We could still survive here. I could afford to pay the rent until you found another job."

That was my opening. That was my chance. I should've told her then and there, I should've told her that I hated my job, that I'd made a mistake by taking it and wanted to quit and look for another position.

But I didn't.

I didn't say anything.

I don't know why. It wasn't like she would've jumped down my throat. She might have tried to argue me out of it, but ultimately she would've understood. I could have walked away clean, no harm, no foul, and everything would have been over and done with.

I couldn't do it, though. I didn't have any work-ethic phobia about quitting, I had no loyalty to some abstract ideal, but as much as I despised my job, as unqualified as I seemed to be for my position, as out of place as I felt among my coworkers, I couldn't shake the feeling that I was *supposed* to do this, that somehow, for some reason, I *should* be working at Automated Interface.

And I said nothing.

Jane's mom dropped by to see us on Saturday morning, and I tried to pretend that I was busy when she came over, hiding in the bedroom and tinkering with a broken sewing machine that had been given to Jane by one of her friends. I had never much liked Jane's mom, and she had never liked me. We hadn't seen her since I'd gotten my job, although Jane had told her about it, and while she pretended to be happy that I had finally found full-time work, I could tell she was secretly annoyed that there would be one less thing she could criticize me for and harp on Jane about.

Georgia—or George as she liked to be called—was part of a dying breed, one of the last of the martini moms, those hard and hard-drinking women who had been so prevalent in the suburbia of my childhood, those gravel-voiced, raucous women who always seemed to adopt the nicknames of men: Jimmy, Gerry, Willie, Phil. It frightened me a little to know that this was Jane's mother, because I always thought that, in regard to women, you could tell how a daughter was going to turn out by looking at the mother. And I had to admit that I did see some of George in Jane. But there was no hardness in Jane. She was softer, kinder, prettier than her mother, and the differences between the two were pronounced enough that I knew history would not repeat itself.

I made a lot of noise, working on the sewing machine, purposely trying to drown out words that I knew I would not want to hear, but in between the pounding and scraping, I could still hear George's alcohol-ravaged voice from the kitchen: ". . . he's still a nobody . . ." and ". . . gutless nothing . . ." and ". . . loser . . ."

I did not come out of the bedroom until she was gone.

"Mom's real excited about your job," Jane said, taking my hand.

I nodded. "Yeah. I heard."

She looked into my eyes, smiled. "Well, I am."

I kissed her. "That's good enough for me."

At work, Stewart's smug condescension gave way to a more direct disdain. Something had changed. I didn't know what it was, whether I'd done something to piss him off or whether it was something that had happened in his personal life, but his attitude toward me became markedly different. The surface politeness was gone, and now there was only undisguised hostility.

Instead of calling me into his office each Monday to give me the week's assignments, Stewart began leaving work on my desk, attaching notes that explained what I was supposed to do. Often, the notes were incomplete or cryptically vague, and though I could usually figure out the gist of the assignment, sometimes I had no idea what he wanted at all.

One morning, I found a batch of ancient computer manuals piled on my desk. As far as I could tell, the manuals explained how to utilize a type of keyboard and terminal that Automated Interface did not possess. Stewart's Post-It note said only: "Revise."

I had no idea what I was supposed to revise, so I picked up the top manual and the note and carried them over to Stewart's office. He was not there, but I could hear his voice and I found him talking with Albert Connor, one of the programmers, about an action movie he'd seen over the weekend. I stood, waiting. Connor kept looking at me, obviously trying to hint to Stewart that I wanted to see him, but Stewart continued to describe the movie, slowly and in detail, purposely ignoring my presence.

Finally, I cleared my throat. It was a soft sound, polite, tentative, quiet, but the supervisor whirled on me as if I had just yelled an obscenity. "Will you stop interrupting me when I'm talking? For Christ's sake, can't you see I'm busy?"

I took a step backward. "I just needed—"

"You just need to shut up. I'm tired of you, Jones. I'm tired of your shit. Your probation period's not over yet, you know. You can be let go without cause." He glared at me. "Do you understand?"

I understood what he was saying. But I also understood that he was bluffing. Neither he nor Banks had as much control over me as they wanted me to believe. If what they tried to make me believe was true, I would've been fired weeks ago. Or, more likely, I never would've been hired at all. Someone above them was calling the shots, and they were hamstrung. They could rant and rave and piss and moan, but when push came to shove, they couldn't do diddly.

Maybe that was why Stewart had been riding me so hard lately.

I stood my ground. "I just wanted to know what I was supposed to revise. I couldn't tell from the note."

Connor was staring at us. Even he seemed taken aback by the force of Stewart's outburst.

"You are supposed to revise the manuals," Stewart said. He spoke slowly and deliberately, angrily.

"Which part of the manuals?" I asked.

"Everything. If you had bothered to look through the books I left on your desk, you would have noticed that we no longer use that hardware system. I want you to revise those operator manuals so that they reflect our current system."

"How do I do that?" I asked.

He stared at me. "You're asking me how to do your job?"

Connor had grown increasingly uncomfortable, and he nodded toward me. "I'll show you," he offered.

I looked at him gratefully, smiling my thanks.

Stewart fixed the programmer with a disapproving glare but said nothing.

I followed Connor back to his cubicle.

It was easier than I'd thought it would be. Connor simply gave me a stack of manuals that had come with the computers Automated Interface had recently purchased. He told me to xerox them, put them in binders, then deliver them to the different departments within the company.

"You mean I'm just supposed to replace the old books with new ones?" I asked.

"Right."

"How come Mr. Stewart told me to *revise* the manuals?"

"That's just the way he talks." The programmer tapped the cover of the top manual he'd given me. "Just make sure you return those to me when you're through. I need them. You should find a distribution list somewhere in your desk that will tell you how many copies each department gets. Gabe always kept an up-to-date distribution list."

Gabe. My predecessor. In addition to being friendly and outgoing, he'd apparently been well-organized and efficient as well.

"Thanks," I told Connor.

"You're welcome."

I licked my lips. This was the first positive contact I'd actually had with one of my coworkers, and more than anything else I wanted to follow up on it. I wanted to build on this tentative base, to try and establish some sort of relationship with Connor. But I did not know how. I could have attempted to continue the conversation, I suppose. I could have asked him what he was working on. I could have tried to talk about something non-work related.

But I didn't.

He turned back to his terminal, and I returned to my office.

I saw Connor later, near the Coke machine, and I smiled and waved at him as I entered the break room, but he ignored me, turned away, and, embarrassed, I quickly got my drink and left.

At lunch, I saw Connor leaving with Pam Greene. They didn't see me, and I stood on the sidelines, watching them take the elevator down. I'd begun

dreading lunch, feeling self-conscious about the fact
that I always ate by myself. I would have much preferred working eight hours straight and getting off an
hour earlier at the end of the day, not taking a lunch at
all. I did not need sixty minutes each day to prove to
me how I was regarded by my coworkers. I was
depressed enough by the job as it was.

What depressed me further was the fact that
everyone—*everyone*—seemed to have someone to eat
with. Even someone like Derek, who as far as I could
tell was almost universally reviled, had someone with
whom he spent his lunch: a squat, toadlike man who
worked someplace upstairs. I alone was alone. The secretaries who were nice to me during working hours all
said good-bye and waved politely before abandoning
me at lunchtime, not even bothering to ask if I would
like to accompany them, perhaps assuming that I
already had something to do with my lunch hour.

Perhaps not.

Whatever the reason, I was ignored, not invited, left
to my own devices.

The secretaries, I must admit, did seem to be nicer to
me than everyone else. Hope, our department secretary, always treated me well. She had the calm, kind,
perpetually friendly air of a stereotypical grandmother,
and she greeted me each day with a cheerful smile and
a heartfelt "Hello!" She asked about my weekend plans
on Friday afternoons; she asked how those plans turned
out on Monday morning. She said good-bye to me each
evening before I left.

Or course, she was equally nice to everyone within
the department. She talked to everyone, seemed to like
everyone, but that didn't make her interest in me any
less genuine or any less appreciated.

Likewise, Virginia and Lois, the women from the
steno pool, were decent to me, friendly in a way
that separated them from everyone else within our
department.

Or within the building.

The guard in the lobby still paid no attention to me, although he seemed to be jovially familiar with everyone else who passed through the doors of Automated Interface.

To Jane, I continued to give a fairly neutral account of my days at work. I told her of my frustration with Stewart, complained about some of my bigger problems, but the day-to-day difficulties, my seeming inability to fit in with my fellow workers, the sense of social ostracism I felt, these things I kept to myself.

It was my cross to bear.

A week after I'd distributed the computer manuals, Stewart walked into my office, waving a sheet of blue interoffice memo paper. I was on break and reading the *Times,* but Stewart slammed down the memo on top of my newspaper. "Read that," he demanded.

I read the memo. It was from the head of the accounting department and simply asked if we could send an extra copy of the computer manual since Accounting had recently received a new terminal. I looked up at Stewart. "Okay," I said. "I'll make another copy and send them a manual."

"Not good enough," Stewart said. "You should've sent them the correct number to begin with."

"All I had to go on was Gabe's distribution list," I told him. "I didn't know they'd gotten another computer."

"It's your job to know. You should have asked each department head how many copies he or she needed instead of relying on that outdated list. You screwed up, Jones."

"I'm sorry," I said.

"You're sorry? This reflects on the whole department." He picked up the memo. "I'm going to have to show this to Mr. Banks. I'll let him decide on the proper course of action to take with you. In the meantime, get that manual to Accounting ASAP."

"I will," I said.

"You'd better."

My workday went downhill from there.

Things did not improve when I got home. Jane was cooking hamburger casserole and watching an old rerun of *M*A*S*H* when I arrived. I'd always hated hamburger casserole, but I'd never told her so and it was not something she'd ever been able to figure out for herself.

I walked over to the TV and switched the channel. I liked *M*A*S*H* but I was a news junkie, and from the moment I got home until the start of prime time, I liked to watch the news. It made me nervous not to know what was going on in the world, to be oblivious to brewing disasters, but it didn't seem to bother Jane at all. Even when the news was on, she paid attention only to movie reviews, and she preferred to watch reruns or films on cable.

It had been the source of many fights.

She knew my position, she knew how I felt, and I couldn't help thinking that her choice of TV fare tonight was a direct provocation, an attempt to goad me. Usually, she had the news on when I came home. The fact that she didn't this evening seemed to me to be a direct slap in the face.

I confronted her. "Why isn't the news on?"

"I had a test today. I was tired. I wanted some light entertainment. I didn't want to have to think."

I understood how she felt, and I should have let it go, but I was still pissed off at Stewart, and I guess I had to take it out on somebody

We got into it.

It was a big fight, almost a physical fight. Afterward, we both said we were sorry, and we kissed and hugged and made up. She went into the kitchen to finish making dinner, and I stayed in the living room and watched the news. I kicked off my shoes and lay down on the couch. I hadn't told her I loved her, I realized. We'd made up, but I hadn't told her I loved her.

She hadn't told me she loved me, either.

I thought about that. I did love her and I knew she

loved me, but we never used those words. Or at least we hadn't for quite some time. We'd said them at first, but strangely enough, though I'd told her that I loved her, I wasn't sure at the time if I meant it. I'd said it, but the words had seemed hollow and clichéd, almost false. The first time, it had been more of a hope than an admission, and I felt no different after than before. There'd been no surge of joy or relief, only a vague sense of unease, as though I had lied to her and was afraid I'd be found out. I'm not sure how she felt, but for me "love" was a transitional word, an acceptable way to escalate the relationship from boyfriend/girl-friend to live-in lovers. It had been necessary, and not necessarily true.

After we moved in together, I stopped saying it.

So did she.

But we did love each other. More than before. It was just that . . . it wasn't the way we'd imagined it. We enjoyed each other's company, we were comfortable together, but when I came home after work I didn't rip off her clothes and throw her on the kitchen floor and rape her then and there. She didn't greet me wearing nothing but a G-string and a smile. It wasn't the intense passionate romance we'd been promised by books and movies and music and TV. It was nice. But it was not all-encompassing, not constantly exciting.

We didn't even make wild passionate love after an argument, the way we were supposed to.

We made love that night, though, before going to sleep, and it was good. It was so good that I wanted to tell her that I loved her.

I wanted to.

But for some reason I didn't.

FIVE

At work, my duties became more substantive. I don't know why this was, whether my success with previous assignments had proved me capable of handling more difficult chores, or whether word came down from on high that I should be pulling my weight and earning my salary by doing real work. Whatever the reason, I was given first one press release to write, then another, and then a full overview for a set of previously written instructions for something called FIS, the File Inventory System.

Stewart made no comment when I turned in the first press release, a two-page piece of unabashed hype modeled after a press release of his own. I attempted to be a little less Madison Avenue in the second release, putting forth the positive attributes of the product in a more objective, journalistic manner. Again, no comment.

The overview was harder to write. I was supposed to describe what the File Inventory System accomplished and how it worked without getting bogged down in too much technical detail, and it took me nearly a week to finish it. When it was done, I made a copy on the Xerox machine and took it over to Stewart, who told me to leave it on his desk and get out of his office.

An hour later, he called.

I picked up the phone. "Hello. Documentation. Bob Jones speaking."

"Jones, I have some things I want to add to your FIS

overview. I'm going to mark up the copy you gave me and let you type in the additions."

"Okay," I said.

"I'll look it over one more time after you're finished. I have to approve it before we send it on to Mr. Banks."

"All right. I'll—" I began.

The phone clicked as he hung up.

I sat there listening to the dial tone. Bastard, I thought. I replaced my handset in the cradle and looked down at the original copy of the overview on my desk. It was strange that he would even call to tell me something like that. It didn't make sense. If he was going to correct my work, why didn't he just do it and order me to type in his revisions? Why had he even called me with this song and dance? There was a reason for this, I knew, but I could not figure out what it was.

Derek was looking at me. "Watch your ass," he said.

I was not sure if that was a threat or a warning—it was impossible to tell from the old man's tone of voice. I wanted to ask him, but he had already turned away from me and was busily scribbling notes on a typed piece of paper.

That was Wednesday. When Thursday and Friday passed, then Monday, Tuesday, and the next Wednesday and I still hadn't heard back from Stewart on the overview, I made a trip over to his office.

He was seated at his desk. His door was open, and he was reading a copy of *Computer World.* I rapped lightly on the doorframe, and he looked up. He frowned when he saw me. "What do you want?"

Nervously, I cleared my throat. "Did you, uh, have a chance to go over my work?"

He stared at me. "What?"

"The overview I wrote for the File Inventory System last week. You said you'd get back to me on it. You said you had some new things to add?"

"No, I didn't."

I shifted uncomfortably. "Well, I thought you said

you had to okay it or approve it or something before it was sent to Mr. Banks."

"What do you want? A pat on the back each time you complete a simple assignment? I'll tell you right now, Jones, we don't work that way around here. And if you think I'm going to allow you to just mope around while you wait for some sort of ego gratification, you've got another think coming. No one here gets medals for simply doing their jobs."

"It's not that."

"What is it, then?" He stared at me, unblinking, waiting for an answer.

I didn't know what to say. I felt flustered. I hadn't expected him to flat-out deny what he'd told me, and I didn't understand what was going on. "Sorry," I mumbled. "I guess I misunderstood what you said. I'd better get back to my desk."

"I guess you'd better."

It might've been my imagination, but I thought I heard him chuckling as I left.

When I returned, there was a note from Hope waiting on my desk, written on a sheet of her pink personalized stationery. I picked up the paper, read the message: "For Stacy's birthday. Sign the card and pass it on to Derek. See you at the lunch!" Paper-clipped to the stationery was a birthday card that showed a group of goofy cartoon jungle animals waving their arms. "From the whole herd!" the front of the card said.

I opened the card and looked at the signatures. All of the programmers except Stacy had signed it, as had Hope, Virginia, and Lois. Each of the signees had also added a short personal note. I didn't know Stacy at all, but I picked up my pen, wrote "Hope you have a great birthday!" and signed my name.

I handed the card to Derek. "What time is the lunch?" I asked.

He took the card from me. "What lunch?"

"Stacy's birthday lunch, I guess."

He shrugged, didn't answer, signed the card, placed

it in its envelope. Ignoring me, he walked out of the office, taking the card with him.

I wanted to say something to him, to tell him what an inconsiderate jerk he was, but as always, I did nothing.

Ten minutes later, my phone rang. I picked it up. It was Banks. He wanted me to come up to his office. I had not been to his office since the first day, and my initial thought was that I was about to be fired. I didn't know why or what for, but I figured that between the two of them, Banks and Stewart had finally come up with a plausible reason why I should be let go.

I was nervous as I waited for the elevator. I didn't like my job, but I certainly didn't want to lose it. I stared at the descending lighted numbers above the metal doors. My palms were sweaty. I wished Banks had not asked me up to his office. If I was going to get fired, I thought, I would have much rather been notified through the mail. I had never been good at personal confrontations.

The elevator doors opened. An older woman in a loud print dress got out, and I stepped in, pressing the button for the fifth floor.

Banks was waiting for me in his office, seated behind his huge desk. He did not say hello, did not stand when I entered, but motioned for me to sit down. I sat. I wanted to wipe my sweaty hands on my pants, but he was looking straight at me and I knew it would be too obvious.

Banks leaned forward in his chair. "Has Ron talked to you about GeoComm?"

I blinked, stared dumbly. "Uh . . . no," I said.

"It's a geobase system that we're developing for cities, counties, and municipal governments. You do know what a geobase system is?"

I shook my head, still not sure where this was leading.

He gave me a look of annoyance. "Geobase is short for geographic database. It allows the user to . . ."

But I was already tuning him out. I wasn't going to

lose my job, I realized. I was being given a new assignment. I was going to be writing instructions for a new computer system. Not just partial instructions, not just one-page rewrites, but an entire manual.

I wasn't going to be fired. I'd been promoted.

Banks stopped talking, looked at me. "Aren't you going to take notes?"

I looked at him. "I didn't bring a notebook," I admitted.

"Here." Sighing heavily, he pulled a pad of yellow legal paper from the top drawer in his desk, handed it to me.

I took a pen from my pocket and began writing.

When I returned to my office an hour later, it was a little after eleven-thirty. Derek was gone. I put my notes and the papers Banks had given me down on my desk and walked over to Hope's station. She was gone, too.

As were the programmers.

And Virginia and Lois.

They'd already left for Stacy's birthday lunch.

I did what I always did, waited until twelve-fifteen, until most of the other people in the building had gone, and then drove to McDonald's, ordering my lunch from the drive-thru and eating in my car at a nearby city park. I don't know why, but I was hurt by the fact that they hadn't waited for me. I shouldn't have expected anything else, but I'd been asked to sign the card, Hope had written "See you at the lunch!" and I guess I'd let myself think that I was actually wanted and welcome. I ate my cheeseburger, taking out the pickle, and listened to the radio as I stared out the car window at a teenage couple making out on a blanket on the grass.

I drove back to work feeling even more depressed.

They arrived back from the lunch a half hour late. I was walking from desk to desk, passing out interoffice phone directories that Stewart had left in my in box and asked me to distribute, when Virginia and Lois passed by me on their way to the steno pool. They were both walking slowly, both holding their hands over their obviously full stomachs.

"I ate too much," Lois said.

Virginia nodded. "Me, too."

"How was it?" I asked. It was a pointed question. I wanted to make them feel guilty for not waiting for me, like Charlie Brown in the Christmas special when he sarcastically thanks Violet for sending him a card she obviously did not send.

Virginia looked at me. "What?"

"How was the lunch?"

"What do you mean, 'How was the lunch?' "

"I was just curious."

"You were there."

"No, I wasn't."

Lois frowned. "Yes, you were. I was talking to you. I was telling you about that accident my daughter got in."

I blinked. "I wasn't there. I was here the whole time."

"Are you sure?"

I nodded. Of course I was sure. I knew where I'd been for lunch, knew what I'd done, but I nonetheless felt chilled, slightly uneasy, and the thought irrationally crossed my mind that there was a doppelganger out there, a double acting in my stead.

"Huh," Lois said, shaking her head. "That's weird. I could've sworn you were there."

I was ignored. By everyone.

I hadn't noticed the extent of it at first because the company was not one big happy family. It was a pretty impersonal place to work, and even friends did not get much of a chance to speak in the hallways beyond a quick "hi."

But people seemed to go out of their way not to notice me.

I tried not to think about it, tried not to let it bother me. But it did bother me. And I was reminded of it each workday, each time I sat in my office with Derek, each time I walked through the halls, each time I took my breaks or went to lunch.

It seemed frivolous to dwell to such an extent on my own problems, to be so chronically self-absorbed. I mean, there were people in Third World countries dying every day from diseases that science had the means to eradicate completely. There were people in our own country who were homeless and starving, and here I was worried that I didn't get along with my coworkers.

But everyone's reality is different.

And in my reality, this was important.

I *thought* of talking about it with Jane, *wanted* to talk to her about it, even *planned* to talk about it, but somehow I never seemed able to bring it up.

On Friday, Hope passed out the checks at four o'clock, the way she always did. I thanked her as she handed me my envelope, and I opened it up to look at the check.

It was sixty dollars less than it was supposed to be.

I stared at the printed number, not sure of what to do. I looked over at Derek. "Is there anything wrong with your check?" I asked.

He shrugged. "Don't know. Haven't looked."

"Could you check?"

"It's none of your business," he told me.

"Fine." I stood up and took my check down the hall to Stewart's office. As usual, he was sitting at his desk, reading a computer magazine. I knocked once on his doorframe, and when he didn't look up, I walked in.

He frowned at me. "What are you doing here?"

"I have a problem," I said. "I need to talk to you."

"What kind of problem?"

There was a chair available, but he didn't offer it to me and I remained standing. "My paycheck's sixty dollars off."

"I don't know anything about it," Stewart said.

"I know. But you're my supervisor."

"What's that supposed to mean? That I'm responsible for everything that goes on in your life?"

"No, I just thought—"

"Don't think. I don't know anything about your little check problem, and to be honest with you, Jones, I don't care." He picked up his magazine, began reading it again. "If you have a question, talk to Accounting."

I looked down at the check, at the attached pay stub, and I noticed something I hadn't seen before. I cleared my throat. "It says here in the hours box that I only worked four days last week."

"There you go, then. That's why your check's short. Case closed."

"But I worked five days."

He lowered his newspaper. "Can you prove it?"

"Prove it? You saw me. Monday I helped you with the IBM memo and retyped that page for the new keyboard. Tuesday I met with you and Mr. Banks to talk about GeoComm. Wednesday and Thursday I worked on the list of processing functions for GeoComm. Friday I turned in what I'd done and started on that Biweekly Report System update."

"I can't be expected to keep track of every little movement made by every little person in this organization. To be honest with you, Jones, I've never known Accounting to make a mistake like this before. If they say you only worked four days last week, then I'm prepared to believe them."

He returned to his magazine.

I stared at him. This was an Orwellian nightmare, a real-life *Catch-22*. I couldn't believe it was happening. I forced myself to take a deep breath. Over the years, I'd grown immune to this sort of reasoning. In the abstract. The three-hundred dollar Pentagon hammers, my dealings with the cable company, all of this had caused me to take for granted the absurdity of the modern world in which I lived. But to come face-to-face with this sort of thinking on such a personal level was not only unbelievable but truly infuriating.

Stewart continued to ignore me, made a big show of licking his thumb and turning the page of his magazine.

He was smiling to himself, and I wanted to smack him, to just walk around the side of his desk, slap him upside the head, and wipe that smirk off his smug pretty-boy face.

Instead, I turned and left, walking straight to the elevator. Accounting was on the third floor, along with Personnel, and I saw Lisa behind the counter as I walked through the third-floor lobby. I ignored her and headed down the main hallway in the opposite direction of the conference room.

I spoke to a clerk, then an accountant, then the finance director, and though I'd half-expected to hear that I had to get Stewart to sign a form verifying my whereabouts on each working day last week, the director apologized for the error and promised to get me a check for the difference by Monday.

I thanked him and left.

I told Jane about it when I got home, related the entire story to her, but I couldn't seem to impart to her the feeling of frustration, the powerlessness I felt in the face of Stewart's disbelief in me and his complete faith in the infallibility of the system. No matter how much I talked, I couldn't make her understand how I felt, and I ended up getting mad at her for not understanding, and both of us went to bed angry.

SIX

I don't know why my job affected my relationship with Jane, but it did. I found myself being unnecessarily curt, getting angry at her for no reason at all. I guess I resented her for not being stuck in a crummy dead-end job like I was. It was stupid and irrational—she was still going to school and working part-time, so of course she couldn't be in the same boat I was in—but I took my frustrations out on her anyway. I felt guilty for doing so. Throughout all those frustrating months when I could not find work, she had been there for me. She had put no pressure on me, she had never been anything but supportive. I felt bad that I was doing this to her, treating her this way.

That made me resent her even more.

Something was definitely wrong with me.

I'd called my parents when I'd first gotten the job but hadn't talked to them since, and although Jane kept pressuring me to do so, I kept putting it off. My mom had been supportive, my dad happy that I'd finally found work, but neither of them had been thrilled, and I'd felt vaguely embarrassed. I didn't know what kind of job they'd expected me to get after graduation, but it was obviously something better than this one, and I felt even more awkward about discussing my work with them now than I had that first time.

I loved my parents, but we didn't exactly have the closest family in the world.

Jane and I were not as close as we had been either. Until recently, we had occupied the same little universe, that of the college student, and our free time had been spent together, doing the same things. But there were differences now, gaps. We were no longer in sync. I worked from eight to five, came home, and my day was done. I relaxed and read or watched TV. She had night classes on Tuesdays and Thursdays and on those evenings did not come home until after nine. On Mondays, Wednesdays, and Fridays she did schoolwork or prepared activities for the kids at the day care center.

Her weekends were spent in the library or in the bedroom, buried in textbooks.

My weekends were free, but I still wasn't used to that. Truth be told, I didn't really know what to do with myself. Throughout my college years, I'd either had a part-time job or, like Jane, I'd done schoolwork when I wasn't in class. Now, having two days with nothing at all to do left me at loose ends. There was only so much work that needed to be done around the apartment, only so much TV I could watch, only so much time I could spend reading. Everything grew old fast, and I was conscious of the weight of all this free time. Occasionally on weekends, Jane and I would go grocery shopping or hit a movie matinee, but more often than not she was doing her school stuff and I was left to my own devices.

It was on one such Saturday that I found myself in Brea Mall, checking out Music Plus, buying tapes I didn't really want because I had nothing else to do. I'd just stopped by Hickory Farms for some free samples when I saw Craig Miller coming out of an electronics store. I felt a sudden lift in my spirits. I hadn't seen Craig since before graduation, and I hurried toward him, smiling and waving as I approached.

He obviously didn't see me and continued walking straight ahead.

"Craig!" I called.

He stopped, frowned, and looked over at me. The expression on his face was blank for a second, as if he didn't recognize me, then he returned my smile. "Hey," he said. "Long time no see." He held out his hand and we shook, though that seemed like kind of a weird and formal thing to do.

"So what are you doing now?" I asked.

"Still going to school. I'm going for my master's in poly sci."

I grinned. "Still hanging out at the Erogenous Zone?"

He reddened. That was a surprise. I'd never seen Craig embarrassed by anything. "You saw me there?"

"You took me there, remember?"

"Oh, yeah."

There was a moment of silence, and it was awkward because I didn't know what to say and it was obvious Craig didn't either. Strange. Craig was a natural motor-mouth and had never been one to let silences remain unfilled. As long as I'd known him, he'd never been without a comment or a reply. He'd always had something to say.

"Well," he said, shifting his weight from one foot to the other. "I better get going. I'm supposed to be home now. Jenny'll kill me if I'm late."

"How is Jenny?" I asked.

"Oh, fine, fine."

He nodded. I nodded. He looked at his watch. "Well, hey, I'd better be going. Nice seeing you again, uh—" He looked at me, caught, instantly aware of his mistake.

I met his eyes and I knew.

He didn't recognize me.

He didn't know who I was.

I felt as though I'd been slapped in the face. I felt like I'd been . . . betrayed. I watched him trying to come up with my name.

"Bob," I prompted.

"Yeah, Bob. I'm sorry. I just forgot for a second." He shook his head, tried to laugh it off. "Alzheimer's."

I merely looked at him. Forgot? We'd hung out

together for two years. He was the closest thing to a friend I'd had at UC Brea. I hadn't seen him in a couple of months, but you didn't completely forget the name of a buddy in less than half a year.

I understood now why he'd been so awkward and formal with me. He hadn't known who I was and had been trying to bluff his way through the conversation.

I thought he'd try to make up for it now. He knew me. He remembered me. I figured he'd loosen up a little, stop acting so stiff and distant, start a real conversation, a personal conversation. But he looked again at his watch, said, "Sorry, I really do have to go. Good to see you." Then he was off, giving me a quick impersonal wave, heading briskly through the crowd, away from me.

I watched him disappear, still stunned. What the hell had happened here? I looked to my left. On the bank of televisions in the window of the electronics store I saw a familiar beer commercial. A group of college chums was getting together with beer and potato chips to watch a Sunday afternoon football game. The young men were all good-looking and good-natured, comfortable enough with themselves and each other to pat one another's shoulders and slap one another's backs.

My college life had not been like that.

The scene of the men laughing as they sat around the television faded into a close-up of an overflowing glass of beer, overlaid with the beer company's logo.

I had not had a group of friends in college, a gang with whom I hung out. I had not had any real friends at all. I'd had Craig and Jane, and that had been it. My Sunday afternoons had been spent not with a group of pals, watching football, but alone in my bedroom, studying. I stared at the TVs as another commercial came on. I had not realized until now how solitarily I had spent the four years I'd attended UC Brea. Those media images of close camaraderie and lasting friendships had been only that for me—images. Their reality had never materialized. I had not known my classmates in college the way I'd known my classmates in grammar school, junior high, and high school. College had been a much colder, much more impersonal experience.

I thought back on my college classes, and I suddenly realized that I'd gone through my entire academic career having had no personal contact with any of my instructors. I had known them, of course, but I'd known them in the same way I knew characters on TV, from observation not interaction. I doubted that a single one would remember me. They'd known me only for a semester and even then only as a number on a roll sheet. I never asked questions, never stayed after for extra help, always sat in the middle of the room. I had been completely anonymous.

I had been planning to hang around the mall a little longer, check out a few other stores, but I no longer felt like doing so. I wanted to be home. All of a sudden I felt strange wandering from shop to shop alone, anonymously, not noticed or known by anybody. I felt uncomfortable, and I wanted to be with Jane. She might be busy studying, she might not have time to do anything with me right now, but at least she knew who I was, and that alone was a comforting thought, incentive enough to make me leave.

I found myself thinking about my meeting with Craig as I drove back to the apartment. I tried to explain it, tried to rationalize it, tried to play it off, but I couldn't. He had not been a mere acquaintance, someone I saw only in class. We had gone places together. We had done things together. Craig was not stupid, and unless he'd had some sort of brain tumor or mental illness or drug problem, there was no way he could have forgotten who I was.

Maybe the problem wasn't with him. Maybe the problem was with me.

That seemed the most likely answer, and it frightened me to think about it. I knew I was not the most interesting person in the world, but was I so hopelessly boring that even a friend could forget who I was within the space of a couple months? It was a terrifying idea, and an almost unbearably depressing one. I was not an egomaniac, and I certainly didn't harbor any illusions about my making a significant mark on the world, but it nonetheless unnerved me to think my existence was so meaningless that it passed entirely unnoticed.

Jane was on the phone when I arrived home, talking to some girl from work, but she looked up when I entered, smiled at me, and that made me feel good.

Maybe I was reading too much into all this, I thought. Maybe I was overreacting.

I went into the bathroom and looked at myself in the mirror. I studied myself for quite a while, trying to be objective, trying to see myself as others might see me. I was not good-looking, but neither was I ugly. My hair, light brown, was neither long nor short, my nose not big and not small.

I was average-looking. I was of average build, average height. I wore average clothes.

I was average.

It was a weird realization. I cannot say that I was surprised, but I had not really thought about it before and I felt strange being able to categorize myself so easily and so completely. I wished it weren't so, wished there were something about me that was unique and exceptional and wonderful, but I knew there wasn't. I was completely and totally ordinary.

Perhaps it explained the situation at work.

I pushed the thought out of my mind and hurried out of the bathroom, back to the living room where Jane was.

I was acutely conscious, the next few days, of everything I did, everything I said, and I was both horrified and discouraged to discover that, yes, I really was thoroughly and consistently unexceptional. My conversations with Jane were banal, my work was never less or more than adequate. No wonder Craig had not remembered me. I seemed to be so average in every way that I was entirely forgettable.

Was I also average in bed?

It was a question that, in one version or another, had been haunting me for some time, even before I'd seen Craig, lurking in the back of my mind when I was with Jane, unfocused but there, a vague threat. Now it had been, if not voiced, at least given shape, and I knew it would not go away. I tried to push it out of my mind, tried not to think of it when we were together, when were eating or talking or taking a shower or lying in bed, but it gnawed at me, growing in my brain from a whisper to a shout until I felt compelled to bring it up.

On Saturday evening, as always, we made love, doing it during the half-hour local news before *Saturday Night Live.* I did not usually analyze our love-making while it was happening, did not examine what we were doing or why we were doing it, but I found myself watching from a distance this time, as though I were a camera, and I realized how limited were my moves, how scripted my responses, how boring and goddamn predictable everything was. I had a difficult time maintaining an erection, and I had to force myself to concentrate in order to finish.

Afterward, I rolled off her, spent, breathing heavily, and stared up at the ceiling, thinking about my performance. I would have liked to believe that it was great, that I was a true stud, but I knew that was not the case. I was average.

My penis was probably the average size.

I probably gave her the average number of orgasms.

I looked over at Jane. Even now, perhaps especially now, hot and sweaty in the aftermath of sex, hair clumped in damp tangles, she looked beautiful. I had always known that she could do a lot better than me, that she was pretty enough, intelligent enough, interesting enough to attract someone superior to myself, but it was suddenly brought home to me in a way that was almost painful.

I touched her shoulder, gently, tentatively. "How was it?" I asked.

She looked at me. "What?"

"Did you . . . come?"

"Of course." She frowned. "What's wrong with you? You've been acting weird all night."

I wanted to explain to her how I felt, but I couldn't.

I shook my head, said nothing.

"Bob?" she said.

I guess what I really wanted was to be reassured, to hear her say that I was not average, that I was special, that I was great, but in my mind I could hear her trying to assuage my fears by saying, "I love you even though you're average." Which was not what I wanted to hear.

Her mother's words echoed in my head: ". . . a nothing . . . a nobody . . ."

That was how I felt.

What would happen, I wondered, if she met someone with more skillful hands, a faster tongue, a bigger penis?

I didn't even want to think about that.

"I . . . love you," I said.

She looked surprised, and her expression softened. "I love you, too." She kissed me on the mouth, on the nose, on the forehead, and we snuggled together and pulled the blanket higher and watched TV until we fell asleep.

SEVEN

Acknowledgment of my mediocrity only seemed to hasten my fade into the woodwork. Even Hope no longer spoke to me unless I addressed her first, and more than once it seemed that she'd forgotten I worked at Automated Interface. It was as if I were becoming a shade within the corporation, a ghost in the machine.

The weather changed, became warmer, became summer. I felt melancholy, sad. Sunny days always made me feel that way. The sharp contrast between the blue beauty of a summer sky and the drab grayness of my life made the difference between my dreams and my reality seem that much more pronounced.

I was working full-time on GeoComm now, writing a real instruction manual, not playing around with the piddly-ass projects to which I'd previously been assigned. I was given access to computer screens by the programmers; I was given demonstrations of the system; I was allowed to play around with the system on one of the terminals in the test facility. I suppose the work could have been considered challenging—*could* have, had I had any interest in it at all. But I did not. Assistant Coordinator of Interoffice Procedures and Phase II Documentation was a job I had taken not out of choice but out of necessity, and its specifics held no allure for me.

The one person who did not ignore me was Stewart. He seemed more hostile than ever. I was a constant source of irritation to him. The fact that Banks, or someone above Banks, had decided to let me work on a legitimate project made him furious, and at least once each day he would come into the office, nod to Derek, then move in front of my desk and stand there, looking down at whatever I was working on. He would not say anything, would not ask me what I was doing, would simply stand there, staring. It annoyed me and he knew it annoyed me, but I refused to give him the satisfaction of letting my feelings show. I would ignore him, concentrate on the work in front of me, and wait him out. Eventually, he would leave.

I'd watch him go, and I'd want to just punch him.

I'd never been a violent person. Even my revenge fantasies had usually involved humiliation, not physical harm. But something about Stewart made me want to just beat the living shit out of him.

Not that I could.

He was in a hell of a lot better shape than I was, and I had no doubt that he could've easily kicked my ass.

I finished documenting the functions from the first GeoComm submenu. I gave the instructions to Stewart, who supposedly gave them to Banks. I heard nothing back from either of them and began work on the system's second submenu.

It was Thursday, the day of Jane's night class, and though we didn't usually have sex on Thursdays because she got home late and tired, I convinced her to do it this time. Afterward, I rolled off her. We'd done it in the missionary position, I realized. We always did it in the missionary position.

We were silent for a moment, lying next to each other. Jane reached for the remote and turned on the TV. A cop show was on.

"Did you come?" I asked her finally.

"Yes."

"More than once?"

She propped herself up on one elbow. "Not this again. Am I going to have to reassure you each time we make love?"

"Sorry I asked."

"What do you want from me? I came, you know I came, and you still have to ask me about it."

"I thought maybe you were faking it."

"I've had enough of this." Angrily, she pulled up the covers, bunching them beneath her chin. "If I knew I was going to have to go through all this crap again, we wouldn't've done it at all."

I looked at her, hurt and trying to show it. "You don't like having sex with me."

"Oh, for God's sake!"

"How am I supposed to feel, huh? I mean, how do you feel about me? Do you still love me? Would you still love me if we met today for the first time?"

"I'm only going to say this once, okay? Yes, I love you. Now that's it. End of discussion. Drop it and go to sleep."

"Okay," I said. "Fine." I was angry with her, but there was really no reason for me to be angry.

We turned away from each other and fell asleep to the sounds of the television.

EIGHT

I began to see flyers for Automated Interface's annual employee picnic tacked up on the bulletin board in the break room, taped to the doors of our department. I ignored the flyers, preferring not to think about the picnic, though I overheard the programmers talking about it. The event seemed to be a biggie, and apparently, from what I gathered, attendance was required.

Required attendance. That was what bothered me. I knew that I would have no one to go with, no friend to sit next to, and the idea of sitting alone at a picnic table while everyone else around me talked and laughed and visited and had a great time worried me.

I worried more and more about the picnic as the flyers proliferated, as conversational references became more common. It was turning into an honest-to-God obsession. As the week, and then the day, grew closer, I found myself hoping absurdly that some sort of natural disaster would occur and prevent the event from taking place.

On Tuesday, the night before the picnic, I even considered calling in sick.

I don't know what prompted this almost pathological fear of the picnic, but I suspect it was a combination of things: my inability to fit in at work, the recent discovery of how hopelessly average I was, the increasing rockiness of my relationship with Jane. My self-esteem and self-confidence were at an all-time low, and I didn't think my ego could stand the sort of bashing the picnic would provide. Like Charlie Brown said, "I know no one likes me. Why do we have to have holidays to remind me of it?"

This wasn't exactly a holiday, but it followed the same principle. I was nothing, I was invisible, and this would only serve to bring it home.

The picnic was scheduled to start at noon and finish at two and was being held in the oversized greenbelt behind the Automated Interface building. At eleven forty-five, the toadlike man from upstairs who ate lunch with Derek stopped by the office, said "Ready?" and he and Derek went out to the picnic. Neither of them spoke to me, neither of them invited me to accompany them, and although I hadn't expected them to invite me to come along, the fact that they didn't pissed me off.

In the hallway, I heard other voices, saw other people pass by, but I remained at my desk. I wondered if I could close the door and stay here, hide and not go. No one would notice if I was missing. No one would know if I didn't show up.

There was an interruption of the Muzak piped over the building's speakers, and a deep-voiced man announced: "The annual employee picnic has now started. All employees must attend. Repeat. The annual employee picnic has now started. All employees must attend."

I *should've* called in sick, I thought.

I waited a moment, then stood slowly and walked out of the office and down the hall to the elevator. The elevator stopped on the other two floors, and by the time we reached the lobby, it was packed. There were even more people in the lobby—employees from the first floor, others who had taken the stairs—and I followed the crowd across the floor of the lobby through the rear double doors. We walked through a short corridor, then through a door that opened outside onto the back of the building. I stood for a moment at the top of the steps, letting everyone pass by me. Rows of picnic tables were now set up on the previously virgin grass.

A portable stage with a canvas roof had been wheeled in from somewhere and sat at the head of the tables, facing the side parking lot. Long banquet tables covered with white tablecloths and piled high with salads, desserts, and main dishes were being added to and overseen by a group of busy women. A series of garbage cans filled with soft drinks and ice cubes lined the area of the lawn nearest the building.

I stood there for a moment, not sure what to do, not knowing if I should go out and grab some chow, or find a place to sit and wait until other people started eating first. From here, I had a clear view of the knolly landscaped greenbelts of the adjacent companies, and it was almost like looking into their backyards. I had a sudden vision of these buildings as giant houses, the greenbelts their yards, the parking lots their driveways.

Most of the people were looking for friends, finding seats, but a few had grabbed plates and gotten into line for the food and I followed their example. I took a can of Coke from one of the garbage cans and piled my paper plate high with hot dogs, chili beans, potato salad, and chips. The picnic table at which Banks, Stewart, the programmers, Hope, Virginia, and Lois sat was full, there was no room for me, so I looked around for an empty seat at one of the other tables. There were several open spots at a table occupied by a group of old women, and I walked over there, carrying my plate. No one was staring at me as I walked across the grass, no one was pointing or giggling, no one was taking any notice of me. I was totally inconspicuous; I blended perfectly into the crowd. But I didn't *feel* as though I blended perfectly into the crowd. Even if no one else was aware of me, I was acutely aware of them.

I reached the table and sat down, smiling at the woman next to me, but she stared past me, ignoring me completely, and I resigned myself to eating alone and in silence.

"Beautiful music," that bastard offspring of Muzak, was issuing from two small speakers on either side of the stage. It wasn't a radio station but a tape and was far worse than even the stringed instrumental renditions of soft pop hits that we usually listened to each day. A uniformed maintenance worker climbed up on the stage and set up a folding table. On top of the table he placed a small cardboard box. He plugged a few wires into the back of one of the speakers, then strung the wires and the Mr. Microphone to which they were connected across the stage floor to the table. I watched him work as I ate, feigning interest, grateful to have something on which to focus my attention.

A few minutes later, a man I didn't know but who seemed to be familiar to most of the other employees hopped up on stage to a round of applause. He waved at the crowd, picked up the Mr. Microphone, and began talking. "I know this is the part of our picnic you've all been waiting for. Especially you, Roy." He pointed toward a balding overweight man at the table closest to him and everyone laughed.

"Yeah, Roy!" someone called out.

The man on stage held up his hand. "Come on, now. What we're going to do this year is start with the smallest prizes first, then after that we'll have the drawing for our grand prize—dinner at Orange County's finest and most expensive restaurant, Elise!"

There were hoots and whistles and catcalls.

I ate my lunch as the man put his hand in the box on the table and drew out names for free car washes, free video rentals, free hamburgers. Then came the grand prize, the dinner at Elise.

I won.

I sat there, unmoving, as the man read my name, my brain not correctly processing the information. When he read my name again, this time with a questioning tone in his voice, as if trying to determine whether or not I was present, I stood. My heart was pounding, my lips dry as I walked onto the stage. I expected there to be silence—no one knew me, after all—but there was polite applause, the type of applause given only out of

obligation and reserved for strangers. The earlier whistles and catcalls were gone. I looked over at my department's table as I accepted the gift certificate and said
"Thank you" into the proffered Mr. Microphone. The
secretaries and programmers were clapping politely,
but Stewart and Banks were not clapping at all. Stewart
was scowling.

I hurried off the stage and immediately sat back
down at my seat.

No one at my table even looked at me.

Later that afternoon, Stewart called me into his
office. "I heard you were at the employee picnic and
you won the grand prize."

He *heard*? He was there.

I nodded, saying nothing.

"You seem to be spending an awful lot of time
socializing on company time. I would think with your
deadlines and all the work you have to do, you'd spend
a little less time with your friends and a little more time
on your assignments."

I stared at him. "Attendance at the picnic was
required. I wouldn't've gone—"

"You do a lot of gabbing with your buddies during
work hours, don't you?"

"What buddies? I don't know anyone here. I come,
do my job, and go home."

He smiled slightly, a hard, mirthless smile. "That's
your problem, Jones. Your attitude. If you put a little
more effort into your work and started thinking of this
as a career instead of just a job, you might get somewhere in life. It would behoove you, I think, to be a
little more of a team player."

I did not even bother to respond. For the first time, I
noticed how empty and bare Stewart's office looked.
There was nothing to indicate its occupant's personal
tastes or interests. There were no framed photos on the
desk, no knickknacks or plants in the room. The few
papers tacked to the bulletin board on the wall were all
memos or official company notices. The pile of maga-

zines on the corner of the desk were all technical journals whose address labels were imprinted with the name and P.O. box of the corporation.

"Jones?" Stewart said. "Are you listening to me?"

I nodded.

"Why haven't you been submitting your biweekly progress report?"

I stared at him. "You told me I didn't have to turn in a report. You said that was only for the programmers."

A trace of a smile touched his lips. "This requirement is clearly stated in your job description, which I suggest you take the time to read."

"If I had known it was required, I would have done it. But you told me specifically that I didn't have to turn in a progress report."

"You do."

"Then why didn't you tell me that before? Why did you wait this long before letting me know?"

He glared at me. "As I'm sure you're aware, your performance review is coming up in a few weeks. I'm afraid I have no choice but to make note of your poor work attitude and continual insubordination."

Insubordination?

This isn't the fucking army, I wanted to say. I'm not your slave, you fascist son of a bitch.

But I said nothing.

When he was through with his diatribe, I went back to my office.

Derek looked up when I returned. That in itself was unusual. But what was even stranger was that he actually spoke to me.

"Were you at the picnic?" he asked.

I was still ticked off at Stewart and was tempted to give Derek a taste of his own medicine, to not answer him, to ignore him and act as though he weren't there. But I couldn't do it. "Yeah," I said, "I was there."

"Do you know who won the drawing? The grand prize?"

Was this a joke? I frowned at him.

"It's for the employee newsletter," he explained. "I've been asked to compile a list."

"I won," I said slowly.

He looked surprised. "Really? Why didn't you go up and collect your prize, then?"

"I did. Here it is." I picked up the certificate from my desk and waved it at him.

"Oh." He started writing, then looked up at me. "What's your first name?" he asked.

This was ridiculous.

"Bob," I found myself answering.

"Last name?"

"Jones."

He nodded. "It'll be in the next issue of the newsletter."

He went back to his work.

He did not speak to me for the rest of the day.

Jane was not there when I came home. There was a note from her on the refrigerator telling me that she'd gone to the library to find some books on the Montessori method of teaching preschool children. It was just as well. I wasn't in the mood to either talk or listen to anyone else. I just wanted to be alone and think.

I popped a frozen burrito into the microwave.

After my short conversation with Derek, I had not been able to concentrate on work for the remainder of the afternoon. I had placed papers before me on my desk and, pen in hand, had pretended to read them, but my mind had been on anything but instruction manuals. I kept going over everything Derek had said, searching for something that would indicate he had been joking or playing with me, not willing to believe that he really had not known my name. I kept wishing he had asked for the spelling. That at least would have allowed me a legitimate out. I could have rationalized that he had known my name but had not known the spelling.

But that wasn't the case.

No matter how much I replayed that conversation in my head, no matter how much I tried to analyze what we both had said, I kept reaching the same conclusion. He had not known my name, though we'd been sharing an office for over two months. He had not seen me win the drawing, though I had stood on the stage in front of him.

I was invisible to him.

Hell, maybe the reason he never talked to me was because he didn't even notice I was there.

The bell on the microwave rang, and I took out my burrito, dropping it on a plate. I poured myself a glass of milk and walked out to the living room, turning on the TV and sitting down on the couch. I tried to eat and watch the news, tried not to think about what had happened. I blew on my burrito, took a bite. Tom Brokaw was reporting the results of a recent AIDS poll, looking seriously into the camera as a the image of a caduceus flashed on the blue screen behind him, and he said, "According to the latest *New York Times*-NBC poll, the average American believes—"

The average American.

The phrase jumped out at me.

The average American.

That was me. That's what I was. I stared at Brokaw. I felt as though I were sick and my illness had been successfully diagnosed, but there was none of the relief that would have accompanied such a medical breakthrough. The description was true, as far as it went, but it was also too general, too benign. There was reassurance in those three words, the implication of normalcy. And I was not normal. I was ordinary, but I was not just ordinary. I was extra ordinary, ultra ordinary, so damn ordinary that even my friends did not remember me, that even my own coworkers did not notice me.

I had a weird feeling about this. The chill I'd felt when Lois and Virginia had insisted they'd seen me at Stacy's birthday lunch was back. This whole thing was getting way too freaky. It was one thing to be just an average guy. But it was quite another to be so . . . so pathologically average. So consistently middle-of-the-road in every way that I was invisible. There was something creepy about it, something frightening and almost supernatural.

On an impulse, I reached over and picked up yesterday's newspaper off the table. I found the Calendar section and looked at the boxed statistics that showed the top five films of the past weekend.

They were the five films I most wanted to see.

I turned the page to look at the top ten songs of the week.

They were my current favorites, ranked in order of preference.

My heart pounding, I stood and walked across the room to the block-and-plank shelves next to the stereo. I scanned my collection of records and CDs, and I realized that it was a history of the number one albums over the past decade.

This was crazy.

But it made sense.

If I was average, I was average. Not just in appearance and personality, but in everything. Across the board. It explained, perhaps, my adherence to the Golden Mean, my unshakable belief in the rightness of the adage "moderation in all things." Never in my life had I gone to extremes. In anything. I had never eaten too much or too little. I had never been selfishly greedy or selfishly altruistic. I had never been a radical liberal or a reactionary conservative. I was neither a hedonist nor an ascetic, a drunk nor a teetotaler.

I had never taken a stand on anything.

Intellectually, I knew it was incorrect to think that compromise was always the ideal solution, that truth always existed somewhere in the middle of two opposing passions—there was no happy medium between right and wrong, between good and evil—but the equivocation that rendered me impotent in regard to minor practical decisions afflicted me morally, too, and

I inevitably vacillated between differing points of view, stuck squarely in the middle and unable to definitely and unequivocally take a side.

The average American.

My extraordinary ordinariness was not just an aspect of my personality, it was the very essence of my being. It explained why I alone among my peers had never questioned or complained about the outcome of any election or the winner of any award. I had always been squarely in the mainstream and had never disagreed with anything agreed upon by the majority. It explained why none of my arguments in any of my high school or college classes had made even the slightest dent in the course of a debate.

It explained, as well, my odd attraction to the city of Irvine. Here, where all the streets and houses looked the same, where homeowners' associations tolerated no individuality in the external appearance of houses or landscaping, I felt comfortable and at home. The homogeneity appealed to me, spoke to me.

But it wasn't logical to think that the fact that I was average rendered me invisible, caused people to ignore me. Was it? Most people, when you came down to it, were not exceptional. Most people were normal, average. Yet they were not ignored by their coworkers, friends, and acquaintances. It was not only the sublime and the horrific that were noticed, not only the individual and idiosyncratic that had their existences validated by attention.

But I was average.

And I was ignored.

I tried to think of some action or event that would disprove my theory, something I'd done that would prove I was not totally ordinary. I remembered being picked on by bullies when I was in the third grade. I hadn't been average then, had I? I had been different enough to have been specifically chosen as the object of harassment by the three toughest kids in the school. One time, in fact, they'd caught me on my way home.

One of them held me down while the other two took off my pants. They played Keep Away, tossing the pants over my head to each other while I tried vainly to intercept their throws. A crowd gathered, laughing, and there were girls in the crowd, and for some reason I liked the fact that the girls were there. I liked the fact that they saw me in my underwear.

I used to think of that later, when I was a teenager, when I was masturbating. It made me more excited to think of those girls watching me trying to get my pants from the bullies.

That wasn't normal, was it? That wasn't average.

But I was grasping at straws. Everyone had little offbeat fantasies and perversities.

And I probably had the average number of them.

Even my out-of-the-ordinary experiences were ordinary. Even my irregularities were regular.

Christ, even my name was average. Bob Jones. Next to John Smith, it was probably the most common name in the phone book.

My burrito was cold, but I no longer felt hungry. I no longer felt like eating. I looked up at the TV. A reporter was describing a mass killing in Milwaukee.

Most people were probably watching the news right now.

The average American was watching news with his dinner.

I got up, switched the channel to *M*A*S*H*. I carried my plate into the kitchen, dumped the leftover burrito into the garbage, placed the plate in the sink. I took a beer out of the refrigerator. I felt like getting good and drunk.

I brought the beer back with me into the living room and sat there watching TV, trying to concentrate on the *M*A*S*H* episode, trying not to think about myself.

I realized that the lines punctuated by the laugh track were the ones I found funniest.

I switched off the TV.

Jane came home around nine. I'd already downed a

six-pack and was feeling, if not better, at least far enough out of it that I no longer cared about my problems. She looked at me, frowned, then walked past me and put her notebooks down on the kitchen table. She picked up the certificate from where I'd left it. "What's this?" she asked.

I'd forgotten about winning the dinner. I looked at her, hoisted my current beer. "Congratulate me," I said. "I won a drawing at work."

She read the name on the certificate. "Elise?"

"Yeah," I said.

"This is great!"

"Yeah. Great."

She frowned at me again. "What the hell's wrong with you?"

"Nothing," I said. "Nothing at all." I finished my beer, put it next to its empty brothers on the table, and headed to the bathroom where I promptly threw up.

We went to dinner at Elise three weeks later.

A child of the suburbs, I could not remember ever eating at a restaurant that was not part of a chain. From McDonald's to Love's to The Black Angus to Don José's, the restaurants I patronized were not unique, individually owned businesses but corporate cookie-cutter eateries, comfortable in the reliability of their conformity. As we walked into the entryway and I saw the elegant decor, the classy clientele, I realized that I did not know how to act here, did not know what to do. Despite the fact that both Jane and I had dressed up— she in her prom gown, me in my interview suit—and outwardly fit in with the restaurant's patrons, I felt jarringly out of place among the other diners. We seemed to be decades younger than everyone else. And instead of actually paying for our meal, we'd be using that stupid gift certificate. I put my hand in my pocket, felt the ruffled edge of the certificate, and I wondered if I'd brought enough money for a tip. I suddenly wished we hadn't come.

We'd made reservations ahead of time, two weeks ahead of time, and we were promptly seated and provided with a calligraphically hand-printed description of the day's dishes. From what I could tell, we had no choice to make; there was only one meal available, a multicourse dinner de jour, and I nodded my approval to the waiter, handing back the description. Jane did the same.

"What would you care to drink, sir?" the waiter asked me.

For the first time, I saw a wine list on the table in front of me, and not wanting to appear as ignorant as I was, I studied the list for a moment. I looked to Jane for help, but she only shrugged, looking away, and I pointed to one of the wines in the middle of the list.

"Very good, sir."

The wine and our first course, some sort of smoked salmon appetizer, arrived minutes later. A dash of wine was poured into my glass, and I sipped it, the way I'd seen it done in movies, then nodded to the waiter. The wine was poured into our glasses. Then we were left alone.

I glanced across the table at Jane. This was the first time we'd had a meal together in over a week. There were legitimate reasons—she'd had to see her mother; I'd had to take the car into Sears to have the brakes checked; she'd had to study at the library—but the real truth was that we'd been avoiding each other. Looking at her now, I realized I didn't know what to say to her. Any conversation starter would be just that, a forced and awkward effort to initiate talk. Whatever rapport we had once had, whatever naturalness had previously existed in our relationship, seemed to have fled. What would have once come easily was now stiffly self-conscious. I realized that I was becoming as estranged from her as I was from everyone else.

Jane looked around the dining room. "This is really a nice place," she said.

"Yes, it is," I agreed. "It really is." I had nothing to

follow this with, nothing more to say, so I repeated it again. "It really is."

The service was amazing. There was a virtual platoon of waiters assigned to our table, but they did not hover, did not make us feel uncomfortable. When one dish was done, a waiter silently and efficiently took it away, replacing it with the next course.

Jane finished her wine soon after the salad. I poured her another glass. "Did I tell you about Bobby Tetherton's mom?" she said. I shook my head and she started describing a run-in with an overprotective parent she'd had at the day care center that afternoon.

I listened to her. Maybe nothing was wrong, I thought. Maybe it was all in my head. Jane was acting as though everything was normal, everything was okay. Maybe I'd imagined the rift between us.

No.

Something had happened. Something had come between us. We had always shared our problems, had always discussed with each other our difficulties at school or work. I had never met her coworkers at the day care center, but she'd brought them alive for me, I knew their names, and I cared about their office politics.

But now I found my mind wandering while she recited the litany of today's injustices.

I didn't care about her day.

I tuned her out, not listening to her. We had always had a balanced relationship, a modern relationship, and I'd always considered her work, her career, her activities, as important as my own. It was not rhetoric, not something I forced myself to do out of obligation, but something I truly felt. Her life was as important as mine. We were equals.

But I didn't feel that way anymore.

Her problems seemed so fucking petty compared to my own.

She chattered on about kids I didn't know and didn't want to know. I was annoyed with her and my annoyance soon graduated to anger. I had not told her about being ignored, about discovering I was some sort of quintessentially average . . . freak, but, damn it, she should have noticed something was wrong and she should have asked me about it. She should have tried to talk to me, to find out what was bothering me and cheer me up. She shouldn't have just pretended that everything was okay.

". . . these parents entrust their children to our center," she was saying, "then they try to tell us how to—"

"I don't care," I said.

She blinked. "What?"

"I don't care about your damn day care center."

Her mouth closed, flattened into a grim line. She nodded, as if this was something she'd been expecting. "Now it comes out," she said. "Now the truth finally comes out."

"Come on, let's just enjoy our meal."

"After that?"

"After what? Can't we just try to have a nice meal together and enjoy our evening?"

"Enjoy it in silence? Is that what you mean?"

"Look—"

"No, you look. I don't know what's wrong with you. I don't know what's been bothering you lately—"

"Why don't you try asking?"

"I would if I thought it would do any good. But you've been living in your own world the past month or so. You just sit there brooding all the time, not talking, not doing anything, shutting me out—"

"Shutting *you* out?"

"Yes. Every time I try to get close to you, you push me away."

"I push *you* away?"

"When's the last time we made love?" She stared at me. "When's the last time you even tried to make love with me?"

I glanced around the restaurant, embarrassed. "Don't make a scene," I said.

"Make a scene? I'll make a scene if I want to. I don't know these people, and I'll never see them again. What do I care what they think of me?"

"I care," I said.

"They don't."

She was right. Our voices were raised now, we were definitely arguing, but no one was looking at us or paying us even the slightest bit of attention. I assumed it was because they were too polite to do so. But a small voice in the back of mind said that it was because they didn't notice me, because I created a kind of force field of invisibility that surrounded us.

"Let's just finish eating," I said. "We can talk about this at home."

"We can talk about it now."

"I don't want to."

She looked at me, and it was like she was a cartoon character or something. I could see in the exaggerated expression on her face the birth of an idea, the dawning of realization. "You don't care about this relationship at all, do you? You don't care about me. You don't care about us. You're not even willing to fight for what we have. All you care about is you."

"You don't care about me," I countered.

"Yes, I do. I always have. But you don't care about me." She sat there, staring at me across the table, and the way she looked at me made me feel not only uncomfortable but profoundly sad. She was looking at me as though I were a stranger, as though she had just discovered that I had been cloned and replaced by a soulless look-alike impostor. I could see the sense of loss on her face, could tell how deeply hurt and suddenly alone she felt, and I wanted to reach across the table and take her hands in mine and tell her that I was the same person I'd always been, that I loved her and was truly sorry if I'd said or done anything to hurt her. But something kept me from it. Something held me back. I was dying inside, desperate to right the things that had gone so wrong between us, but something made me look away from her and down at my plate.

I picked up my fork, began eating.

"Bob?" she said.

I looked at my plate.

"Bob?" Questioningly, tentatively.

I did not answer, kept eating.

After a moment, she too picked up a fork and started eating.

Smoothly, silently, a waiter took my plate, replaced it with another.

NINE

August became September.

I arrived at work one morning to find a manila interoffice envelope and a small rectangular cardboard box sitting on my desk. I was early; Derek had not yet come in, and I had the office to myself. I sat down and picked up the envelope, staring at the rows of crossed-off names on its front. The envelope's itinerary for the past month was printed plainly on its cover, in different ink, with different signatures, and it made me realize just how much I hated my job. As I scanned down the list of names and departments now hidden behind ineffectual lines and halfhearted scribbles, I found that there was not a single individual I felt warmly toward.

I also realized how long I'd been here.

Three months.

A fourth of a year.

Pretty soon it would be a half a year. Then a whole year. Then two.

I dropped the envelope without opening it, feeling unaccountably depressed. I sat there for a moment, staring at the ugly blank office wall in front of me, then reached for the box. I picked it up, pulled off the top, looked inside.

Business cards.

Hundreds of cards, making up a single solid block of white, filled the inside of the small box. On the face of the front card, I saw my name and my title printed next to the Automated Interface logo and the corporation's address and P.O. box number.

My first business cards.

I should have felt happy. I should have felt excited. I should have felt something positive. But that huge stack of wallet-sized cards filled me instead with an emotion akin to dread. The cards bespoke commitment, a belief on the part of the corporation that I would be there for a long time to come. The cards seemed at that moment as binding as a contract, as adhesive as glue, an investment in obligation. I wanted to scream. I wanted to throw the cards away. I wanted to send them back.

But I did nothing of the sort.

I took a few others out of the box and put them in my wallet and placed the rest in the upper right drawer of my desk.

The drawer closed with a metallic clank that sounded disproportionately loud and had about it a tone of finality.

I found myself focusing on the permanently jammed keyhole in the center of the drawer. So this was it. This was my life. Here I would spend the next forty years or so, then I would retire and then I would die. It was an overly pessimistic view of the situation, maybe a little melodramatic. But it was essentially true. I knew what I was like. I knew my personality and patterns. Theoretically, I could move on to another job. I could even go back to school eventually, get another degree. There were many options available to me. But I knew that none of those things would happen. I would simply adjust to my situation and live with it, the way I always had. I was not an initiator, a doer, a get-up-and-goer. I was a stayer and a stick-it-outer.

And then my life would be over.

I thought back to the dreams I'd had in grammar school and junior high, my plans of being an astronaut and then a rock star and then a movie director. I wondered if it was this way for everyone, and I decided that it probably was. No little kid *wanted* to be a bureaucrat or a technocrat or a middle management supervisor—

or an Assistant Coordinator of Interoffice Procedures and Phase II Documentation.

These were the jobs we settled for when our dreams died.

And that's all they had been—dreams. I was not going to be an astronaut; I was not going to be a rock star; I was not going to be a movie director. This was where I was, this was who I was, and the reality of the situation depressed the hell out of me.

Derek came in just before eight, ignored me as usual, and immediately started making phone calls. At nine, Banks called and said he wanted to have a meeting with me and Stewart, and I went upstairs to his office where the two of them berated me for half an hour and told me how unsatisfactory my GeoComm documentation had been until now.

I spent the rest of the morning and the afternoon rewriting the GeoComm function descriptions I'd already written.

Exactly five years ago this month, I realized, I had started attending UC Brea. What a difference those five years had made. Then I'd been just out of high school, my whole future ahead of me. Now I was rapidly speeding toward thirty, locked into this horrible job, my life a dead end.

Typing my revisions into WordPerfect on the PC, I accidentally pressed a wrong key and deleted ten pages of work. I looked up at the clock. Four-thirty. A half hour to go. There was no way I'd be able to retype all of that in a half hour.

This was the bottom, I thought. This was hell. There was no way things could get worse than this.

But, as usual, I was wrong.

The apartment was dark when I got home, and it still smelled of breakfast. Faint traces of toast and egg and orange juice lingered in the still air. I reached next to the door and flipped on the light switch.

The living room was empty. Not just empty as in no

people, but empty as in no furniture. The couch was gone, as was the coffee table. The TV was still there, but the VCR was gone. Both the ficus and the Boston fern were gone, and the walls were bare, all of the framed art prints missing.

I felt as thought I'd stepped into another dimension, into the twilight zone. An overreaction, maybe, but the look of the apartment was so shocking, so unexpected, that my mind could not focus on particulars, could only take in the totality of the situation, and that totality was so overwhelming that I could not put anything into perspective.

But I knew instantly what had happened.

Jane was gone.

I pulled off my tie as I hurried into the kitchen. Here again, things were missing: the toaster, the cookie jars.

There was a note on the kitchen table.

A note?

I stared down at the folded piece of paper with my name on it, stunned. This was not like Jane at all. This was totally out of character. This was just not the sort of thing she'd do. If she was unhappy, if she had a problem, she'd talk to me about it and then we'd fight it out. She wouldn't just pack her stuff and sneak away and leave me a note. She wouldn't just give up. She wouldn't walk away from me, from us, from what we had together.

The first thing I probably should've thought was that somebody had taken her, that she'd been kidnapped by the same person who had ransacked our apartment.

But somehow I knew that wasn't the case.

She'd left me.

I don't know how I knew, but I knew. Maybe I had seen it coming but hadn't wanted to acknowledge it. I thought back, remembered her telling me that communication was the most important thing in a relationship, that even if two people loved each other, there was no relationship if they couldn't communicate. I recalled her trying to talk to me for the past few months, trying to get me to talk to her and tell her what was bothering me, what was wrong.

I remembered the night at Elise.

We hadn't really talked much since that evening. We'd fought about not talking a few times, she accusing me of emotional secrecy, of not opening up and sharing my feelings with her, my lying and claiming that there were no feelings to share, that everything was fine. But even our fights had been tepid, lukewarm affairs, not the passionate battles of the past.

I looked again at the folded square of white notebook paper with my name on it.

Maybe she would have told me of her plans to leave at one time. But we definitely had not been talking much lately, and in that context the note made perfect sense.

I reached down, picked up the paper, unfolded it.

Dear Bob,
    These are the hardest words I've ever had to write.
    I didn't want to do it this way, and I know it's wrong, but I don't think I could face you right now. I don't think I could go through with it.
    I know what you're thinking. I know what you're feeling. I know you're angry right now, and you have every right to be. But it's just not working out between us. I've turned this over and over again in my mind, wondering if we should try to work it out or if we should just spend some time apart, in a trial separation, and I finally decided that the best thing to do would be to make a clean break. It'll be hard at first (at least it will be for me), but I think in the long run it will be for the best.
    I love you. You know that. But sometimes love isn't enough. For a relationship to work, there has to be trust and a willingness to share. We don't have that. Maybe we never had that. I don't know. But I thought we did at one time.
    I don't want to place blame here. It's not your fault

this happened. It's not my fault. It's both our faults. But I know us. I know me, I know you, and I know that even though we'll say we'll work on our relationship, nothing will change. I think it's better to say good-bye now before things get too ugly.

I'll never forget you, Bob. You'll always be a part of me. You were the first person I ever loved, the only person I've ever loved. I'll remember you always.

I'll love you always.

Good-bye.

Beneath that was her signature. She'd signed her full name, both first and last, and it was that bit of formality that hurt more than anything else. It's a cliché to say that I felt an emptiness inside me, but I did. There was an ache that was almost physical, an undefined hurt that had no set center but seemed to alternate between my head and heart.

"Jane Reynolds."

I glanced again at the paper in my hand. Now that I looked at it, now that I reread it, it wasn't just the signature that struck me as being too formal. The entire letter seemed stiff and stilted. The words and sentiments hit home, but they still seemed familiar and far too pat. I'd read them before in a hundred novels, heard them said in a hundred movies.

If she loved me so much, why were there no tears? I wondered. Why weren't any of the letters smeared; why wasn't the ink running?

I looked around the kitchen, back into the living room. Someone had to have helped her move the furniture, the couch, the table. Who? Some guy? Someone she'd met? Someone she was fucking?

I sat down hard on one of the chairs. No. I knew that wasn't the case. She was not seeing someone else. She would not have been able to hide something like that from me. She would not even have tried. *That* she would've told me about. That she would've talked to me about.

Her dad had probably helped her move.

I walked out of the kitchen, through the living room to the bedroom. In here the loss was less, but more personal, and all the more painful for that. No furniture had been removed. The bed was still in place, as was the dresser, but the bedspread and the lace doily covering the top of the dresser were gone. In the closet there were only my clothes. The framed photographs on the nightstands had been taken.

I sat down on the bed. My insides felt like the apartment—physically, structurally unchanged, but gutted, hollowed out, soulless, the heart removed. I sat there as the room darkened, late afternoon turning to dusk, dusk to evening.

I made my own dinner, Kraft macaroni and cheese, and afterward watched the news, *Entertainment Tonight,* and all the other shows I usually watched. I was paying attention to the TV, yet not paying attention; waiting for a phone call from Jane, yet not waiting. It was as though I was possessed of multiple personalities—all with conflicting thoughts and desires—and was aware of all of them at once, but the overall effect was one of numbed lethargy, and I sat on the couch and did not move until the late news came on at eleven.

It was strange walking into the dark, empty bedroom, strange not hearing Jane in the bathroom, brushing her teeth or taking a shower, and with the television turned off I realized how quiet the apartment was. From down the street somewhere, muffled and indistinct, I could hear the sounds of a frat party. Outside, life continued on as usual.

I took off my clothes, but instead of dropping them on the floor and then crawling into bed like I usually did, I decided to put them in the hamper, as Jane had always nagged me to do. I carried my pants and shirt into the bathroom, opened the plastic top of the dirty clothes basket, and was about to drop them in when I looked down.

There at the bottom of the hamper, rolled up next to one of my socks, was a pair of Jane's panties.

The white cotton ones.

I dropped my clothes on the floor. I swallowed hard. Suddenly, staring down at Jane's rolled-up underwear, I felt like crying. I took a deep breath. I remembered the first time I'd ever seen her. She'd been wearing white panties and a pair of jeans with a rip in the crotch to school. I had been sitting across from her in the library and I had been able to see that white peeking through the hole in the blue, and nothing had ever turned me on so much in my life.

My eyes were wet as I bent over, reached into the hamper for the panties. I picked them up gingerly, handling them as though they were breakable, and carefully unrolled them. They felt damp to my touch, and when I lifted them to my face, the cotton smelled faintly of her.

"Jane," I whispered, and it felt good to say her name. I whispered it again. "Jane," I said. "Jane . . ."

TEN

Jane had been gone for three weeks.

I settled into my chair and looked at the calendar I'd tacked up on the wall to my left. There were fifteen red X's drawn through the month's workdays.

As I did each morning, I crossed out another date, today's date. My eye was drawn back to that first X—September 3. I had not heard from Jane since she'd left. She had not called to see how I was; she had not sent me a letter to tell me that she was all right. I'd expected to hear from her, if not for sentimental reasons, then for practical reasons. I figured there were logistical things she'd need to discuss—belongings she'd forgotten and wanted me to send, mail she wanted forwarded—but she had cut off all contact cold.

I worried about her, and more than once, I thought about going to the Little Kiddie Day Care Center, or even calling her parents, just to make sure she was okay, but I never did. I guess I was afraid to.

Although I could tell from the drastic decrease in mail that she had put in a change-of-address request at the post office, she still occasionally received bills or letters or junk mail, and I saved it all for her.

Just in case.

After work, I stopped by Von's for milk and bread, but I felt so depressed that I ended up buying half a gallon of chocolate ice cream and a bag of Doritos as well. All of the checkout stands were crowded, so I picked the one with the shortest line. The cashier was young and pretty, a slim brunette, and she was bantering happily and easily with the man ahead of me as she ran his items over the scanner. I watched the two of them with envy. I wished I had the ability to start up a conversation with a perfect stranger, to discuss the weather or current events or whatever it was that people talked about, but even in my imagination I was unable to do it. I just could not seem to think of what to say.

Jane had been the one to start the first conversation between us. If the responsibility had been left up to me, we probably never would have gotten together.

When I reached the cashier, she smiled at me. "Hello," she said. "How are you today?"

"Fine," I told her.

I watched in silence as she rang up my items on the cash register. "Six forty-three," she said.

Silently, I handed her the money.

I'd never thought about it before, but as I put the ice cream in the freezer, the Doritos and bread in the cupboard, I realized that there'd always been something within me that distanced people. Even my relationships with my grandparents were overly formal; we never hugged or kissed, though they were naturally affectionate. Ditto with my parents. Throughout my life, our "friends of the family," my parents' friends, had always been nice to me, cordial to me, but I never got the impression that any of them liked me.

They didn't dislike me.

They just didn't notice me.

I was a nobody, a nothing.

Had it always been this way? I wondered. It was possible. I had always had friends in elementary school, junior high school, high school, but never very many of them, and as I thought back now, I realized that nearly all of them had been, like myself, totally nondescript.

On an impulse, I went into the bedroom, opened the closet door, and found the pile of sealed boxes under my hanging clothes—the record of my past. Dragging the boxes to the center of the room, I ripped off the masking tape and opened their tops one by one, digging through the contents of each until I found my high school yearbooks.

I took the books out, began looking through them. I hadn't seen the yearbooks since high school, and it was strange to see again those places, those faces, those fashions and hairstyles from half a decade back. It made me feel old and a little sad.

But it also made me feel more than a little uneasy.

As I'd suspected, there were no photographs of me or my friends in any of the sports, clubs, or dance pictures. There were not even any of us in the random shots of the campus that were sprinkled throughout the books. We were nowhere to be seen. It was as though my friends and I had not even existed, as though we had not eaten lunch at the school or walked across campus from class to class.

I looked up the names of John Parker and Brent Burke, my two best friends, in the section of the senior yearbook dedicated to individual photographs of each class member. They were there, but they looked different than I recalled, the cast of their features slightly off. I stared at the pages, flipping back and forth from Brent to John and back again. I had remembered them as looking more interesting than they apparently had, more intelligent, more alive, but it seemed my memory had altered the facts. For there they were, staring blandly into the camera five years ago and out of the pages at me now, their faces devoid of even the slightest hint of character.

I turned to the blank green pages at the front of the book to see what they'd written to me on this, the eve of our graduation.

"I'm glad I got to know you. Have a great summer. John."

"Have a cool summer and good luck. Brent."

These were my best friends? I closed the yearbook,

licked my dry lips. Their comments were just as impersonal as those of everyone else.

I sat there for a moment in the middle of the floor,
staring at the opposite wall. Was this what it was like
for people with Alzheimer's? Or people going crazy? I
took a deep breath, trying to gather my courage to open
the yearbook again. Had it been them or myself? I
wondered. Or both? Was I now as big a blank to them
as they were to me, merely a name from the past and a
hazily remembered face? I opened the yearbook again,
turned to my own photo, stared at my picture. I found
my visage not bland, not blank, not nondescript, but
interesting and intelligent.

Maybe I had grown more average over the years, I
thought absurdly. Maybe it was a disease and I'd
caught it from John and Brent.

No. I wished it were something as simple as that. But
there was something far more comprehensive, far more
frightening here.

I skimmed the rest of the yearbook, scanning the
pages, and a familiar envelope fell from between the
last page and the back cover. Inside the envelope were
my grades. I opened the envelope, scanned the thin
translucent sheets of paper. My senior year: all C's.
Junior year: the same.

I hadn't been average in English, I knew. I'd always
been an above-average writer.

But my grades did not reflect that.

I had gotten C's across the board.

A wave of cold passed over me, and I dropped the
yearbook and hurried out of the bedroom. I went into
the kitchen, took a beer out of the refrigerator, popped
open the top and chugged it down. The apartment
seemed silent again. I stood in the kitchen, leaning
against the sink, staring at the door of the refrigerator.

How deep did this thing go?

I didn't know and I didn't want to know. I didn't
even want to think about it.

The sky was darkening outside, the sun going down,

and the inside of the apartment was filling with shadows, the furniture that I could see through the living room doorway shifted slowly into silhouette. I walked across the kitchen, turned on the light. From here, I could see where the couch had been, where the prints had hung. I looked into the living room and all of a sudden I felt lonely. Really lonely. So damn lonely that I almost felt like crying.

I thought of opening the refrigerator and getting out another beer, maybe getting drunk, but I didn't want to do that.

I didn't want to spend the evening in the apartment.

So I got out of the house and drove, hitting the Costa Mesa Freeway and heading south. I only realized where I was going when I was halfway there, and by that time I did not want to turn back, although the ache within me grew even more acute.

The freeway ended, turned into Newport Boulevard, and I drove to the beach, our beach, parking in the small metered lot next to the pier. I got out of the car, locked it, and wandered aimlessly through the crowded streets. The sidewalks were teeming with beautifully tanned bikini-clad women and handsome athletic men. Roller skaters glided through the throng, maneuvering around the walkers.

Again, from the Studio Cafe, I heard that music, Sandy Owen, although this time the music did not seem magically transcendent but sad and melancholy and, once more, wholly appropriate: a different sound track for a different night.

I looked toward the pier, toward the blackness of the ocean night beyond.

I wondered what Jane was doing.

I wonder who she was with.

ELEVEN

Derek retired in October.

I did not attend his going-away party—I was not even invited—but I knew when it was being held because of the notices on the break room bulletin board, and I called in sick on the day that it took place.

Odd as it seemed, I missed him after he was gone. Merely having another body in the office, even if it was Derek's, had somehow made me feel less alone, had been like a tie to the outside world, to other people, and the office, in his absence, seemed very empty.

I was starting to worry about myself, about my lack of human contact. The evening after Derek's departure I realized that I had gone for a whole day without speaking, without uttering a single, solitary word.

And it had not made a damn bit of difference to anyone. No one had even noticed.

The next day, I woke up, went to work, had a few words with Stewart in the morning, stated my order to the clerk at Del Taco at lunch, said nothing to anyone during the afternoon, went home, made dinner, watched TV, went to bed. I had probably spoken a total of six sentences the entire day—to Stewart and the Del Taco clerk. And that was it.

I needed to do something. I needed to change my job, change my personality, change my life.

But I couldn't.

"Average," I thought, was not really an accurate description of what I was. It was true as far as it went, but it didn't imply enough. It didn't quite cut it. It was too benign, not pejorative enough. "Ignored" was more appropriate, and that was how I began thinking of myself.

I was Ignored.

With a capital *I*.

I made a point the next day of passing by the desks of the programmers, the desks of Hope, Virginia, and Lois. I said hello to each, and each one of them ignored me. Hope, the kindest, nodded distractedly at me, mumbled something vaguely salutatory.

It was getting worse.

I was fading away.

On my way home, on the freeway, I drove wildly, cutting in front of cars, not letting people pass, slamming on my brakes when I felt the drivers were following too close behind me. I received horn honks and middle fingers in return.

Here I was noticed, I thought. Here I was not invisible. These people knew I was alive.

I cut off a black woman in a Saab, was gratified to hear her honk at me.

I swerved in front of a punk in a VW, smiled as he screamed at me out the window.

I started buying lottery tickets each Wednesday and Saturday, the two days on which the game was played. I knew I had no chance of winning—according to an article in the newspaper, I had a better chance of being hit by lightning than winning the lottery—but I began to see the game as the only way of escaping the straitjacket that was my job. Each Wednesday and Saturday night as I sat in front of the television, watching the numbered white Ping-Pong balls flying about in their glass vacuum case, I not only hoped I would win, I actually *thought* I would win. I began to concoct elaborate scenarios in my head, plans of what I would do with my newfound wealth. First, I would settle some scores at work. I would hire someone to dump a thousand pounds of cowshit on top of Banks's desk. I would hire a thug to make Stewart dance naked in the first-floor lobby to Led Zeppelin's "Whole Lotta Love." I would yell obscenities over the corporation's PA system until someone called Security and had me forcibly removed from the building.

After that, I would get the hell out of California. I did not know where I'd go; I had no real destination in mind, but I knew that I wanted out of here. This place had come to represent everything that was wrong with my life, and I would ditch it and start over somewhere else, somewhere new, somewhere fresh.

At least that was the plan.

But each Thursday and Monday, after watching the lottery drawing and comparing the chosen numbers with those on the ticket in my hand, I inevitably ended up back at work, a dollar poorer and a day more depressed, all my plans shot to hell.

It was on one of these Mondays that I came across a photo someone had accidentally dropped on the floor of the elevator. It was an eight-by-ten, a picture of the testing department that had obviously been taken in the sixties. The men all had inappropriately long sideburns and wide, loud ties, the women short skirts and bell-bottomed pantsuits. There were faces I recognized in the photo, and that was the weird thing. I saw long-haired young women who had become short-haired old women; smiling, easygoing men whose faces had since hardened permanently into uptight frowns. The dichotomy was so striking, the differences so obvious, that it was like seeing a horror movie makeup transformation. Never before had I seen such a depressingly clear example of the ravaging effects of time.

For me, it was like Scrooge seeing the Ghost of Christmas Yet to Come. I saw my present in that photo, my future in the now-hardened faces of my coworkers.

I returned to my desk, more shaken than I would have liked to admit. On my desk, I found a stack of papers and, on top of that, a yellow Post-It upon which

Stewart had scrawled a short note: "Revise Termination Procedures for Personnel. Due tomorrow. 8:00."

The 8:00 was underlined.

Twice.

Sighing, I sat down, picked up the papers. For the next hour, I read through the highlighted paragraphs in the provided pages and looked over the margin notes that Stewart wanted me to incorporate into the text. I made my own notes, hacked out a rough draft of the corrections, which I paper-clipped to the proper pages, then carried my materials down the hall to the steno pool. I smiled at Lois and Virignia, said hi, but both of them ignored me, and I retreated to the word-processing desk in the corner and sat down at the PC.

I turned on the terminal, inserted my diskette, and was about to start typing the first of the corrections when I stopped. I don't know what came over me, I don't know why I did it, but I put my fingers to the keys and typed: "A full-time employee can be terminated in one of the three ways—hanging, electrocution, or lethal injection."

I reread what I'd written. I almost stopped there. I almost moved the cursor to the beginning of the line and pressed the delete key.

Almost.

My hesitation lasted only a second. I knew I could be fired if I distributed these corrections and someone read them, but in a way I would have welcomed that. At least it would have put an end to my misery here. It would have forced me to find another job someplace else.

But I knew from experience that no one *would* read what I was writing. The people to whom I gave my updates seldom even inserted them in the appropriate manuals, let alone read them. Hell, even Stewart seemed to have stopped going over my work.

"An employee terminated for poor work performance can no longer be drawn and quartered under the new regulations," I typed. "The revised guidelines state clearly that such an employee is now to be terminated by hanging from the neck until dead."

I grinned as I reread the sentence. Behind me, Lois and Virginia were talking as they did their own work, discussing some miniseries they'd seen the night before. Part of me was afraid that they would come up behind me, look over my shoulder and read what I'd written, but then I thought no, they'd probably forgotten I was even there.

"Unapproved, non-illness-related absences of over three days will be grounds for termination by electrocution," I typed. "Department and division supervisors will flank the electric chair as the death sentence is carried out."

I waited for repercussions from my Termination Procedure stunt, but none came. A day passed. Two. Three. A week. Obviously, Stewart had not bothered to read the update—although he'd had a bee up his butt about getting it done instantly, that day, as if it were the most important thing in the world.

Just to be safe, just to make sure, I asked him about it, caught him by Hope's desk one morning and asked if he'd gone over the update to make sure it was correct. "Yeah," he said distractedly, waving me away. "It's fine."

He hadn't read it.

Or . . . maybe he had.

I felt a familiar churning in the pit of my stomach. Was what I wrote as anonymous as what I said or did? Was my writing ignored, too? I had not thought of that before, but it was possible. It was more than possible.

I thought of my C's in English on that report card.

On my next set of screen instructions for GeoComm, I wrote: "When all on-screen fields are correct, press [ENTER] and your mama will take it up the ass. She likes it best that way."

I got no comment on it.

Since no one seemed to notice me, I took it a step

further and began coming in wearing jeans and
T-shirts, comfortable street clothes, instead of the more
formal dress shirt and tie. There were no reprimands,
no recriminations. I rode up on the elevator each
morning, denim-clad amidst a sea of white shirts and
red ties, and no one said a word. I wore ripped Levi's
and dirty sneakers and T-shirts from old rock concerts
to my meetings with Stewart and Banks and neither of
them noticed.

In mid-October, Stewart went on a week's vacation,
leaving a list of assignments and their deadlines on my
desk. It was a relief to have him gone, but his absence
meant that what miniscule interaction I had with other
people was for that week suspended. I spoke to no one
at all while he was gone. No one spoke to me. I was
unseen, unnoticed, entirely invisible.

Friday evening I got home and I desperately wanted
to talk to someone. Anyone. About anything.

But I had no one to talk to.

Out of desperation, I looked through an old magazine and found a number for one of those porno calls,
the ones where women talk to you about sex for a
three-dollar-a-minute toll. I dialed the number, just
wanting to speak to a person who would speak back.

I got a recording.

TWELVE

When I arrived at work the next Monday morning, someone was sitting at Derek's desk.

I literally stopped in my tracks, I was so surprised. It was a guy about my age, a little older maybe, with a brown beard and thick, longish hair. He was dressed in regulation white shirt/gray pants, but his tie was wide and silk and brightly colored, with a print of toucans standing on pineapples. He grinned when he saw me, and his smile was wide, generous, and unaffected. "Hey, dude," he said.

I nodded hello, unsure of how to respond.

"David's the name." He stood, extended a hand, and we shook. "I've been transferred here from Bookkeeping. You must be Bob."

Again I nodded. "You're taking over Derek's job?" I asked dumbly.

He laughed. "What job? That position's gone. It was nothing but a title, anyway. They just let that guy hang on until retirement out of pity."

"I always wondered what he did."

"So did everyone else. How did you get along with him?"

I shrugged noncommittally. "I didn't know him too well. I just started working here a few months ago—"

"Come on. The guy's a dick with feet."

I found myself smiling. "All right," I admitted. "We weren't bosom buddies."

"Good," David said. "I like you already."

I walked over to my desk and sat down, feeling

good. It had been so long since I'd had an actual conversation with anyone that I was emotionally charged by even this small contact, my spirits absurdly buoyed by the fact that I had a new office mate who had actually noticed me.

Maybe my condition was reversible.

"So what is your job?" I asked.

"Still bookkeeping," he said. "Only for your department now. I think they invented this job so they could kick me upstairs a floor. None of the old farts in my department like working with me."

I laughed.

"I'm stone serious."

I smiled. The people in his department might not like working with him, but I could tell that I would.

I was right. David and I hit it off immediately. We were close in age so there was that generational connection, but he was also friendly and easygoing, one of those people who were naturally open and accessible, and from the beginning he talked to me as though we'd been close for years. There was nothing about himself he could not discuss with me, no opinion that he would refrain from expressing. The wall of formality that seemed to exist between me and everyone else did not exist between David and myself.

He not only noticed and accepted me, he seemed to like me.

It was Wednesday before he asked The Question. I knew it would come up eventually, I'd been prepared for it, but it was still something of a surprise. It was afternoon, I was proofreading the GeoComm instructions I'd printed out earlier in the day, and David was taking an early break, leaning back in his chair and munching on Fritos.

He popped a chip in his mouth and looked over at me. "So do you have a wife or girlfriend or anything?"

"Girlfriend," I said. "Ex-girlfriend," I corrected myself. I felt a funny sort of fluttering in my stomach.

My feelings must have shown on my face, because

David quickly backed off. "Sorry, man, I didn't mean to pry. If you don't want to talk about it . . ."

But I did want to talk about it. I hadn't talked about our breakup to anybody, and I found that I had a sudden need to tell someone what had happened.

I told David everything. Well, not everything. I left out the part about my being Ignored, but I told him how we'd begun drifting apart ever since I got this damn job, and about how I'd been too stubborn to meet her halfway and how one day I'd come home and she'd been packed and gone. I'd expected to feel better after talking about it, but in truth I felt worse. The memories were recent, the events still fresh, and dredging them up only made me relive the pain, not exorcise it.

David shook his head. "That's cold. She just hit the road and left a note?"

I nodded.

"Well, what happened when you went after her? What did she say when you confronted her?"

I blinked. "What?"

"What happened when you tracked her down?" He looked at me, frowned. "You did go after her, didn't you?"

Should I have? Was that what she'd wanted? Proof that I cared, that I loved her, that I needed her? Should I have gone after her like some sort of hero and tried to win her back? I had this sinking feeling that I should have, that that was what she'd wanted, that that was what she'd expected. I looked at David, slowly shaking my head. "No, I didn't."

"Oh, man. You blew it. Now you'll never get her back. How long's it been?"

"Two months."

He shook his head. "She's found someone else by now. Your window of opportunity's closed, dude. Didn't you even try to call her?"

"I didn't know where she'd gone."

"You should've called her parents. They'd know."

"She said she just wanted to cut off all contact cold,

not see each other anymore. She said it'd be easier that way."

"They always say things like that. But what they say and what they mean are two different things."

There was movement in the doorway. Stewart. "Hey, girls," he said, peeking his head into the office, "stop your talking. Get back to work."

I quickly picked up my pen, began going over the instructions.

"I'm on break," David said, eating a Frito. "I still have five minutes to go."

"Then you take your break in the break room where you won't disturb—" There was a pause as he blanked on my name. "—Jones."

"Fine." David got up slowly, grinned at me as he followed Stewart out the door.

I smiled back, but I felt sick inside.

What they say and what they mean are two different things.

I had the horrible feeling that he was right.

There was traffic on the freeway, a three-car accident in the fast lane, and it was nearly six-thirty by the time I got home. I parked in the garage and trudged up the stairway to my apartment. I opened my mailbox and rifled through the envelopes as I unlocked the door. There was a bill from the gas company, this week's *Pennysaver* . . . and something that felt like a card.

A card? Who would be sending me a card?

Jane?

My hopes soared. Maybe she'd gotten tired of waiting for me to make contact. Maybe she'd decided to contact me. Maybe she missed me as much as I missed her.

I quickly ripped open the envelope and saw the words "Happy Birthday!" above a picture of hot-air balloons sailing into a blue sky. I opened the card.

Preprinted on the white background in laser-jet

perfection was the message "Happy Birthday From Your Friends at Automated Interface, Inc."

My heart sank.

A form birthday card from work.

I crumpled up the card, threw it over the stairway railing, and watched it hit the ground.

In two days it would be my birthday.

I'd almost forgotten.

THIRTEEN

I spent my birthday typing and filing, filing and typing. David was sick, and I was alone in the office all day.

I spent that night watching television.

No one at work did anything for my birthday. I hadn't expected them to, but I had half expected a call from Jane—or at least a card. She knew how important birthdays were to me. But of course there was nothing. What was even more depressing was that my parents didn't acknowledge my birthday either. No present, no card, not even a phone call.

I tried to call them, several times, but the line was always busy and I eventually gave it up.

In five years, I thought, I would be thirty. I remembered when my mom had turned thirty. Her friends had thrown her a surprise birthday party and everyone had gotten drunk and I'd been allowed to stay up way past my bedtime. I'd been eight then, and my mom had seemed so old.

I was getting old, too, but the strange thing was that I didn't feel it. According to the professor of a Cultural Anthropology class I'd taken, American culture has no rite of passage, no formal initiation into manhood, no clear demarcation between childhood and adulthood. Maybe that was why, in many ways, I still felt like a kid. I did not feel the way my parents had probably felt at my age, did not see myself the way my parents had probably seen themselves. I might be living an adult life, but my feelings were a child's feelings, my attitudes and interests those of a teenager. I had not really grown up.

And my twenties were half over.

I thought about Jane all night, thought about what this birthday could have been, what it should have been, and what it wasn't.

I went to bed hoping against hope that the phone would ring.

But it didn't.

And sometime after midnight I fell asleep.

FOURTEEN

Thanksgiving came and went and I spent the holiday in my apartment by myself, watching the *Twilight Zone* marathon on Channel 5 and wondering what Jane was doing.

I'd tried ringing my parents the week before, calling them several times, planning to wrangle a Thanksgiving dinner invitation out of them, but no one was ever home when I called. Although they'd invited me and Jane over for the past three Thanksgivings, we had never gone, begging off because of school, work, whatever excuse we could think up. Now this year, when I finally wanted to go, when I needed to go, no invitation was offered. I wasn't exactly surprised, but I couldn't help feeling a little hurt. I knew my parents weren't trying to be mean, weren't going out of their way to purposely not invite me—they'd probably assumed that once again Jane and I had plans of our own—but I didn't have any plans and I desperately wanted them to provide me with some.

I still hadn't told them I'd broken up with Jane. I hadn't even called them since the split. My parents and I had never really been close, and talking about something like this with them would have made me feel extremely uncomfortable. I knew they'd ask a million questions—How did it happen? Why did it happen? Whose fault was it? Are you guys going to patch things up?—and I didn't want to have to talk to them about things like that. I just didn't want to deal with it. I'd rather they find out later, secondhand.

I'd been planning to lie if I'd gone down to San Diego to spend Thanksgiving with them, to tell them that Jane got sick at the last minute and was spending the holiday with her family. It was a pretty flimsy and pathetic excuse, but I had no doubt that my parents would buy it. They were pretty gullible about things like that.

But I never did get ahold of them. I could have invited myself, I knew. I could have just shown up on their doorstep Thursday morning. But somehow I didn't feel comfortable doing that.

So I stayed home, lounged on the couch, watched *The Twilight Zone.* I made macaroni and cheese for my Thanksgiving meal. It was pretty damn depressing, and I could not remember having ever felt so alone and so abandoned.

I was almost grateful for Monday.

On Monday morning, David was there before I was, feet up on the desk, eating some type of muffin. I was glad to see him after the four days I'd just spent in semi-isolation, but at the same time I felt an emotional weight, a feeling almost like dread, settle upon me as I sat down at my desk and surveyed the array of papers before me.

I liked David, but, God, I hated my job.

I looked over at him. "This is hell," I said.

He finished the last of his muffin, crumpling the cupcake paper and tossing it into the trash can between our desks. "I read this story once where hell was a hallway filled with all the bugs you'd killed in your life: all the flies you'd swatted, all the spiders you'd squished, all the snails you'd dissolved. And you had to keep walking back and forth down this hallway. Naked. Back and forth. Back and forth. Forever." David grinned. "Now *that* would be hell."

I sighed. "This is close."

He shrugged. "Purgatory, maybe. But hell? I don't think so."

I picked up a pen, looked at the latest batch of Geo-

Comm instructions I'd written. I was sick of documenting that damn system. What had once seemed like a great step forward, a huge increase in responsibility, was now a burden around my neck. I was starting to long for the days when my job had been less defined and my tasks varied with the day. My work might have been more pointless and frivolous then, but it had not been so stultifyingly the same.

"I think it might be," I said.

It was four o'clock and the employees who were on flexible work schedules were starting to leave, passing by our office and heading down the hall toward the elevators, when David leaned back in his chair and looked over at me. "Hey, what're you doing after work?" he asked. "Anything?"

I knew where this was leading, and my first instinct was to beg off, to invent an excuse why I couldn't go with him, wherever he was going. But it had been so long since I had done anything or gone anywhere with another person that I found myself saying, "Nothing. Why?"

"There's this club I go to in Huntington Beach. Stocked with babes. I thought you might wanna come."

The second level. An invitation.

Part of me wanted to say yes, and for a brief second I thought that this might turn the tide, this might save me. I'd go out clubbing with David; we'd become good buddies, close friends; he'd help me meet some women; my entire life would change in one smooth, easy stroke.

But my true nature won out, and I shook my head and smiled regretfully. "I wish I could, but I have plans." I said.

"What plans?"

I shook my head. "I can't."

He looked at me, nodded slowly. "I understand," he said.

* * *

David and I were not as close after that. I don't know if it was his fault or mine, but the bond that had existed between us seemed to have been broken, the closeness dissipated. It wasn't like it had been with Derek, of course. I mean, David and I still talked to each each other. We were still friendly. But we were not friends. It was as though we had approached friendship but had backed off, deciding we were better suited to acquaintanceship.

The routine returned. It had never really gone away, but since David had started sharing my office I had been able, to some extent, to ignore it. Now that I was fading into the periphery of David's life, however, and he into mine, the mind-numbing dullness of my workday once more took center stage.

I was an uninteresting person with an uninteresting job and an uninteresting life.

My apartment, too, I noticed, was bland and characterless. Most of the furniture was new, but it was generic: not ugly, not wonderful, but existing somewhere in the netherworld of plainness in between. In a way, gaudiness or ugliness would have been preferable. At least it would have stamped an imprint of life upon my home. As it was, a photograph of my living room would have fit neatly and perfectly into a furniture catalog. It had the same featureless, antiseptic quality as a showroom display.

My bedroom looked like it had come straight out of a Holiday Inn.

Obviously, whatever character the place had had was attributable to Jane. And obviously it had departed with her.

That was it, I decided. I was going to change. I was going to make an effort to be different, be original, be unique. Even if civil-service chic became all the rage, I would never again fall into a rut of quiet unobtrusiveness. I would live loud, dress loud, make a statement. If it was my nature to be Ignored, I would go against my nature and do everything I could to make myself noticed.

I went that weekend to furniture stores, charged a couch and bed and end tables and lamps—mismatched items from the wildest and most disparate styles I could find. I tied them in the trunk of the Buick, tied them to the roof, took them home and put them in places where they weren't supposed to be: bed in the dining area, couch in the bedroom. This wasn't ordinary; this wasn't average or mundane. No one could ignore this. I walked around my apartment, admiring the extravagantly gauche decorations, satisfied.

I went to Marshall's, charged a new wardrobe. Loud shirts and outrageously designed pants.

I went to Supercuts, got a modified mohawk.

I had done it. I had changed. I had made myself over. I was a new me.

And at work on Monday, nobody noticed.

I walked through the parking lot and into the lobby feeling almost foolishly conspicuous, my band of centered hair standing tall and stiff on my otherwise bald head, my pants baggy and shiny red, my shirt lime-green, my tie fluorescent pink. But no one gave me a second glance. There was not even a pause in the conversation between two fifth-floor secretaries waiting for the elevator as I walked up and stood next to them. Neither of them glanced in my direction or paid me any attention at all.

Even David did not notice the difference. He said hi to me when I walked into the office, finished his breakfast muffin, then settled down to work.

I was Ignored no matter what I did.

I sat down at my desk, discouraged and depressed, feeling like an asshole with my hair and my clothes. Why was this happening to me? Why was I Ignored? What was wrong with me? I touched my mohawk, as if to reassure myself that it was real, that I was real, that I had physical substance. My hand felt hard lacquered hair.

What was I?
That was the real question.
And for that, of course, I had no answer.

The week passed slowly, with seconds that seemed
like hours, hours that seemed like days, days that were
of interminable length. David was out for the second
half of the week, and by the time Friday rolled around I
had been so consistently disregarded and overlooked
that I was about ready to attack one of the secretaries to
prove to myself and everyone else that I existed, that I
was there.

On my way home, I tried to speed, to drive crazily
and recklessly, but my heart wasn't in it and I failed to
make even a small dent in the consciousness of my
fellow freeway travelers.

Inside my apartment, the garishly clashing color
scheme of the living room only made me feel tired and
even more depressed. I stared at the Monster Roster
poster hung at an inappropriate angle above my pink
butterfly chair. I had somehow managed to make the
gaudy look mundane, the garish unobtrusive.

I loosened my tie and sat down on he couch. I felt
drained. The weekend loomed before me: two days of
freedom in which I would constantly be confronted
with my anonymity. I tried to think of something I
could do, some place I could go where I wouldn't be
continually faced with the meaningless obscurity that
was my existence.

My parents, I thought. I could visit my parents. I
wasn't ignored by them. I was not just a forgettable
face to my mom, not just a nobody to my dad. I might
not be able to talk to them about my situation, but just
being with them, just being with people who noticed
and paid attention to me, would help.

I hadn't tried calling them after Thanksgiving,
feeling vaguely pissed off at their treatment of me and
wanting to punish them for it, but Christmas was fast

approaching and I needed both my mom and my dad to give me some idea of what they wanted this year.

I figured that was as good an excuse as any to give them a ring.

I walked over to the phone, picked it up and dialed. Busy. I hung up, dialed again. We weren't close, my parents and I. We did not see eye to eye on most things; we did not even like each other a lot of the time. But we loved each other. We were family. And if you couldn't turn to your family in time of need, who could you turn to?

The line was still busy. I hung up the phone. I had a plan. I would be spontaneous. I would surprise them by driving down right now and showing up on their doorstep for dinner.

Average people weren't spontaneous.

I packed a toothbrush and a change of clothes, and ten minutes later I was on the freeway, headed for San Diego.

I considered pulling off at San Juan Capistrano, then at Oceanside, then at Del Mar and trying to call again. Now that I thought about it, my parents probably wouldn't like it if I just showed up on their doorstep without warning. But I had momentum, I didn't want to get sidetracked, and I stayed on the highway, moving south.

It was close to nine when I pulled up in front of my parents' home. *Our* home. It hadn't changed much since I was a child, and that was reassuring. I got out of the car and walked up the short cement path to the porch. Although I had been here less than a year ago, it seemed like it had been forever, and I felt as though I were returning after a long, long absence. I stepped onto the porch, knocked, rang the bell.

A strange man answered the door.

I jumped, startled.

From behind the stranger came the voice of another stranger, a woman. "Who is it, dear?"

"I don't know!" the man called back. He was

unshaven, overweight, wearing low-slung jeans and a tank top T-shirt. He looked at me through the screen. "Yes?"

I cleared my throat. There was a funny feeling in my stomach. "Are my parents here?" I asked.

The man frowned. "What?"

"I came to visit my parents. They live here. I'm Bob Jones."

The man looked puzzled. "I don't know what you're talking about. I live here."

"This is my parents' house."

"Maybe you have the wrong street or something."

"Taz!" the woman called.

"In a minute!" the man called back.

"I don't have the wrong street. This is my parents' house. I was born here. My parents have lived here for the past thirty years!"

"I live here now. What did you say your parents' names were?"

"Martin and Ella Jones."

"Never heard of them."

"They own this house!"

"I rent from Mr. Sanchez. He's the owner. Maybe you should talk to him."

My heart was pounding. I was sweating, though the weather was chilly. I tried to remain calm, tried to tell myself that there was a rational explanation for this, that it was all part of a simple misunderstanding, but I knew it was not true. I swallowed, tried not to show my fear. "Could you give me Mr. Sanchez's address and phone number?"

The man nodded. "Sure." He started to turn around, then stopped. "I don't know, though. Mr. Sanchez might not appreciate me giving out personal stuff—"

"A daytime number, then. Don't you have his work phone number?"

"Yeah, sure. Hold on a sec."

The man retreated into the house—*our house*—to find a pen and paper, and I realized that a work number wouldn't do me any good. It was Friday night. Unless I wanted to wait until Monday, I was screwed. On an impulse, I looked toward the wood frame house next door. The name on the burnt wood novelty shingle hanging from the lighted porch was CRAWFORD. The Crawfords! I should have thought of them before. If Mr. and Mrs. Crawford still lived next door, they would know what the hell had happened. They would know why my parents were not here, why this strange man and his wife were living in our house.

Without waiting for the man to return, I hopped off the porch and started across the lawn toward the Crawfords'. "Hey!" the man called out behind me. I heard his wife yell something.

I stepped over the low hedge that separated our house from the Crawfords' and walked up their porch, ringing the doorbell. A moment later, I was gratified to see Mrs. Crawford open the door. I was afraid she'd be frightened by my mohawk, and I purposely tried to look as nonthreatening as possible, but she opened the door all the way, totally unafraid. "Yes?"

"Mrs. Crawford! Thank God you still live here. Where are my parents? I just went next door and there's a strange man living in our house who said he's never heard of us."

Now there was fear in her eyes. She moved slightly behind the door, ready to slam it at the slightest provocation. "Who are you?" Her voice sounded older than I remembered, weaker.

"I'm Bob."

"Bob?"

"Bob Jones. Don't you remember?" I could see that she didn't. "I'm Martin and Ella's son!"

"Martin and Ella had no son."

"You used to babysit me!"

She started to close the door. "I'm sorry—"

I was so frustrated that I felt like screaming at her, but I kept my voice even. "Just tell me where my parents are. Martin and Ella Jones. Where are they?"

She looked at me, squinting for a moment as thought she almost recognized me, then shook her head, obviously giving up her memory search.

"Where are they?"

"The Joneses died six months ago in an automobile accident. Drunk driver."

My parents were dead.

I stood there as she closed the door on me, not moving, not reacting, not doing anything. The door clicked shut, followed by the snick of a dead bolt. In my peripheral vision, I could see the curtains move on the window to the right side of the door, could see Mrs. Crawford's face peek through the opening. I was vaguely aware that the man living in my parents' house—Taz—was calling to me, saying something.

My parents were dead.

I wanted to cry but I couldn't. I had not had enough time to think about their lives to be able to react to their deaths. I had not had time to prepare for and cultivate a sense of loss. The shock had been too sudden. I wanted to feel sad, but I didn't. I simply felt numb.

I turned slowly around, walked out to the sidewalk.

I hadn't been invited to my own parents' funeral.

I wished that my parents and I had been closer, but I'd always assumed there'd be time for that, that eventually it would happen, that age would provide common ground, that years would bring togetherness. It was not something I'd actively planned for or sought out, just a general feeling, but now those vague hopes had been permanently dashed. I should've made an effort, I thought. I should've known that something like this could happen to them, and I should've put aside the babyishness, the pettiness, and not let our disagreements divide us. I should've gotten closer to them while I'd had the chance.

Taz was still calling to me, but I ignored him and got in my car, turning the key in the ignition. I glanced back toward the Crawfords' as I pulled out, and now both Mrs. and Mr. Crawford were looking openly through the parted curtains.

Six months ago. That would've been June. Jane and I had still been together then. I would've just gotten my job two months before.

Why hadn't someone notified me? Why hadn't I been called? Hadn't someone found my name and address somewhere amidst their personal effects?

I had not really thought of myself as being ignored by my parents, but as I thought back to my childhood, I was surprised to find my memories slightly hazy. I could not recall any specific instances in which I'd done things with my mom or gone places with my dad. I remembered teachers, kids, pets, places, toys—and events related to each of them—but of my parents there was only a general sense that they'd done a good job of raising me. I'd had a fairly normal, happy childhood—at least I'd thought I had—but the warm, loving recollections I should've held, the remembrances of individual events I should've possessed, were nowhere to be found. There was no personalization to my parental memories.

Maybe that's why we hadn't been closer. Maybe I'd been merely a generic child to them, a personalityless blank they were obliged to feed, clothe, and raise.

Maybe I'd been Ignored since birth.

No, that couldn't be true. I had not been ignored by my parents. They'd always bought me birthday and Christmas presents, for Christ's sake. That proved that they thought about me. They'd always invited me home for Easter, for Thanksgiving. They cared about me.

Jane had cared about me, too, though. That didn't mean I wasn't Ignored.

Six months ago.

That was about the time I'd first started to notice my condition, that I'd first become aware of my true nature. Maybe it was connected. Maybe when my parents died, when the people who knew me and loved me best passed away, what had always been dormant within me had been activated. Maybe it was their knowledge of my existence that had kept me from being completely Ignored.

I'd been fading even faster since I'd lost Jane.

I pulled onto Harbor Drive, pushing the thought out of my mind, not wanting to think about it.

Where were my parents' belongings? I wondered. Had they been auctioned off? Donated to a charity? There were no other relatives except me, and I hadn't gotten anything. Where were all our pictures and photo albums?

The photo albums.

It was the photo albums that did it. It was the photo albums that were the trigger.

I started to cry.

I was driving toward the freeway, and suddenly I couldn't see because of the tears in my eyes. Everything was runny, blurry, and I pulled to the side of the road and wiped my cheeks and eyes. I felt a sob in my throat, heard a sound come out of my mouth, and I forced myself to stop it, to knock it off. This was not the time to be maudlin and sentimental.

I took a deep breath. I had no one now. No girlfriend, no relatives, no friends. Nobody. I was all alone and on my own, and I was Ignored. I had only myself—and my job. As strange and ironic as it was, it was now only through my job that I had any sort of identity at all.

But that was going to change. I was going to find out who I was, what I was. I was through living in darkness and ignorance. And I was through with letting opportunities pass me by. I had learned from my mistakes, I had learned from my past, and my future was going to be different.

I put the car into gear and headed toward the freeway. It would be nearly midnight before I got back to Brea.

I stopped by a Burger King and got a Coke for the long trip home.

FIFTEEN

Monday.

I was ten minutes late for work due to a three-car pileup on the Costa Mesa Freeway, but I didn't sweat it. No one would notice if I was late.

I'd spent the weekend calling my parents' friends, the ones I remembered, asking if they knew what had happened to my parents' personal effects. None of them had known. Several of them wouldn't even talk to me.

None of them remembered me.

No one had known or was willing to tell me which mortuary had handled the arrangements and at which cemetery my parents were buried, so I went to the library, xeroxed the appropriate pages from the San Diego Yellow Pages, and called every damn funeral home in the book. Of course, it turned out to be the last one. I asked the funeral director if he knew what had happened to my parents' belongings, and he said no, he didn't. I asked him who had paid for the funeral, and he said that information was confidential. He was understanding and apologetic and told me that if I could bring proof that Martin and Ella Jones were my parents he would be happy to divulge the information to me, but he could not tell me over the phone. Proof? I asked. Birth certificate, he told me.

My parents had kept my birth certificate.

He did tell me where my parents were buried, and I thanked him and wrote it down and hung up.

My past was gone, I realized. I had no roots, no history. I now existed entirely in the present.

David was hard at work on something when I walked into the office, and he did not even look up as I entered the room. I walked past him, took off my coat, and sat down at my desk. On top of the desk was a huge stack of papers. Adjacent to the papers was a hastily scrawled note on FROM THE DESK OF RON STEWART stationery that read: "Please document these procedures by 12/10." It was initialed "RS."

December 10. That was today.

The note was dated November 2.

I stared, read the note again. The bastard had deliberately done this to get me in trouble. I quickly shuffled through the pile of papers. There were memos from Banks and from Banks's superiors dated several months back asking that this or that procedure be documented. I had never seen any of them before. I had never heard anything about these procedures.

Stewart had set me up.

I was furious, but I was so preconditioned that I actually got out a pen and began looking over the top page. There was no way I could complete even a third of these today, and after a few frustrating minutes I realized that I could not do this. I had to get out of here. I threw down my pen, grabbed my coat, and headed out the door.

At that point, I really didn't care whether or not I got fired. I just had to get away from that office.

Outside, the early morning gloom was starting to lift, sunshine showing through the clouds, blue usurping the place of gray. I was parked out in the boonies of the Automated Interface parking lot, and by the time I reached my car I was already starting to sweat. I threw my coat on the passenger seat, rolled down the front windows, and backed out, leaving the lone open space amidst the endless rows of shiny cars. I pulled onto Emery, heading south. I turned right on the first cross street with a stoplight, then left on the next street. I did not know where I was going, had no definite destination in mind, was simply planning to lose myself in the comforting sameness of Irvine's mazelike streets, but I found myself heading more or less in an westerly direction.

I ended up at South Coast Plaza.

I parked out by Sears and trekked across the asphalt to the main entrance. I walked into the mall, grateful for the relaxed coolness of air-conditioning after the humid heat outside.

Even though the Christmas season was here, there did not seem to be as many people in the mall as there should have been. The parking lot had been crowded, but inside South Coast Plaza the crowds were curiously sparse.

Muzak carols were playing over the mall's speakers; elf figures and toy sleighs and fake snow adorned the window fronts. In front of Nordstrom, a huge flocked Christmas tree was festooned with garlands and tinsel and every type of ornament imaginable. Christmas had always been my favorite time of year. I'd always loved the feel of the season, the mood, everything from the nativity scenes to the festive fantasy trappings of Santa that had put a secular face on this sacred occasion. But this year it just didn't feel like Christmas. I had no presents to buy; I was expecting no presents myself. Last year, Jane and I had spent almost every spare November and December moment shopping for gifts, planning our celebration, enjoying each other and the promise of the season. This year I was alone and lonely, with no plans, no purpose.

I stood next to the Christmas tree and scanned the faces of the passersby, but even the frank and open stares with which I greeted people did not phase them. Theoretically, the women and children in the mall should have noticed me. Shopkeepers should have eyed me with suspicion. Even during the height of the punk movement it had not been normal to see mohawked, Day-Glo-dressed men loitering around

South Coast Plaza, and those days were long gone. Someone who looked like me definitely should have attracted attention.

But, of course, I didn't.

Not everyone was ignoring me, though.

Standing next to one of the small benches between Rizzoli's bookstore and the Garden Bistro restaurant was a sharp-eyed man a few years older than myself who was staring intently, watching my every move. I did not notice him at first, but I kept seeing him out of the corner of my eye, unmoving, and I began to have the uncomfortable feeling that I was being observed, spied upon. I put the two together and casually looked to my left, toward the man. I caught his eye, and he looked away, pretending to be interested in the Garden Bistro's menu. Now it was my turn to watch him. He was tall and thin, with short black hair that accentuated the hard, cold severity of his face. He stood stiffly, in a manner that was almost regal, but there was an indefinable air of the plebeian about him.

I wondered why he had been staring at me, how he had noticed me, and I started walking toward him, intending to ask, but he quickly moved away, making a beeline toward the center of the mall, hurriedly moving past two women and cutting in front of them to get away from me.

I considered following him, and I started to do so, but then he pushed through a small group of people and started up the stairs to the mall's second level, and I knew that I would not be able to catch up. I watched him hurry up the steps. Strange. I had never seen the man before in my life. Why had he been looking at me? And why had he acted so guilty and suspicious when I caught him staring? It might have been my clothes and hair that caught his attention. That was a logical assumption. But then why had no one else noticed me?

I stared at the top step, where I had last seen the man

before he'd hurried toward the Sears wing of the mall. It was probably nothing, probably just my imagination, an overreaction to the fact that someone had actually seen me.

But I felt uneasy as I walked into Nordstrom.

I stayed in the mall all day. I had nowhere to go, nothing to do; I didn't feel like driving around and I certainly didn't feel like going home. So I wandered in and out of the various stores, bought a lunch at Carl's Jr., read some magazines at B. Dalton, looked through the CDs at Music Plus.

Business picked up in the late afternoon, after the schools let out. I was in Miller's Outpost, had pretty much seen everything I wanted to see, and was about to leave, when I happened to glance behind me.

And saw the sharp-eyed man staring at me from between the racks.

This wasn't just coincidence.

Our eyes locked for a second, and I felt a cold chill pass through me. Then he turned away, moving quickly up the aisle toward the front of the store. I headed after him, but by the time I reached the store's open entrance he had already blended into the crowd, disappearing into the stream of package-carrying customers passing through the mall.

I wanted to stop him, but what could I do? Run after him? Yell?

I stood there for a moment, unmoving, watching as the man tried desperately to get away from me, thinking how frightened I'd been when I'd looked into his hard, cold eyes.

But why should I be frightened of him when he was obviously just as frightened of me?

But if he was so frightened of me, why was he stalking me?

Stalking.

Why had I thought of that word?

I started walking. Something about the man seemed familiar to me on a subconscious level. There was something almost, but not quite, recognizable in his features that I had not noticed until I'd seen him up close, and that something bothered me, nagged at me, all the way out to the parking lot and all the way home.

SIXTEEN

I expected to be quizzed on where I'd been, and I'd prepared an elaborate story to justify my absence. But none of it was necessary. No one asked about my day off. In fact, when I mentioned to David that I was feeling much better today, he looked at me with surprise. "You were sick?"

"I wasn't here yesterday," I told him.

"Huh," he said. "Didn't even notice."

Stewart might not have noticed that I'd been gone, but he noticed that I'd missed his deadline and he called me into his office soon after lunch. He faced me from across the desk. "Jones? You've failed to complete an important assigned task, despite having had a very generous deadline to work with."

Generous deadline? I stared straight at him. He and I both knew what he had pulled.

"This is going to be noted on your six-month review."

I mustered my courage. "Why are you doing this?" I asked.

He stared at me innocently. "Doing what? Enforcing department standards?"

"You know what I'm talking about."

"Do I?"

I met his eyes. "You have it in for me, don't you?"

He smiled that smug jock's smile. "Yes," he admitted. "I do."

"Why?"

"I don't like you, Jones. I've never liked you. You represent everything I despise."

"But why?"

"Does it matter?"

"It does to me."

"Then it doesn't matter. Get back to work, Jones. I'm pretty dissatisfied with your performance so far. So is Mr. Banks. We all are."

Fuck you, I wanted to say. But I said it only with my eyes and turned and left the office.

I was Ignored because I was average. It seemed the most logical answer, the most reasonable assumption. Having come of age in the latter half of the twentieth century, I was a product of the mass media standardization of culture, my thoughts and tastes and feelings shaped and determined by the same influences that were acting upon everyone else of my generation.

But I didn't buy it.

For one thing, I wasn't completely average. If I had been, if everything had been that consistent, my existence would have been understandable, predictable. But there were glaring inconsistencies in the theory. My television viewing might correspond exactly with the Nielsen ratings, the shows ranked the same order in the newspaper and in my mind, but my taste in books was nowhere near mainstream.

Then again, while my reading tastes might be different from those of the general public, perhaps they were precisely average for white males of my socio-economic and educational background.

How specific did this thing get?

It would take a statistician years to sort through this information and pick out a pattern.

I was driving myself crazy with this endless speculation, trying so desperately hard to find out who or what I was.

I looked around my apartment, at the outlandish furnishings that my influence had somehow made mundane. I had an idea, and I went into the kitchen and dug through the junk drawer until I found my AAA map of Los Angeles. I spread the map out, located the Los Angeles County Museum of Art.

There was a car parked on the street in front of my apartment. A white Dodge Dart. I didn't think much of it at first, but when the car pulled behind me as I drove out of the driveway . . . then followed me down College Avenue, down Imperial Highway and onto the freeway, I began to feel a little unnerved. I knew it was probably nothing. I'd simply seen too many movies. And my solitary existence had only contributed to my paranoia. But I couldn't help noticing that the car remained behind me: changing lanes when I changed lanes, speeding up when I sped up, slowing down when I slowed down. There was no reason for anyone to be following me—such an idea was obviously ludicrous—but I still felt uneasy and a little bit frightened.

In my rearview mirror I saw that a black four-door pickup had zoomed into the space between me and the Dart, and I used this opportunity to get away, flooring the gas pedal, suddenly swerving in front of a VW and exiting the nearest off-ramp. I waited at the intersection of the street at the bottom of the off-ramp, not moving even when the light changed to green, but the Dart did not reappear behind me.

I'd lost him.

I got back on the freeway, heading toward L.A.

The art museum was crowded, and it was hard to find a parking spot. I finally had to shell out five bucks and park at a rip-off lot across the side street from the La Brea Tar Pits. I walked through the park, past the outrageously colored replicas of long-extinct mammals, and up to the museum, where I paid another five bucks for a pass.

Inside, the museum was cool and dark and silent. There were people here, but the building was so big that they seemed few and far between, and even the most flamboyant among them were cowed into quiet by the hushed and intimidating atmosphere.

I walked from room to room, wing to wing, floor to floor, past English furniture and French silverware and Indian statues, scanning the paintings on the walls, looking for one of the big names, one of the heavy hitters. Finally I found one. Renoir. A painting of people eating at an outdoor café.

There were no other guests in this gallery or even this wing, only a lone uniformed guard standing silently by the entryway. I stepped back, into the center of the room. This, I knew, was class. This was culture. This was Art with a capital A.

I stared at the painting and felt cold. I wanted to experience the magic, the sense of awe and wonder, the feeling of transcendence that people were supposed to have when confronted with great works of art, but I felt only a mild enjoyment. I looked at the other paintings on display. Before me were the treasures of the world, the very finest objects that man had produced in the history of the planet, and all I could muster was a halfhearted interest. My senses were muffled, subdued, stifled by the nature of my being, by the fact that I was completely and utterly ordinary.

The extraordinary had no power to touch me.

It was what I'd thought, what I'd feared, and although it only confirmed what I'd expected, that confirmation hit home with the force of a death announcement.

I looked again at the Renoir, moved closer, studied it, examined it, trying to force myself to feel something, anything, trying desperately to understand what others might see in the work, but it was beyond me. I turned to go—

—and saw someone standing in the entryway of the gallery, staring at me.

The tall, sharp-eyed man I'd seen at the mall.

A wave of cold passed over me, through me.

And then he was gone, disappearing behind the wall to the left of the door. I hurried over to the entryway, but by the time I reached it there was no sign of him. There was only a lone couple, dressed in matching black turtlenecks, walking toward me from the far end of the wing.

I was tempted to ask the guard whether he'd seen the man, but I realized instantly that he wouldn't have. The guard was facing into the room, away from where the man had been, and he would not have seen a thing.

The museum suddenly seemed darker, colder, bigger than it had, and as I walked alone toward the front of the building, past silent wings and empty rooms, I realized that I was holding my breath.

I was scared.

I walked faster, wanting to run but not daring to, and it was only when I was safely outside, in the sunshine, surrounded by people, that I was again able to breathe normally.

SEVENTEEN

On Monday, David was gone. I was not told why and I did not ask, but his desk was cleared off, the metal shelves behind him empty, and I knew without being told that he no longer worked for Automated Interface. I wondered if he'd quit or been fired. Fired, I assumed. Otherwise he would've told me.

Or maybe not.

What they say and what they mean are two different things.

I found myself thinking about what he'd said about women when I'd told him that I hadn't made an effort to contact Jane after she'd left me. It had been bothering me ever since he'd said it, nagging at the back of my mind, making me feel, not exactly guilty, but . . . responsible somehow for the fact that she hadn't come back. I thought for a moment, then stood, closed the door to the office, and sat down at David's desk, picking up the phone. I still remembered the day care center's phone number after all this time, my fingers punching the seven digits almost instinctively.

"May I speak to Jane?" I asked the old woman who answered the phone.

"Jane Reynolds?"

"Yes."

"She quit four months ago. She no longer works here."

I felt as though I'd been kicked in the stomach.

I hadn't seen, talked to, or communicated with Jane since we'd broken up, but somehow the idea that she'd

been near, that she'd continued carrying on her normal
life, even though I was no longer part of that life, had
been comforting to me, calming. I might not be with
her, but just knowing that she was there reassured me.
Now, I suddenly discovered, she'd dumped *all* of her
old life at the same time she'd dumped me.

Where was she now? What was she doing?

I imagined her cruising across the country on the
back of some Hell's Angel's Harley.

No. I pushed the thought out of my mind. That
wasn't Jane. And even if it was, it was none of my
business. We weren't together anymore. I had no right
to be affected by the details of her new life.

"Hello?" the old woman said. "Are you still there?
Who is this?"

I hung up the phone.

I saw him outside my apartment that evening. The
sharp-eyed man. He was standing in the shadows under
a tree, his left side lightly and partially illuminated by
the streetlamp halfway up the block. I saw him through
the front window as I was closing the drapes, and the
sight of him scared the shit out of me. I had been trying
not to think about him so I would not have to rationalize his existence to myself, but seeing him there,
waiting in the dark, staring at my apartment, watching
me, made me very afraid. It was clear now that he was
spying on me—

stalking me

—though I had no idea why. I hurried to the door,
opened it, and bravely stepped out on the porch, but
when I looked toward the tree he was gone. There was
no one there.

I closed the door, chilled. The thought occurred to
me that he wasn't human. Maybe he was like the hitch-
hiker who kept following the woman in that *Twilight
Zone* episode. Maybe he was Death. Maybe he was a
guardian angel. Maybe he was the ghost of a person my

family had wronged who was now fated to follow me everywhere.

Now I was just being stupid.

But was I? If I could accept the idea that I was Ignored, why couldn't I accept the idea that he was a ghost or some other sort of supernatural being?

I had a tough time falling asleep that night.

I dreamed of the sharp-eyed man.

I began skipping out, taking days off work. As long as I was there to fill out my time card on Friday, it didn't really seem to make any difference whether I showed up the rest of the week.

I never felt like going home, and at first I hung out at the various malls: Costa Mesa's South Coast Plaza, Santa Ana's Main Place, Orange's Orange Mall, Brea's Brea Mall. But I soon tired of that, and I eventually found myself driving around Irvine, hovering about the city like a moth near a porch light.

I started parking the car and walking through Irvine's shopping districts, taking comfort in the uniformity of the shops, feeling relaxed in the midst of all this harmonious homogeneity. I settled into something of a routine, eating lunch at the same Burger King each day, stopping in at the same music, book, and clothing stores to browse. As the days passed, I began to recognize faces on the street, other men, like myself, who were dressed as if for work but were obviously not working and obviously not job-hunting. Once, I saw one of the men steal from a convenience store. I was standing across the street, at the crosswalk, waiting for the light to change, and I watched a tall, well-dressed man walk into a 7-Eleven, pick up two cartons of Coors from the display in the front window, and walk out, apparently without paying. The two of us passed each other on the sidewalk in front of the convenience store.

I found myself wondering if he'd left any finger-prints in the store, if he'd touched anything else besides the beer. He had to have touched the door to open it. If I went into the store and told the clerk, could the police dust for prints and catch the man that way?

I opened my right hand, moved it up in front of my face, looked at my fingers. Every individual in the world was supposed to have a unique fingerprint, distinctive only to him or her. But as I stared at the lightly ridged whorls of skin that covered the tip of my index finger, I wondered if that was true after all. I had the sneaking suspicion that my fingerprints were not unique, were not truly my own. If nothing else about me was original, if nothing else about me was inimitable, why should this be different? I'd seen pictures of prints before, in magazines, on the news, and the differences between them were always so slight as to be nearly unnoticeable. If the print patterns were so limited to begin with, how reasonable was it to think that no two, in the entire history of man, were ever alike? There had to be sets of fingerprints that looked the same.

And mine were no doubt the most common kind.

But that was stupid. If that were the case, someone would have noticed it by now. Police would have discovered even a small contingent of identical fingerprints, and that would have automatically invalidated the use of prints as weapons in crime detection and as evidence in court.

But maybe the police *had* discovered that all fingerprints were not unique. And maybe they had kept it quiet. After all, the police had a vested interest in maintaining the status quo. Fingerprinting worked in the majority of cases, and if a few people fell through the cracks . . . well, that was the price that had to be paid for an orderly society.

I suddenly felt chilled, and at that moment the entire criminal justice system seemed a lot more sinister to me than it had only a few seconds before. In my mind I saw innocent men convicted of crimes, jailed, perhaps even executed, because their prints matched those of the real murderers. I saw computers displaying a list of people with fingerprints identical to those found on a murder weapon and the police picking a scapegoat using eenie-meenie-minie-moe.

All of Western civilization operated on the assumption that everyone was different, everyone was unique. It was the basis of our philosophical constructs, our political structure, our religions.

But it wasn't true, I thought. It wasn't true.

I told myself to stop thinking about that, to stop projecting my own situation onto the entire world. I told myself to enjoy my day off.

I turned away from the 7-Eleven and walked over to the music store to do some browsing. At noon I ate lunch at Burger King.

EIGHTEEN

Christmas came. And New Year's.
I spent both holidays alone, watching TV.

NINETEEN

The work was piling up, and I knew that even if my absences weren't noticed, my lack of output would be. At least by Stewart. I decided to spend a whole week in my office, catching up on my assignments.

It was halfway through the week when I walked over to the break room to buy a Coke—or a Shasta—and I heard Stewart's voice: "He's gay, you know."

"I thought maybe he was." Stacy. "He's never tried to hit on me."

I walked into the break room and Stewart grinned at me. Stacy, Bill, and Pam all looked away, and their impromptu group began immediately and guiltily dispersing.

I realized that they had been talking about me.

I felt my face redden. I should have been outraged by their intolerance and homophobia. I should have given an angry speech denouncing their unenlightened narrow-mindedness. But I felt embarrassed and humiliated, ashamed that they thought I was homosexual, and I blurted out: "I'm not gay!"

Stewart was still grinning. "You miss David, don't you?"

This time I said it: "Fuck you."

His grin grew. "You'd like to, wouldn't you?"

It was like a school yard argument, the trading of insults by junior high school students. I knew that intellectually. I understood that. But I was also a part of it, and emotionally I felt like I was once again a skinny kid on the playground being picked on by a bigger bully jock.

I took a deep breath, willed myself to remain calm. "This is harassment," I said. "I'm going to talk to Mr. Banks about your behavior."

"Oooh, you're going to go tell Mr. Banks on me," he said in an exaggeratedly whiny crybaby voice. His voice hardened. "Well, I'm going to make a report of your insubordination and have you bounced out of this corporation so fast your head will spin."

"I don't give a shit," I said.

The programmers were not looking at us. They had not left—they wanted to see what was going to happen—but they were off in other corners of the room, pretending to look at the selections in the vending machines, flipping through the pages of the women's magazines left on the tables.

Stewart smiled at me, and it was a hard smile, a cruel smile, a triumphant smile. "You're out of here, Jones. You're history."

I watched him walk out of the break room, away from me, down the hall. There were other people in the corridor, employees from other departments, and I noticed for the first time that though he was nodding at those he passed, no one was nodding back, no one was smiling, no one was saying hello, no one was acknowledging him in any way.

I thought of his spare, impersonal office, and it hit me.

He was Ignored, too!

I watched him turn the corner into his office. It made perfect sense. The only reason he was noticed at all was because he was a supervisor. It was only his position of power that kept him from fading into the woodwork completely. The programmers and secretaries paid attention to him because they had to, because it was part of their job, because he was above them in the corporate hierarchy. Banks paid attention to him because Banks was responsible for the whole division and had to keep close tabs on what everyone was doing, particularly the department heads.

But no one else was aware of his existence.

Maybe that was why Stewart disliked me so much. He saw in me the things he hated most about himself. Odds were that he didn't even know he was Ignored. He was sheltered by his position and probably wasn't aware of the fact that no one outside of our department paid any attention to him at all.

The thought occurred to me that I could kill him and no one would notice.

I instantly tried to take the thought back, tried to pretend I hadn't had it. But it was there in my mind, defying my attempts to erase it even as I desperately tried to think of something else. I don't know to whom I was denying this thought. Myself, perhaps. Or God— if He or She was listening in on my mind and monitoring the morality of my random ideas and notions. It wasn't just a random notion, though. And as I tried not to think about it and only thought about it more, I realized that while I wanted to find the idea horrifying and completely repugnant, it actually seemed . . . attractive.

I could kill Stewart and no one would notice.

I thought of the man stealing Coors from the 7-Eleven and not getting caught.

I could kill Stewart and no one would notice.

I was not a murderer. I owned no guns. Killing went against everything I'd ever been taught or believed in.

But the idea of doing away with Stewart had a definite appeal. I would never really go through with it, of course. It was just a fantasy, a daydream—

No, it wasn't.

I wanted to kill him.

I began thinking about it logically. Was Stewart truly Ignored? Or was he just kind of a boring guy who wasn't very popular? Could I be certain that if I killed him I would get away with it?

It didn't matter if he was Ignored. *I* was Ignored. People might notice that he was dead, but they wouldn't know that I was the killer. I could murder him in his office and walk down the hallway, go down the elevator, and pass through the lobby all covered with blood and no one would pay any attention to me at all.

The programmers left the break room and I was alone, standing in the center of the room, surrounded by the humming refrigerator and the vending machines. Things were moving too fast. This wasn't who I was. I wasn't a criminal. I didn't kill people. I shouldn't even want to kill people.

But I did want to.

And, as I stood there, I knew that I would do it.

TWENTY

On the day of the murder I went to work in a clown suit.

I don't know what possessed me to go to that extreme. Maybe, subconsciously, I wanted to be found out and stopped, prevented from going through with it. Maybe I wanted someone to force me to do what I knew I should do and couldn't.

But that didn't happen.

There'd been fewer preparations necessary than I'd expected. As the days passed and the certainty grew within me that I was going to kill Stewart, I started to formulate a plan. At first, I thought I'd have to learn all of the of the exits and entrances within the building, the location of each fire alarm, the exact shift hours of each downstairs security guard, but I soon realized that it would not be that complicated. I was not robbing Fort Knox here. And I was practically invisible already. All I really had to do was get in, do it, and get out.

The major problem would be Stewart himself. I was not invisible to him—he saw me—and he was in a hell of a lot better shape than I was. He could kick my ass with one hand tied behind his back.

And if he knew what I was—what *we* were—he could kill *me* and get away with it. No one would know. And no one would care.

I'd have to have the element of surprise on my side.

I followed him about for a few days, trying to learn his patterns, his routine, hoping I could figure out from this how, and where, I could most effectively strike at him. I was sneaky about it, not obvious. Since no one ever noticed where I went or what I did, I staked out a corner by the programmers' section where I could keep an eye on Stewart's office. I watched him come and go for two days, and was gratified to learn that his habits were very regular, his daily routine practically set in stone. From there, I moved to the main hallway, making sure I was walking down the hallway at the times he left his office so that I would be able to see where he went and what he did.

He went into the bathroom each day after lunch, at approximately one-fifteen, and he stayed in there a good ten minutes.

I knew that that was where I would kill him.

It was the perfect spot, the bathroom. He would be vulnerable and unsuspecting, and I would have the element of surprise. If I could catch him while his pants were down it would be even better, because he would be partially incapacitated: he wouldn't be able to kick me or run away.

That was the plan.

It was simple and to the point, and I knew that that was why it would work.

I set a date: January 30.

Thursday.

On January 30, I woke up early and put on my clown clothes. The clothes had been a last-minute decision. I'd stopped by a costume rental shop on my way home the night before. I'd pretented to myself that it was a disguise, but I knew that was bullshit. In a business environment, a clown suit was not an effective disguise, it was a red flag. And I'd paid for the rental with my Visa card. There was a record of this. There was a paper trail. Evidence.

I think, subconsciously, I wanted to get caught.

I took my time painting my face with the greasepaint supplied by the costume shop, making sure I covered every inch of skin with white, making sure the red smiling mouth was perfectly painted on, making sure the nose was precisely in place.

It was already after eight before I left the house.

Next to me, on the passenger seat of the car, was the carving knife I'd taken from the kitchen.

It was like I was someone else, like I was in a movie and watching myself secondhand. I drove to Automated Interface, parked way the hell out in God's country, walked through the rows of cars to the building, walked through the lobby, took the elevator upstairs, and went into my office. I carried the knife all the way, holding it out in front of me, practically advertising what I intended to do, making no effort to hide it, but no one stopped me, no one saw me.

I sat at my desk, unmoving, the knife in front of me, until one o'clock.

At five after, I stood, walked down the hallway to the bathroom, went into the first stall. I'd expected to be nervous, but I was not. My hands were neither sweaty nor shaking, and I was calm as I sat down on the toilet. This was the time to back out. Nothing had happened. I could call it off right now and no one would know. No one would get hurt.

But I wanted Stewart to get hurt.

I wanted him dead.

I made a deal with myself. If he walked into my stall, I would kill him. If he walked into one of the other stalls, I would call the whole thing off now and forever.

I grasped the knife tighter. Now I was starting to sweat. My mouth was dry, and I licked my lips, trying to generate some saliva.

The bathroom door opened.

My heart was pounding, whether from excitement or fear I couldn't tell. The sound seemed extraordinarily loud in my head and I wondered if Stewart could hear it.

Footsteps crossed the tile floor toward the stalls.

What if it wasn't even Stewart? What if it was

someone else and they opened the door of my stall and saw me there, a deranged clown with a knife? What would I do? What could I do?

The footsteps stopped outside my stall.

The metal door was pulled open.

It was Stewart.

For a split second, his face registered surprise. Then I stabbed him. The knife did not slide easily into his body. It hit muscle and rib and it was tough going, and I pulled it out and pushed it in again, only this time with more of a thrusting motion. I guess the shock must've worn off then because he started to scream. I shoved my left hand over his mouth to keep him quiet, but even without the screams the loud, rough sounds of our struggle echoed in the empty bathroom. He was pressed against the side of the stall, and he was kicking and fighting and trying desperately to get away. There was blood everywhere, flowing, spurting, on him, on me. A kick connected with my right knee and almost brought me down. His fist hit the side of my head. I realized instantly that I'd made a mistake, but it was too late to turn back now, and I continued to stab.

It didn't feel good, the way I'd thought it would. I didn't feel satisfied, didn't feel as if justice was being served. I felt like what I was. A cold-blooded killer. In my plans, in my fantasies, this had been the payoff scene of a movie, and I'd been cheering the hero— me—as he finally meted out retribution to the villain. But in reality it was not that way. It was brutal and messy and ugly: he trying furiously to save his life, me no longer wanting to kill him but fully committed to that course of action and unable to stop.

He fell, hitting his head on the bottom edge of the metal door and causing a new geyser of blood to gush forth from his forehead. He was dying, but not quickly and not without a struggle, and I was being hurt. If he had been quicker or I had been slower, he would have knocked the knife out of my hand or wrestled it away from me and that would have been the end.

He punched me in the balls and I tripped backward, but I fell onto the toilet, and I lunged forward and stabbed him in the face.

His body convulsed crazily for a few seconds, then was still.

I withdrew my knife from his nose. It was followed by a wave of blood and some sickly gray clumpy stuff that washed over my shoes.

How was I going to explain all this to the costume rental shop? I thought stupidly.

I stood, pulled off some toilet paper, and wiped the blood from the knife. I stepped over Stewart's body and closed the stall door behind me. His head and one arm were sticking out from underneath the side of the stall, his hand practically touching the edge of the adjacent urinal, but I didn't care. There was no way I could hide the body at this point or even remotely disguise what had happened.

I felt nothing. No guilt, no fear, no panic, no exhilaration. Nothing. I realized that I was probably suffering from some kind of shock, but I didn't feel like I was suffering from shock. I seemed to be thinking clearly, my mind functioning normally.

It had not happened the way I'd thought it would happen, but I decided to stick with my original plan. I walked out of the bathroom and down the hall to the elevator. I walked through the lobby and outside, but by the time I started looking around for my car I had already passed it. I was on the sidewalk and looking at cars parked on the street. I guess I was more in shock than I thought.

It hit me then.

I started trembling, and I dropped the knife. I could no longer see because of the tears in my eyes. I could still feel the knife stabbing through muscle and hitting bone, could still feel my hand over his mouth as he bled and drooled all over me and tried desperately to escape. Would I ever be able to erase those images and sensations from my consciousness?

I walked slowly and dazedly down the sidewalk. I probably would have felt foolish had I thought about the way I was dressed, but right now my appearance was the last thing on my mind.

I had killed a man. I had taken a human life.

I realized that I knew nothing about Stewart's existence away from work. Was he married? Did he have a family? Would there be a young son and daughter waiting at a house with a white picket fence for their father to come home for dinner? I felt guilty, horrible, and within me was a black blank feeling that went far beyond depression. The strength and will I'd felt at the moment of the murder was gone, replaced by a tired, lethargic despair.

What had I done?

Behind me, on the street, I heard sirens.

Police.

"Bob!"

I turned around at the sound of my name.

And saw the sharp-eyed man running toward me across the sidewalk.

I had a momentary sensation of panic, a quickflash feeling of fear, but though I wanted to run, I did not. I turned fully, faced the man.

He slowed as he approached, grinning at me. "You killed him, didn't you?"

I tried to keep my face innocently neutral, tried not to let the alarm show on my face. "Who?"

"Your boss."

"I don't know what you're talking about."

"Yes, you do, Bob. You know exactly what I'm talking about.

"No, I don't. And how do you know my name?"

He laughed, but strangely enough there didn't seem to be any maliciousness in the laugh. "Come on. You know I've been following you, and you know why."

"No, I don't know why."

"You've passed the initiation ceremony. You're in."

The fear returned. I suddenly wished I hadn't dropped the knife. "In?"

"You're one of us."

It was like I'd suddenly figured out how to do a complicated math problem that had been frustrating me. I knew what he was. "You're Ignored," I said.

He nodded. "But I prefer to call myself a terrorist. A Terrorist for the Common Man."

I felt strange, unlike I'd ever felt before, and I didn't know if the feeling was good or bad. "Are . . . are there more of you?"

He laughed again. "Oh, yes. There are more of us." He stressed the word "us."

"But—"

"We want you to join us." He moved forward, next to me. "You're free now. You've cut off your ties to their world. You're part of our world now. You never were one of them, but you thought you had to play by their rules. Now you know you don't. No one knows you; no one will remember you. You can do what you want." His sharp eyes focused on mine. "We've all done the same thing. We've all done what you've done. I offed my boss and *his* boss. I thought I was all alone then, but . . . well, I found out that I wasn't. I found others. And I decided that we should band together. When I saw you that first time, at South Coast Plaza, I knew you were one of us, too. But I could tell that you were still searching. You hadn't found yourself yet. So I waited for you."

"You don't even know me."

"I know you. I know what foods you like; I know your taste in clothes; I know everything about you. And you know everything about me."

"Except your name."

"Philipe." He grinned. "Now you know everything."

It was true. He was right. And as I stood there and looked at him and that strange feeling settled inside me, I knew that the feeling was good.

"Are you in?" he asked.

I looked back down the street, toward the mirrored facade of the Automated Interface building, and I nodded slowly. "I'm in," I said.

Philipe pumped his fist in the air. "Yes!" His smile grew broader. "You're a victor now, not a victim. You won't regret this." He spread his arms wide. "The town," he crowed, "is ours!"

PART TWO

We Are Here

ONE

I felt no guilt. That was the weird thing. Aside from those first few initial qualms, I felt no guilt over what I'd done. I wanted to; I tried to. I even attempted to analyze why I didn't. Murder was wrong. I'd been taught that since I was a child, and I believed it. No human being had the right to take the life of another. To do so was . . . evil.

So why didn't I feel bad?

I suppose it was because deep down, despite my surface reservations against murder, I felt that Stewart had deserved it. How I could think that, how I could believe that arrogance toward an underling qualified one for the death penalty, I could not rationally say. It was an instinctive feeling, a gut reaction, and whether it was Philipe's persuasive arguments or my own rationalizations, I soon came to think, to believe, that what I had done was not wrong. It might have been illegal, but it was fair, it was just.

Legality and illegality.

Did such concepts apply to me?

I thought not. I began to think that perhaps, like Philipe said, I had been put on this earth for a purpose, that my anonymity was not a curse but a blessing, that my invisibility protected me from the mundane morality that ruled the lives of everyone else. I was average, Philipe kept telling me, but that made me special, that gave me rights and licenses that went far beyond those accorded to the people who'd surrounded me all my life.

I was born to be a Terrorist for the Common Man.

Terrorist for the Common Man.

It was an attractive concept, and it was obviously something to which Philipe had given a lot of thought. He introduced me to my fellow terrorists that first day. I was still stunned, still not fully functioning, but he led me back to my car and had me drive, following his directions, to a Denny's coffee shop in Orange. The other terrorists were already there, taking up two pushed-together tables in the back of the restaurant and being completely ignored by both the waitresses and the other customers. We walked over to where they sat. There were eight of them, not counting Philipe. All men. Four of them, like Philipe and myself, appeared to be in their twenties. Three of them looked to be in their thirties, and one was an old man who could not have been a day under sixty-five.

I looked at the men and I realized what had struck me before about Philipe, why there had been something familiar about him. He looked like me. They all looked like me. I don't mean that we had the same physical features, the same-sized noses or the same color hair, but there was a similarity in our expressions, in our attitudes, an undefinable quality that marked us as being of a kind. We were all Caucasian. I noticed that immediately. There were no minorities among us. But our similarity went far deeper than mere race.

We were all Ignored.

Philipe introduced me to the others. "This is the man I've been telling you about," he said, gesturing toward me. "The one I've been cultivating. He finally did his boss today. Now he's one of us."

Nervous, embarrassed, I looked down at my hands. I saw dried blood in the short lines of my knuckles, around the edges of my fingernails. I realized I was still wearing the clown suit.

The others stood, all smiling and talking excitedly, and they shook my hand and congratulated me one by one as Philipe introduced them. Buster was the old man, a former janitor. The young guys were John, James, Steve, and Tommy. John and Tommy had both worked for chain department stores before hooking up with Philipe. James had been a circulation manager for the *Pennysaver*. Steve had been a file clerk working for a temporary agency. Two of the thirtysomethingers, Bill and Don, had both held middle-management positions—Bill with the County of Orange, Don with a private investment firm. The other, Pete, had been a construction worker.

These, then, were my peers.

"Sit down," Philipe said. He pulled out a chair, looked at me. "You hungry? Want something to eat?"

I nodded, sitting down in the chair next to him. I *was* hungry, I realized. I hadn't eaten breakfast or lunch, and all of this . . . excitement had left me with a huge appetite. But none of the waitresses had even looked in this direction since we'd walked in.

"Don't worry," Philipe said, as if reading my thoughts. He walked to the middle of the room and stood directly in front of a plump older waitress who was heading back toward the kitchen. She stopped just before running into him, an expression of surprise crossing her features as she saw him for the first time. "Could we get some service?" Philipe said loudly. He pointed to our table, and the waitress's gaze followed his finger.

"I'm sorry," she said. "I—" She caught herself. "Are you ready to order?"

"Yes."

She followed Philipe back to our table. He ordered a patty melt and a cup of coffee, I ordered a cheeseburger, onion rings, and a large Coke. The other men had already eaten but asked for refills of their drinks.

I looked around the table at my fellow Ignored. Everything was happening so fast. My brain was registering the information, but my emotions were lagging a beat or two behind. I knew what was happening but not

how to feel about it. I found myself staring at John and
Tommy, or Tommy and John—I couldn't remember
who was who—trying to recall if I'd seen either of
them on the streets of Irvine during the days I'd
ditched work. There was something about them that
made them seem more familiar to me than the others.

Had I seen them before?

Had one of them stolen the Coors from the
7-Eleven?

"Okay." Philipe smiled at me. "I know this is all new
to you, so instead of me trying to explain everything,
why don't you just ask what you want to ask."

I looked from one face to another. I saw no unfriend-
liness there, no suspicion, no superiority, only sympathetic understanding. They all knew what I was
going through, what I was feeling. They'd been there
themselves.

None of them looked like terrorists, I found myself
thinking. Philipe was probably the hardest among
them, but even he did not look mean enough or suffi-
ciently fanatic enough to be a true terrorist. They were
like kids, I thought. Pretending. Playacting.

I realized that, as they'd introduced themselves to
me, they'd all told me what they *had* been doing, what
their jobs *had* been, but none of them had said what
they were doing now. I cleared my throat. "Where do
you, uh, work?" I asked. "Do you . . . do you all work
together someplace?"

"Work?" Buster laughed. "We don't work. We're
through with that shit."

"We don't need to work," Steve said. "We're terrorists."

"Terrorists? What does that mean? What do you do?
Do you all live together someplace, like a commune?
Or do you guys meet, like, once a week, or what?"

I was facing Steve when I asked the question, but he
immediately looked toward Philipe. They were all
looking toward Philipe.

"It's not like a job," Philipe said. "It's not what we *do*. It's what we *are*."

The others nodded in agreement, but none of them volunteered to expand on that.

"You asked what we did," Philipe continued, "where we work. That's the problem. Most people identify themselves with their jobs. Without their jobs, they're lost. That's the source of their identity. That's who they are. A lot of them don't know anything *but* work. They need that sort of structure to give their lives purpose, to feel fulfilled. But how fulfilling can a job as a secretary be? With free time, you can do anything! Your limits are those of your imagination. Most people don't have any meaning in their lives. They don't know why they're here, and they don't care. But we have a chance to be different. We don't need to just keep busy, to put in our time until we die. We can live!"

I thought of my long weekends, my boring vacations. I'd always been one of those people who were lost without imposed structure. I looked around the table, at the faces of my fellow Ignored. They, I knew, were that way, too.

But Philipe was right. This was a chance to break out. We had already killed. Each of us at the table, as nice as we seemed, as friendly as we looked, had murdered someone. What else was left after that? What other taboo could there be? We had already proved that we were not bound by the strictures of society.

I nodded at Philipe.

He smiled at me. "We're freer than everyone else," he said. "Most people think that what they do is important, that they matter. But we know better. There are sales clerks who come back to work immediately after they have a baby because they're convinced that their work is so important and valuable, their contribution so unique, that things could not go on without them. The truth is that they're just cogs in the machine. If they quit or died, someone else would immediately take their place and it wouldn't make a damn bit of difference to anybody.

"That's why we've been blessed. We've been shown that we are disposable, dispensable, unimportant. We've been freed for other, greater things."

"So what do we do?" I asked. "I mean as terrorists, what do we do?"

"Whatever we want," Buster said.

"Yeah, but what do we want?"

Again, all eyes turned to Philipe.

He straightened in his seat, obviously enjoying the attention. This was his idea, his baby, and he was proud of it. He leaned forward, elbows on the table, talking in the furtive yet passionately committed manner of a rebel leader giving a pep talk to his troops. He saw our role as that of avengers, he explained. We had experienced the persecution of the known, of the intellectual and physical elite. We knew what it was like to be overlooked and disregarded and unseen. Because of that, he said, because of our experiences, because of our oppression, because we had seen society from the yoke end of the plow, we knew what needed to be done. And he knew how to do it. With planning, with organization, we could bring about changes, great changes.

Everyone nodded enthusiastically, like true believers at a tent revival, and I, too, felt a proud stirring inside myself. But at the same time I found myself wondering if we all truly had such utopian goals in our hearts.

Or if we just wanted to be a part of something for once in our lives.

"But are we really . . . terrorists?" I asked. "Do we blow things up and kidnap people and . . . perform terrorist acts?"

Philipe nodded excitedly. "We're starting small, working our way up. We haven't been together that long, but we've already vandalized a McDonald's, a K-Mart, a Crown Books, and Blockbuster Video, some of the most recognized and well-known franchises in the country. Originally, as I said, our intention was to strike a blow against our oppressors, to cause financial damage to name brands, those who extol the known over the unknown, but we realized almost immediately that terrorism is nothing more than guerilla PR. What it does is draw attention to an issue. Individual acts of terrorism can't bring about any permanent, lasting change, but they can alert the masses to a problem and focus public attention on it. To answer your question, in our case the word 'terrorists' is perhaps an over-statement. We haven't actually blown anything up or hijacked an airplane or anything." He grinned. "Yet."

"Yet?"

"As I said, we're working our way up, conducting a campaign of gradual escalation."

"And what do we hope to accomplish by this?"

Philipe leaned back in his chair with a satisfied smile. "We'll become known."

The waitress came with food and drinks, and I hungrily scarfed down my lunch while the conversation between everyone else drifted back from the rhetoric they'd been spouting for my benefit to more everyday topics of trivial personal matters.

Philipe did not participate in the conversation. He stayed out of it, above it, and I thought that he seemed so much more knowing and sophisticated than the rest of us.

I finished my pie. Two of the waitresses pulled venetian blinds over the windows on the west side of the restaurant. I looked up at the wall clock above the cash register. It was after three.

There was still one thing I did not know, that I had not asked and that no one had voluntarily answered. I put down my fork, took a deep breath. "So what are we?" I asked. "Were we born this way? Did we become this way over the years? What . . . what *are* we?" I looked around the table, but no one would meet my eyes. They all looked uncomfortable.

"We're different," Philipe said.

"But what are we?"

There was silence. Even Philipe, for the first time since he'd called out my name on the street, looked unsure of himself.

"We're Ignored," Buster said.

"I know that—" I began. Then I stopped, thought, looked at him. "Where did you get that word, 'Ignored'? Who told you that?"

He shrugged. "I don't know."

Philipe saw what I was getting at. "Yes!" he said excitedly. "We all thought of that word, didn't we? It occurred to each of us independently."

"I'm not sure what that means," I said. "Or if it means anything. But it seems too weird to just be a coincidence."

"It means we were meant for this," Philipe said. "It means we were meant to be terrorists."

"Manifest Destiny!" said Tommy or John.

I felt uneasy with this kind of talk. I did not feel as though I had been *chosen* for anything, I did not think God had picked the ten of us for some special purpose, and the idea that there was a power guiding us, a reason and a will dictating our actions, made me very uncomfortable.

Philipe looked at his watch. "It's getting late," he said. "I think we'd better hit the road." He pulled a twenty out of his pocket and tossed it on the table.

"Will that cover it?" I asked.

Philipe smiled. "It doesn't matter. They won't notice if it doesn't."

We split up in the parking lot, agreeing to meet again the next morning at the municipal courthouse in Santa Ana. Philipe said he had a plan to throw a monkey wrench into the American legal system, and he wanted to start small, with a test, to see if it would work.

Philipe was planning to get a ride home with Steve, but he turned back to me as he headed across the asphalt toward Steve's Toyota. "Are you coming with us?" he asked.

"Of course," I said.

Of course.

I had killed a man this morning and then spent my afternoon casually hanging out with a group of people I didn't know from Adam who called themselves terrorists, and I was already thinking of myself as one of them, was already taking part in their activities as if it were the most natural thing in the world.

"Pick you up at seven-thirty, then," Philipe said. "We'll grab some breakfast first."

I nodded. "Okay."

I drove home.

They were at my apartment at seven-fifteen the next morning. All of them. Waiting on my doorstep. I'd just finished taking my shower and was getting dressed, and I answered the door wearing only my jeans. I was glad to see them. I'd spent most of the night tossing and turning, trying to figure out why I wasn't more suspicious or more curious or more ... something, why I had just accepted the terrorists and fell into step with them; but when I saw them again, all that worrying and speculation seemed irrelevant. I was one of them. That was why I felt this way. I had never been part of anything before in my life, and it felt good to know that there were others just like me.

I was absurdly glad to see them, and I grinned hugely, unable to help myself, as I invited them in. All eight men crowded into my mismatched living room.

"Wow," James said admiringly. "This place is great."

I looked around my apartment, seeing it through his eyes, and for the first time since I'd redecorated I thought that, yeah, it was pretty great.

I finished dressing and combing my hair, and we went to McDonald's and grabbed some Egg McMuffins for breakfast. We took three cars. I rode with James and Philipe in Philipe's Dart.

It was as though we'd known each other forever. I was not treated as an outsider or a newcomer, and I did not feel like an outsider or a newcomer. I'd been instantly assimilated into the group, and I was comfortable and at home with my newfound friends.

No, not my friends.

My brothers.

Court did not begin until nine, but we arrived earlier, at eight-thirty, and Philipe withdrew a large canvas bag from the Dart's trunk. We asked what it was, but he smiled and would say nothing, and we followed him into the building and up the stairs to a traffic courtroom, sitting down in the theaterlike section in the back that was reserved for defendants and members of the public.

"What are we going to do?" James asked.

"You'll see," Philipe told him.

The court started to fill up with other traffic violators and their families. A clerk came out and read off a list of names. A bailiff entered the courtroom, and then the judge, introduced by the bailiff as the Honorable Judge Selway. The first case was called, and a policeman and a dreadlocked black man who identified himself as a taxi driver began discussing the circumstances of an illegal turn.

There was a pause in the discussion.

"Judge Selway is a putz!" Philipe yelled.

The judge and the rest of the court staff scanned the seats. There was a crowd of people in the court, but they were all scattered, and in our section there were only us and a Hispanic couple.

"Your daughter fucks cotto salamis!" Philipe yelled. He nudged me, grinned. "Go on," he urged. "Say something."

"They'll arrest us for contempt!" I whispered.

"They don't see us. They forget we're here the second after they look at us." He nudged me again. "Go on. Go ahead."

I took a deep breath. "Get a dick!" I called out.

The judge pounded his gavel. "That's enough!" he

announced. He said something to the bailiff, who walked up to the railing in front of us.

"Pussy!" Buster said loudly.

"Cocksucking fuckwad!" Tommy called.

The judge banged his gavel again. The bailiff looked at us, through us, past us. The Hispanic couple looked around as if searching for the source of this disturbance.

"Your mother takes it up the ass!" I cried. I turned, grinned at Philipe. It felt good to shout like this.

"Pussy!" Buster yelled again.

"Eat shit!" I screamed. There was anger in my voice, as there was in the voices of the others. I hadn't realized I was angry at anything, but I was, I discovered. I was very angry. I was exceedingly angry. I was angry at fate, angry at the world, angry at everything that had made me this way, and years of rage and frustration came out in my cries.

"I pissed in your sister's mouth and she begged for more!" I yelled.

"You're a fat-assed, pantywaisted, tater-twanging, wuss-boy!" James called.

Philipe opened his canvas bag.

Removed several cartons of eggs.

I laughed, excited.

"Do it quickly," he said, passing the cartons down the row.

We began throwing. An egg hit the bailiff's hat, knocking it off. Another, immediately after, broke against his bald head. The judge ducked under a hail of eggs that splattered against his desk and the wall behind him. I let one fly, aiming for him, and hit him squarely in the chest, the yellow yolk brightly obvious against the black robes. Declaring a recess, the judge hurried out of the court into his chambers.

We were out of eggs almost immediately, and Philipe grabbed his bag and stood. "Okay, guys. Let's go."

"But we're just getting started," Steve complained.

"We're not invisible," Philipe said. "We're Ignored. If we stay here any longer, they'll catch us. Let's cut out now." He walked out of the courtroom and the rest of us followed.

"Pussy!" Buster yelled before leaving.

I heard the bailiff yell something, and then the door closed behind us.

We were high on adrenaline, our spirits soaring, and we fairly floated down the hall, laughing and talking together excitedly in a close-knit bunch, going over what had just happened, repeating our favorite lines, calling out things we should have said but hadn't been able to think of at the time.

"It worked," Philipe said wonderingly. He turned toward me. "Imagine if we interrupted a major trial, something all of the media was covering. Think of the exposure we could get. We'd make the newscasts for sure."

"So what's next?" Steve asked as we pushed open the glass doors and walked out through the front entrance of the building.

Philipe grinned, put his arm around Steve's shoulders, around James's. "Don't worry, boys. We'll think of something. We'll think of something."

TWO

My brothers.

We got along instantly, and although there were definitely some terrorists whose company I preferred, I basically liked them all. To be honest, I was so ecstatic to find people of my own ilk, others who were Ignored, that I probably would have been happy even if I'd hated Philipe and his followers.

But I didn't.

I liked them.

I liked them a lot.

I got the feeling that, despite all of Philipe's talk, they had not been very organized before now. But something seemed to come together with my arrival, something seemed to coalesce. I brought nothing special to the group, no ideas or ambitions, but it was as if I was some sort of catalyst, and what had been just a loosely knit gathering of men joined by the circumstances of their existence suddenly started to become a cohesive unit.

Philipe spent most of his time that first week with me, finding out the details of my background, trying to indoctrinate me and make sure I saw things from his perspective. It seemed important to him that I buy into his concept of Terrorism for the Common Man, and although I already did, and told him so repeatedly, he still felt the need to go over it with me, explain it to me, as though he was a missionary and I was an unbeliever he had been assigned to recruit.

I worried at first that Stewart's murder would

somehow be traced to me, that the police would put two and two together and notice that I hadn't shown up for work since he had been killed. When Philipe came for me on Saturday morning and knocked on my door, I half thought that it was the police, come to question me. But Philipe explained that none of the other terrorists had been caught or even questioned, and that it was highly likely that my coworkers had forgotten all about me and had not even mentioned me to the police.

I saw no mention of Stewart's murder in either the *Orange County Register* or the *Los Angeles Times*.

We spent that week on vacation, having fun while Philipe formulated plans for upcoming terrorist projects, and I thought that it was the best week I'd ever had in my life. There was a short January heat wave, and we went to the beach. Since no one noticed us, Philipe said, we could stare to our hearts' content, and there were women galore, all available for our visual enjoyment. We compared breasts and bikini lines, rated postures and posteriors. We would pick out one woman and all concentrate on her, watch her swim and sunbathe, watch her adjust her top, watch her surreptitiously scratch her crotch when she thought no one was looking. All this time, one or another of us would provide running commentary on her each and every move. On a dare and in a mood of lunatic bravery, Buster ran down the beach and pulled loose the bikini ties of all women who were sitting alone on their blankets.

We went to Disneyland and Knott's Berry Farm, sneaking in the reentry gates one by one while the guards were looking in another direction. We went to malls and shoplifted, daring each other to steal bigger and bulkier items, running like hell and laughingly losing ourselves in the crowd when Buster was spotted carrying a monstrous boom box out of Radio Shack. We went to movies, one person paying, then opening the exit door so the rest of us could sneak in. It was like being a kid again, or like being the kid I never was, never had the guts to be, and it was wonderful.

Through it all, we talked. We talked about our families and our lives and our work, about what it was like to be Ignored, about what we could do as Terrorists for the Common Man. Only Buster and Don had ever been married, it turned out. Buster's wife had died and Don's had run off with a securities consultant. Of the others, only Philipe and Bill had even had girlfriends. The rest had been as ignored by women as they had been by society at large.

I still didn't believe that Manifest Destiny crap, but I had started to think that, yeah, maybe there was a reason we'd been created like this. Maybe some higher power did have a special purpose for us, although whether that purpose was to initiate greatness or merely to serve as comic relief to the footnotes of contemporary culture remained to be seen.

We always met at my place. I offered to drive, to pick up Philipe at his house, but he always said no. Ditto for the others. I didn't know if they weren't ready to completely trust me yet, if this was some type of security measure or paranoia on their part, or if things just happened to work out this way, but that first week I never saw where any of my fellow terrorists lived. They seemed to like my apartment, though, to find it comfortable, and that made me feel good. A couple of times we rented videotapes, and we watched them in my living room, and once they all stayed overnight, crashing on my couch and on the living room and bedroom floors.

It felt good to be a part of something.

It was on the second Saturday that Philipe suggested that we begin another vandalism campaign in an attempt to draw attention to our plight. We were at my place again, chowing down on a Taco Bell lunch, and I pushed my chair back onto two legs, steadying myself with one foot. "Okay," I said. "Let's do it. What's the plan?"

Philipe shook his head. "Not now. This isn't a social

outing we're going on. This is terrorism. I need time to
make some preparations."

"What are we going to hit? Where are we going to
start?"

"Where? City Hall. Orange City Hall."

"Why there?"

"It's where I used to work. I still have a key and a
security card. We can get in."

"You used to work for the city of Orange?"

"I was one of the assistant city managers," he said.

That surprised me. I was not sure what I'd thought
Philipe had done before becoming a Terrorist for the
Common Man, but it was not that. I guess I'd seen him
doing something more glamorous or more dangerous.
Something in the movie business maybe. Or working
for a detective agency. This made more sense, though.
Philipe might seem like a leader to us, but he was still
Ignored, a faceless nonentity to the rest of the world.

"When?" Pete asked.

"Tuesday."

I looked around the group, nodded. "Tuesday it is,"
I said.

We drove to the meeting separately. Philipe didn't
want us all riding together.

There were cars in the parking lot when I arrived,
and the other terrorists were milling around by the
building's back door, where Philipe had told us to
meet. Only Philipe himself was missing, and I parked
my car, got out, and walked over to the group. None of
us spoke, and there was a feeling of hushed expectancy
among us.

Buster had brought a friend, a man also in his mid to
late sixties who was wearing the uniform of a Texaco
attendant. The name tag on the old man's uniform read
"Junior," and I couldn't help smiling at the incongruity
of the name and the face. The old man smiled back at
me, happy to be noticed in even this small way, and I
immediately felt sorry for laughing at him.

"My friend Junior," Buster explained. "He's one of us."

Apparently Junior had not yet been introduced to the others, because at this announcement they all gathered around, shaking his hand, welcoming him, the artificially imposed silence of a few moments before effectively broken. I did the same. It felt strange to be on the inside looking out. I had been in Junior's shoes only recently, and it seemed weird and slightly disorienting to view all this from the opposite angle.

Junior ate it up. He had apparently been told by Buster beforehand about the terrorists—he did not seem confused or surprised upon meeting us—and there was a smile on his face and tears in his eyes as he shook our hands and repeated our names.

It was at that moment that Philipe arrived. Resplendent in an expensively tailored suit, his hair neatly trimmed, he looked almost presidential, the model of a modern leader, and he strode across the parking lot with the air and authority of one used to being in charge.

The rest of us grew quiet as he approached. I felt a strange excited shiver pass through me as Philipe stepped confidently up the curb. It was the type of moment I'd experienced before only as an observer, not as a participant. I felt the way I had in movies when the music swelled and the hero performed heroically. For the first time, I think, I realized that we were part of something big, something important.

Terrorists for the Common Man.

It was more than just a concept to me now. I finally understood what Philipe had been trying so hard to explain.

He looked at me and smiled, and it was as if he knew what I was thinking. Taking out his key and security card, he inserted both into the electronic slot on the wall next to the door, and the door clicked. He pushed it open.

"Let's go in," he said.

We followed him inside the building. He paused, closed and locked the door behind us, and we proceeded down a darkened corridor to an elevator. Philipe pushed the Up button, and the metal doors instantly slid open, the light inside the elevator cubicle seeming harsh and far too bright after the darkness.

"Second floor," Philipe announced, pushing the button.

The second floor was even darker than the first, but Philipe forged ahead and turned on a bank of lights and a series of recessed fluorescents winked on, illuminating a huge room fronted by a built-in counter and partitioned off into smaller sections by modular wall segments.

"This way!" he said.

He led us behind the counter, through the modular maze of workstations, to a closed wooden door in the far wall. He opened the door, turned on the lights.

I had a queasy momentary sense of déjà vu. We were in a conference room, bare save for a long table with a television and VCR on a metal stand at its head. It looked almost exactly like the room in which I'd been introduced to Automated Interface.

"This looks just like the conference room at my old firm," Don said.

"It looks like the training room at Ward's." Tommy.

"It looks like the county's multipurpose room." Bill.

Philipe held up his hands. "I know," he said. He paused, looked around the room at the rest of us. "We are Ignored," he said. He looked around the table. His gaze landed on Junior, and though he said nothing, he smiled, silently welcoming the old man to the fold. Then he continued, "We are of a kind. Our lives have traveled along parallel paths.

"There is a reason for this. It is not by chance or accident that our experiences echo each other's, and it is not by chance or accident that we met and joined together. It is by design. We have been chosen for a special purpose, and we have been given this talent to use.

"Most of you did not realize at first that it was a talent. You thought it was a curse. But you've seen what we can do together. You've seen the places we can go, the actions we can perform. You've seen the opportunities available to us." He paused. "We are not the only people who are Ignored. There are other Ignoreds whom we don't know and may never know, living out their lives of quiet desperation, and it is for those people, as much as for ourselves, that we must fight. For we have the opportunity, the ability, and the obligation to claim rights for a minority that the rest of the world does not even know exists. We are here tonight not only because of what we are, but because of what we have chosen to be: Terrorists for the Common Man!"

Again, a tingle of excitement ran through me. I almost felt like cheering, and I knew the others did, too. Yes, I thought. Yes!

"What does that mean? Terrorists for the Common Man? It means that it is our responsibility to act on behalf of the forgotten and the disregarded, the unknown and the unappreciated. We will give a voice to the people who have no voice. We will bring recognition to the people who aren't recognized. We have been ignored all our lives, but we will be ignored no more! We will make the world sit up and take notice and we will shout to anyone who will listen, 'We are here! We are here! We are here!' "

Steve pumped his fist in the air. "Yeah!"

I felt like doing the same.

Philipe smiled. "How do we accomplish this? How do we grab the attention of a society that has so far paid no attention to us at all? Violence. Creative, constructive violence. We kidnap and take hostages, we blow up buildings, we do anything we have to do to get our point across and make Middle America sit up and take notice. Playtime's over, kiddies. We're in the big leagues now. And it's time for us to get to work."

From the inside of his expensive suit, Philipe withdrew a hammer. Calmly, coolly, he turned around and smashed the screen on the TV. There was a loud pop, and glass shattered outward, accompanied by a small shower of sparks.

He used the hammer to smash the VCR as well.

"This will get in the *Orange City News*," he said. "There will be a short blurb of an article stating that a person or persons unknown broke into City Hall and destroyed audiovisual equipment. That's it." He knocked the TV onto the floor. "All of our previous attempts have been amateurish and unfocused. We have not gotten the attention we deserve because we did not choose our targets wisely and did not properly identify ourselves." Once again, he reached into his jacket. "I have had cards made up. Professionally typeset business cards that list the name of our organization. We'll leave these at the scenes of our crimes so they'll know who we are."

He passed the cards around, and we all got a look at them. White with red lettering, they said:

> THIS IS A BLOW FOR THE IGNORED
> TERRORISTS FOR THE COMMON MAN

"Yes!" Steve said. "Yes!"

"Now the more damage we do, of course, the bigger the articles about us will be, the more attention our acts will get." He walked around the table, past us. "Come on."

We followed him out to the room with the workstations. He bent down to turn on a computer terminal that was sitting atop a desk. "They forgot about me," he said. "They didn't think to change my password. Their mistake." He pulled up an initial security screen, typed in an ID and password, and a list of property records appeared on the screen. In one column were the names of the parcel owners, in another the assessed valuation of each property.

Philipe pressed two keys.

The records were deleted.

"Gone," he said. "Now we'll be portrayed as expert computer hackers who deleted hundreds of important government records. It'll probably make the *Register*. Maybe the Orange County edition of the *Times*."

He straightened up, pulling the terminal onto the floor, where it fell with a crash. He kicked in the screen, then used his arm to clear the top of the desk, sweeping everything onto the floor.

"We can do anything we want," he said, "and they'll never be able to catch us!" He jumped on top of the desk, held his hammer high. "Let's tear this fucking place apart!"

Like Willard's rats, we set about following his order. I tipped over one of the modular walls, smashed a terminal myself. I pulled open file drawers, yanking out anything I could lay my hands on. It felt good, this destruction, invigorating, and we spread out, taking out our aggression and frustrations on the anonymous inanimate objects of Orange City Hall.

We trashed the entire floor.

A half hour later, sweaty and out of breath, huffing and puffing, we met by the elevator.

Philipe surveyed the damage, grinned hugely. "This will be noticed," he said. "This will be reported. This will be investigated. We're off to a good start." He pressed the elevator button, the metal doors opened, and we stepped inside.

In the instant before the doors slid shut, he threw his key and security card out onto the second-floor carpet.

"There's no turning back now."

THREE

I was like an adolescent who suddenly becomes enormously wealthy or an ordinary man who becomes dictator. I was drunk with possibilities, greedy to use my newfound power.

We all felt that way, I guess, but we didn't really talk about it. The feeling was too new, too strong and pure, and I don't think any of us wanted to dilute its potency by discussing it. For my part, I felt excited and absurdly happy, almost intoxicated. I felt invincible, as though I could do anything. As Philipe had predicted, our trashing of Orange's city hall made not only the Orange city paper but the *Times* and the *Register*. Although our fingerprints were all over everything from the back door of the building to the vandalized workstations, although Philipe had tossed his key and security card on the floor in front of the elevator, although we had scattered our new business cards about the area, each of the articles clearly stated that the police had no suspects and no clues.

We had been ignored once again.

I should have felt remorse, I suppose. I had been brought up to have respect for other people's property, and until now I had never even thought about destroying something that did not belong to me. But Philipe was right. Breaking the law was justified if it led to the eradication of an even greater wrong. Thoreau had known this. So had Martin Luther King. And Malcolm X. Civil disobedience was an American tradition, and we were just the latest soldiers in a long battle against hypocrisy and injustice.

I wanted to vandalize someplace else.

Anyplace. I didn't care where.

I just wanted to smash and break things.

We met the next day at my apartment. Everyone was talking about what we'd done, each man rehashing his own personal contribution. No one seemed more hyped than Junior, our newest terrorist. He kept giggling, the laugh of a schoolboy, not an old man, and it was obvious that this was the most exciting thing to have happened to him in years.

Philipe stood by himself, next to the doorway to the kitchen, and I moved next to him. "What are we going to do next?" I asked.

He shrugged. "Who knows? You got any ideas?"

I shook my head slowly, surprised not only by his answer but his attitude. The rest of us were pumped up, high from our first outing and ready for more, but Philipe seemed . . . I don't know. Bored? Disappointed? Disillusioned? All of those and none of them. I looked at him, and the thought crossed my mind that he was manic depressive. That didn't fit, though. Manic depressives were either up or down; there was no middle ground. Philipe was more even-keeled than that.

Maybe, I thought, he was feeling remorse.

Maybe he was feeling what I was supposed to feel.

I still wanted to hit someplace else, to strike another blow against the empire, but I decided that maybe this wasn't the time to bring it up. On the table to my left was the Show section of the *Register*, the entertainment section, and I picked it up, glancing at the top article on the front page. Fashion Island, in Newport Beach, was hosting its annual jazz concert series. I'd been there last spring, with Jane. Throughout March and April each year, jazz artists gave free Thursday evening concerts in an outdoor stage area set up near The Broadway.

"Let me see that," Philipe said. He took the paper

from me. He had been reading over my shoulder and had obviously found something that caught his interest. He looked over the front page, and a grin spread across his face. His eyes, dull a few moments before, were animated and excited. "Yes," he said.

He strode into the middle of the room, held up the newspaper. "Tomorrow," he announced, "we're going to a jazz concert!"

We'd planned to arrive early, but by the time we battled the work traffic on the freeway and made it to Fashion Island, it was five-fifty. The concert was scheduled to start at six.

Bleachers and folding chairs had been set up for the audience, but both were filled and people were starting to stand around the periphery of the concert area. We stood in front of a men's clothing store, watching the people pass by. It was an upscale crowd of beautiful people, the type of people I'd always hated. The women were all model-thin with short skintight dresses and designer sunglasses, the men blond and athletic and young and successful. Most of them were talking business.

Apparently Philipe felt the same way I did. "Obnoxious jerks," he said, surveying the crowd.

An announcer introduced the band, and an eclectic group of longhaired men and short-haired women took the stage. The music started, a Latin-fusion hybrid. I looked toward Philipe. He obviously had something planned for tonight, but none of the rest of us knew what it was. I felt a rush of adrenaline as I saw him straighten, walk forward.

He moved beside a smug-looking woman wearing designer-label tennis clothes, a trendy chatterbox who had not stopped talking to the identically dressed woman next to her since the concert began. He turned to face her. "Would you please be quiet?" he said. "We're trying to hear the concert."

He slapped her hard across the face.

She was too stunned to react. By the time she realized what had happened, Philipe had again stepped back to where the rest of us were standing. The woman looked at us, through us, past us, searching for the person who had hit her. There was fear on her face, and her right cheek was bright red where it had been slapped.

She and her friend quickly moved away, toward a security guard standing near the bleachers.

Philipe grinned at me. I heard Bill and Junior giggling behind me.

"What should we do?" James asked.

"Follow my lead," Philipe said. He moved forward, into the crowd, in the direction of the folding chairs. He stopped next to a young Turk in a power tie who was discussing stock options with a friend.

Philipe reached out, grabbed a handful of the man's hair, and yanked. Hard.

The man screamed in pain and whirled around, fists clenched.

Steve punched him in the gut.

The man fell to his knees, gasping for air and clutching his stomach. His friend looked at us with frightened eyes and began backing away.

Bill and John advanced on him.

I felt strange. Following the rush of our city hall escapade, I'd wanted to do something else along those lines, I'd wanted to see some type of action, but this sort of random violence made me feel extremely uncomfortable. It shouldn't have—I'd already killed a man, I'd already vandalized a public building, I didn't like these yuppies here to begin with—but I still felt as though we were in the wrong. If there had been more provocation, if there was some way I could justify our actions, I might feel better about it, but as it was, I felt sorry for the woman Philipe had slapped, for the man he had attacked. I'd been the victim too often myself not to sympathize with other victims.

The first man was starting to get up, and Philipe

pushed him back down onto the cement. He turned to me. "Go with Bill and John. Get his friend."

I stood there.

"Get him!"

Bill and John had tackled the other man. Someone else had come to his rescue. This was turning into an honest-to-God brawl.

"Get in there!" Philipe ordered.

I didn't want to "get in there." I didn't want to—

An Armani-suited jerk bumped into me. He was heading toward the fight, ready to get into it. He obviously hadn't seen me and had run into me accidentally, but he didn't even bother to apologize. "Get the fuck out of my way," he said instead, pushing a fisted hand toward my face.

That did it.

The crowd suddenly had a face to me. The man in the Armani suit instantly came to symbolize everything that was wrong with these people, everything that I hated about them. They were no longer innocent victims of Philipe's random attacks. They were deserving recipients of justice.

These were the people who had kept us down, kept us Ignored, and after all this time, we were finally striking back.

I punched Armani hard in the back.

He stumbled, grunted, whirled around, but Don was already on him, hitting him in the stomach. Armani doubled up, but took it, and was about to retaliate when Buster, behind him, kicked the back of his left knee.

He went down.

"Retreat!" Philipe announced suddenly. "Move back!"

I didn't know why he said that, what he had planned or decided, but like the others, I instantly, instinctively obeyed. All ten of us gathered around Philipe. He grinned hugely. "Look," he said.

My gaze followed the nod of his head. The fight was still going on, although between whom I did not know.

Two security guards had rushed over and were trying to break it up.

No one had noticed our absence.

I got the point.

Philipe caught my eye, grinned, nodded when he saw that I understood. "We'll spread out, start up conflicts throughout the crowd. Bill and John, you go to the other side of Nieman Marcus. James, Steve, Pete, start something near Silverwood's. Buster and Junior, you do something by the far bleachers. Tommy and Don? You two attack near the sign-up table for the drawing. Bob and I will take this area."

The plan worked perfectly. We would pick one man and then set upon him, pummeling him. Others would join in, expanding the fight, and we would bow out.

Soon there were several pockets of turmoil in the crowd, a free-for-all melee with us unseen at the center of the storm.

The band had stopped playing by this time, and an announcement was made from the stage that unless order was restored immediately the concert would be canceled.

The fighting continued, with an ever-increasing number of security guards emerging from some reserve area in an attempt to bring the crowd under control.

Philipe surveyed the scene, nodded with satisfaction, dropped a handful of cards on the ground, placed some on the bottom bleacher seats. "Good enough," he said. "Let's go. We're outta here."

The next day we made the front page of the *Register*. GANG VIOLENCE ERUPTS AT FREE CONCERT, the headline read.

Junior laughed. "Gang violence?"

There was no mention of our exploits in the *Times*.

"The concert was sponsored by the *Register*," John said. "That's why."

"First lesson," Philipe said. "Avoid partisan media events."

We all laughed.

"We should start a scrapbook," James suggested. "Cut out all the articles about us."

Philipe nodded. "Good idea. You're in charge of that." He turned toward me. "And since you have the best VCR here, you're in charge of taping local news broadcasts, in case we ever make it onto TV."

"Okay," I said.

He continued looking at me. "By the way, you know what today is, don't you?"

I shook my head.

"It's your one-month anniversary."

He was right. How could I have forgotten? Exactly one month ago today, I had killed Stewart. The morning's lighthearted mood disappeared instantly for me. My hands grew sweaty, the muscles in my neck tense as I thought of that scene in the bathroom stall. In my mind, I again smelled the blood, felt the knife push thickly through muscle, deflect off bone.

At this time of day, one month ago, I had been sitting at my desk in my clown suit. Waiting.

The clown suit was still on the floor of my bedroom closet.

"Let's go back there," Philipe said. "See what's happened since then."

I was horrified. "No!"

"Why not? You can't tell me you're not even curious."

"Yeah," Don said. "Let's go. It'll be great."

"What did he do a month ago?" Junior asked.

"He killed his boss," Buster explained.

The old man's eyes widened. "Killed his boss?"

"We all did," Buster told him. "I thought you knew that."

"No. I didn't." He was silent for a moment. "I did, too," he admitted. "I killed my boss, too. But I was afraid to tell you."

Philipe continued to look at me. "I think we should go back to your company," he said. "I think we should go back to Automated Interface, Incorporated."

Even hearing that name sent a strange shiver through me. "Why?" I asked. My hands were trembling. I tried not to let it show. "What good would it do?"

"Catharsis. I think you need to go. I don't think you'll get over it until you confront it."

"Is this because of last night? Because I didn't want to just start beating on people for no reason?"

He shrugged. "Maybe. You can't have pussies in a terrorist organization."

I thought of a thousand retorts to that, a thousand things I could say, a thousand things I should say, but for some reason I backed off. I looked away from him, looked down at my shoes, shook my head. "I don't want to go."

"We're going," he said flatly. "Whether you want to or not. I'll drive."

James, on the couch, glanced up from the newspaper article. "Are we all going?"

"No, just Bob and me."

I wanted to object, wanted to refuse, but I found myself nodding. "Okay," I said.

Philipe talked on the drive over. This was the first time we'd been alone, with none of the others anywhere around, since he'd first approached me on the street after Stewart's murder, and he seemed anxious to explain to me the importance of what he termed "our work."

"I know," I said.

"Do you?" He shook his head. "I never know about you," he said. "John, Don, Bill, and the rest, I always know where they stand, I always know what they're thinking. But you're a mystery to me. Maybe that's why it's so important for me to make sure you understand why we're doing what we're doing."

"I understand."

"But you don't approve."

"Yes, I do. It's just . . . I don't know."

"You know."

"Sometimes . . . sometimes some things seem wrong to me."

"You still have your old values, you still have your old system of beliefs. You'll get over that eventually."

"Maybe."

He looked sideways at me. "You don't want to?"

"I don't know."

"But you're with us? You're one of us?"

"Always," I said. "What else do I have?"

He nodded. "What else do any of us have?"

We drove the rest of the way in silence.

It felt strange to be driving back to Automated Interface again, and my palms were sweaty as we pulled into the parking lot. I wiped them on my jeans. "I don't think we should do this."

"You think they're going to see you and immediately put two and two together and arrest you for killing your supervisor? These people don't even remember you. They probably couldn't describe you if their lives depended on it."

"Some of them could," I said.

"Don't count on it."

The parking spaces were all filled, so Philipe pulled into a handicapped visitor's spot near the entrance. He switched off the ignition. "We're here."

"I don't—"

"If you don't face it, you won't get past it. You can't let the memory of what happened here ruin your whole life. You did the right thing."

"I know I did."

"Then why do you feel guilty?"

"I don't. I just . . . I'm afraid."

"There's nothing to be afraid of." He opened his door, got out of the car. Reluctantly, I did the same. "It's places like this that have made us what we are," Philipe said. "These are the places we need to strike against."

"I was always Ignored," I pointed out. "My job didn't make me Ignored."

"But it made you worse," he said.

I could not really argue. I did not know if I believed him, but I could not refute him.

"You had to waste that fucker. You couldn't have done anything else. That's why you are who you are. That's why you're here with me now. That's why you're a terrorist. It's part of the plan."

I smiled. "A Dan Fogelberg reference?"

"If it applies, use it." He grinned. "Let's go in."

We walked up the sidewalk, through the entrance, into the lobby. The guard was at his post. As always, he ignored me. I was about to walk past him to the elevator when I suddenly stopped. I turned toward Philipe. "I hate that guy," I said.

"Then do something about it."

"I will." I walked up to the guard's desk. He still didn't see me.

I leaned forward, knocked the cap off his head. "Asshole," I said.

Now he saw me.

He leaped out of his chair, reached over the desk to grab my arm. "Who do you think you are, you—"

I backed up, moved next to Philipe, and suddenly the guard looked confused.

He could no longer see me!

"It's good to be back," Philipe said. "Isn't it?"

I nodded. It did feel good. And I was glad Philipe had forced me to return. We continued on toward the elevator. I hazarded a glance back at the guard. He seemed not only confused but frightened.

"We can do anything," Philipe said. He looked at me meaningfully. "Anything."

The elevator doors opened, and we stepped inside. I pressed the button for the fourth floor. Flush with my success, primed by encouragement from Philipe, I considered killing Banks. I'd been invisible to him for quite some time before I left, but when he had been able to see me, he hadn't liked me. He'd been Stewart's ally. He'd even made fun of my haircut once.

I could give him a haircut.

I could scalp the fucker.

Then I thought of Stewart and the horrible way he'd died, the way he'd tried to kick me and hit me as I stabbed him, the way the blood gushed out of his body onto me, and I knew I would not be able to kill again.

The elation fled as quickly as it had come. Why was I here? What could I possibly hope to accomplish at Automated Interface? Philipe had said in the car that he wanted us to monkey-wrench, but I was not in a position to cause any serious damage. I didn't know enough to do any real harm.

We got out on the fourth floor. I walked over to the programming section. The lights were off in Stewart's old office. Obviously he had not been replaced. Otherwise, everything was as I'd left it. I took Philipe past Stacy's desk, and Pam's and Emery's. None of the programmers even looked up at us.

It felt oppressive to me here, the atmosphere thick and heavy, the air way too warm, and I told Philipe that I wanted to leave, but he said that first he wanted to see where I'd killed Stewart.

I took him into the bathroom.

It was weird being back again. The body was gone, of course, and the blood was cleaned up, but the place still seemed tainted to me, dirty. With trembling hands, I opened the door to the first stall. Philipe made me go over the whole thing, in detail, and he nodded, touching the metal wall into which I'd slammed Stewart, crouching down to examine the toilet where I'd fallen.

When I finished, he said, "Don't feel bad; you did everything you were supposed to.

I didn't buy that, but I nodded.

He pushed me gently out of the stall. "Excuse me," he said.

"What?"

"I have to take a piss."

He closed the door to the stall. I heard the sound of a zipper going down, heard piss hitting the toilet water.

That did it.

Coming here, seeing everything, going over it all again—none of that had done anything to erase the unease I felt. But hearing Philipe taking a leak in the same stall where I'd killed Stewart, that put those feelings to rest. In some bizarre way, it made me realize that the past was over, the future was here, and the future was good.

The future was us.

I was grinning when Philipe flushed the toilet and came out.

"Everything okay?" he asked.

"Everything's fine," I told him.

"Let's check out your office."

I led him down the hall. Like Stewart's office, mine was empty. A replacement for me had not been found yet. Hell, maybe they hadn't even noticed that I was gone. The papers on top of my desk were untouched, exactly the way I'd left them a month ago.

He looked around the small cubicle. "God, this is depressing."

"Yeah," I agreed.

"Didn't you hate working here?"

I nodded.

He looked at me, tossed me a book of matches. "Do something about it."

I understood what he wanted me to do, and the thought made my blood pump faster. Yes, I thought. This was right.

He backed out of the office, into the hallway.

This is something I had to do on my own.

I stood there for a moment, then lit a match, touched it to the edge of a memo, the edge of a procedural manual. The flames spread slowly, from one paper to another across the top of the desk. I thought of my cards, my business cards, and I quickly opened the drawer where I'd put them and took them out. The entire top of the desk was burning now, and I turned over the box and dumped the cards on the fire. They caught and curled and blackened and were gone.

My old life was over.

Really over.

I could not go home again.

I moved back into the hallway, nodded to Philipe, and the two of us walked slowly and calmly down the hallway, dropping terrorist cards, as around us fire alarms sounded and sprinklers went off.

FOUR

Again I wondered what I was. What we were. Did we possess different genes or chromosomes than everyone else? Was there a scientific explanation for all of this? Were we descendants of aliens or a separate race of being? It seemed silly to think that we were not human, particularly since we were so prototypically, so stereotypically, average in every way, but there was obviously something that set us apart from those around us. Could it be that individually, coincidentally, we had so conformed to the norms of society, our backgrounds and environments had so shaped us, that we had collectively turned out this way and were now ignored by a culture trained to look for the unusual and overlook the obvious? Or were we truly of a kind—did we send out some sort of subliminal psychic signal that was picked up by those around us and caused us to be ignored?

I had no answers, only questions.

I was not sure that the others thought about this as much as I did. They didn't seem to. Philipe probably did. He was deeper than the rest of us, brighter, more ambitious, more serious, more philosophical. The others, in a way, were almost like children, and it seemed to me that as long as they had Philipe to be their parent and do their thinking and planning for them, they were happy. Philipe kept insisting that because we were Ignored, because we fell through the cracks, we did not have to conform to other people's perceptions or standards or ideas of what we should be. We were free to be ourselves; we were free to be individuals. But the other terrorists were not individ-_ uals. Instead of defining themselves in terms of their jobs, they now defined themselves as terrorists. They'd simply switched one group identity for another.

But I dared not tell Philipe that.

I let him think we were what he wanted us to be.

After our trip to Automated Interface, Philipe and I were closer. There was no official hierarchy among the terrorists—Philipe was the leader and the rest of us were his followers—but if there had been, I would have been vice president or second in command. I was the one he asked when he wanted a second opinion on something; I was the one whose advice he heeded most often. All of the other terrorists, all of them except Junior, had been with Philipe longer than I had, but it was pretty well accepted that, among equals, I was somewhat more equal. There was no resentment of this, just acceptance, and everything continued along smoothly the way it always had.

During the next few weeks, we went to all of the terrorists' former places of work.

We vandalized them big-time.

But though we left our cards everywhere we went, we received no credit.

We did get several more news articles for our scrapbook, though. And while we didn't make the television news, Philipe assured us that we would get there eventually, and I had no doubt that he was right.

I started taking walks. After a busy day, after the other terrorists had left or had dropped me off at my place, I was often still not tired. And I usually did not feel like being cooped up alone in my apartment. So I began taking walks. I had never really walked much before. The frat-rat neighborhood in which my apartment was located was not the best in the world, for one thing, and I would have felt exposed and rather self-conscious walking by myself. But now that I knew that no one noticed me, that no one saw me, I felt safe and comfortable strolling about the streets of Brea.

Walking relaxed me.

One night, I walked all the way to Jane's parents' house, on the other side of town. I don't know what I expected—Jane's car in the driveway, perhaps; a glimpse of her through an open window—but when I reached the house it was dark, the driveway empty.

I stood across the street for what seemed like hours, thinking about the first time I'd picked up Jane for a date, about the time we'd spent afterward in my car, parked two doors down, out of sight of her parents' windows. At one point in our relationship, before we'd moved in together, this house had been almost like a second home to me. I'd spent as much time here as I had at my own apartment.

Now it seemed like the house of a stranger.

I stood there, waiting, watching, trying to gather up enough courage to walk up to the front door and knock.

Was she living with her parents again? Or was she staying somewhere else? Even if she was living in another city, another state, her parents would know where she was.

It didn't look like her parents were home, though.

And if they came home and I asked them about Jane, would they tell me? Would they recognize me? Would they even see me?

I stood there for a while longer. The night was chilly, and my arms began to get cold. I wished I'd brought a jacket.

Finally I decided to leave. Jane's parents still had not come back, and I did not know when they would. Maybe they'd gone on a vacation. Maybe they'd gone to visit Jane.

I turned away from the house, began walking back the way I'd come. The streets were empty, there was no one outside, but the drapes of the houses I passed were backlit with the blue glow of television. What was it that Karl Marx had said? Religion was the opiate of the masses? Wrong. Television was the opiate of the masses. No religion had ever been able to command as large and loyal an audience as that electronic box. No pope had ever had the pulpit of Johnny Carson.

I realized that I had not watched TV since I'd become a terrorist.

Did that mean that no one was watching TV? Or did that mean I was no longer average?

There were so many things that I did not know and would probably never know. I thought, fleetingly, that perhaps our time would be better spent trying to find out the answers to these questions rather than trying to draw attention to ourselves. But then I thought, no, drawing attention to our cause, letting people know we existed would eventually attract the interest of other, greater minds. People who might be able to change us, rescue us from our plight.

Rescue us.

Was that still how I thought? Despite Philipe's assertion that we were special, chosen, luckier than everyone else, despite my adamant professions of belief, would I still trade it all instantly to be like everyone else, to fit in with the rest of the world?

Yes.

It was after midnight when I arrived back at my apartment. I'd done a lot of thinking on my way home, run through a lot of scenarios in my head, made a lot of plans. Before I could change my mind, before I could chicken out, I dialed the number of Jane's parents. The phone rang. Once. Twice. Thrice.

On the thirtieth ring, I hung up.

I took off my clothes and got into bed. For the first time in a long time, I masturbated.

I fell asleep afterward and dreamed of Jane.

The night after we trashed the body shop where Junior had worked—pouring oil and transmission fluid onto the cement floor, smashing windows and equipment, sledgehammering cars—Philipe decided that we should take some time off, enjoy some R & R. We deserved it. John suggested that we go to a movie, and that idea was greeted with unanimous approval.

We met the next day at the theater complex.

There were a total of four movies playing on six screens, and though ordinarily we were in agreement on almost everything, we could not seem to decide what movie to see. Tommy, Junior, Buster, James, and Don wanted to watch a new comedy. The rest of us wanted to check out a horror flick.

My guess was that two movies would tie for first place in the box office rankings this weekend.

Philipe bought a movie ticket, and while the usher at the door tore his stub, the rest of us filed silently past, unnoticed, into the multiplex. The horror movie had started a few minutes ago, the comedy was not scheduled to be shown for another ten minutes, so we split up, going into our respective theaters.

The movie was okay, not great, although Bill seemed to like it quite a bit. I found myself wondering what the results of *Entertainment Tonight*'s movie track poll would be.

I had a feeling that one out of four people would rate the movie "above average or outstanding."

After we got out, the four of us hung around outside the theater, waiting. Bill said he was hungry, so we looked at the schedule mounted in the ticket booth to see how long it would be until the comedy got out. When we found out that it would be another twenty minutes we walked slowly down the block to a Baskin-Robbins. Two blond bimbos, giggling and talking in Valleyspeak, moved around us, past us.

"I'd like to feed that girl my ice-cream cone," Steve said.

"Which girl?" John asked.

"Either. Both."

We laughed.

Philipe stopped walking. "Rape," he said, "is power."

The rest of us stopped walking, looked at each other. We couldn't tell if he was joking or serious.

"Rape is a weapon."

He was serious. I stared at him in disgust.

"Don't give me that Holy Joe look. That's what this is all about. Power. It's what we, as Ignored, don't have. It's what we have to learn to take."

"Yeah," Steve said. "Besides, when's the last time you had some pussy?"

"Great idea," I said sarcastically. "That's how you can get women to notice you. Rape them."

"We've done it before." Philipe stared at me calmly.

That stopped me. I looked from Philipe to Steve to the rest of them, shocked. I had killed; I had assaulted; I had vandalized. But all of that had seemed perfectly justifiable to me, perfectly legitimate. This, however . . . This seemed wrong. And the fact that my friends, my brothers, my fellow terrorists had actually raped women made me see them in a different light. For the first time, I felt that I did not know these men. For the first time, I felt out of sync with them.

Philipe must have sensed my discomfort. Maybe it showed on my face. He smiled at me gently, put an arm around my shoulder. "We're terrorists," he said. "You know that. This is one of the things terrorists do."

"But we're Terrorists for the Common Man. How is this going to help the common man? How is this going to advance our cause?"

"It lets these bitches know who we are," Steve said.

"It gives us power," Philipe said.

"We don't need that kind of power."

"Yes, we do." Philipe squeezed my shoulder. "I think it's time for your initiation."

I pulled away. "No."

"Yes."

Philipe glanced around. "How about her?" He pointed down the sidewalk to where an Asian woman was stepping out of a lingerie shop, carrying a small bag. The woman was gorgeous: model-tall, with finely sculpted features, dark almond-shaped eyes offset by luscious red lipstick, long straight black hair that hung

almost to her waist. Her thin shiny pants were purple
and skintight, and I could clearly see the outline of
French-cut panties beneath.

Philipe saw the look on my face. "Take her down, bud."

"But . . ."

"If you don't, we will."

The others nodded enthusiastically.

"It's broad daylight."

"No one will see you."

He was right, I knew. I would be as ignored raping a
woman as I was at everything else. The woman began
walking away from us, past the Baskin-Robbins,
toward an alley in the center of the block.

But that didn't make it okay.

"That woman's going to be raped," Philipe said.
"Either you do it or we do it. The decision's yours."

I fell for the argument, believing in my arrogance that
being raped by me was somehow preferable to being
raped by Philipe or Steve or John. I was a nice person, I
rationalized, a good person performing a bad act. It was
less horrible to be raped by me than one of the others.

John giggled. "Pork her. And throw her a hump for me."

I took a deep breath and walked casually down the
sidewalk toward the woman. She did not see me until I
was upon her, did not react until I had grabbed her arm
and pulled her into the alley, my hand held over her
mouth. She dropped her bag. Black lace panties and a
red silk teddy spilled out.

I felt horrible. I suppose somewhere deep down in
the dark, unexplored recesses of my macho heart of
hearts I'd thought she might enjoy it just a little bit,
that even if the experience was emotionally wrenching,
it might still somehow be physically pleasurable. But
she was crying and terrified and obviously in anguish,
and I knew even as I pressed against her that she would
hate it and hate me.

I stopped.

I couldn't go through with it.

I let the woman go, and she fell onto the asphalt,

sobbing, sucking in air with great gasps. I moved away from her, stood, and leaned back against the alley wall. I felt like shit, like the criminal I was. My stomach was churning, and I felt like throwing up. What in the hell was wrong with me? How could I have ever consented to something like this? How could I be so morally weak, so pitifully unable to stand up for my beliefs?

I was not the person I'd thought I was.

In my mind, I saw Jane, yanked into an alley, raped by some stranger.

Did this woman have a boyfriend? A husband? Did she have children? She had parents.

"You had your chance," Philipe said. He was running into the alley, unbuckling his pants.

I lurched toward him, felt dizzy, felt like throwing up, had to lean against the wall again for support. "No!"

He looked at me. "You knew the rules of the game."

He grabbed the front of her pants, pulled, and a snap flew off.

The other terrorists were laughing. The woman was whimpering pitifully, struggling on the ground, trying desperately to keep her pants from being pulled down, trying to reclaim some of her stolen dignity, but Philipe dropped to his knees and roughly shoved her legs apart. I heard the sound of material ripping. She was screaming, crying, tears streaming down her reddened face, and she looked for all the world like a frightened little girl. There was terror in her eyes. Pure, abject terror.

"Let her go!" I said.

"No."

"I'm next!" Steve said.

"Me," Bill said.

I staggered out of the alley. Behind me, I heard their laughter, heard her screams.

I couldn't fight them. There was nothing I could do.

I walked down the sidewalk to the left, sat down on the narrow ledge beneath the Baskin-Robbins window. The glass felt cool against my back. I realized that my hands were shaking. I could still hear the woman's screams, but they were muffled by city sounds, by traffic, by people. The door to the ice cream parlor opened, and Bill walked out, a huge chocolate sugar cone in his hand.

"Done?" he asked me.

I shook my head.

He frowned. "No?"

"I couldn't do it," I said, sickened.

"Where is everybody?"

"There."

"Oh." He licked his ice cream, then headed toward the alley.

I closed my eyes, tried to concentrate on the noise of the traffic. Was Philipe evil? Were we all evil? I didn't know. I'd been taught my entire life that evil was banal. It was the Nazis and their institutionalized horror that had given rise to such a theory, and during my life I'd heard ad nauseum that evil was not brilliant and spectacular and grandiose, but small and mundane and ordinary.

We were small and mundane and ordinary.

Were we evil?

Philipe thought we were good, believed we could do anything that we wanted and that it was all right. There was no moral authority to which we had to answer, no system of ethics to which we were obliged to adhere. We were above all that. We decided what was right for us, what was wrong.

I had decided that this was wrong.

Why didn't we all agree on this? Why were our beliefs different? In almost everything else, we thought, we felt, as one. But at this moment, I felt as estranged from my fellow Ignored as I ever had from normal men and women.

Philipe would say that I was still holding on to the mores and conventions of the society that I had left behind.

Maybe he was right.

They emerged from the alley a few minutes later. I

wanted to go back there, check on the woman, make sure she was all right, but I stayed where I was, leaned my head back against the Baskin-Robbins window.

"Their movie's probably out by now," Philipe said, adjusting his belt. "We'd better get back to the theater."

I nodded, stood, and we started walking back down the street the way we'd come. I peeked into the alley as we walked past but saw nothing. She must have run out the other end.

"You're one of us," Philipe said. "You were part of it, too."

"Did I say anything?"

"No, but you're thinking it." He looked at me. "I need you with us."

I did not respond.

"You'll murder but you won't rape?"

"That was different. That was personal."

"It's all personal! We're not fighting individuals, we're fighting an entire system. We have to strike where and when we can."

"That's not how I see it," I told him.

He stopped walking. "You're against us, then."

I shook my head. "I'm not against you."

"Then you're with us."

I said nothing.

"You're with us," he repeated.

I nodded. Slowly. I was, I supposed. I had no choice. "Yeah," I said.

He grinned, put an arm around my shoulder. "One for all and all for one," he said. "Like the Three Musketeers."

I forced myself to smile, though it felt sickly and anemic on my face. I felt soiled and dirty and unclean and I didn't like his arm around me, but I said nothing.

I was with them. I was one of them.

Who else did I have?

What else could I be?

We walked down the sidewalk to the theater.

FIVE

We lived in our own world, a netherworld that occupied the same space as the normal one but existed a beat or two behind. It reminded me of an old *Outer Limits* episode I once saw, where time stood still and everyone in the world remained frozen in place except a man and woman who were somehow unaffected, untrapped, living outside of time, between the seconds.

Only the people we ran into weren't frozen in time.

They just didn't notice us.

It was a weird feeling, not being seen by the people with whom I came into contact. I'd been conscious of being Ignored for quite a while, but this feeling was different. It was as if I were really invisible, a ghost. Before, I'd felt a part of the world. I was unnoticed, but I existed. Now, though . . . Now, it was as though I did not exist, not on the same level as everyone else. It was as if normal life was a movie and I was a viewer: I could see it but not participate in it.

The only time I honestly felt alive was when I was with the other terrorists. We seemed to validate each other's existence. We were a pocket of reality in an unreal world, and as this feeling of alienation from human society grew within me, I began to spend more and more time with the terrorists, less and less time by myself. It was comforting to have the others around, reassuring to know that I was not alone, and as the days and weeks passed, we began sleeping over more often at each other's houses and apartments, not splitting up at night but staying together twenty-four hours a day.

It was not just the eleven of us huddling against a cold, hostile world, though. We had fun together. And there were perks, small advantages to being Ignored. We could go to restaurants, order whatever we wanted, eat to our heart's content, stay as long as we wanted, and we never had to pay. We could go to stores, take what we needed in food and goods. We could go to movies and concerts for free.

But there was still something unsettling about it all, still something missing—in my life, at least—and despite our best attempts to believe otherwise, despite our earnest efforts to reassure ourselves that we were happy, that we were luckier than everyone else, I don't think any of us really thought that was the case.

We were never bored, however, and we did not lack for things to do. We were the national average and America was made for us. We loved shopping at malls. We loved eating at restaurants. Amusement parks amused us, tourist attractions attracted us, popular music was popular with us, hit movies were a hit with us. Everything was aimed at our level.

And when we tired of legitimate ways of whiling away our hours, we could always rob, steal, and vandalize.

We could always be terrorists.

After the rape, we laid low for a couple of weeks. There was no mention of the rape in the papers or on the TV news—I was not even sure it had been reported—but it was not the possibility of getting caught that compelled Philipe to make us take time off anyway.

It was because he wanted to win back my confidence.

It was stupid, but it was true. My opinion was important to him. Most of the others were thrilled by what had happened. They had already snagged *Playboy*s and *Penthouse*s, *Hustler*s, and *Cavalier*s, and were busily picking out the types of women they wanted to take down next, but Philipe made it clear that there were to be no more sexual assaults. At least not for a while. Instead, he attempted to convince me that rape was a legitimate weapon at our disposal. He seemed aware of the fact that my opinion of him had dropped, that I no longer had the respect for him that I'd previously had, and he seemed desperately anxious to reinstate himself in my eyes.

That was an ego boost, of course. Such personal attention made me feel important. And, I had to admit, his arguments were persuasive. I understood where he was coming from, and I even agreed with him—on a purely theoretical level. But I also believed that it was wrong to punish innocent individuals for general wrongs perpetuated by the group to which they belonged, and I think I made him see my point. I got him to agree that the rape of the Asian woman had been only peripherally political, and he said that from now on we would only use rape if it would legitimately and specifically accomplish one of our goals.

If we just wanted to get ourselves off, we'd go to prostitutes or something.

We both thought that was fair.

It was in July that we performed our first big terrorist act, that we finally got on TV.

We were staying at Bill's place, a comfortable three-bedroom house in Fountain Valley, and we were awakened by the sound of a chain saw. The noise was loud, outrageously so, and frighteningly close. Instinctively scared, my heart pounding, I jumped out of my sleeping bag and opened the door of the bedroom.

Philipe stood in the hallway, wielding a gas-powered chain saw that smelled of burning oil, and waving it above his head like Leatherface. He saw me and grinned.

James emerged from the bedroom behind me, wide-eyed and frightened. The others came into the hall from the living room and the other bedrooms.

Philipe lowered his chain saw, turned it off. His grin

grew wider. "Get dressed, kiddies. We're going into town."

At his feet, I saw hammers and screwdrivers, a tire iron, an ax, a baseball bat. My ears were still ringing from the chain saw noise. "What?" I said.

"Get dressed and get ready," he said. "I have a plan."

We drove into L.A. in a caravan of three cars, Philipe's Dodge leading the way. It was Sunday, and the traffic was light. There'd been wind the night before, and for once we could see both the San Gabriel Mountains and the Hollywood Hills. The Los Angeles skyline looked the way it did in movies and on TV, backed by pale blue sky, only a faint haze of smog obscuring the details of the buildings.

We followed Philipe's car off the freeway and down Vermont Avenue, through gang-graffitied neighborhoods, past run-down grocery stores and dilapidated hooker hotels. We turned left on Sunset and headed through Hollywood to Beverly Hills. The chain saw and tools had been put in my trunk, and they rattled as I bumped over each dip in the road, shifted as I turned each corner. Buster, next to me in the passenger seat, held his Nikon camera on his lap. Philipe had told him to bring it.

"What do you think he has planned?" Buster asked.

I shrugged. "Who knows?"

"Isn't this great? Don't you love it?" The old man chuckled. "If anyone'd told me that at my age I'd be cruising around with a . . . a gang, kicking ass and raising hell, I'd've thought . . . well, I'd've said they were full of horse pucky."

I laughed.

"I feel so . . . so young. You know?"

Truth to tell, I felt the same way myself. I *was* young—compared to Buster, at least—but being a terrorist made me feel excited, exhilarated, exuberant. I felt good this morning, jazzed, almost giddy, and I knew the others felt the same way.

"Yeah," I said, nodding. "I know what you mean."

We passed a brown WELCOME TO BEVERLY HILLS sign, passed several import car dealers. Philipe's right-turn signal started blinking, and a hand shot out from the driver's side of his car, pointing up and over his roof toward the street sign on the corner: RODEO DRIVE.

He turned onto the street, parked his car.

I pulled in behind him and got out. I'd heard of Rodeo Drive, of course, but I'd never been there, and it wasn't quite what I'd expected. The stores seemed ordinary, mundane, more like the normal stores you'd see in the downtown of any average city than the glitz and glamor you'd expect from the most exclusive shopping district in the world. The entire area seemed a little shabbier than I'd been led to believe, and though the names were there on the storefronts—Gucci, Cartier, Armani—I still found myself a little disappointed.

Philipe walked back to my car, accompanied by Don, Bill, and Steve. "Open the trunk," he said. "Let's get that stuff out."

"What's the plan?" I asked, unlocking the trunk.

"We're going to rob Frederick's of Hollywood."

I frowned. "Frederick's of Hollywood? Why? What's the point? What'll we do with stolen underwear?"

"Why? For fun. The point? To show them that we can. The underwear? We'll keep what we want and toss the rest. Donate it. Leave it on the street or something, give it to the Goodwill."

"Like Robin Hood!" Steve piped up.

"Yeah, like Robin Hood. Taking from the known and giving to the Ignored." Philipe grabbed his chain saw out of the trunk. "Frederick's of Hollywood has national name recognition, and because it sells sexy lingerie, it's titillating enough to be newsworthy. It'll be noticed."

The other terrorists had just walked up behind us. "What?" John asked. "We're going to hit Frederick's?"

"Yeah," I said. I picked up the baseball bat.

"Let's loot the whole fuckin' street!" Junior said,

and there was a gleam in his eye that I hadn't seen there before and didn't much like.

Philipe shook his head. "The cops'd be here by then. We'll pick one store, do what we can, and get the hell out."

I looked up Rodeo Drive. It was after ten, but all of the stores were still closed. I was not sure if they opened after noon or if they were closed all day Sunday. I saw one man and two couples walking up the sidewalk on the left side of the street. A few cars passed by.

"Come on," Philipe said. "It's getting late. Let's do it." He stepped aside, and the others began grabbing tools from the trunk.

None of us knew where Frederick's was, so we walked up the street until we found it. I couldn't help thinking how comical we looked—eleven men, walking along Rodeo Drive on Sunday morning carrying bats, axes, and chain saws—but, as always, no one paid any attention to us at all.

A police car cruised by, signaled left, turned down a side street.

We stopped halfway up the block, in front of a window displaying lifelike female mannequins wearing red G-strings and lace push-up bras and black crotchless panties. The rest of us looked toward Philipe. He nodded, motioning toward Don, who held the ax. "You do the honors," he said.

"What should—"

"Smash the glass."

Don stood before the door, hefted the ax over his shoulder, brought it down squarely at chest level. The glass shattered, thousands of small safety shards falling inward. Lights went on in the store, and an alarm. A bank of security cameras swiveled conspicuously in our direction. Philipe reached through the door, turned the lock, pushed open the frame, and walked inside. A few remaining pieces of glass fell from the sides of the door.

Philipe said nothing but started his chain saw.

I didn't know if anyone else planned to do anything about those security cameras, so I walked over to the shelf on which they were stationed and began smashing them with the bat. I didn't care if we were Ignored, after five minutes on videotape, we would be identified. I finished with the cameras, looked around, spotted the alarm—a small white plastic box in the corner above the fitting rooms—and walked over, jumped up, and smashed the thing to hell.

When I turned around, Philipe was chain-sawing through the checkout counter, having already knocked over the cash register. Bill and Don were breaking display cases; James and John and Steve were pushing over racks; the others were filling bags and baskets with lingerie. I walked over to a mannequin, unsnapped its bra, ripped off its panties.

Philipe suddenly turned off his chain saw. The silence was jarring. We all looked toward him. He cocked his head, listening.

Outside, from several streets over, we heard sirens.

"They respond fast in good neighborhoods," Buster said.

"Out!" Philipe ordered. "Everyone out!"

We moved quickly toward the front of the store, scattering our cards on the floor and on what remained of the register.

"Drop your weapons," Philipe said. "Leave them. We can't afford to draw attention to ourselves on the street. Cops'll be swarming all over this area in a few minutes."

"What do we do with this stuff?" Tommy asked, holding up his bag of lingerie.

"Toss it," Philipe told him. "Throw it out on the street. Throw everything you can onto the street. It'll make a better picture on the news."

We all grabbed handfuls of teddies and chemises. As we left the store, we tossed them into the air, onto the sidewalk, into the street.

Two police cars rounded the far corner.

"Stay cool," Philipe said. "Act casual. Here they come."

We were the only ones walking on Rodeo Drive, but the cops did not notice us. They sped past, pulled to braking catty-corner stops in the middle of the street in front of Frederick's, and emerged from their vehicles drawing revolvers. Two more patrol cars came speeding down the street from the opposite direction.

We said nothing, did not talk, walked slowly but surely toward our cars. I got out my keys, unlocked and opened my door, got in. I reached across the seat and opened the passenger door for Buster. Through the windshield, I saw three policemen, guns drawn, walk into the store, while five others stood in a semicircle in the street out front.

Following Philipe, we turned the cars around and returned down Sunset the way we'd come.

Back home in Orange County, we went to our usual Denny's to celebrate. Philipe placed himself in the path of our usual waitress, confronted her, asked her to take our orders. As always, she was surprised to see us, and as always, she took and brought our orders and then immediately forgot about us.

We hogged the back booth, laughing and talking loudly. We were pumped, both proud of and excited by what we had done. The damage we'd caused at our former places of employment had been more extensive, more thorough, but none of those incidents had had the marquee value of this exploit, and we continued to speculate on what was happening right now in Beverly Hills, what the police were doing, what they were saying to the press as we ate our lunches.

Junior was laughingly describing a particularly exotic undergarment he'd come across in his looting, when I suddenly thought of something. "Let's write a note," I said. "A letter."

"We left cards," Don said.

"The cards haven't worked yet. It's time to try something new."

The others looked toward Philipe. He nodded, slowly. "Not a bad idea," he admitted. "We need to take credit for this. Even if they pick up on the cards, this is added insurance.

"You write it," Philipe told me. "Address it to the Beverly Hills police chief. Tell him who we are, what we're doing. Make it clear that we'll strike again. I want those bastards thinking about us."

I nodded.

"I want to proofread it before you send it out."

"Okay."

He smiled to himself, nodding. "Pretty soon everyone is going to know about the Terrorists for the Common Man."

The ransacking of Frederick's made the local NBC and ABC newscasts. Both segments were short, long on snickering innuendo and short on factual details, but they received prominent placement and were repeated on both eleven o'clock newscasts. I taped all showings.

The CBS station didn't lower itself to cover such sensationalism.

I wrote the letter that night, Philipe read it, we all signed it, and I sent it off.

We waited.

A day. Two. Four. A week.

There was nothing on the news, no follow-up story on television or in the papers.

Finally, following Philipe's directions, I made an anonymous call to the Beverly Hills Police Department from a pay phone outside a 7-Eleven. I claimed responsibility for the looting of Frederick's of Hollywood in the name of the Terrorists for the Common Man.

The sergeant on the other end of the line laughed at me. "Nice try, bud. But we caught the perps on that three days ago. Better luck next time."

He hung up.

Slowly, I placed the receiver in its cradle. I turned to face the others. "He said that they caught the guys who did it three days ago."

"That's impossible!" Junior said.

Steve frowned. "Call them back. Tell 'em they got the wrong men."

Philipe shook his head. "That's it. Case closed."

"I don't even think they got my letter," I said.

"They got it," Philipe said softly. "They just ignored it. I was afraid of that."

He walked away from us, into the 7-Eleven, and we stood there, confused and silent, waiting for him, as around us a group of kids who'd gotten off school went into the convenience store to play video games, paying no attention to us at all.

SIX

Philipe went out alone that night and did not return until it was almost dawn, but he was back to his normal self the next day. We'd spent the night at my apartment, and in the morning we went outside before deciding where we were going to eat breakfast. I'd been home so infrequently the past few months that I never bought groceries anymore, and there was no food in the apartment. Philipe, as always, took charge of the situation. "All right," he said, and there was no trace in his voice or attitude of the melancholy defeatism of the night before. "We have three choices. We can grab some fast food. We can go to a coffee shop." He paused. "Or we can get new cars."

Buster frowned. "New cars?"

Philipe grinned. "Our wheels are looking pretty raggedy. I think it's time we get some new ones. I myself would like a Mercedes."

"What do you mean?" Don asked. "We're supposed to steal ourselves some cars?"

"I have a plan," Philipe said. "I'll tell it to you over breakfast." He looked around the group. "Who votes for Jack-in-the-Box; who votes for IHOP?"

He did indeed have a plan. And it was a good one.

We ate breakfast at the International House of Pancakes, commandeering two tables that we pushed together in the rear of the restaurant, and he explained what he wanted to do. The plan was definitely workable, brilliant in its simplicity, and it was exciting to realize that we were probably the only people in the world who could pull it off.

After breakfast, we went looking for cars. The dealerships were closed, would not open until ten, but that did not prevent us from doing a little window-shopping. We drove to the Cerritos Auto Square, a two-block section in the city of Cerritos that had been specifically set aside for car dealers. We walked past the Mazda showroom, the Jeep dealer, Porsche, Pontiac, Mercedes, Nissan, Volkswagen, Chevrolet, Lincoln, and Cadillac. By the time we finished walking past the Cadillac lot, it was ten o'clock and the showrooms were opening for business.

"We drove here in three cars; we'll pick out three new ones today," Philipe said. "Has everybody decided what they want? I'm still going with the Mercedes. I like the light blue one we saw."

We decided on the Mercedes, a red Jeep Wrangler, and a black 280Z.

We paired off. Philipe and I would get the Mercedes, Bill and Don would take the Jeep, and John and Steve would go for the Z. The others would drive our old cars home.

"How come we're not in on it?" Junior complained.

"Next time," Philipe promised.

We split up, and I accompanied Philipe to the Mercedes dealer. Salesmen were pouncing on people the second they stepped onto the lot, but we had no such problem. Philipe, in fact, had to hunt down a salesman in the office, an oily sleaze wearing an inappropriately expensive suit and a gaudy set of large gold rings. He introduced himself as Chris, enthusiastically pumped both of our arms, asked what sort of car we were interested in. Philipe pointed toward the blue car we'd looked at earlier. "That one there," he said.

Chris looked him over, took in his jeans, his faded T-shirt, his windbreaker, and smiled indulgently. "That's our top of the line. May I ask what price range you're looking at?"

Philipe turned away. "I came here to buy a car, not be harassed about my appearance." He motioned for me to follow him. "Come on, let's go to the Porsche dealer."

"I . . . I'm sorry," the salesman said, his phony smile faltering.

"It was a toss-up anyway. You just threw it into the Porsche's corner. Thanks. You made my decision for me."

"Wait!" the salesman said.

"Yes?" Philipe looked at him coolly.

"Give us another chance. I know you'd be much happier with a Mercedes-Benz, and I can really get you a hell of a deal."

Philipe appeared to think for a minute. "All right," he said. "Let's test-drive that blue one there."

"Yes, sir. I'll just go get the keys."

Philipe and I looked at each other as Chris hurried into the office. I quickly turned away so I wouldn't burst out laughing.

The salesman sped back, almost out of breath. He handed the keys to Philipe. "Let's take her for a spin, Mr. . . ?

"Smith," Philipe said. "Doug Smith."

We walked across the lot and got into the car, Philipe in the driver's seat, the salesman in the passenger seat next to him, me in the back. Philipe and I put on shoulder harnesses. The salesman did not, obviously wanting room to move around in order to properly deliver his sales pitch. Sure enough, he shifted his position, half turned toward Philipe. "Air-conditioning is standard," he said. "As is the AM/FM radio/cassette player."

Philipe started the car.

"Pull out there," he said, pointing to the lot's front gate. "We'll go around the block."

Philipe followed his instructions. The salesman droned on about the car's features.

We came to a stoplight. "Hang a left here," the

salesman said. He grasped the dashboard with one hand as Philipe maneuvered the turn. "Note how she handles on the curve."

Philipe slammed on the brakes.

Chris flew sideways, nearly thrown out of his seat, hitting the side of his head on the padded dash.

"Good brakes," Philipe said.

The salesman, obviously shaken, was moving back in his seat, trying to regain his composure. "You shouldn't—"

"Get out of the car," Philipe said.

"What?"

"I have a gun in my pocket. Get out of the fucking car or I'll blow a hole through your fucking gut." Philipe had slipped a hand into his windbreaker pocket and he was holding it there, finger pointing outward.

All trace of unctuousness was gone from the salesman's voice. He was a frightened baby, and he was practically blubbering as he fumbled with the door lock. "Don't shoot me," he begged. "I'll go . . . Take the car . . . Do what you want . . . Just don't . . . shoot me. . . ." He successfully managed to open the door and stumbled outside, closing the door behind him.

Philipe took off.

He was laughing as he sped down the street toward the freeway. "What a dick!"

Through the back windshield, I could see the salesman running crazily down the sidewalk away from us. "You think he'll remember us?"

I looked up front, saw Philipe's eyes in the rearview mirror.

"Sorry," I said. "Dumb question."

We were the first of the new car owners to make it back to Bill's house, our prearranged meeting place. The others were already there, waiting outside on the porch, and they came walking across the lawn to admire the Mercedes.

John and Steve arrived with the Z about fifteen min-

utes later. Bill and Don and the Jeep pulled up soon
after that.

Buster looked at the old cars, the new cars, and
shook his head. "It's a damn fleet," he said.

Don patted the hood of the Jeep. "We're moving up
in the world."

Philipe had gone inside the house to get a beer, and
he came back out, drinking straight from the bottle. He
stood next to Junior, eyed the new cars, and shook his
head. "You know," he said, "it's a shame to let these
new wheels go to waste. Let's do something with
them."

"Like what?" Pete asked.

"Road trip!" John said.

"I was thinking of something a little more appropriate, a little more fitting for the Terrorists for the
Common Man."

"Like what?" Pete asked.

"Like knocking over some banks."

There was silence.

"Banks?" James repeated nervously.

"Well, ATM machines. Same difference."

No one said anything.

"What are you, a bunch of old ladies? Come on, you
pussies. We just stole a hundred thousand dollars worth
of vehicles here, and you're afraid of kyping a little
cash from a teller machine?"

"Bank robbers?" James said.

"Don't think we can do it?"

"We can do it," I said. "We've killed and not been
caught. We've vandalized; we've stolen from stores;
we've looted Rodeo Drive. We can sure as hell pick off
a few bank machines."

"That's true," James admitted.

"He has a point," Steve said.

Junior let out a whoop. "Let's do it!"

"Let's do it," Philipe agreed.

We went first to a hardware store, walked out with
sledgehammers and crowbars, exiting through the

unattended nursery section on the side of the building. Then we drove around Orange County, picking out banks that were not in open, populated areas, that had instant teller machines hidden by trees or bushes. Following Philipe's lead, we walked straight up to the machines, pushed aside whoever was there, and smashed the hell out of the metal withdrawal drawers. At that point, an alarm usually went off and the other customers began running, but we continued to bash in the machine until the entire front facade was gone, and then took the money from within before leaving our cards and walking calmly back to the cars.

We hit six banks that first day.

Ten more the next day.

Our haul was somewhere around forty thousand dollars.

We split it up, then deposited it in the ATMs of our own banks.

The ATM robberies were high profile, big news, and we began reading about ourselves in the newspapers consistently, seeing the aftermath of our exploits on TV. It was downright creepy. There were the people who'd watched us commit our crimes, who were witnesses to what we'd done, and they remembered nothing. Some recalled seeing a group of people, but had no specific descriptions to provide. Some out-and-out lied, usually white middle-aged macho men who invariably recalled seeing black or Hispanic gang members.

"Yeah!" Philipe would jeer, throwing pretzels at the television. "Blame the minorities!"

It was even more unnerving a few days later watching the police arrest two Hispanic men for committing the robberies. The men looked rough, were definitely not upstanding-citizen material, and if I had not known better, I, too, would probably have believed them guilty.

I thought of Frederick's of Hollywood, of the "perps" who had been "caught."

"I guess they needed scapegoats," James said quietly.

"Fuck 'em," Philipe said. "Let's prove those men innocent. Let's knock off a few more ATMs."

"One of these days those video cameras are going to capture our pictures," Don said. "What'll we do then?"

"They've got our pictures already. But no one can remember what we look like. Don't worry."

The next day we did rob three ATMs, all of them in the city of Long Beach, and that night at my apartment we tuned into the news, VCR at the ready, to see the results. The ATM robberies were not the top story—that went to a shooting outside a Westwood theater showing a new gang-themed movie—but they were second, and an obviously frustrated police spokesman said that the men arrested yesterday in connection with the crimes were now being released.

Philipe grinned. "Kicked their ass."

"But we're still not getting credit," I said. "We're a goddamn crime epidemic, and we're still not getting the credit for it."

"Maybe the police are just trying to keep our names out of the news," Buster suggested. "Maybe they don't want to give us any publicity."

"Maybe," I said.

James was sitting in one of the chairs, staring thoughtfully at the television as a camera showed the police rounding up suspects in a drug sweep in Compton. He looked up. "You know," he said, pointing to the TV, "we could solve this gang problem."

Philipe turned to face him. "What?"

"We could get into places even the cops couldn't go. We could walk in, confiscate drugs and weapons, walk out."

"We're not superheroes, dipshit. We're average, we're not memorable, we don't make an impression, but we're not fucking invisible."

"What's with you?" I asked Philipe. "It was just a suggestion."

He stared at me, and for a moment our eyes locked. I

had the feeling that he expected me to understand why he was angry, what was bothering him, but I was completely at a loss, and he broke contact and looked away.

I felt as though I'd missed something. "Are you okay?" I asked.

He nodded. He looked suddenly tired, worn out. "I'll see you guys tomorrow," he said wearily. "I'm going to bed."

Before anybody could say anything, he was heading down the short hallway to the bedroom.

"What the hell was that about?" Tommy asked.

I shrugged. "I don't know."

John looked around conspiratorially. "You think he's like . . . ?" He tapped his forehead, rolled his eyeballs.

Junior looked at him disgustedly. "Shut the hell up."

I went into the kitchen, pulled a beer out of the refrigerator, opened it, drank. My face felt warm, hot, and I stood in front of the open refrigerator door, letting the cool air wash over me.

Steve walked into the kitchen. "Can I get one of those?"

I pulled out a beer, handed it to him.

He stood there for a moment, twisting the bottle in his hands, fidgeting indecisively. "Look," he said finally, "I know how you feel about it, but I think you should change your mind."

I looked at him over the refrigerator door. "About what?"

"About rape." He held up his hand to ward off my response. "I know what you're going to say, but I'm just asking you to see it from our side. It's been a long time since most of us have had sex. Not that we ever got a lot to begin with. And I know you know what I'm talking about there. You know how it is." He paused. "All I'm saying is . . . well, don't cut off our only chance. You're close to Philipe. He listens to you. And right now he's put the kibosh on the sex because you don't like it."

I sighed. I really didn't feel like getting into this right now. "It's not sex I don't like. It's rape."

"Well, you don't have to do it. You don't even have to know about it when we do it. We'll keep you completely in the dark, if that's what you want. Just don't . . . just don't try to make us behave exactly the way you behave." He was silent for a moment. "Some women like to be raped, you know. Some fat chick, she knows she's not going to get sex on her own. She'd be grateful if we gave it to her. She'd love it."

"Then ask her if she wants to. If she consents, there's no problem."

"But she won't consent. The rest of the world . . . they're not as uninhibited as we are. They're not as free. They can't say what they feel; they have to say what's expected of them. But that fat girl? She probably fantasizes about being reamed by a group of healthy young studs like us." He grinned. He tried to make his smile winning, but it came out rather sickly and pathetic.

I looked at Steve and I felt sorry for him. He was serious about what he was saying, about the arguments he was putting forth. To him, Philipe's elaborate theories about our existence and our purpose in life were nothing more than justifications for his own petty actions and small desires. His mind, his world, his worldview were that limited.

Maybe none of it did have a purpose, I thought. Maybe there was no reason for anything. Maybe the others were right and we should do whatever we wanted to merely because we had the ability to do so. Maybe there should be no brakes on our behavior, no artificially imposed boundaries.

Steve was still fidgeting with his beer bottle, anxiously awaiting my response. He really believed that my opposition to rape was the reason he wasn't getting any sex. I looked at him. There were differences between us. Big differences. We were both Ignored and were alike in a lot of ways—in most ways, perhaps—

but there were definitely differences in our value systems, in what we believed.

On the other hand, here I was: murderer, thief, terrorist. Who was I to moralize? Who was I to tell the others what they could and couldn't do, what they should and shouldn't do? I closed the refrigerator door. "Go ahead," I told Steve. "Rape away."

He stared at me, surprised. "What? You mean it?"

"Fuck whoever you want. It's none of my business."

He grinned, clapped a hand on my shoulder. "You're a hero and a he-man."

I smiled wanly. "I know."

Together, we walked back out into the living room.

We woke up late the next morning, all of us, and after a hurried catch-as-catch-can breakfast, we cruised over to the mall and caught a matinee of a bad science-fiction movie. After the flick ended, we walked out into the sunlight. Philipe blinked back the brightness, drew a pair of sunglasses out of his shirt pocket and put them on. He was silent for a moment. "Let's go to my place," he said.

We were suddenly silent.

His place.

Philipe's place.

I could tell the others were as surprised as I was. Over the past months, we'd gradually gotten around to visiting everyone's house or condo or apartment. Everyone's, that is, except Philipe's. There'd been reasons, of course. Good reasons. Logical reasons. But I'd always had the feeling that Philipe had *arranged* for it to be inconvenient to stop by his house, that he had, for some strange reason, not wanted us to see where he lived, and I suspected that everyone else felt the same way.

Philipe looked at me archly. "Or not," he said. "If you don't want to, we can go to your place instead."

"No," I told him hurriedly. "Your place is fine."

He chuckled, obviously enjoying my shocked surprise. "I thought so."

We followed him to his house.

I don't know what I expected, but it was certainly not the bland tract home in which he lived. The house was in Anaheim, in a typically average neighborhood, surrounded by rows of other houses that looked exactly the same. Philipe pulled into the driveway, parked, and I pulled in next to him. The other cars parked on the street.

I was . . . disappointed. After all the waiting, after all the secrecy, I had expected something else. Something more. Something better. Something that was actually worth keeping secret.

But maybe that's why he *had* kept it secret.

Without waiting for us, Philipe got out of the car, strode up the front walk, unlocked the front door of the house, and went inside. I hurried after him.

The interior of the house was as disappointing as the outside. More so, if that was possible. The large, drab living room contained depressingly few pieces of furniture. There was a clock and lamp on a plain wooden end table, a nondescript couch, a long, unadorned coffee table, and a television set in a wooden cabinet. Period. There was one picture on one wall, a standard come-with-the-frame print of a young boy walking down a country lane with a fishing pole in his hand and a dog at his side. Other than that, the room was devoid of decoration. The entire scene looked unnervingly like something out of my grandparents' old house.

I said nothing, tried not to let the feelings show on my face, but I felt a strange hollowness inside me. And a nasty little unbidden twinge of superiority. I'd thought that Philipe's taste would be . . . different. Bolder, newer, younger. More extravagant, more flamboyant. Something. Not this quiet old lady's home with its June Cleaver furniture and its stultifying ordinariness.

"I have to take a whiz," Philipe said, heading into the

hall. I nodded as the other terrorists filtered in behind me. They were silent as they entered the house. Only Buster spoke, commenting on how much he liked the place. I saw James roll his eyes.

Philipe returned. "Make yourselves at home," he said. "There's food and drink in the fridge. I just have to do a few things." He disappeared again into the hall-way, and Junior, Tommy, and Pete crossed into the kitchen. John turned on the TV, found a daytime talk show. I sat down on the couch.

Next to me on the floor, half hidden under the end table, was a pile of lined notebook paper, filled with writing. The top sheet looked like the rough draft of a term paper or report. I reached down, picked up the paper, glanced at the corrections and crossed out lines, read what was written: "We've been blessed. We've been shown that we are disposable, dispensable, unim-portant. We've been freed for other, greater things."

It was the speech Philipe had made at Denny's that first day. The brilliant, stirring, spontaneous talk he had given.

He'd written it all out ahead of time and memo-rized it.

I reached down, picked up a handful of papers, quickly scanned the sheets: "We are of a kind. Our lives have traveled along parallel paths" . . . "Rape is a legitimate weapon" . . . "It's places like this that have made us what we are. These are the places we need to strike against."

Almost everything he'd ever said to us, every argu-ment he'd propounded, every idea he'd described, every theory he'd explained, was there, in that pile of papers, worked out and written down.

Junior, Tommy, and Pete came out of the kitchen, Coke cans in hand. "No beer," Junior said. "We got what we could."

Carefully, surreptitiously, I put the papers back on the floor where I'd found them. I felt cold, empty. I still respected Philipe, still thought he was the only one among us with vision and ideas and the will and courage to carry them out and see them through, but there was something sad and rather pathetic about those worked-over speeches in that old-lady house, and I couldn't help feeling depressed.

A few minutes later, Philipe emerged from the hallway with two packed suitcases. "All right," he said. "I'm ready. Let's go."

"Go?" I said. "Go where?"

"Anywhere. I'm through with this dump. It's time to move on."

I glanced toward James, Steve, the others. They seemed just as surprised and taken aback by this as I was. I turned again toward Philipe. "You want to move? Get a new house?"

"Not a bad idea. But, no. I want to travel."

"Travel?"

"I think we need to go on a trip."

"Why?"

"We've been a little too active lately. I think we need to take a breather, let things cool down. We're starting to attract attention."

"I thought attracting attention was what we wanted."

"This is the wrong kind of attention."

"What does that mean?"

He looked at me solemnly, evenly, and I understood from that look that he did not want to talk about this in front of the others. "It means we need to take a vacation for a while."

"How long is a while?" Buster asked.

Philipe shook his head. "I don't know."

We were silent then. I imagined us taking off, moving away from the city to some small town in the great Northwest, some little logging community where the pace of life was slow and everybody knew everybody else. Would we blend into the background everywhere, I wondered, or just in cities? Would people in a small town eventually get to know us? Would we be noticed?

Probably not.

"Let's go," Philipe said. "We'll stop by everyone's place. Pick up what you need and what we can carry in the cars, and we'll hit the road."

"Where?" Pete asked.

"It doesn't matter."

"North," I said.

Philipe nodded agreeably. "North it is."

We decided to limit everyone to two suitcases—the amount we could fit easily into the trunks of the cars— and we stopped by Tommy's, James's, John's, and Junior's places before we got to my apartment. I didn't know what I wanted to bring, but I didn't want to waste time thinking, trying to decide, so I quickly looked through the cupboards and closets, dug through the dresser, picking up shampoo and underwear and shirts and socks. In the dresser, I came across Jane's old pair of panties, and a feeling of nostalgia or déjà vu or melancholy or something flashed through me, and I had to sit down on the bed for a moment. I held the panties in my hand, turned them in my fingers. I still didn't know where Jane was. I'd tried calling her parents the week after my walk to their house, but when her father had answered the phone I'd hung up.

I wanted to get in touch with her now, to let her know I was leaving. It was stupid, but for some reason, it seemed important to me.

"Almost done?" Bill called from the living room.

"Almost!" I called back. I stood, dropped the panties into the suitcase and closed it.

I took a last look around my bedroom. I didn't know if we were really going on a vacation, if we would be gone only until things cooled down, or if we were going to be gone for good and I would never see this place again. An absurd sadness came over me at the thought that we might not be coming back. A lot of my memories were here, and I suddenly felt like crying.

"Bob?" John called.

"Coming!" I took a last look around the bedroom, closed the second suitcase, picked both suitcases up, and walked quickly out the door.

SEVEN

We were gone for three months.

We traveled north, through California, stopping at tourist spots along the way. We went to San Simeon, tagging along for free with a group of paying customers. We visited the Winchester Mystery House, leaving the tour group unseen and spending several nights in that spooky old mansion. We went to Santa Cruz to ride the roller coaster, stopped by Bodega Bay to see the birds.

We lived for the most part in motels, those glorious monuments to facelessness. We never saw the chefs who cooked our meals nor the purveyors of room service who brought them. We were gone when the maids made our beds and exchanged our dirty towels for clean ones.

The rooms themselves were interchangeable, decorated by anonymous firms who dealt in bulk with the stylishly sensible. There were always twin double beds separated by adjoining nightstands topped with securely anchored night-lights, a long dresser atop which perched a swivel television, bolted in place. There was always a Gideon Bible.

I wanted to hate living this way, knew that I should, but I did not. I loved it. We all did. We did not tire of either the food or the accommodations. This was our milieu, this was our native element, and we basked in it. The ordinary, the average, the standardized, this was what we felt comfortable with, and though we avoided five-star inns and stayed primarily in moderately priced motels, from our point of view we were in hog heaven.

We did not pay for food or lodgings, but aside from that and a few five-finger discounts on souvenirs, we suspended our illegal activities. We really were on vacation—from both our regular lives and our roles as terrorists—and it felt great.

We moved up into Oregon, through Washington, into Canada, before finally starting back down again. I had never before been out of California, and it seemed exciting to me to leave the state. I was seeing things I had never seen before, that I had only read about, and it made me feel more sophisticated, more cosmopolitan, and gave me a sense of satisfaction.

I loved traveling, loved going to all these places, but it was our nightly bull sessions that I really looked forward to, that gave me a sense of purpose. For it was here, for the first time, that we discussed who we were, what we were, how we felt, what it meant to be Ignored. We tried to find meaning in our existence, and for once it was not Philipe telling us how we were supposed to feel, but all of us expressing our thoughts and emotions and trying together to make some sense of our lives.

I had never before been a part of a group, had never before belonged to any clique or circle, and it felt good. I knew now what people saw in teams and fraternal organizations, the bonding they felt being with like-minded individuals, and it was wonderful. I was free to be myself because I was with others who were just like me. The atmosphere was relaxed and easygoing. We talked seriously and honestly, but we were not solemn, and we had fun together. We would often brag to each other about our sexual prowess, a juvenile, junior high school kind of exaggeration. We all knew none of it was true, and I suppose it should have seemed pathetic, as old as we were, but somehow it made us feel better. Philipe would tug on his pant leg just below the knee, pretending that his penis hung that far down, and say, "Why did God bless me so?"

Buster would say, "Is that all you've got? When I lie down, dogs mistake it for a fire hydrant."

And all of us would laugh.

We were together so often, so rarely apart, that for a long time I did not have the opportunity to speak with Philipe alone about why he'd really wanted us to get away from Southern California. I was tempted to ask him on several occasions, but we were always within earshot of the others, and I remembered that look he'd given me in his house, and I always decided to wait for a more opportune time.

That time finally came when we were at Mt. Shasta. For once, *all* of the others had started up the self-guided tour trail while Philipe was still sitting in the car, looking at a map to try to figure out where we should go next, so I stayed with him, waiting until the others were out of sight before bringing it up.

"So," I said, "why did we really go on this trip?"

He folded the map, looked up at me. "I was wondering when you were going to ask about that."

"I'm asking now."

He shook his head slowly, thoughtfully. "I don't know."

"You know."

"No, I don't. Not really. I just had this feeling—" He broke off. "Do you ever have, like hunches or intuition or . . . premonitions? Things that you know are going to come true and do come true?"

I shook my head.

He licked his lips. "I do. I don't know if it's just coincidence or what, but I get these feelings sometimes. . . . Like when I killed my boss: I knew months ahead of time that I was going to kill him, even before I wanted to, and of course it came true. And when I met you. Something just told me to go to South Coast Plaza that day. I don't know why. And when I got there, I had the hunch that I was supposed to look for somebody. It was like . . . like I was being guided or something."

I laughed. "You're getting a messiah complex."

"Maybe I am," he admitted.

My smile faded. "I was just joking."

"I'm not." He looked up at me. "I feel that way sometimes. Like I'm a man thrust into a god's role—and I'm not prepared for it." He dropped the map on the seat next to him and got out of the car. He closed the door, locking it. "Anyway, that's how I decided on this trip. Something just told me it was time to go. I had this vague feeling that we were being watched, that someone was closing in on us, and we had to get out of there. I didn't know for how long. I just knew we had to leave. Fast."

"Who do you think's after us? The cops?"

"Maybe." He shrugged.

"But you don't think so."

He looked at me. "I don't think so."

"Are we ever going back?"

"Yeah," he said. "Soon. I think it's blowing over. I think it'll be safe again in a few weeks."

We walked down the guide trail where the others had gone. I glanced over at Philipe as we started down a series of log-and-gravel steps. "Your house," I said.

He looked at me.

"Was it your mother's?"

"No. Mine. I bought it."

"I'm sorry. It just kind of looked like it might be your parents' place."

We were silent for a moment.

"Where is your mother?" I asked.

"I don't know."

"Well, when's the last time you saw her?"

"I don't know."

"What about your father?"

"I don't want to talk about it."

We were quiet then, the only sound the crunching of

the gravel on the path beneath our feet and the occasional far-off cry of a bird.

"I'm Ignored," Philipe said. "You're Ignored. We've always been that way; we'll always be that way. Don't try to look for answers in childhood or family histories. They're not there."

I nodded, said nothing.

Ahead, on the path, we saw the others, and we hurried to catch up to them.

We added two members to our little group.

Paul we picked up in Yosemite, on our way back home. He was standing buck-naked on a footbridge beneath Yosemite Falls, yelling obscenities at the top of his lungs. A constant stream of tourists crossed the bridge, looking up at the falls, taking pictures. People from other states, other countries. English, German, Japanese.

Paul stood there, cock and balls bouncing with each bump and jostle. "FUCK! FUCK! FUCK! SHIT! SHIT! SHIT!"

We stood for a moment at the foot of the bridge, watching him.

"That's amazing," Philipe said. "They're running into him, and he's yelling in their ears, and they still don't see him."

Steve and Bill were laughing. They seemed to think it was the funniest thing they'd ever seen.

To me, it was eerie, like something out of a David Lynch movie. The man stood on the bridge, absurdly visible in his nakedness, while the crowd of Bermuda-shorted tourists took no notice of him, passing him by, bumping into him, even pushing him casually aside in order to take a clearer photograph. The sound of the falls was deafening, masking all ordinary conversation, but faintly, in tandem with the movements of this naked man's mouth, came a barely audible voice, quietly screaming: "PRICK! PRICK! PRICK!"

It was an obvious cry for help, a desperate plea to be

noticed from a dangerously disturbed man, and all I could think was that if the rest of us had not found each other, if the terrorists had not come together, that could be one of us.

"He's insane," James said. And he, too, seemed to sense the seriousness in the situation. "He's gone completely insane."

I nodded.

"No," Philipe said.

He followed the flow of foot traffic onto the bridge and walked up to the man. He spoke to him, said something the rest of us could not make out. And then the man stopped screaming and was crying, sobbing, and laughing at the same time. He hugged Philipe, his entire body shaking.

Philipe led him off the bridge.

The man dried his eyes with his hands, wiped his nose on his arm as he saw us. He looked from one of us to another, and an expression of understanding crossed his features. "Are you . . . are you all Ignored?"

We nodded.

The man fell to his knees, began sobbing again. "Thank God!" he cried. "Thank God!"

"You're not alone," Philipe told him, placing a hand on his shoulder. He looked at us. "His name's Paul."

Paul was not insane, as James and I had originally feared. He did have a few problems adjusting at first— he had definitely been alone for far too long—but by the time we returned to Southern California, he was pretty well recovered.

Our second new recruit we found after we got back to Orange County.

We saw him for the first time in Brea Mall, a week or so after we got back, sitting on the floor in front of the magazine rack at Waldenbooks, reading a *Penthouse*. He was young, not more than nineteen or twenty, and he was dressed in jeans and a T-shirt, his long hair pulled into a ponytail. We were walking toward the food court when Philipe spotted him and suddenly stopped. Philipe stood outside the store, staring at the man, and after a few moments, obviously seeing our presence, he looked up, returned the stare.

"Another one," Philipe said. "Let's see how far along he is." He told the others to move on, told me to stay with him. "We'll meet at the food court in a half hour," he said.

As soon as the others left, Philipe walked straight up to the magazine rack, smiled at the man on the floor, picked up a *People.* The man, panicked, shoved his *Penthouse* in front of a *Redbook* and hurriedly left the store.

"That's what you were like at first," Philipe told me. He put down his magazine. "Come on. Let's follow him."

It was surprisingly easy to keep track of the man. His attempts to ditch us were almost cartoonlike. He'd stride quickly through the crowd of shoppers, looking constantly over his shoulder to see if we were following; he'd dart behind couples and groups of teenagers, only to move out into the open again to see if we were coming.

I must admit, the man's obvious fear of us gave me a little thrill of power, made me feel strong and forceful. I walked through the mall more confidently, hyperaware of my own authority, and in my mind I was like an Arnold Schwarzenegger character, single-mindedly stalking an enemy.

"He hasn't gone through the initiation yet," Philipe said as we followed the man through Sears. "He's not yet one of us."

"The initiation?"

"He hasn't killed yet."

The man exited Sears and started running down the first aisle of the parking lot. I was about to run after him when Philipe put a hand in front of me, holding me back. "Stay here. We'll never catch him. Just try to see what kind of car he drives."

We stood on the sidewalk in front of the store. The

man moved between two cars about halfway up the aisle, and a moment later, a yellow VW Bug pulled out.

"He'll drive by us," Philipe said. "He wants to see us. Try to get his license plate number."

Sure enough, instead of exiting down the aisle away from us, he came speeding in our direction. In the second before he turned, I saw through the windshield wild eyes staring out from beneath a large forehead.

Then he was gone.

"Did you get the number?"

"Part of it," I said. "PTL something. I think the next number was a five, but I'm not sure. It could've been a six."

"Close enough. I saw a Fullerton College parking decal on his bumper. It should be pretty easy to find a yellow Bug in the Fullerton College parking lot with a license plate that starts with PTL."

We walked back into the mall, through Sears, toward the food court.

"How do you know he hasn't killed his boss?" I asked.

"You can tell. Something happens during the initiation. Something physical or biological. Something changes within us the first time we kill someone. There's a definite difference in the way we act. I can't really explain it, but I know it. It's real, concrete." We saw the others, and he motioned for them to join us. "We'll follow this guy, keep tabs on him. In a few weeks or so, he'll be ready to join."

"You don't know anything about him," I said. "You don't know him, you don't know his family, you don't know his work situation. What makes you think he *will* kill his boss?"

"We all do," Philipe said, and there was a hint of sadness in his voice. "We all do."

A week or so later, we staked out the Fullerton College parking lot. We found the VW with no problem, and the rest of us waited in our cars while Tommy, the youngest of us, stood near the Bug.

A few minutes after noon, the man came walking up from the direction of the math building, a load of books beneath his arm. Several other students came out as well, talking in groups or pairs, but our man walked alone.

He reached the VW, unlocked the door.

"Hey!" Tommy said. "Is that your car?"

The man stared at him for a moment. Contrasting emotions were visible on his face: surprise, relief, fear. It was fear that won out, and before Tommy could say anything else, the man had gotten into the Bug, locked his door, and started the engine.

"Wait!" Tommy called.

The man took off.

The rest of us emerged from our hiding places. "He's getting close," Philipe said knowingly. "Next time he'll be ready."

Through sheer luck, we picked the perfect day. It was about two weeks later, and again we staked out the parking lot. This time the man was not in class but sitting in his car.

He was wearing a Frankenstein mask.

I felt a chill pass through me. I knew exactly what he was going to do. I'd been there. I understood how he felt, what he was going through, but it was strange seeing it this way, watching it as a third party. I felt almost as though I were viewing a film of my own stalking of Stewart. I remembered how alone I'd thought I was, how invisible I'd perceived myself to be, and I knew that this guy felt the same way. He had no clue that we were watching him, that we knew what he was going to do and were waiting for him to do it.

I wanted to walk up to his car right now, let the man know he wasn't alone, let him know that I and all the others had gone through the same thing. But I also understood, as Philipe had made clear, that this was something he had to go through himself. This was his initiation.

He got out of the Bug clutching a sawed-off shotgun.

We watched him walk across the parking lot toward the quad.

A few minutes later, there came from one of the buildings the sound of a thunderous shotgun blast, followed soon after by another. Faintly, from far off, filtered as though through water, we heard screams.

"Okay," Philipe said. "I'll take it from here. You guys meet me at Denny's. I'm going to talk to this guy, then bring him around."

We nodded. "All right," Steve said.

In the rearview mirror of the Buick, I saw the man, dazed and confused, stumbling out to the parking lot, still wearing the Frankenstein mask. He had dropped the shotgun somewhere.

Philipe walked up to him, smiling, waving.

By the time the two of them arrived at Denny's an hour later, he was one of us.

The man's name was Tim, and he fit in as well and as quickly as I had. He understood us, was one of us, and he was tremendously excited by the idea that we were Terrorists for the Common Man. He thought that was a brilliant concept.

He also found us a place to live.

We had been staying, since our return, at a series of hotels and motels. Philipe had not wanted us to go back to our old homes, believing that they were not safe, and we'd been searching for a new place to live, someplace where we could all live together.

Tim told us that he'd been living in a model home for the past two months.

"They built a new subdivision off Chapman in Orange, where it goes over the hill toward Irvine. It pretty much sucks in the daytime, since people are tromping through all the time. But at night, it's empty and it's great. It's furnished with *Architectural Digest*-type furniture, and it has a really neat bathroom with a sunken tub. It's a terrific place to live. My house is on a cul-de-sac with four other models. All of them are two stories and have from three to six bedrooms. We could just take over the whole place."

"That sounds great," I said.

"It's in a nice new area, and there's a gate to keep vandals out. It's the perfect place to stay."

"It does sound good," Philipe admitted. "Let's check it out."

It was a weekday and there was no one house-shopping, but we still passed through the sales office unnoticed, unaccosted by any of the salespeople. We all grabbed brochures, and we walked into the gated cul-de-sac to check out the first model.

All of the houses were wonderful, all very expensive and very expensively furnished. There were five huge houses, and thirteen of us, so there was plenty of living space. Philipe took the largest house, Tim's house, and said that he would be sharing the place with both Tim and Paul so that he'd be there if they needed any help or had any questions. I took the mock-Tudor next door with James and John.

We went back to our current place of residence—the Holiday Inn in Tustin—and gathered up our belongings and personal effects. It was getting late. It was already after five, and I wanted to go straight back to the house, but James wanted to do some shopping, pick up some snacks, and John was going to hitch a ride with Steve and pick up his van, which was still at our previous motel, so I gave James the keys to the Buick and caught a ride back with Junior, who was driving the new Jaguar he had obtained last week in our latest raid.

Junior and I drove to the new housing development, and we each took our own suitcases from the tiny trunk.

"You still have anything back at the hotel?" he asked me.

"Another box."

"Me, too. You want a ride back tomorrow?"

I nodded.

"I'll stop by then and pick you up before I go."

"Thanks," I said.

"See you later."

"Later." I walked down the empty sidewalk to my new house. It was starting to get dark, and whatever automatic timer turned on the outside lights had already kicked in. The porch light was on, as was a light on the edge of the garage that illuminated the driveway.

Tim had said that he'd steal keys for the houses from the sales office, and the keys to my place were in the lock. I pulled out the keys, pressed down on the over-sized latch, and walked inside.

My house.

Our house, really. But for some reason, I thought of it as my house, and thought of John and James as my guests.

I put the suitcase down in the foyer and turned on the lights. Recessed fluorescents in the hall and entryway came on, as did the standing lamps in the living room and den, and the chandelier in the dining room. I stood there for a moment, took a deep breath. The house even smelled good.

I heard a noise from upstairs, what sounded like a knock.

"Hello!" I called. "Anybody home?"

I waited, listening.

Nothing.

I picked up my suitcase, carried it upstairs, and dumped it on the floor of the master bedroom. There might be a fight later over who got this room, but I figured it was first come, first served, and I wasn't about to give up my claim.

As Tim had said, and as we'd discovered earlier in the afternoon, the bathroom was marvelous. The tub was sunken on a raised dais and was the size of a Jacuzzi. At the head of the tub was a windowsill filled with plants. The frosted glass window overlooked the front yard.

I had to whiz, and I did so in what had to be the

quietest toilet I'd ever used. I walked back out to the bedroom, plopped down on the bed. I felt good. Happy. Each of the houses was unique, the furnishings and decorating provided by different firms whose names were announced by small plaques next to the ash cans outside the front doors, but they had obviously been intended to please as many people as possible, and that cross section of the public that they were aimed at was us.

I loved these houses.

And mine in particular.

Once again, I heard a knocking sound. I sat up, listened. It seemed to be coming from the room next to mine. What the hell was it? Rats? Bad plumbing? I got out of bed, smiled. Maybe I'd have to complain to the company. I walked out into the hall, into the next room. It was obviously supposed to be a girl's bedroom. There were ballet prints on the wall, dolls on the white desk, stuffed animals on the pink bedspread. I scanned the room, seeing nothing that could possibly have caused the sound I heard. Maybe it was something in the wall between the two rooms—

A woman jumped out of the closet.

I screamed, backed up, almost tripped over my feet. She stood there, next to the bed, glaring at me. There was anger in her eyes, but there was also fear, and neither of us made a move toward the other one.

"Who are you?" I asked.

"Who are *you*?"

She could see me, I suddenly realized. She could hear me.

I looked at her more carefully. She was older than me, between thirty-five and forty, probably, and despite the wild eyes and hair, there was something demure about her, a perceptible shyness. Her forcefulness seemed fake, her aggressiveness forced.

"Are you Ignored?" I asked.

She stared at me. "How . . . how did you know that word?"

"I'm Ignored, too. We're all Ignored."

"All?"

"There are thirteen of us. We've come to live here."

She stared at me for a few more seconds, then sat down hard on the bed. She looked at the wall, I looked at her. She was attractive. There was an agreeable softness to her features, an intelligence evident in her eyes. Her lips, dark red, neither too large nor too small, seemed somehow very sensuous. Her hair was light brown, her medium-sized breasts perfect.

Was I attracted to her? Not really. She was pretty, but the sort of spark that had flashed between Jane and me the first time we'd met was not there between this woman and myself. Nevertheless, I felt a stirring in my groin. It had been so long since I'd been alone in a room with a woman, talking to a woman, that even this casual contact aroused me.

"What's your name?" I asked.

"Mary."

"Do you live here?"

"I used to. I guess I don't anymore."

I didn't know what to say to her, and I wished Philipe was here with me. I took a deep breath. "Where are you from?"

"Here. California. Costa Mesa."

"Are you alone?"

She looked at me suspiciously. "Why?"

"I mean, are there any others like you?"

She shook her head slowly.

I thought that I should ask her to join us, but I wasn't sure if I was really in a position to do so. That was for Philipe to decide. I looked at her, she looked at me. We stared dumbly at one another. She was the first female Ignored I'd seen, and the fact that she even existed surprised me and threw me off guard. I guess I'd assumed that being Ignored was strictly a masculine condition, that whether by design or accident, everyone who was Ignored was male.

I was glad I was wrong, though. Already I was

thinking ahead, thinking that we could find girlfriends, lovers, wives. All of us. We could live relatively normal emotional and sexual lives, have healthy, happy relationships.

But what would the children be like? If being Ignored was genetic, was the gene for it recessive or dominant? Could we have normal children? Or would our offspring be even worse off than we were? Would they be completely invisible?

All this I thought in the few brief seconds that we stood staring at each other. Then she stood, broke the spell, and started toward the door. "I . . . I guess I'd better be going."

"Wait!" I said.

She stopped in midstride. "What?"

"Don't go."

She stared at me, frightened. "Why?"

"Let me talk to the others."

"What for?"

"Just let me talk to them."

She backed up, sat down again on the bed. She nodded slowly.

"I'll be back in a few minutes," I said. "Will you stay here?"

"Where else do I have to go?"

I moved out of the room, hurried downstairs, and ran over to Philipe's house to tell him about Mary.

"A woman?" he said, excited.

"A woman?" Paul repeated, frightened.

"I think we need to discuss it," I said.

Philipe nodded. "You're right." He immediately had Tim run from house to house and get the others, and a few minutes later, we met in Philipe's living room. John, James, and Tommy had still not returned, but the rest of us were there, and we sat on chairs and couches and on the floor.

I quickly told about finding her in the closet, about our brief conversation.

"She'd been living there?" Philipe asked.

"I guess so."

He turned to Tim. "And you never saw her?"

Tim shook her head.

There was a quick discussion.

I cleared my throat. "I say we let her in."

"No." Paul.

"I say we rape her and leave her on the side of the road." Steve.

"Let's vote on it," Buster said.

I stood. "What's there to vote on? She's one of us. God, what do you think this is, a fraternity? A social organization? I don't even know if she wants to be a terrorist. I haven't asked her. But she should be. Everyone who's Ignored should be." I shook my head. "You know, we can tell her she can't hang around with us if we want to be that petty and elitist, but we don't decide who's Ignored and who isn't. You either are or you aren't. And she is. I think that qualifies her to be one of us."

"Bob's right," Philipe said. "She's in."

"Besides," James added, "it's not as if women are breaking down our doors to hang with us. We'd better take what chances we get."

"Let's go introduce ourselves," Philipe said. "If she hasn't run away already."

We walked, all ten of us, next door. I went first, and I hurried up the stairs before the rest of them and peeked into the girl's bedroom where I'd left her. She was still sitting on the bed, unmoving.

"We're all here," I said. "Would you like to meet the others?"

Mary shrugged. Her fear seemed to have left, but in its place was a strangely detached apathy.

Philipe, as always, did the talking. He explained about Terrorism for the Common Man, about what we were, and he asked her if she would like to join us.

"I don't know," she said.

"Would you rather be alone?"

She shrugged.

Philipe looked at her thoughtfully. "I've seen you somewhere before. I never forget a face. Where did you used to work?"

She shifted uncomfortably. "Why?"

"Harbor," he said, pointing at her. "You used to work Harbor Boulevard."

"I don't know what you're talking about."

"I saw you there."

"You did not."

"You were a streetwalker. I saw you there."

She seemed to deflate, as though air had been let out of her. She slumped down on the bed and nodded, her lower lip trembling slightly. "I only tried it for a while," she said. "I . . . I thought it would . . . I thought someone would notice me." Tears welled in her reddening eyes. "But no one ever did. No one saw me—"

"I saw you," Philipe said quietly. He sat down next to her. "I thought you might be one of us, and I started keeping tabs on you. Then you disappeared and I forgot all about you. What happened?"

A tear spilled out, coursing down her right cheek. She wiped it away. "I killed my first and only customer." She began sobbing, great heaves racking her body, tears streaming from beneath the hands covering her face.

Philipe put an arm around her, drew her to him. "It's all right," he said soothingly. "It's okay."

The rest of us stood around uncomfortably.

"I stabbed him!"

"It's okay," he said. "We make no judgments here. We've all done something similar."

She looked up, wiped her eyes.

"I killed my boss and his boss," he said. "Slit their throats."

"You don't care what I've done?"

"We've all done the same."

She sniffled. "Then . . . then you'll take me?"

"You're one of us," Philipe said. "How could we not?"

EIGHT

We lived happily in our model homes, leaving each morning before they opened at ten, returning after they'd closed at five. It was like a commune, I guess. One for all and all for one.

We shared everything, even sex, but the sex was unaccompanied by either feeling or commitment. It was a purely physical act, like eating or defecating, invested with no meaning. I joined in more out of obligation than desire, but although it was physically pleasurable, it was not rewarding, and I always felt empty inside afterward.

We started off simply taking turns with Mary. If it had been a long time since we'd had sex, it had been just as long for her, and she was hungry for it. She made it clear very quickly that she was not interested in having a relationship with any of us, but that she would not object to nonbinding, no-strings-attached sex.

So Philipe would have her one night, me the next, John the next, and on down the line. Buster usually passed, saying he did not want to violate the memory of his late wife, but Junior jumped into the swing of things wholeheartedly, picking up sex manuals and toys and trying every act and position that he could possibly perform.

Then there were the combinations. I didn't like these much, they made me uncomfortable, and I did not participate, but most of the others did. Even James and John, in my house, shared a bed together one night with Mary, and I heard the sounds of their sexual triad as I lay alone in the master bedroom trying to fall asleep.

I met Mary at the breakfast table the next morning. James and John were still slumbering, and I poured her a cup of the coffee I'd made and sat down at the dining room table next to her. We were silent for a few moments.

"I know you don't approve," she said finally.

"It's not my place to approve or disapprove."

"But you don't. Admit it."

"I just don't understand why you . . . why you do it."

"Maybe I like it."

"Do you?"

She sipped her coffee. "Not really," she admitted. "But I don't dislike it either. It's just kind of there. Everyone else seems to enjoy it, though."

"Doesn't it make you feel like, you know, like . . . a whore?"

She shrugged. "That's what I am."

"No, you're not." I put down my coffee. "You don't need to have sex with us to get us to notice you, you know. We'd notice you anyway."

"But this way you notice me more." She smiled. "Besides, I don't see you turning down any freebies."

I said nothing. There was nothing to say. I suddenly felt depressed, and I decided to go for a walk. I pushed back my chair, touched her shoulder, and walked outside. Behind Bill and Don's place, construction had started on the third phase of the subdivision, and the workers had already arrived and were starting up the cement mixer, climbing the frames of the houses.

I jogged around the circle, then let myself out through the gate and went running along Chapman until I came to a recently built gas station. I went in, picked up a Hostess fruit pie, and walked out. I stood there for a moment, staring out at the work traffic on the street. I didn't feel like hanging out with the other terrorists today. I needed a break. We'd spent too much time together lately, almost all day every day since the trip, and I found myself wishing that things were back to the way they used to be, with us doing things together but still having places of our own that we could retreat to.

I missed having time to myself.

I would have time to myself today, I decided. I was going to take a vacation from being a Terrorist for the Common Man. I was going to be plain old Ignored me.

I jogged back to the model homes, ran up Philipe's walk, let myself in. He and Paul were watching *Good Morning America*, eating Eggo waffles on the couch.

"Hey," Philipe said. "What's up?"

"I'm going to take off by myself today," I said. "I want to be alone. I need some time to think."

"Okay. We had nothing earth-shattering planned anyway. When'll you be back?"

"I don't know."

"See you then."

I went back to my house, grabbed my wallet and keys, and took off in the Buick.

I just drove. All day, I drove. When I needed gas I stopped and got some. When I was hungry I stopped at Burger King for lunch. But otherwise I kept moving. I went up Pacific Coast Highway all the way to Santa Monica, then cut inland and followed the foothills and mountains clear to Pomona. It felt good to be alone and on the road, and I cranked up the radio and rolled down the windows and sped down the highway, the breeze in my face, pretending I was not Ignored but normal and a part of the world through which I was driving and not just an invisible shadow at its fringes.

It was late when I got home, and though there were still lights on in two of the other homes, my house was dark. It was just as well. I didn't feel like chatting with James or John tonight. I just wanted to go to bed.

I slipped quietly through the front door and up the stairs to my bedroom.

Where Mary and Philipe sat, naked, on my bed.

I started to leave the room.

"Where are you going?" Philipe said.

I turned reluctantly toward him. "To find someplace to sleep."

"You're going to sleep here with us."

I shook my head.

"Why not?"

"I don't want to."

"This isn't rape," Philipe said. "You can't have any objections to this. We're all consenting adults here."

"I'm not consenting."

"I'm telling you to consent."

"But—"

"No buts. You're still hung up on your old morality. You still don't seem to realize that we've moved on, we've left all that behind. The normal rules don't apply to us. We're beyond all that."

But I was not beyond all that.

I shook my head, backed out of the room.

I spent the night downstairs on the couch.

NINE

It was now November. We'd had some of our cars for nearly half a year by this time, and the newness of them had worn off. We were even starting to get a little tired of them. So Philipe decided that we would junk the ones we had and get some more.

And get some publicity in the process.

We held a demolition derby with the Jeep, the Mercedes, and three of the sports cars. Stealing roadblocks from the police, we closed off a stretch of the 405 Freeway near Long Beach one Wednesday night, illuminated the site with flares, and three at a time pretended to be on a bumper car course, speeding forward, throwing the vehicles into reverse, sideswiping whichever car we could. The Porsche was the first to crap out, pummeled from all sides by Philipe in the Mercedes and me in the Jeep, and Junior and his car were replaced by Steve in the 280Z. This time they both ganged up on me, and though I put up a brave fight, forcing Steve onto an off-ramp and ramming Philipe almost into a light pole, I was eventually slammed into the center divider, and the Jeep died.

Philipe was the winner of the derby, and though that qualified him under our quickly made-up rules to keep the Mercedes, he elected to leave it on the freeway with the others. He pointed it down the empty middle lane, put on the cruise control, and hopped out of the car.

The Mercedes drove straight for a few moments, then drifted sharply to the right and went over a small asphalt bump and then down an embankment. We heard it crash and die, and we waited for an explosion but there was none.

"That's it," he said. "Game over. Let's go home."

Behind the line of flares was a massive traffic jam, and we walked past the roadblocks, between the honking cars, and over the center divider to where we'd left our getaway vehicles.

We drove home in a good mood.

Our little exploit made the local news, and we gathered in Philipe's house and cheered when film footage of the wrecked cars came on TV.

"The reason for the unauthorized roadblock and the origin of the automobiles is described as a mystery by police," the reporter said.

Mary, sitting on the arm of Don's chair tonight, was grinning. "This is great," she said. "This is really great."

I dutifully videotaped the newscast.

Afterward, the male anchor made a joke about our cars to his female coanchor, and then the weather report came on.

The other terrorists were talking excitedly about both the demolition derby and the newscast, but I stood there with the video remote in my hand, watching the weather forecast. We were not Terrorists for the Common Man, I realized. We were nothing so noble or romantic. Nothing so important. We were a pathetic group of unknowns trying desperately, in any way we could think of, using any means at our disposal, to leave a mark on society, to let people know that we were here, to get publicity for ourselves.

We were clowns. Comic relief for the real news.

It was a rather stunning realization, and not one for which I was really prepared. I had not given this terrorist business much thought since those first few weeks. I had simply bought into Philipe's concept and assumed that what we were doing was real, legitimate, worthwhile. I had never stopped to analyze what exactly we were accomplishing. But now I looked back on everything we'd done and saw for the first time how little that actually was, and how embarrassingly pitiful were our delusions of grandeur.

Philipe was angry at what he was, and it was this anger that drove him, that fueled his passion and his efforts to do something big, something important with his life. But the rest of us had no such driving force. We were sheep. All of us. Myself included. I might have been angry myself at first, but I no longer felt that way. I no longer felt anything, and whatever fleeting pleasure I had derived from our exploits had long since faded.

What was the point to it all?

I turned off the VCR, put the tape back in its box, and wandered back home alone. I took a long, hot shower, then put on a robe and walked into the bedroom. Mary, wearing only a pair of white silk panties, was lying on the bed waiting for me.

"Not tonight," I said tiredly.

"I want you," she said, in a husky voice filled with false lust.

I sighed, took off my robe. "Fine."

I stretched out on the bed next to her, and she climbed on top of me, began kissing me.

A moment later I felt pressure at the foot of the bed. Rough hands suddenly reached up, held my penis.

Male hands.

I squirmed, trying to get away. I felt sickened. I knew I should be more open-minded, but I wasn't.

I felt a mouth on my organ.

I was tangled up in Mary, and I tried to get away, but her arms and legs were wrapped around me and I could not struggle out of her embrace.

There was a muffled male grunt, a grunt I recognized, and I realized that it was Philipe at the end of the bed, working on me.

I closed my eyes, filled with a deep black despair.

Jane, I thought.

Philipe's mouth moved off of me, and a second later Mary stiffened, moaned, increased the pressure against my body. The pressure increased, decreased, increased, decreased, and then she jerked forward with a gasp, slumping against me.

Now I did roll over and away, feeling lower than I ever had in my life. I hated Philipe, and part of me wanted to kill him, wanted to sit up, take his neck in my hands, and squeeze the life out of him.

I wanted him to go away, did not want to look at him, but he stood next to the bed and stared down at me.

"Get out," I said.

"It wasn't that bad. I could tell you enjoyed it."

"That's an automatic response."

Philipe crouched down next to me. There was something like desperation in his eyes, and I understood that deep down, despite all his talk of freedom from conventional morality and beliefs, he felt the same way I did.

I thought of his old-lady house.

"You might've hated it," he said. "But you felt alive, didn't you? It made you feel alive?"

I looked at him, nodded slowly. It wasn't true, and we both knew it wasn't true, but we both pretended that it was.

He nodded back. "That's what's important," he said. "That's what's really important."

"Yeah," I said. I turned away from him, closing my eyes, pulling the covers up around me. I heard him talking to Mary after that, but I could not hear what either of them said, and I didn't want to.

I closed my eyes tightly, kept myself wrapped in the covers, and somehow I fell asleep.

TEN

I wondered sometimes what had happened to Jane.

No. Not sometimes.

All the time.

There was still not a day that went by that I did not think about her.

It had been over a year and a half now since we'd broken up, since she'd left me, and I wondered if, in that time, she'd found someone else.

I wondered if she ever thought about me.

God knows I thought about her. But I had to admit that as time passed, her image in my memory began to fade. I could no longer recall the precise color of her eyes, could no longer call to mind the unique details of her smile, the specific mannerisms that were hers and hers alone. Everywhere I looked, in every crowd, there seemed to be at least one young woman who looked like Jane, and I found myself wondering whether I would recognize her if I saw her again.

If she'd changed her hairstyle or was wearing a different type of clothes, I could probably pass right by her and not notice.

The thought of that made me incredibly sad.

God, I hated being Ignored.

I hated it.

I don't mean to say that I disliked my fellow terrorists or that I didn't enjoy being with them. I did. It was just that . . . I didn't *want* to like being with them. I didn't want to enjoy the things I enjoyed. I didn't want to be who I was.

But that was something I would never be able to change.

After the experience with Mary and Philipe, I gave up on sex. I took myself out of the loop. Mary still spent different nights at different houses, but her trips to my house were limited to John's and James's bedrooms. She was polite to me, and I was polite to her, but for the most part we tried to ignore each other and stay out of one another's way.

Philipe's attitude toward me seemed to have changed as well. We were not as close as we had been. If we had had hierarchical ranks, I would probably still be his second in command—but he would resent me for it.

As with Mary, Philipe and I were polite, outwardly friendly, but whatever real camaraderie we had once shared was gone. Philipe also seemed harder now, more businesslike, less inclined to joke around or have fun. And it was not just with me. He was that way with everybody. Even Junior remarked upon it.

But of course no one dared say anything to his face.

I got the impression that Philipe had come to the same conclusions about the efficacy of our organization as I had. He spent most of the next week by himself, locked in his room, in his house. We did go out to a few Garden Grove car dealerships on Saturday and pick up some new vehicles, but other than that we laid low, and Philipe we saw only at dinner.

He called us together the next Thursday for a meeting in the sales office. He sent Paul around to the different houses with written invitations for each person, and he made it clear that this was a mandatory meeting, that he had something important to announce.

At eight o'clock, the appointed time, I walked across the street with James and John. Apparently, Philipe or Paul or Tim had stolen a key or found some way to pick the lock because the door to the office was open, and all the lights were on. On a table in the middle of the room, spread over a map of the subdivision, was a map of Orange County. Around the table were thirteen chairs.

We sat next to Tim and Paul and Mary, waiting for the others.

Philipe did not begin speaking until we had all arrived and were seated. Then he jumped right in. "You know why we're together," he said. "You know our purpose. But lately we seem to have lost sight of that purpose." He looked around the room. "What have we been doing? We call ourselves terrorists, but who have we terrorized? What terrorist acts have we actually performed? We've been playing at being terrorists, having fun, doing what we wanted with the liberty afforded us and pretending that our actions have meaning."

The liberty afforded us.

Philipe had practiced this. He had written it out ahead of time. A wave of cold passed through me. I suddenly knew what was coming next.

"We need to take our roles seriously. If we're going to call ourselves terrorists, then we need to act like terrorists. We need to draw attention to our cause in the way we originally planned. We need to make a statement. A bold statement that will capture the attention of the country." He paused, and there was an excited sparkle in his sharp eyes. "I think we should blow up Familyland."

There was a sick sinking feeling in the pit of my stomach as I heard the name of the amusement park. I looked around our group and I saw that James and Tim and Buster and Don felt the same way. But on the faces of the others, Steve and Junior in particular, I saw looks of excited anticipation.

Philipe pointed down at the map on the table in front of us. "I've devised a plan, and I think it will work."

He outlined his idea. Explosives, he said, would be obtained from the road construction crew currently blasting through south county hills in an effort to build a new highway. We would then arrive at Familyland, in teams of two, coming at different times, in different cars, from different entrances. We would each be equipped with explosives and remote detonators, and at a prearranged time we would get on different rides, plant the explosives, and then meet on the train, where, while passing through Dinosaur Country, we would detonate the explosives simultaneously. We would get off the train at the Old Town entrance and then walk calmly and individually out to our respective cars before driving home.

He would, ahead of time, send letters to the police and the media, taking credit for the attack in the name of the Terrorists for the Common Man.

"Wow!" Steve said, grinning. "Killer idea!"

There was no discussion of the plan. Philipe announced that that was all, the meeting was over, and like a general, he nodded brusquely to us and, hands clasped stiffly behind his back, walked off alone into the night.

The rest of us looked at each other, looked at the map on the table, but said nothing.

We split up.

And we, too, walked alone into the night.

ELEVEN

It was almost as if I were in a trance, as if I had no will of my own.

For the next two weeks, the other terrorists and I prepared for the attack on Familyland. I didn't want to, I thought it was wrong, but I was a sheep and said nothing, and I followed Philipe's directions and did as I was told. At night, alone in my bed, I told myself that I wanted to leave, that I wanted to get away from the terrorists, that I just wanted to go back to the way things were before and live out my anonymous life in peace.

I told myself that.

But it wasn't true.

I was opposed to Philipe's plan; I really thought that what we intended to do was wrong, but I also enjoyed being part of a group effort, having a role in such a project.

I still enjoyed being a terrorist.

I made my opposition known, tried to convert the other Ignored to my point of view, but I had no sway with Philipe anymore and the others were not brave enough to buck him.

We set the date for the Saturday after Thanksgiving. Familyland would be crowded that day. It would be big news. We would get lots of publicity.

On Thursday, Mary made Thanksgiving dinner, and we ate it at Philipe's house, wasting most of the day watching TV, alternating between football games and the *Twilight Zone* marathon. Philipe joined us for dinner, but spent the rest of the time upstairs, alone, working.

Friday evening, the night before the attack, we met again in the sales office—or as Philipe referred to it, the War Room. This time he had spread out a map of Familyland, and he had marked specific points in the amusement park with red pins.

He wasted no time with pleasantries or formalities. "Here are the assignments," he said. "Steve and Mary, Bill and Paul, Junior and Tim, Tommy and Buster, Don and James, Pete and John, Bob and me. Here are the cars we're going to take, and the routes, and the rides we're going to go on. . . ."

He described in detail the plan, then made each of us repeat our part aloud. I was to accompany Philipe in the Mercedes. We were to arrive at noon, then walk in through the reentry gate, me carrying the explosive pack, Philipe the detonator. We were to hang around for two hours, going on rides, going in shops, pretending to be normal tourists, then at precisely two-fifteen we were to get on Mr. Badger's Crazy Journey. Near the end of the ride, while the car was maneuvering through hell, I was to jump quickly out of the car, place the explosives behind one of the little devil figures, then hop back in. We would finish the ride, walk to the train station near the roller coaster, and get on the train. We would stay on the train, circling the park, until all of the terrorists were on board. Then Philipe would detonate our explosives, the others assigned detonators would set off theirs, and we would get off the train at Old Town and leave the park.

I watched Philipe as he talked, as he made the others repeat the time sequences of their portions of the plan, and I wondered why he had chosen me to be his partner. Not because I was his right-hand man, that was for sure.

Probably to keep an eye on me because he didn't trust me anymore.

After the meeting, as we were getting up and leaving, he called my name, asked me to stay. I waited around while the others walked across the cul-de-sac to their respective homes.

Philipe pulled the red pins from his map, picked up the map from the table, folded it. "I know your opinion of this," he said. "But I want you with us."

He spoke as he was folding the map, not looking up at me, and I realized that, in his own way, he was trying to make up with me. He was trying to apologize. I leaned against the wall near the door, not knowing what to say.

He stared down at the pins in his hand, jiggled them. "It's not easy being who we are," he said. "What we are. There are no rules, no traditions. We're making them up as we go along. Sometimes we make mistakes. Sometimes we can't tell they're mistakes until after the fact." He looked up at me. "That's all I had to say."

I nodded. I was not sure what he wanted from me. I was not even sure what he'd said.

We stared at each other for a moment.

Then I walked out of the office, back to my house.

We drove to Familyland in silence, and the silence was tense. Philipe turned on the radio. A station I didn't like. But I left it on because it was better than the quiet.

We parked near a light post with an "H" hanging from the pole and walked across the lot to the entrance.

The second we walked into the amusement park, I was struck by the enormity of what we planned to do, and I had to stop for a moment and close my eyes and catch my breath. I felt a little dizzy. I opened my eyes again, and saw hordes of people walking down Old Town, past the magic shop, past the Hall of History. A trolley passed by, pulled by a horse, its bell dinging. In front of me, at the end of the street, I could see the graceful fairy-tale spires of the Castle.

A family passed by us, the boy asking his father if he could have some ice cream.

This was serious. This was the real thing. I had not bargained for anything like this. I don't think any of us had. Except maybe Philipe.

I had killed before, but that was different. It was personal. This would be the cold-blooded murder of innocent strangers. Mothers. Families. Kids.

I did not want to be a Terrorist for the Common Man, I realized. Maybe Prankster for the Common Man. Monkey-wrencher for the Common Man. But that was as far as I was willing to go.

"I can't do it," I told Philipe.

"You can and you will."

"What if I don't?"

"Then I'll kill you. I'll set off this detonator, and the explosives you're carrying will blow your ass to hell."

"You'd do that?"

"Try me."

I shook my head. "I can't kill innocent people."

"No one's innocent."

"Can't we just set these off somewhere where they won't really hurt anyone? We'd still be making a statement, we'd still get the attention we want, but we wouldn't have to kill anybody."

"They'll take us a lot more seriously if we do kill someone."

"You sent letters off, didn't you?"

"And our cards. Yesterday. To the park's headquarters, to the Anaheim police, and to all the local newspapers and TV stations."

"That should be good enough. They'll get the letters; we'll plant the explosives; they'll search for them and find them; we won't have to blow up anything. We'll still get the attention for our cause—"

"Why are you like this?" Philipe asked.

"Like what?"

"Why do you care so much about these people? Have

they ever cared about you? Have they ever noticed you?"

"No," I admitted. "But they haven't done anything to hurt me either."

"It has to be personal with you, doesn't it?"

"Yes."

"I really hate that about you," he said. He looked down Main Street. He took a deep breath, sighed. "But sometimes I wish I was that way too."

"Do you really want to go through with it?" I gestured around us. "I mean this is *Familyland*. Do you really want to do anything to hurt Familyland?"

He was about to reply, about to say something, when he stiffened, looking furtively around.

"What is it?"

"Something's changed. Don't you feel it?"

I shook my head.

"They know. They're looking for us."

"What—?"

"The letters must have gotten there early. Fucking post office." He stared up the street, scanning the crowd. "Shit. I see them."

Panic welled within me. "What are we going to do?"

"Get the others and get the hell out of here."

I looked around, saw a lot of short-haired, gray-suited men on the sidewalks and in the street. Some of them seemed to be wearing walkie-talkies on their belts, speaking into transistor headsets. They'd infiltrated the crowd without me even noticing.

We hurried through Old Town toward Futureland, where Bill and Paul were supposed to be planting explosives under a seat in the Journey to Jupiter ride. "Who are those guys?" I asked.

Philipe shook his head. "I don't know."

"I didn't see them until you said something. They're almost as hard to notice as we are."

"That's what scares me."

We found Bill and Paul waiting in line for Jupiter. We told them what was happening and the four of us hurried over to the Submarine ride to find Steve and Mary.

The gray-suited men were all around.

"Do they work for Familyland?" Bill asked. "Or are they cops?"

"I don't know," Philipe repeated. He sounded tense.

The men were everywhere, but they didn't notice us. I was not even sure that they knew who or what they were looking for. We rounded up Steve and Mary and were about to head over to the Enchanted Mountain when, from hidden loudspeakers all over the park, a calm and reassuring, serious yet friendly voice announced: "Due to unforeseen circumstances, Familyland will be closing in five minutes. Please proceed to the main gate."

Around us, rides were shutting down. People were being quickly and efficiently herded by cheerful young red-coated men and women toward the park entrance.

"—All guests will be issued complimentary return passes for two days at Familyland, the Home of Fun!"

The message was repeated.

"Get a move on," Philipe said. "They're closing in on us. Without a crowd for us to hide in, they'll see us for sure."

We found Pete and John waiting by the African Princess, Don and James standing in front of the High Seas Adventure ride. By now the park was almost emptied of normal tourists. Teams of the gray-suited men, accompanied by what looked like uniformed policemen, were patrolling the walkways and thoroughfares, walking into the rides and shops and attractions.

Philipe looked at his watch. "That's it," he said. "The others should still be outside. Let's get the fuck out of here."

All ten of us ran back through Wild West Land. We hurried past the shops and arcades.

And saw Tommy and Buster walk through the front entrance of the park into a deserted Old Town.

They got several yards up the street before they were

spotted. Then the gray suits were talking frantically into headsets and walkie-talkies, uniforms were drawing guns, crouching into firing positions.

"Run!" Philipe yelled.

"Get out!" I screamed.

We were all yelling, shouting at the top of our lungs for them to hightail it out of here, but they could not hear us and seemed oblivious to the fact that Familyland was practically deserted save for themselves and the gray suits and the uniforms.

A couple of the suits looked in our direction as we screamed, but we ducked into a doorway, were quiet for a moment, and were forgotten.

"Stay where you are!" someone announced over a loudspeaker.

We came out of our hiding place and saw Tommy running like hell back toward the entrance, having obviously figured out that something was wrong. Buster, though, looked confused. He stood in place, turning back toward Tommy, then back toward the men, not moving in either direction.

"Surrender your weapons!" the loudspeaker said.

For a second, it looked like a scene in a silent comedy. Buster stood there, puzzled, glanced around as if searching for someone else they might be addressing, then pointed quizzically toward himself as if to say, "Who? Me?"

Then there was a shot.

And Buster went down.

"No!" I screamed.

I started toward him, but Philipe grabbed my collar and pulled me back. "Forget it," he hissed. "It's too late for him now. We have to save ourselves."

"He might still be alive!"

"If he is, they have him. Come on."

We cut through the open patio of a restaurant, ran down a side path past some restrooms and a diaper-changing station, through a gate marked EMPLOYEES ONLY.

"What about Tommy?" Mary asked.

"He'll make it back," Philipe said. "He's smart."

We were behind Familyland's false front, in what looked like a parking lot between office buildings, and we ran toward where we knew the main public parking lot was located. We sprinted past one of the buildings and through an unattended open gate, and found ourselves in front of Familyland. We were far away from where our cars were located, but amazingly, idiotically, they did not seem to have staked out the parking lot, and we ran unchecked to our cars.

Tommy was waiting by the Mercedes, and Junior and Tim were parked nearby. All looked worried and frightened, and Philipe shouted at them to get the hell out of here and make sure they were not followed.

I got in the Mercedes with Philipe, and we flew over the parking lot's speed bumps, bottoming out as we skidded onto the main road. Philipe turned, then sped over the freeway, zigzagged through a residential neighborhood, and drove all the way down Lincoln to Los Alamitos before doubling back and hitting Chapman and heading home. We were not followed.

The rest of them were already waiting for us when we arrived, and Philipe parked in front of the sales office and told everyone to pick up personal effects, it was time to move.

"Where are we going?" Mary asked.

"We'll find someplace."

"Maybe they won't find us here."

"We can't take that chance," he snapped. He looked quickly around the group. "Everyone still have the explosives and detonators?"

We all nodded.

"Good. Let's take this place out. I don't want any trace of us left."

"It's daytime," Tim said. "The models are still open."

"Just do it."

We each booby-trapped our own houses. James,

John, and I quickly dumped all the trash cans—the used Kleenex, the empty food cartons, the old newspapers—on the kitchen floor. I poured lighter fluid all over the trash, then sprayed the rest on the downstairs carpets.

When we were all packed and in our cars, a block or so away from the houses, we set off the detonators.

We hadn't planned it that way, but the houses went off in sequence, from left to right, and the sight was truly awesome. The explosives we'd gotten were obviously extremely powerful. Walls blew outward, flames exploded from underneath suddenly rocketing roofs, and in a matter of seconds our homes looked like wildly burning piles of junk timber.

The salesmen were running out of the office, yelling at each other, running around wildly. I knew that one of them had to have already called the police and the fire department, and I honked my horn, pointing toward the road, and Philipe nodded. He stuck his head out the window of his car. "Follow me!" he yelled.

He sped out of the subdivision, down Chapman, and the rest of us followed. Just past Tustin Avenue, a fleet of cop cars and fire engines passed us, going in the opposite direction.

We got on the Costa Mesa Freeway, heading south.

We took the 55 to the 405 and did not stop until Philipe turned in at a gas station in Mission Viejo. He had obviously been thinking while he'd been driving, and he came back to each of our cars and told us to fill up. We were going to go down to San Diego for a few days, he said, stay in a motel, lay low. He still seemed shaken, frightened, and he told us to pay cash for the gas and not just steal it—we couldn't afford to leave a trail.

"You know San Diego," Philipe told me. "You lead the way. Find us an anonymous motel."

We drove downstate, and I led the way to motel row. We picked the Hyatt, one of the bigger and more impersonal places, and stole the keys off a maid's cart, taking rooms on one of the middle floors. After dumping our suitcases in our respective rooms, we met in Philipe's suite to watch the Los Angeles news on cable.

There was no mention made of what had happened at Familyland.

We watched the five o'clock news, the five-thirty news, and the six o'clock news, switching from channel to channel.

Nothing.

"Those fuckers," Mary said. "They covered it up."

"What happened to Buster?" Junior asked. It was the first time he'd spoken since we'd left Familyland, and his voice was quiet and unnaturally subdued.

"I don't know," Philipe admitted.

"You think he's dead?"

Philipe nodded.

"Who but us would even notice or care that he's gone?" James said.

We were silent after that, each of us thinking about Buster. I found myself remembering how happy he'd been on that day we'd trashed Frederick's of Hollywood, how he'd said he felt so young being with us.

I felt like crying.

"Even if no one noticed that he was killed, the fact that Familyland kicked everyone out and closed down is news in itself," Philipe said. "Either the company has enough clout to keep that out of the news . . . or someone else does."

"Who?" Steve asked.

He shook his head. "I don't know," he said. "But I have a bad feeling about it."

We spent the next day at the motel, monitoring newscasts, reading papers.

The day after that, we went to Sea World.

Philipe got over his nervousness and paranoia extraordinarily quickly, and by that second day it had disappeared without a trace, leaving no residue. It was at his urging that we went to Sea World. He and the others treated it like a normal day, a normal outing, enthusiastically reading the list of times for the dolphin and killer whale shows when we arrived, rushing over to look at the shark tank. I could not believe that they could so easily forget Buster, that they could react so casually to his death, that they could carry on as if nothing had happened, and it depressed the hell out of me. Buster's passing might not be noted by the world at large, but I'd at least expected it to have some effect on his fellow Ignored. Were we all this expendable? Were all of our lives this meaningless and inconsequential?

It was at Shamu's show that I was finally compelled to mention it. We were sitting in the front row of the grandstands, had just been soaked with water after the killer whale had done a belly flop in the pool directly in front of us, and the other terrorists were laughing uproariously. "This is great!" Paul said. "I'm sure glad we came to San Diego."

"We came here because we fucked up when we tried to blow up Familyland and Buster was shot to death and the scary ass-fuckers who blew him away were going to do the same thing to us. We're not here on a fucking vacation!"

"What's with you?" Philipe said. "Chill out."

"Chill out? Two days ago, you made us blow up our damn houses because you thought those suits were chasing us—"

"That was two days ago."

"Now Buster's dead and we're here having a great time at fucking Sea World!"

"It's not as if he died in vain."

"What?"

"He gave himself for the cause."

"Oh, so now we should be happy to sacrifice ourselves for 'The Cause.' We're supposed to accept that as part of the cost of doing business. I thought the whole point of all this was to free us up so that we would not be cogs in a machine, just small parts of a large organization. I thought we were supposed to be fighting for individual rights. Now we're just supposed to submerge our individuality in another group. Yours." I met his eyes. "I, for one, do not want to die. For anything. I want to live." I paused dramatically. "Buster did too."

"Buster's gone," Philipe said. "There's nothing we can do to bring him back." He fixed his gaze on me. "Besides, why should we feel bad? Why should we feel guilty? We were always there for him when he was alive. We were his friends, his family, we provided a place where he belonged, and he knew it. He was happy with us."

I didn't want to believe Philipe, but I did. God help me, I did. I tried to tell myself that he understood the way I thought, that he was able to manipulate me because he knew me so well, but I could not make myself believe it. Philipe was right. Buster had been happier in the last year of his life than he had ever been before, and it was all due to us.

Philipe looked at me calmly. "I think we need to kill a celebrity."

I blinked, caught off guard. "What?"

"I've been thinking about it. As you said, we fucked up Familyland. We haven't accomplished anywhere near what we set out to do as terrorists. But I think killing a celebrity would get us a forum. We'd be able to take our case to the public."

"I don't want to kill," I said. "Anyone."

"Yes, you do."

"No, I don't." But, again, that secret something inside me agreed with the reasoning of Philipe's argument, thought it was a justified course of action.

"I don't either," Tim said. "Why don't we just find a female celebrity and rape her?"

"Why don't we kidnap a celebrity and hold him hostage?" Mary suggested. "We'll get a lot of publicity that way. And we won't have to take a life."

"We've all taken lives," Philipe said in a cold, hard voice. "You all seem to conveniently forget that. We're not virgins here. None of us are."

"But some of us have learned from our mistakes," I said.

"What do you want to do, then? Nothing? Big change calls for big action—"

"What change? Who are we fooling here? You think killing someone famous is going to change who or what we are? We're Ignored. We'll always be Ignored. That's the fact, jack, and you'd better get used to it."

Around us, the crowd cheered wildly as Shamu jumped through a series of fiery hoops.

"Celebrity," Philipe said with disgust. "That's the very concept we're fighting against. That's the very core of our complaint. Why should some people be more recognized than others? Why can't everyone be noticed equally? The ironic thing is that killing a celebrity *makes* you a celebrity in this sick society. Mark David Chapman? We know that name because he killed John Lennon. John Hinckley? He tried to kill Ronald Reagan and was obsessed with Jodie Foster. James Earl Ray? Lee Harvey Oswald? Sirhan Sirhan? If we kill a celebrity, someone big enough, we will strike a blow against the enemy camp, and we'll be known, we'll be able to let people know we exist, we're here."

"If we're caught," Pete said quietly.

"What?"

"We'll only have a forum if we're caught. That's the only way the media will pay any attention to us. Otherwise, we'll be just as unknown as ever. The police probably get stacks of letters claiming to take credit for something like this. Even if we sent a letter or made a phone call, it would just get lost in the shuffle."

It was obvious Philipe had not really considered that aspect, and it threw him for a second, but he recovered almost immediately. "Then Mary's right. We should kidnap a celebrity. That way we could let the cops hear his voice, know he's alive. *Then* they'd pay attention to us. We'd threaten to kill the celebrity unless our demands were met. That would get us some results."

"We could videotape him, too," I suggested. "Send the video to the cops."

Philipe turned to look at me, and a slow smile spread across his features. "Good idea." He grinned at me and I found myself grinning back, and the old magic was there. Suddenly we were a team again.

The Shamu show ended, and after a sustained cheer, people started leaving, getting up, gathering their purses and souvenir bags, streaming down the bleacher steps, maneuvering around us. We stayed where we were.

"So where are we going to go?" Junior asked. "Hollywood? Beverly Hills?"

Philipe shook his head. "Those are for tourists. Celebrities only show up there when there's a premiere or something, and that would be way too crowded and security would be way too tight. I'm thinking Palm Springs. They live there. They'll be more accessible, more off their guard."

"Sounds good," I said.

Steve nodded. "Yeah. Let's do it."

Philipe looked around the group. "Are we all agreed?"

There was a chorus of "yesses" and "yeahs," much nodding of heads.

"Tomorrow then," he said. "Tomorrow we'll pack our stuff and head out to Palm Springs." He grinned. "We're going to catch us a movie star."

TWELVE

Palm Springs.

It was exactly the way I'd imagined it would be.

Maybe a little hotter.

If Rodeo Drive had seemed shabbier than it was supposed to, Palm Springs more than lived up to its hype. The sun was bright, the sky free from smog or clouds, and everything seemed cleaner, clearer, sharper than it did in Los Angeles or Orange County. The streets here were wide, the buildings low and sleek and new, the people good-looking and well-heeled. The only concessions to the season were geometric Christmas tree shapes hung high on the streetlamp posts and occasionally frosted windows on some of the smaller stores. If it was not for those subdued reminders, I probably would have thought it was summer.

We were down to four cars now, and we cruised up and down the main streets—Gene Autry Trail, Palm Canyon Drive—in a single line, looking for a place to set up camp. We finally decided on a bland-looking Motel Six near the freeway, far off the main drag, and we found rooms, dumped our boxes and suitcases, and headed back into town for supplies.

We picked up food and rope and a video camera.

"So where are we going to find our celebrity?" I asked back at the motel. "What are we going to do? Are we going to just look for houses with gates and guardhouses and break in and peek through windows until we spot someone famous?"

"Not a bad idea." Philipe laughed. "But I thought

we'd start by staking out the local nightspots. We might be able to spot someone at a dance club or a restaurant. Then we can follow them home and nab them."

"What'll we do then?" Tommy asked. "Bring them back here to the hotel?"

"Maybe," Philipe said. He thought for a minute. "Or maybe we can find someplace else to live." He turned to Tim. "This afternoon, I want you and Paul to see if you can find a model home or someplace that's for rent or . . . somewhere where we can stay."

"What'll you do?"

"The rest of us'll split up, walk around, hit boutiques and restaurants, keep our ears and eyes open, see if we can't figure out where the action'll be tonight. We may be able to cut down on trial and error just by doing a little local research."

We ate lunch at a Del Taco, then headed off in our different directions. In our car were Philipe, myself, John, and Bill, and we parked near a series of interconnected shops done up in a Southwestern motif. Next door was a library, and Philipe told me to go there, look through local newspapers and magazines, see if any public events involving celebrities were going on this week.

"Like what?" I asked.

"Golf matches, store openings . . . I don't know. Anything. Just look for famous names."

The other three were going to split up and casually go through the shops. We were to meet back at the car in an hour.

In the library, I went directly to the periodical reading section and grabbed all of the copies of the three local newspapers for the past week. I carried my cache to a study carol against the back wall of the library and started quickly scanning headlines, reading ads, looking at pictures.

On the third page of the fourth paper, I saw a photo that made me stop.

It was a photo of a man. Joe Horth, according to the caption. The mayor of Desert Palms.

And he was Ignored.

I don't know how I knew it, but I did. There was something in the cast of the features, some familiarity of expression, some essential lack of charisma, that I instantly recognized, that translated even through the blurry black dot pointillism of the newsprint. I continued to stare at the picture. I had never seen a photograph of someone who was Ignored before, and I hadn't realized that it would appear so obvious.

I quickly read the accompanying article. I knew I should continue to dig through the newspapers for celebrity news, but this was too important to put off, and I tore out the page, folded it in half, and carrying it in my hand, hurried out of the library.

I ran past the fronts of the adjacent shops, looking through the windows until I saw Philipe. He was in a faux antique store, pretending to examine Victorian greeting cards while obviously listening in on the conversation of two trendily dressed young women.

I burst into the shop. A bell rang above the door, but only Philipe turned to look at me.

"I've found something," I said.

"What?" He put away the card in his hand, placing it back on the rack.

"I have a line on a new one."

"A new what?"

"A new terrorist. Someone Ignored."

"Oh." He looked disappointed. He glanced behind me, over my shoulder. "Where is he? . . . She?"

"He. Joe Horth. The mayor of Desert Palms." I held up the newspaper. "Here."

"Desert Palms?"

"Next town over. From what I gather, it's even more exclusive than Palm Springs. It's newer, not as well known, but it's full of heavy hitters."

He took the page from me. "Let me see that." Philipe looked at the picture, read the story, and I saw excitement spread quickly across his face. "He's going to be giving a speech at the Desert Disabled Foundation dinner tonight. Celebrities always show up for charity events like this. They get free publicity and look like they're good-hearted humanitarians." He folded the paper. "This guy may be able to give us an in with one of them. You've stumbled upon something here. This is good. This is really good."

"Where is the dinner?"

"Some place called La Amor. Seven o'clock." He put the paper in his pocket. "We'll find out where it is. We'll get some monkey suits. We'll be there."

The dinner was invitation only, but we crashed La Amor with no problem. There was a uniformed man stationed at the door to keep out nonmembers and non-invitees, but we easily walked past him and immediately found seats at the bar.

The restaurant was big and looked like a nightclub out of some forties film. Tables were arranged in an amphitheaterlike semicircle radiating outward from a stage on which an orchestra played jazz standards. Ceiling lights were dim, and individual art deco lamps shed illumination on the tables. Waiters wore tuxedos. Waitresses wore short skirts.

Philipe had been right. Charities did bring out the big guns. Bob Hope was there. And Charlton Heston. And Jerry Lewis. And a host of other lesser lights all conspicuously visible among the noncelebrities.

We sat together at the bar, watched the proceedings from afar, hearing only snatches of conversation—most of which had to do with the work of the foundation—as one couple and then another came up and ordered drinks.

As always, we took our cue from Philipe, and he remained strangely quiet. It seemed almost as though he was awed being in such a place, with such company.

Dinner was served, although since we didn't have a table we didn't get to eat. The orchestra stopped play-

ing, took a break, and the clink of glasses and silverware, the low hum of conversation, took the place of
the music.

The bartender set up drinks on trays for waiters to
take to the tables, and we stole some for ourselves.

Halfway through dinner, the speeches began. The
speakers were uniformly boring and almost indistin-
guishable from one another. First the president of the
foundation spoke. Then the founder. Then a local business leader who'd raised a lot of money. Then the
father of a disabled boy.

Then Mayor Joe Horth.

We all focused on the stage as the mayor stepped to
the podium and began speaking. The other guests paid
even less attention than they had to the other speakers.
That was expected, though, and not surprising. What
was surprising was what the mayor had to say.

He started off praising the Desert Disabled Foundation and its cause, stating how much he had enjoyed
working with all of the people attending the dinner.
Then he said that he regretted that this would be the
last foundation event he would be attending as mayor.
He had decided to resign.

The announcement was clearly meant to be a surprise, but it was met with indifference. No one was
listening.

We were listening, though, and I could tell by the
look on Philipe's face that he had noticed the same
thing I had: the mayor did not want to leave office.

Philipe turned toward me. "What do you think it is?"
he asked. "A scandal?"

I shrugged.

"He's being forced out. He doesn't want to leave."

I nodded. "I think so, too."

He shook his head. "Weird."

There was a commotion near the door. An excited
buzz began in that section of the room and spread to
the rest of the restaurant, and like a wave moving outward, heads turned toward the door. A phalanx of large

tuxedoed men pushed the crowd back, and between the bodies I could see a familiar round head nodding to the assembled dinner guests.

Frank Sinatra.

He was in the open now, coming toward us, smiling and heartily shaking hands. Bob Hope was suddenly next to him, saying something, and Sinatra was laughing. He put a friendly arm around the comedian's shoulder, then shouted an enthusiastic greeting to an elderly man seated at one of the upper tables. The man waved back, shouted something unintelligible in return.

"Sinatra," Junior said, impressed. He looked excitedly toward Philipe. "Let's nab him."

"Wait a minute." Philipe was still staring intently at the podium, where the mayor was being lectured by three imposing-looking men in their early to mid fifties.

"Sinatra!" Junior repeated.

"Yeah." Philipe waved him away distractedly and stood, moving through the crowd toward the podium. Curious, I followed.

The three men gathered around the mayor were obviously very wealthy, obviously very powerful, and they were openly treating Horth as though he were a flunky, a servant. We could not hear what was being said, but the attitudes were obvious. The mayor was obsequious and subservient, the businessmen commanding and authoritative. No one save us was paying attention to them, and they knew it. This was a private scene being played out in public, and it had the feel of a commonplace occurrence. I felt sorry for Joe Horth and angry on his behalf.

Philipe moved closer, stepping almost right up to the podium. The mayor turned, saw him, saw me, and gave a small start. He instantly turned back toward the businessmen, pretending to give them his full and undivided attention.

"The bar!" Philipe shouted. "Meet us at the bar!"

The mayor gave no indication that he heard.

"We can help you! We're Ignored, too!"

At that word, "Ignored," Joe Horth whirled to face us. The expression on his face was unreadable. He was distraught, obviously, and agitated, but there was also hope and what looked like a wild sort of exhilaration mixed in there. He stared at us. We stared back. The three men, obviously sensing from the mayor's behavior that something was amiss, looked into the crowd at us.

Philipe turned quickly, grabbed my shoulder, and pulled me back toward the bar. "Come on," he said.

A moment later, we were with the others. "Sinatra's up there at that big table," Junior said, pointing. "Bob Hope's with him and so's some other famous guy but I can't remember his name. I say we take 'em all."

"We're not taking anybody," Philipe said.

"But I thought we wanted publicity."

"We wanted publicity so we could draw attention to the plight of the Ignored, so we could help others like ourselves. Not so we could become famous. We were going to use the attention to throw a spotlight on a problem that, no pun intended, has been ignored until now. I don't know if the rest of you picked up on this, but it's obvious to me that our friend the mayor is being forced out of office by some high-profile money men because he's Ignored. I guess they want someone in there who's a little more charismatic, who can get more attention for them. What we have here is a chance to help someone who's Ignored, to do some real good. What we have here is a chance to keep one of us in a position of power."

I had not heard Philipe speak so idealistically for a long time, and a small thrill of excitement passed through me.

This was why I had become a terrorist.

"Joe Horth can do more good for the Ignored as mayor of Desert Palms than publicity from any kidnapped celebrity could. This is real progress. This is a real coup."

I looked toward the podium. One of the businessmen had left. The other two were still lecturing the mayor. "Do you think he's offed his boss yet?" I asked.

Philipe shook his head. "I don't know. I don't think so." He watched Horth. "There's something different about him. I'm not even sure he has to."

"Why?"

"I don't know."

I didn't understand it, but I believed him.

It was nearly half an hour later that the mayor came walking up to us at the bar. He was nervous and sweating, and he kept looking behind him as if to make sure he wasn't being followed. He was obviously surprised to see so many of us. He kept staring at Mary.

"Glad you could join us," Philipe said, extending his hand.

Horth shook it. "Who . . . who are you guys?"

"We're Ignored," Philipe said. "Like you. We call ourselves Terrorists for the Common Man."

"Terrorists?"

"And we've come to help you out." He stood, and the rest of us did, too. "Come on. Let's go back to our rooms. We have a lot to talk about. We have a lot to discuss. We have a lot to plan."

Dazed, confused, the mayor nodded, and all fourteen of us walked unnoticed through the crowd, past the doormen, and outside into the cool night air.

THIRTEEN

As I had, as Junior had, as Paul had, as Tim had, Joe Horth fit in with us perfectly. We were instantly close. He knew us, we knew him, and although in the past that immediate camaraderie had always made me feel warm and good and nice, watching it work this time, being so acutely aware of it, gave me the creeps.

What were we?

It always came back to that.

We brought Joe to our motel, but he immediately suggested that we come with him to his house, and there was no argument. While the rest of us packed, gathered our stuff, Philipe talked to him about the terrorists, explained what we were about, what we hoped to accomplish. The mayor listened eagerly, enthusiastically, and he seemed genuinely excited by what Philipe had to say.

"We think we can help you," Philipe told him.

"Help me?"

"Help you keep your job. And you, in turn, can help us. This could be the beginning of a true coalition. What we have here is the opportunity to give political power to a group that's never even been recognized, much less catered to."

The mayor shook his head. "You don't understand. The only reason I have this job is because I'll do what they say. And they know it. They want someone to follow their orders and be as unobtrusive as possible—"

"Who's 'they'?" Steve asked.

"Why, our local business leaders and the desert's

most prominent and respected citizens." Joe's voice was sarcastic. "I dared to make a small decision on my own, without their approval, and that's why I'm out."

"We'll see about that," Philipe said.

"What exactly did you do?" I asked.

"I broke a tie on the city council and voted to approve funding for a new softball diamond at Abbey Park. I was supposed to have tabled the discussion, held it off until the next meeting, and first asked them how I should vote."

"No, you weren't," Philipe said. "You did the right thing. And now we're here to back you up."

"I have a meeting with them tomorrow," Joe said. "Come to the meeting with me."

"We will," Philipe promised, and there was a hint of steel in his voice. "And we'll see if we can't get these guys to back down."

Joe's house was a nondescript dwelling on a street of mildly upscale tract homes. Exactly the sort of place that we found most comfortable. He had no wife, no roommate, no live-in lover, so all of the rooms were free, but with so many people the place was still pretty crowded. If we were going to sleep here, most of us would end up on the floor in sleeping bags.

We were tired, though, and didn't care about the close quarters. I wound up sleeping in the living room with Philipe and James and Mary—Mary on the couch, the rest of us on the floor.

"You think I should go in there and fuck him?" Mary asked as we settled in.

"Give it a day," Philipe said. "He needs a little time to adjust."

"So what's the plan?" I asked.

"Me, you, and Steve will go to this meeting with Joe, scope it out, see where things stand. Then we'll be able to decide what we're going to do."

"What do you *think* we're going to do?" I asked.

He did not answer.

* * *

We woke up early, spurred by Joe's alarm, and after all of the showers had been taken, we headed to the International House of Pancakes for breakfast. Joe offered to pay, but Philipe explained that we didn't have to pay, and after we ate, we simply left.

The mayor took us on a short tour of his city—Philipe, Steve, and I riding in his car, the others following—and we cruised through downtown Desert Palms, past the new mall, through the growing section of corporate office buildings. "Ten years ago," he explained, "none of this existed. Desert Palms was a few shacks and stores outside of Palm Springs."

Philipe looked out the window. "So, basically, these rich guys owned a lot of worthless desert land out here, and they stacked the city council with their people and got the land zoned the way they wanted, got the city to chip in for redevelopment projects, and they got even richer."

"Pretty much."

"How did they find you? What did you used to do?"

Joe smiled. "I was the personnel assistant for what passed for city hall back then."

"And no one ever noticed you or paid attention to you, and then suddenly someone offered to support you in the race for mayor and you were treated like a king."

"Something like that."

"You must've done something else besides vote for a softball diamond," I said. "They couldn't want you out just because of that."

"It's the only thing I can think of."

Steve shook his head. "I don't understand how they can tell you you can't be mayor anymore. The people around here voted for you. What if they want to vote for you again? You should just tell these guys to beat off, you don't need them."

"But I do need them."

"Why?"

Philipe snorted derisively. "Are you kidding? How

do you think someone gets elected in these small elections? You think candidates personally meet all the people in their districts? You think voters know where the candidates stand on all the issues? Be serious. People vote on name recognition. Candidates *get* name recognition through ads and posters and newspaper exposure. Money *buys* ads and posters and newspaper exposure. You get it? If these guys back you, you're in. That's it. Your name's plastered on red, white, and blue poster board on every telephone pole in the city."

Joe nodded. "Exactly."

"But he must have name recognition already. He's been mayor for a long time."

"Who's the mayor of Santa Ana?"

"I don't know."

"See? You're from Santa Ana and you don't even know. Besides that, Joe's Ignored. You honestly think people are going to remember who he is?"

"Oh," Steve said. He nodded. "I understand."

We drove back to the mayor's house. The meeting was scheduled for eleven o'clock in one of the corporate offices we'd passed on our tour. Philipe told the others they could hang around, go shopping, do whatever they wanted, but they had to be back by one o'clock because we were going to have a strategy meeting to decided on our next course of action.

Joe changed into nice clothes—a suit and tie—and Philipe, Steve, and I piled into his car. The four of us drove downtown.

The office building into which we walked reminded me uncomfortably of Automated Interface and I found myself thinking of Stewart's dead, bloodied body, but I forced myself to push those thoughts aside, and we followed Joe through the lobby, to an elevator. He pushed the button for the fifth floor.

The metal doors opened on a long, plushly carpeted hallway. We walked down the hall to an office. The plaque on the wooden double doors read: TERENCE HARRINGTON, CHAIRMAN OF THE BOARD.

Joe knocked timidly.

Philipe reached over, rapped more loudly.

The mayor licked his lips. "Let me do the talking."

Philipe shrugged, nodded.

The door swung open. There was no one behind it; it had been opened electronically. We stepped into what looked like an unusually opulent doctor's waiting room. Another set of doors immediately opened at the room's far end. Through the doorway, we could see an extraordinarily large desk, behind which sat one of the business-suited men from the foundation dinner.

"Obviously designed to be intimidating," Philipe whispered.

"It is," Joe replied.

We walked through the waiting room into the office beyond. All three power brokers from last night were there, two of them sitting in high-backed chairs flanking the man behind the desk. Three other equally important-looking men sat on a couch to the left of us.

The office itself was like something out of a movie. One wall had a fully stocked bar next to a partially opened door that led into what I assumed was a bathroom. The opposite wall was a floor-to-ceiling bookcase into which was set a combination high-tech stereo/television. Behind the desk was all window, a breathtaking panoramic view of the desert and Mount San Jacinto.

"Come in." The man behind the desk smiled, but there was no warmth or humor in it. "Sit down."

There were no chairs for us to sit in.

The man laughed.

The man—Terence Harrington, I assumed—was big, tall, with a florid face and the jowls of a bulldog. He wore his thinning gray hair long, combed across the bald spot on his head. I looked from him to the two men flanking him, both of whom were staring at us. The one on the left had a military brush cut and was chewing on the end of a huge unlit cigar. The one on the right had a thick white mustache and was rattling some sort of hard candy between his teeth.

The antipathy between us was immediate and was born full-blown. It was like we were magnets with opposing fields—we hated each other instantly. I looked at Philipe, at Steve, and for the first time in a long time we were in tandem. We knew instantly what each other was thinking, feeling. We knew what each other wanted because we all wanted the same thing.

We wanted these fuckers dead.

It was an unsettling realization, a frightening realization. I wanted to be able to get on my moral high horse and say that I could not condone violence, that I did not wish to harm anyone ever again, but that was not true, and we all knew it. The reaction within us was animal, instinctive.

We wanted to kill these men.

I glanced toward the three other men on the couch. They were obviously very powerful, obviously very rich, but they looked to me like members of an old movie comedy team: one was short, one was fat, one was bald with an unusually shiny head. All were staring at us disinterestedly.

Joe faced Harrington. "You wanted to see me?"

"I want you to give us your resignation. We already have one typed up. All you have to do is sign it. We're going to hold a special election in mid-January and install our new mayor, and we need your resignation by the end of this week."

"You can take that resignation and shove it up your ass," Philipe said.

He'd spoken softly, but his voice seemed loud in the room. All eyes turned toward him, and I realized with a start that this was the first time the power brokers had noticed him. The antipathy we'd felt, the disgust, had all been directed at Joe. The men had not even noticed us until now.

"And who, may I ask, are you?" Harrington's voice

was also low, but it was filled with a sense of coiled menace.

"It's none of your fucking business, you pig-eyed sack of shit."

Harrington turned his attention back toward Joe. "Aren't you going to introduce us to your friends, Mayor Horth?" The threat had not left his voice.

Joe was obviously frightened, but he held his ground. "No."

"I see."

The man with the cigar stood. "You're through, Horth. You're an ineffectual know-nothing nobody. We want a new mayor. We want a real mayor. We're tired of putting up with your incompetence."

Harrington pushed one of a panel of buttons on his desk. Through what I'd thought was the bathroom door strode two men, a tall, good-looking banker type in his mid-forties, and an average-looking man of approximately the same age. Harrington pointed toward the nondescript man. "We're running Jim this time. This is the new mayor of Desert Palms."

Jim was one of us.

Jim was Ignored.

I stared at Jim. He stared back. He knew I knew what he was, and I'm sure he knew Philipe and Steve did, too, but there was no way in hell that Jim was going to do anything to screw up his chances here. This was his shot, his opportunity to be someone, and he wasn't about to fuck it up just to align himself with us. I knew how he felt, and I couldn't blame him, but I also knew something he didn't know. Something that Joe had found out the hard way.

No matter what happened, he would still be Ignored.

"We'll finally have a real mayor," Cigar said. "Someone who can get things done."

"Come on," Philipe said. "We've heard enough. Let's go."

Joe looked as though he'd been about to say

something, but he apparently changed his mind and turned toward the door.

"You haven't signed—"

"And he's not going to," Philipe said.

Harrington's red face was turning even redder. "Who the hell do you think you are?"

"I'm Philipe. Terrorist for the Common Man."

"You don't know who you're dealing with here!"

"No," Philipe said. "*You* don't."

We hurried out the door. My heart was pounding, and I was shaking like a leaf. I was scared and angry at the same time, pumped up with adrenaline. I half expected the men to come after us and beat the shit out of us. I half expected a phalanx of armed guards to come running down the hallway. But none of this happened. The elevator doors opened when we pushed the button, we rode the elevator downstairs, went through the lobby, out into the parking lot, and got into Joe's car.

The mayor was nervous as he fumbled with his keys. "Shit!" he said. "Shit!"

"Calm down," Philipe told him.

"They know where I live!"

"We'll move to a motel. They'll never find us."

"You don't know them. They will find us."

"They didn't even see us until I spoke. We'll just blend into the woodwork and they'll never be able to track us down."

"You think so?" Joe sounded hopeful.

"I know so."

Joe started the car, put it into gear, and we sped out of the parking lot, bouncing onto the street.

Philipe nodded to himself. "We can get these guys," he said, and there was genuine excitement in his voice. "We can nail their asses to the wall."

"Terrorists for the Common Man!" Steve pumped his fist in the air.

I, too, felt the excitement. "Yeah!" I said.

Joe let out an enthusiastic whoop, caught up in the moment.

Philipe grinned. "We're gonna get those fuckers."

The other terrorists were all waiting when we got home. Philipe gathered everyone into the living room and described what had happened at the meeting.

"So what do we do?" Don asked.

"We kill them," Philipe said.

There was silence, I was remembering Familyland. I knew the others were, too.

"We take them out of the picture. We let the people of this city actually vote for the best candidate. We restore democracy to Desert Palms."

James looked at Tim. Both looked at me. I wanted to be able to stand up and articulate their obvious misgivings, but I did not share those misgivings. I had been in that office with Philipe. I knew where he was coming from. I agreed with him.

"We'll find a motel in Palm Springs or one of the other nearby cities, lay low for a week, let them think we left. Then we'll strike." He withdrew a gun from his inside jacket pocket. It was silver and gleamed in the room's refracted light.

"Yeah!" Joe said excitedly. "Blow those fuckers away!"

Steve grinned.

"We all need to be armed."

"What's with all this killing?" Tim asked. "I don't see why we need to kill anybody. Violence won't solve—"

"It's a tool," Philipe said. "The primary tool used by terrorists."

"It's the only thing they'll understand," Joe said. "It's the only way to stop them."

"I say we put it to a vote," James said.

Philipe shook his head. "We're going to get those fuckers. You can choose to help or not. But we're going to do it."

"Not," Tim said.

Philipe shrugged. "That's your right."

Tim looked at me, but I could not meet his eyes. I keep my gaze focused on Philipe.

"Pack everything up," Philipe ordered. "Like Joe said, they know where he lives. They'll be after us soon. We have to get out of here."

That night, sleeping alone in my spacious hotel room bed, I found myself mentally replaying everything that had happened in Harrington's office. I remembered what Philipe had told Steve that morning in the car, about how people voted not on issues but name recognition.

Was all politics this way? I had the feeling that it was. I tried to think of the name of my congressman but could not. I could name only one of California's two senators, I realized, although both of them sent me biannual "Senate Updates" and both did their damnedest to get their names in the newspaper at any opportunity.

I felt chilled. Was this democracy? This sham, this substanceless pretext of power supposedly in the hands of the people?

I fell asleep, and I dreamed that we flew to Washington, D.C., and went to the White House and walked right in. No security guards saw us; we were ignored by the Secret Service men.

I was in the lead, and I pushed open the door to the Oval Office. The President was meeting with his advisers, only it wasn't really a meeting. They were telling him what to say, what to do, what to think. The President was surrounded by a platoon of men who were lecturing him from all sides, and he looked toward us and his eyes were wide and frightened, and I knew that he was one of us.

I awoke with my pillow drenched with sweat.

FOURTEEN

We spent Christmas in Palm Springs, at the Holiday Inn.

The place didn't matter so much to us, but the rituals did—we were all uniformly in agreement on that—and on December 24, we hit the Palm Springs Mall and picked up presents for each other. Philipe set a limit: each of us could get only one gift per terrorist. There was to be no favoritism.

That night, Mary prepared roast beef and mashed potatoes with gravy, and we drank mulled wine and watched videotapes of *How the Grinch Stole Christmas* and *A Charlie Brown Christmas* and *Scrooge* and *It's a Wonderful Life.*

We went to sleep with visions of sugar plums dancing in our heads.

The next morning, we opened our presents. I received books and cassettes and videotapes and clothes and, from Philipe, an automatic rifle.

Mary prepared a turkey dinner, which we ate sometime in the midafternoon.

I could not help thinking of my previous Christmas, spent alone in my apartment. I felt better here with the others, but I still found myself thinking of even earlier Christmases, those spent with Jane and my parents. Then I had been really, truly happy. I had not realized it then, but I knew it now, and that knowledge depressed me. Not for the first time, I wished that I could turn back the clock and return to those days, that

I could know then what I knew now, and that I could do everything over again.

But that was impossible, and I knew that it would only depress me further to look back at the past, and I forced myself to concentrate only on the present and the future.

Mary saw me sitting alone in the corner of the suite that we'd commandeered for Christmas Day, and she came over and planted a chaste kiss on my forehead. "Merry Christmas," she said.

I smiled at her. "Merry Christmas." I gave her a hug, kissed her on the cheek, and took the hand she offered me, walking back into the thick of the festivities, where Tommy was trying to teach Junior how to play Nintendo.

FIFTEEN

Business in the desert cities did not stop for the week between Christmas and New Year's Day, and we took the opportunity to do a little spying on the enemy. Joe told us who the power brokers were and where they worked, and we spent the week walking into some of the newer and more exclusive office buildings, checking out the lairs of our adversaries.

None of the security guards stationed at the entrances to the banks or corporate offices saw us, and we walked easily past them, into the buildings, choosing doors at random, going in. Some were locked, of course, but others weren't, and behind them we saw deals being made, bribes being offered and accepted. We saw secretaries having sex with bosses, saw an executive with a photo of his wife and daughter on his desk fellating a younger man.

Sometimes these people would jump up in shock and outrage and horror when we barged in.

Sometimes they did not see us at all, and we stood watching as though we were invisible.

None of the power brokers were ever in, though. They *did* take the week off, no doubt spending it with their families, and it was lucky for them that they did, because we always arrived armed, ready to take out whomever we could.

New Year's Day was on a Saturday this year, and Philipe had Joe call Harrington on the Thursday prior and set up a meeting on the first. Harrington didn't want to have it on that day, he wanted to stay home, watch the games, but Joe said it was then or never, and the businessman finally agreed.

Joe hung up the phone. "He asked me if I'd finally come to my senses and decided to resign," he said. "I told him that's what we're going to talk about."

"Good," Philipe said, nodding. "Good. That gives us a full day for target practice."

We spent Friday in the desert, shooting at cans.

All of us.

Even Tim.

Saturday, we awoke early, too restless and anxious to sleep. Part of it was because the specifics of what we intended to do were still hazy in our minds—Philipe might know exactly how we were going to take out the power brokers, but he hadn't yet shared it with the rest of us and we were vague on the details.

That ended at breakfast.

Over McMuffins picked up by Joe, with the sounds of the Rose Parade coming from the TV, Philipe outlined precisely what each of us was to do in what he called "the operation." The plan was simple and—because of who we were, because of *what* we were—foolproof.

Joe was scheduled to meet with Harrington and the others at Harrington's office at eleven, but we were in front of the building by nine, sitting in our cars, watching, waiting. The first man, the one with the cigar, arrived around ten. They were all there by ten-thirty.

"He's not coming," Joe said at ten-fifty.

"Who?" Philipe asked.

"Jim. The Ignored guy who's supposed to be the new mayor."

"What do you expect? He has no say in any of this. He's just a puppet." Philipe opened the door, got out of the car, motioned for the terrorists in the other cars to do the same. They emerged carrying revolvers and shotguns and automatic rifles.

"All right," Philipe said. "You know the plan. Let's get in and get it done."

"Wait a minute." Joe cleared his throat.

"What?"

"I want Harrington. He's mine."

Philipe grinned. "You got it." He looked around the assembled group. "Are we all ready?"

"No." Mary, holding on to the trunk of our car, shook her head. She had driven over with us, riding in the backseat next to Joe. She'd spent the night with him.

Philipe turned to face her, annoyed. "What is it now?"

She looked pale. "I . . . I can't do it. I can't go through with it."

"Bullshit," Philipe said.

"No. Really." She seemed as if she were about to throw up.

"You were in on Familyland—"

"I can't do it, okay?"

Philipe looked at her, then nodded. "Okay." He sighed. "Wait here with the cars."

She smiled weakly. "You want me to drive the get-away vehicle?"

He looked at her, then grinned slightly. "If you can handle it."

"Yes, boss."

Once again, he looked over the group. "Anyone else want to bow out?" His gaze settled on me, moved to Tim, to James. We all shook our heads. "All right, then," he said. "Let's get these fuckers."

We strode into the building. Don and Bill staked out the south stairway, Tommy and Tim the north. Paul and John stayed in the lobby, in front of the elevators. The rest of us went up.

I held tightly to my automatic rifle and stared at the ascending numbers lighting up sequentially above the elevator door. My hands were sweaty and felt slippery on the gunmetal.

How had I gotten into this? I thought. How had this

happened? I felt in my gut that I was doing what needed to be done—it seemed like the right thing to me—but at the same time I could not help thinking that something here was way off base. This was not *supposed* to feel right to me; I should not want to kill these men.

But I did.

I started thinking about all the ways in which I and the others were average, ordinary. Did average, ordinary individuals want to go around killing people?

Maybe they did.

I thought again that something had slipped off track somewhere along the line.

Then the elevator doors opened and we were on the fifth floor. Most of the lights were off. Only a few soft recessed fluorescent bulbs illuminated the long hallway. We walked slowly toward the office, our weapons at the ready.

"Harrington's mine," Joe repeated.

Philipe nodded.

We moved into the darkened waiting room, and the door into the inner office opened slowly.

"You go in first," Philipe whispered. "Tuck your gun in your belt. Hide it."

Joe turned toward us, scared. "You're not going to leave me alone?"

"No. I just want to hear what they have to say."

Joe nodded.

"Mayor Horth!" called out someone inside the office.

"Go!" Philipe whispered.

The rest of us gathered around the door, hiding in the shadows. Harrington stood as Joe entered the room. He looked large and threatening, silhouetted against the panoramic desert view, and when he spoke his voice was tight, tense, filled with a barely contained rage. "You little shit," he said.

"What?"

"Who the fuck do you think you are, ruining our New Year's like this? You think you can pull this crap without us teaching you a lesson? I don't know what got into your pea-brain, but you've obviously forgotten who you are and who we are and who calls the shots around here."

"He calls the shots around here. He's the mayor." Philipe stepped out of the shadows into the room, revolver drawn. The rest of us fell into step behind him.

All of the men in the room looked from Joe to the rest of us. "Who are these guys?" the bald man asked.

Cigar squinted, looked closely at me, at Steve, at Junior, at Pete. "It's more of them," he said. "A whole gang of them."

" 'Them'?" Philipe said mockingly.

"You're certainly not one of us."

"Then what are we?"

"You tell me."

"We're Terrorists for the Common Man."

Cigar laughed. "And what the fuck's that supposed to mean?"

"It means we're going to blow you away, you ego-centric asshole."

Philipe raised his gun and fired.

Cigar went down screaming, blood gushing from the hole blown in his chest. For a brief fraction of a second, I saw what looked like a light-colored organ or piece of tissue through the ragged opening, then the blood was everywhere, pumping out in a sickening, amazing geyser. Cigar began thrashing crazily on the floor, blood spurting all over the carpet, all over the pants and shoes of his panicked, terrified buddies.

"Take 'em out," Philipe said coldly.

And we began shooting.

I aimed for the bald man. He was scrambling across the boardroom, trying to get away, and it was as though I was at a shooting gallery. I watched him move jerkily back and forth across the width of the room, like a target on a track, and I trained my automatic rifle on him, followed him for a few seconds, and shot. The first bullet hit him in the arm, the second in the side, and then he was on the floor and howling with agony, and I took a sight on his head and pulled the trigger and blood and brains shot out of his collapsing skull and then he was still.

I didn't want to feel good, but I did. I felt great. I glanced to the right of the bald man, saw the short guy rolling on the floor, holding his leg and screaming, begging for his life in high womanly tones. Red streaks smeared over the white shag where his blood soaked into the carpet. Pete stood above him, a rifle pointed at his head.

"No!" he screamed crazily. "No! No! No! No!—"

Pete pulled the trigger and the short guy's head exploded in a spray of red-and-white mist.

I was still high, still pumped, and I looked around for someone else to shoot, but the others had gotten them all.

Joe fired his last bullet into Harrington's already unmoving body.

There was silence all of a sudden.

After the screams, after the shots, the quiet seemed spookily unreal. There was a muffled ringing in my ears. The air was filled with smoke, the floor with blood, and the room smelled of metal and cordite, fire and shit.

As quickly as it had come, the elation fled, replaced by repulsion and horror. What had we done? I caught James's eye. The expression on his face was a mirror image of the one that must have been on my own.

"Let's go," Philipe said quickly. "Let's get out of here. Now."

Joe looked around the blood-spattered office. "But shouldn't we—?"

"Now!"

He strode through the doors the way we had come. I followed immediately behind him, my stomach churning.

I made it all the way to the hallway before I puked.

SIXTEEN

The murders were news. Big news. They were the top story on the front page of *USA Today*, on the NBC, CBS, and ABC national newscasts, in *The Wall Street Journal*.

The men we'd killed had not only been important residents of Desert Palms, they'd been big deals in the world of business, and their deaths caused the stock markets of Tokyo and Wall Street to dip for a few days before turning back up. It turned out that Cigar, whose real name was Marcus Lambert, had not only owned Lambert Industries, *the* major tool manufacturing firm in the United States, but had been the major stockholder in literally dozens of multinational corporations. The others had not been quite as powerful, but their deaths as well caused a ripple effect in the world financial markets.

We cut out articles and videotaped newscasts and added to our library of media coverage.

Joe was like a new man. The whipped dog we had met that first night at La Amor had been replaced by a cocky bantam rooster. In a lot of ways, I liked the old Joe better, and I knew most of the other terrorists felt the same way. He'd been timid and frightened, but he'd been kind and generous and humble. Now he seemed overconfident, cocksure, and self-important, and there was a hardness within him that made a lot of us uncomfortable.

The day after "the action," Joe convened a meeting of the city council, and he asked publicly for the resignation of the city manager and the chairman of the planning commission. He called for a vote on several ordinances that he'd been told to support in the past, and he voted against them.

We sat in the audience and watched. Philipe was paying particularly close attention to the proceedings, and he frowned to himself each time the mayor spoke. Finally, after Joe had broken a tie vote on widening a three-block section of road, I tapped Philipe on the shoulder. "What is it?" I asked.

"I'm trying to figure out what's wrong."

I followed his gaze, watched Joe lead a discussion on neighborhood watch programs. "What do you mean?"

"They hear him: they pay attention to him." He looked at me, gestured around the room. "Not just the city council, but the reporters, the people who came to watch. They see him."

I'd noticed that, too.

"And he's changed. I mean, he's killed his boss— with a little help from us—but he hasn't . . . " Philipe shook his head, trying to find the right words. "He's drifted farther away from us instead of coming closer. He's . . . I can't explain it, but I know it. I know what happens after the initiation, and it hasn't happened to Joe."

"You know what I think?" Junior said.

"What?"

"I think he's half-and-half."

Philipe was silent.

Bill jumped in, nodding excitedly. "Yeah. It's like his dad was Ignored and his mom wasn't. Like Mr. Spock or something."

Philipe nodded slowly. "Half-and-half," he said. "I can see it. It would explain a lot."

I cleared my throat. "Do you think we can trust him? I mean, do you think he'll remember where he came from or do you think he'll just shine us on? Do you think he's still on our side?"

"He'd better be," Philipe said.

"And if he isn't?"

"We'll take him out. And we'll put Jim in his place. Just like the money men originally planned."

Three days later, Jim showed up at the mayor's office. He was not only cowed and humbled but frightened, and we had a hard time convincing him that we did not blame him for anything.

He had called Philipe to ask for the meeting, had called from a pay phone because he thought we were going to track him down and kill him for his affiliation with Harrington and Lambert and the power elite. He wanted a truce, he said. He wanted to meet with us, get things straightened out.

There was no truce to be called, nothing to be straightened out, but Philipe agreed to meet with him, and set the time and place.

"Don't tell Joe," he told me as he hung up the phone.

"Why?"

"Because."

"Because why?"

"Because."

When Jim stepped into the mayor's office the next morning at the appointed time, he looked bad. He'd obviously been living hand-to-mouth, and he'd obviously been under a lot of strain. His clothes were dirty, his face gaunt. He smelled as though he hadn't bathed in quite some time.

Philipe told him about the terrorists, explained what we did and who we were. He put no pressure on Jim, but he made it clear that Jim was free to join us if he so desired.

It was then that Joe walked into the room.

The mayor stood in the doorway for a moment, stunned and unmoving. Then he rushed forward, his face crimson with anger. "Get the hell out of my office!" he demanded, pointing toward the door. "Get the hell out of my city!"

"This is Jim," Philipe said conversationally. "Our newest terrorist."

Joe looked from Philipe to Jim and back again. "Do you know who that is?"

"I just told you. He's the newest Terrorist for the Common Man."

"That's the son of a bitch Harrington was going to put in my place!" The mayor moved in front of Jim, faced him. "Who are you and where are you from?"

"My name's Jim Caldwell. I'm from San Francisco."

"Why were you going to sell us out?"

"I wasn't going to sell you out. Those guys found me working in a gas station and asked me if I wanted to be mayor. What was I supposed to say?"

"Don't be so hard on him," I said. "You know how it is."

"I know how it is? I know he was going to take over my job!" He confronted the new man. "Why did you come here?"

"I had to leave San Francisco because I killed my supervisor in the plant where—"

Philipe held up a tired hand. "Save it. We know the story."

"I want him out of here!" Joe roared.

"I don't give a fuck what you want." Philipe's voice was low and cold, the way it had been when he'd spoken to Harrington. He fixed the mayor with a steely stare.

Joe backed off a little, but his tone was no less belligerent. "*I'm* mayor here," he said. "Not you."

"That's right," Philipe said, moving slowly toward him. "You're mayor here. You're mayor of this shitty little Palm Springs suburb and you have the power to widen streets and build baseball diamonds." He brought his hand down flat on the top of the desk. The slap sounded like a bullwhip. "Don't try to tell me who the fuck you are. You'd be nothing if we hadn't taken up your cause." He pointed to Jim. "You'd be him!"

"I thank you for what you've done. But I'm afraid this is my town. I'm mayor—"

"Yes. You're mayor. You're not king."

"I want you all out of my office."

Philipe stood for a moment, shook his head slowly, then reached into his pocket and withdrew his revolver. "I knew it would come to this. You're so fucking predictable."

Now there was a quaver in Joe's voice. "What do you think you're doing?"

I glanced toward Tim, toward James. None of us knew where this was going. My mouth felt dry.

"Jim's mayor here now," Philipe said. He calmly checked the chambers of the gun. "How do you like that? I'm not even going to bother making you resign or sign a piece of paper. I'm just going to remove you from office and replace you."

"You can't do that! The people elected me!"

"And I'm unelecting you." Philipe smiled coldly. "You think anyone's going to know the fucking difference?"

I felt chilled. This was a Philipe I had not seen before. This was not the idealist who'd recruited me into the terrorists or who'd quixotically decided to save Joe Horth's job. This was not the desperate seeker who'd had sex with Mary and me and everyone else. This was not even the half-crazed fanatic who'd wanted to blow up Familyland, or the dispassionate killer who had murdered his supervisors and gunned down Joe's tormentors. This was a Philipe on the edge, a Philipe with no motive, no plan, a Philipe with no reason behind his actions, a Philipe flying blind, acting on instinct, and it scared the shit out of me.

"Philipe," I said.

"Shut up."

Jim backed away. "I don't want to be mayor," he said. "I just came up here to make sure you all weren't after me. I didn't want—"

"You shut up, too." He stared Joe down. "Well, what's it going to be, *mayor*?"

Joe cracked. "I'm sorry," he said. He licked his lips. "I was just . . . I . . ." He stared helplessly at Philipe.

Philipe remained impassive for a moment. He blinked hard a few times, then he nodded. "Okay," he said. "All right." He replaced the gun in his pocket. "Does that mean it's agreeable with you if we recruit Jim to our side?"

"Go right ahead." The mayor faced Jim, held out a hand, forced himself to smile. "I'm sorry," he said. "No hard feelings?"

"No hard feelings."

"That's what I like to see." There was still something strange about Philipe's behavior, something unsettling about the way he was acting. I remembered how I'd once thought he might be manic depressive.

Mentally ill?

I looked at James, he looked at me, and I knew he was thinking the same thing I was. He looked away.

Philipe continued nodding. "Friends again. That's what I like to see. Friends again."

We spent the day with Jim, hanging out, telling him about our old lives and our new ones. He hit it off instantly with Mary, and the attraction was obviously mutual. James and I shared knowing smiles as the two found not-so-subtle ways to stand or sit next to one another. I had the feeling that the rest of the terrorists were going to be seeing a lot less of Mary in their beds in the near future.

Philipe remained tense, seemed coiled like a snake. All day long, he was hyper, moving around, walking in and out of where we were, popping abruptly into conversations and just as abruptly out. He seemed to be waiting for something, anxious for its arrival.

After dinner, after dark, there was a windstorm, and we were all sitting in Joe's living room, watching TV, when Philipe suddenly jumped to his feet and hurried over to the front door, yanking it open. He stood for several seconds in the doorway, breathing heavily. He shook his head. "I have to go," he said. "I have to get out of here."

I got up, frowning, and went over to him. "Go where? What are you talking about?"

"You wouldn't understand."

"Try me."

He thought for a moment, then shook his head. "Thanks," he said. "But . . . no." He started outside, turned around on the porch. "Don't follow me," he said. "Don't anyone try to follow me."

And then he was gone, into the night, into the dark, and I was left staring at the open doorway where he had stood, hearing only his retreating footfalls as they were overtaken by the sounds of the desert wind.

SEVENTEEN

Philipe did not return for a week.

When he did, he was his old self again, cheerful, enthusiastic, filled with plans for what Joe could do to simultaneously aid the Ignored and further his own political career.

We had been dormant in his absence, not sure if he was coming back, not sure what we would do if he didn't. I hadn't realized until that point how dependent we'd all been on him. Despite our arguments and disagreements, despite my periodic attempts to distance myself from him, I was just as reliant upon Philipe as the others were, and I knew that none of us had the vision or leadership qualities needed to fill his shoes and take charge of the organization.

Then, just as it was starting to look as though we really would have to start making some decisions on our own, Philipe was back, acting as though nothing unusual had occurred, once again laying out plans and telling everyone what to do.

I wanted to talk to him about what had happened, wanted to talk to the others as well, but for some reason I didn't.

Joe was our liaison with the real world. He was definitely Ignored, but somehow, whether by virtue of his nature or his position, he could get non-Ignored to pay attention to him. He could communicate with them and they would listen.

After his return, the first thing Philipe asked Joe to do was to look for any Ignored who might already be working for the city and promote them to positions of power. "They'll never be promoted from within their own departments because they're not noticed. No one pays attention to them and no one considers them when positions are open."

"I'm not sure I can tell who's Ignored," Joe said hesitantly.

"I can," Philipe told him. "Get me a printout of all city employees and their personnel histories. We'll start out that way, narrow it down. Then you can call them all into the council chambers for a meeting, introduce me as an efficiency expert or something, give me a chance to look them over. If we find any, we'll talk to them, decide where to put them."

"But what do we do after that?"

"We'll see."

There was no one Ignored working at city hall, it turned out. A canvass of the company to whom the city contracted out tree-trimming and park maintenance service likewise proved futile.

We were rarer than we'd thought.

But none of this deterred Philipe. He got us all together, asked us pages upon pages of questions that he'd written out on a variety of basic topics, and from our answers he devised a test that he called the EAP, the Educational Aptitude and Proficiency exam. He got Joe to get the city council to pass an ordinance requiring the school district to administer the exam in all Desert Palms schools before the end of the current school year.

"We'll be able to catch them young," Philipe explained.

In the meantime, he and Joe pored over stacks of personnel printouts and labor distribution reports in order to determine which city employees were the most average and unexceptional in the amount of hours they put into their jobs and the amount of work that they produced. Philipe's goal was to eventually, through attrition, get rid of those employees with poor performance records, demote those with high performance records, letting them carry the heaviest load and do the majority of the work, and promote those who were the most average, the most ordinary, the most like us.

"Mediocrity should be rewarded," he said. "It's the only way we'll ever be able to get any respect."

For the rest of us, our days became less structured. Without a specific short-term goal toward which we were working, we began to drift. Once again, we started going to movies in the afternoon, hanging out at malls. We walked into expensive five-star resorts, swimming in their luxurious pools. In the evenings, we'd hit the nightclubs. We found that it was fun to annoy celebrities, tripping them as they danced, watching them fall and flail awkwardly to the secretly delighted stares of the ordinary men and women around them. We flipped up celebrity women's skirts and pantsed the more pretentious men, exposing who wore underwear and who didn't. I'd always thought of the Palm Springs area as sort of a retirement community for old-line celebrities, but it was surprising how many young movie actors and soap opera stars and contemporary entertainers frequented the local clubs on weekends.

In the women's restroom of one club, Steve and Paul raped a blond bimbo who was currently starring in a Saturday night CBS sitcom. Afterward, showing off her silk thong panties as a trophy, Steve said, "She wasn't that great. Mary's as good as her any day."

"Famous people are no different than us," Paul agreed. "I don't see why people treat them like they are."

I said nothing.

Philipe and Joe, when they heard about the rape, were furious. Philipe lectured all of us about committing crimes in Desert Palms. "You don't shit where you eat," he said. "Do you think you assholes can comprehend that?"

It was interesting to note the change in Philipe since

"the action." He'd become downright conservative lately, eschewing the tools of terrorism that he'd championed in the past and opting for maneuvering within the strict boundaries of the system.

I had to admit, I liked this conventional approach.

It was about a month later that I was walking back from a bookstore down a nearly empty street and a woman bumped into me. She let out a short startled cry, then stood there, puzzled and frightened, looking around.

She didn't see me.

At all.

My first thought was that she was blind. But almost immediately I realized that that was not the case. She was simply unable to see me—I was completely invisible to her. I stood there, watching as she continued to look frantically around, then hurried away, continuing to glance over her shoulder for the invisible intruder.

I was stunned, not sure how to react. I thought for a moment, then looked up and down the street, searching for someone else. I saw a derelict sitting at a bus stop farther up the block and hurried over. He was a heavily bearded man in a dirty overcoat and was staring straight out at the street, eyes focused on the building opposite. I licked my lips, took a deep breath, and began walking back and forth in front of him. His eyes did not follow me.

I stopped. "Hello," I said.

No response.

I clapped my hands loudly next to his ears.

Nothing.

I pushed his shoulder.

He jumped up, startled, and let out a sharp exhalation, looking wildly around.

He could not see me either.

Or hear me.

"They're back!" he screamed crazily, and ran up the street away from me.

I sat down hard on the bench.

We'd graduated to the next step.

When had this occurred? Had it happened over-night, or had we been gradually fading away from public view?

A bus passed by. The driver did not see me on the bench, did not stop.

We were, I realized, completely free. Even the minor restrictions imposed on us by our extremely limited visibility had now been lifted. We could do anything, whatever we wanted, whenever we wanted, and no one would ever know.

But. . .

But I wasn't sure I wanted to tell the others. I wasn't sure I wanted them to know this. I had the sense that it might set us back, that wherever we were now, what-ever point we had reached in our evolution, would be forgotten and we would have to redo what we had already done. We would try desperately to take advan-tage of our invisibility and end up playing pointless games.

Besides, I had to admit the prospect of having the freedom that I now possessed frightened me. I did not like flying without a net, did not trust myself.

And I trusted the others even less.

Were we responsible enough to possess such unchecked autonomy?

I walked back to Joe's, still not sure what I was going to say, still not sure if I was going to say any-thing. John and Bill and Don were gone, but Philipe, thank God, was home for lunch. The others were lounging around the living room, talking, reading magazines, watching TV.

I had to tell them something, I decided. But I would soft-pedal it.

"I don't want to frighten anybody," I said. "But I was just walking back from the bookstore and I bumped into this woman, and she didn't see me."

Paul snickered, looked up from his *Time*. "Big revelation."

"No. I mean she didn't see me at all. It wasn't that she didn't notice me. She could look right through me." I glanced around the room. I cleared my throat nervously. "Doesn't it seem like we're getting ... worse? James said one time that we could be like invisible superheroes, catching crooks and all that. Don't you think we could do that now? Or am I the only one who's noticed this?"

Silence greeted my words. Philipe looked uncomfortable.

I told them about my experiment with the derelict.

"I've noticed a difference, too," Pete said quietly. "I didn't want to say anything, I thought it might be just my imagination, but ever since we offed those power guys it's felt different to me."

Tommy faced Philipe. "Is this like a progressive disease? Is that what we have?"

Philipe sighed. "I don't know. I've noticed it, too, though. I just didn't want to say anything. I didn't want to frighten anyone."

Mary, on the couch, reached for Jim's hand, held it. On TV, a commercial for a new brand of tampon came on. This was going in a different direction than I'd thought. On the street, I'd felt as though I'd been let out of a cage and forced to fly in open, unrestricted air. Now I felt as though the walls of a prison were closing in on me. I felt isolated; alone, despite the presence of the others.

"What are we going to do?" Tommy asked.

Philipe stood. "What *can* we do?" He took a deep breath. "I have to get back to work. I'll talk to Joe, see what he thinks. He's half-and-half, maybe he has a different perspective on this."

"Maybe he won't be able to see us for much longer, either," Mary suggested.

Philipe walked out of the living room, not looking at us. "I have to go to work," he said.

* * *

We were invisible, but it didn't seem to matter much. At least not as much as I'd thought it would. Here, in the sun, amidst the wealth, with Joe as our go-between to normal society, that lost sense of alienation I'd felt temporarily disappeared.

Joe could see us as well as he always could.

We were not fading away to him.

Not yet.

Philipe continued working full-time on legislative ways to better our position and bring us attention. The rest of us fell into our old patterns.

One night after we'd gone to Sizzler and loaded up on all we could eat at the salad, taco, and pasta bar, we were walking back along the crowded side-walk to Tower Records to steal some tapes and CDs when Philipe pulled me aside. "I need to talk to you," he said.

"About what?"

He stopped walking, letting the others get a little further ahead of us. "We're being followed," he said. There was a pause. "I think they're on to us."

"Who's on to us?"

"The suits."

Goose bumps spread down my arms. "They've found us?"

"I think so."

"When did you discover this?"

"A week ago, maybe."

"Did you just 'feel' it, or did you see them?"

"I saw them."

"Why haven't they done anything? Why haven't they captured us or killed us?"

"I don't know."

I looked around to see if any were near us now, but saw only casually dressed tourists and locals. "Who do you think they are?"

He shrugged. "Who knows? The government, may-be. The FBI or CIA. We'd be great spies for them. For all I know, they created us. Maybe our parents were given some sort of drug, exposed to some type of radiation—"

"Do you think so? Do you think that's why we're Ignored?" I should have been horrified, angry at the idea, but instead I felt excited, thinking that finally there was a chance I might get a concrete explanation for why we were the way we were.

He shook his head slowly. "No. But I do think that they found out about us. I think they know what we are and who we are and I think they're watching us." He was silent for a moment. "I think we should take them out."

"No," I said. "No more. I've done enough killing for two lifetimes. I'm not going to—"

"You liked it when we took out the money men. Don't deny it."

"That was different."

"Yeah. Those guys wanted to fire Joe and put in a new mayor. These guys killed Buster. And they're going to kill us. That's the difference."

"Look, I don't—"

"Shh!" Philipe said quietly, harshly. "Keep your voice down."

"Why?"

"I don't want the others to hear."

"Why?"

"I don't want to worry them."

"*Worry* them? After all they've been through?"

"Because. That's why. Is that a good enough reason for you?" He looked at me. "I told you I get feelings? Hunches? Well, right now I have this feeling that we shouldn't tell the others."

We were quiet for a moment. "What are these 'hunches'?" I asked. "What are they really? Are they like . . . ESP or something?"

"I don't know."

"I don't believe you."

He was silent. "Yeah, I guess they are like ESP," he

said finally. "Or maybe more like fortune-telling. They're always about the future and they always come true. I don't see pictures or images. I don't get coherent messages read to me. I just . . . know things."

"Why did you go off into that sandstorm last month? Why did you disappear for a week?"

"I had to."

"What did you do while you were gone?"

"It's none of your business."

"It is my business."

He looked at me, his eyes boring into my own. "No. It's not."

"It's related, isn't it? It has something to do with your 'hunches.' "

He sighed. "Let's just say that I had to go out and . . . do something. If I didn't, something really bad would have happened to us. To all of us. It wouldn't make any sense to you if I told you the specifics—it doesn't make any sense to me—but it's true, and I know it's true, and . . . it's just something that happened."

"Why don't you talk to the rest of us about this stuff? We—"

"Because you wouldn't understand. And because it's none of your business."

We had been walking slowly along the sidewalk and were now in front of Tower Records. The others had already gone in, but Pete was standing in the doorway waiting for us. "I know you guys are discussing something I wasn't supposed to hear," he said. "But are you talking about the suits?"

"Why?"

"I know they're here. I saw one outside Sizzler."

Philipe pulled him away from the door. "How many of the others know?"

He shrugged. "I don't know. None of them, probably. I haven't talked about it with anyone. I thought I should talk to you first."

Philipe grinned. "You're a rock, Pete."

I looked around again.

"They're not here now," Philipe said.

"So what are we going to do?" Pete asked.

"Take them out."

I shook my head. "They're not alone. They're working for somebody. They've already checked in by now, called or radioed to their bosses to tell them where we are. We could kill them, but more would come. We have to get out of here."

Philipe thought for a moment. "You may be right," he said. "One thing's for sure, though. We have to tell the others. Then we'll vote on it. But we can't just stay here and do nothing. It's not safe. We either take them out or hit the road, or both."

"Agreed."

"All right, then. Let's head for home. Meeting time."

We voted to stay.

And hide.

The polling was unanimous, except for Philipe. Everyone else seemed to be tired of killing, and despite what had happened to Buster, no one was in the mood to seek revenge. We were scared and wanted only to lay low.

"But where'll we go?" Mary asked.

"There are a lot of nice homes in a new subdivision on the south end of town," Joe suggested.

"How's the access?" Philipe asked. "Any gates? How many roads in and out? Will we be able to keep the place secure?"

"Don't worry."

"The suits aren't playing games," Philipe said. "If they're here, they're here for a reason. They've already killed one of us—"

"Joe can tell the police chief about these guys," Tim pointed out. "He can have them hauled in for harassment or something. We can find out who they are, why they're after us."

Joe nodded. "I will."

Philipe paused for only a second. "All right," he

said. "But be careful. If they know you're one of us, they may try to take you out, too."

"Don't worry."

Philipe nodded. "Okay. From now on, we'll have someone on watch at all times, twenty-four hours a day." He turned toward Joe. "Show us where this place is."

We drove to the subdivision, took an empty ranch-style house at the end of a cul-de-sac so we could spot all comers. Joe did talk to the police chief and arranged for a patrol car to be stationed at the entrance of the subdivision. He gave the police a description of the suits, confirmed that the local police knew nothing about them, and made sure that the police would pick up any suits they could find for questioning.

"I think you're safe," Joe said.

"Maybe," Philipe told him. "But I'm still keeping a man on watch. Just in case."

It happened that night.

Once again, it was during a sandstorm. We were at the house. We'd been planning a barbecue, but the sandstorm had come and we'd moved inside, where Mary put the half-cooked chicken into the oven. We were sitting around waiting for the food, talking, drinking beer, watching a videotape of *Top Gun*, when I suddenly noticed that Philipe was gone.

He might've been in the bathroom, he might've been in the kitchen, but something told me that he wasn't, and I quickly searched the rooms of the house and determined that he was not there. I opened the front door, looked outside. Through the blowing sand, I could see that all of our cars were still parked out in front.

And then I saw Philipe.

He was inside the house next door. I could dimly make out his silhouette through one of the side windows.

Something about that alerted me, sent up my antennae. I had a sickening feeling in the pit of my stomach, and I ran outside, jumped the small wooden fence that separated the two homes, and sped up to the porch next door. The front door was wide open, despite the sandstorm, and I walked right in. I hurried past the window where I'd seen Philipe, through a den, into a hallway. Philipe was before me, walking toward the far end of the hall.

In his hand was a carving knife.

"Philipe!" I yelled.

He ignored me, kept walking.

"Philipe!" I ran forward.

He was mumbling, talking to himself. I heard him say, "Yes," and the way he said it sounded as though he were talking to someone.

God?

Chills cascaded down my arms as I remembered him suggesting, when I first joined the terrorists, that God had chosen us for this work.

"Yes," he said again, and he seemed to be answering a question. "I will."

But he'd claimed that he didn't hear voices.

"No," he said to his unseen questioner.

"Philipe!" I grabbed his shoulder. He whirled around, swung at me with the knife, but when he saw who I was, pulled back, missing me.

Then he punched me in the nose.

I fell back against the wall, stunned and hurt, blood spilling from my nostrils and backing up into my throat. I spit, stood, tried to breathe. Philipe was gone, no longer in the hallway, and a split second later I heard a child's staccato screams.

I ran through the open doorway at the end of the hall. Philipe was on his knees in the center of a pink girl's room, flanked by twin beds. He was covered with blood, his eyes white and crazy in the midst of the red, and he was hacking at two small unmoving children on the ground before him.

"My name's not David!" he screamed. "It's Philipe!"

He swung the knife, sliced into a shoulder. "My name is Philipe!"

I was pushed aside as a woman ran screaming into the room. Her screams stopped abruptly as the horror of the scene imprinted itself onto her brain. She fainted dead away, not collapsing gently and gracefully to the floor as women did in movies but falling flat and heavy, her head hitting the wooden floor with a hard thud, her outstretched right hand flopping into a puddle of her daughters' blood.

There was a pink dresser next to the door. On top of the dresser were two piggy banks, and I picked one up and heaved it at Philipe's head.

It hit, bounced off, and broke on the floor, pennies spilling into the blood. Philipe shook his head, blinked, and at the same time seemed to see for the first time the knife in his hand, the dead girls before him and me standing by the door. It was as if he had awakened from a trance, and he looked at me with weak, frightened eyes. "I didn't . . . I had no . . . I had to—"

"Save it," I said.

"Help me clean this up. Help me get rid of this." He stared up at me frantically, beseechingly, holding out his bloody hands, palms up.

Part of me felt sorry for him, but it was a small part of me. "No," I said disgustedly.

"Something would've happened to us if I didn't—"

"What?" I demanded. "What would have happened to us?"

He started to cry. It was the first time I had ever seen Philipe cry and the sight tore at me, but the other sights in the room tore at me more. I could not forgive him for this. I could not justify what he had done. I would never defend him simply because we were both of a kind. Our kinship could not excuse this butchery.

"I'm out of the terrorists," I said.

"Don't tell the others—"

"Fuck you."

I walked out of the bedroom, out of the house,

through the sandstorm back to Tim's. I told everyone what had happened, what I had seen, and hushed and silent, they went next door. Steve and Junior stayed to help Philipe clean up the mess. The rest returned, shocked into silence.

"I'm out," I said when they got back. "I resign."

"You can't resign," Pete said.

"Why not?"

"You're Ignored. You can't just stop being Ignored by saying so."

"Yeah, I'll always be Ignored. But I'm no longer a Terrorist for the Common Man. I'm resigning from the terrorists. I can't follow Philipe. He's crazy."

"But we've all killed," Paul said. "Doesn't that mean we're all crazy?"

"If you can't see the difference, I can't explain it to you." I looked around at my friends, my brothers, my sister. "I'm leaving," I said. "Does anyone want to come with me?"

"Where are you going?" James asked quietly.

"I don't know."

"I'm not going anywhere," Joe said. "I'm mayor here. This is my town."

I nodded. "I understand."

"I don't want to leave either," Tim said. "I'm not with Philipe, but I'm staying."

Mary stepped forward. "We'll come with you," she said. "Jim and I will come." She looked toward Jim, and he nodded.

"I'm coming," James said.

"Me, too." Don.

In the end, Bill and John and Tommy and Pete and Paul voted to stay with Philipe. I knew Steve and Junior would do the same, so I didn't even bother waiting until they came back to ask them.

"How quickly can you pack?" I asked.

James gave me a wan grin. "I never unpacked."

We were gone before Philipe and the other two had returned. I promised to call, to keep in touch, but at that moment I was not sure if I would. Too many conflicting emotions were churning within me. More than anything else, I wanted to be free of this burden of being Ignored. I wanted to be just a regular person again, to not have to worry about the suits or think about killings or plan ways to overthrow "the system." I did not want the mantle of responsibility that I had been forced to carry ever since I'd met Philipe. I just wanted to live my life in peace and quiet.

We walked through the blowing sand to Jim's van. Already, I was starting to regret my decision to break away. The horror of what I'd seen had already begun to fade, and I found myself starting to rationalize Philipe's actions, telling myself he was sick, he couldn't help it, he didn't know what he was doing.

Already, I was starting to miss Philipe.

I thought of Sea World.

No, I told myself. I couldn't let *these* memories fade. I'd made a decision and I was going to stick by it.

We left the subdivision, headed through the city toward Interstate 10. The winds had died down, and above us the stars were visible. A full moon, partially risen, made the sand dunes look blue.

"So where are we going?" James asked again.

I shook my head. "I don't know. Got any ideas?"

"Back home?"

"Home where?"

"Our old homes, our real homes. Your apartment, my condo."

"What if the suits are staking them out, waiting for us to come back?"

"After this long? Be serious."

"Okay," I said. "Sounds good to me. What about the rest of you?"

"I do kind of miss my house," Don admitted.

We voted, and the vote was unanimous. "All right," I said. "We'll do it." We pulled into an Arco gas station near the highway to tank up for the long drive back to

Orange County. I walked into the AM/PM Mini-Mart to snag some snacks while James pumped the gas.

The man behind the counter was Ignored.

We stared at each other. There was no one else in the small convenience store but us, and I stood there, stunned, facing the man behind the counter. He was young and clean-shaven, with long brown hair, and he looked a little like Tim.

"You," he said finally. "You're Ignored."

I nodded. For some reason, I thought of Philipe's policy about not taking on anyone who had not yet killed his boss. This guy was still working. He had obviously not taken out his boss.

"My name is Dan," he said.

"Hi," I said warily. I had been planning to steal some Twinkies and cookies and potato chips, but I thought now that I would pay for them. I didn't want to get this guy into trouble. He was one of us.

"Are you from Thompson?"

Thompson? I shook my head, not understanding.

"Are you going there?"

"Excuse me?"

"Thompson."

I stared at him blankly.

His eyes widened in surprise. "You don't know about Thompson?"

"No." I looked out the window, saw James replacing the nozzle on the gas pump. I had no idea what the hell this guy was talking about. The thought occurred to me that he was out of it, like Paul when we'd found him.

"I'm from Thompson."

That meant nothing to me.

"Thompson is *our* city."

"Our city?"

He nodded. "Our city."

I stared at him, suddenly realizing what he was talking about. I cleared my throat. "You mean . . . a city of people like us?"

"Of course. It's the city of the Ignored."

The city of the Ignored.

I had sudden visions of a vast underground world, a honeycomb of caverns and tunnels that housed a massive secret society. I thought of the buried city under Seattle. I'd seen it as a child on an old *Night Stalker* TV movie, and something about that entombed metropolis, coexisting with the urban world above, appealed to me. For some reason, that was how I imagined the city of the Ignored.

The city of the Ignored.

A city where everyone was exactly like us.

The very thought of it made my blood pump faster.

Dan nodded, grinning. "I was born there. I left a few years ago, figured I'd bum around the country, get some life experience. I'm a writer. Writers need lots of life experience."

"But . . . but this city . . . Thompson?"

"Yeah."

"It's filled only with people who are Ignored?"

"Yeah." He shook his head. "Shocked the hell out of me when I saw you walk through that door. You're the first Ignored I've seen in the past three years. I thought all of them lived in Thompson."

"There's more of us in the van. And there's even more in Desert Palms. The mayor's Ignored."

"No shit?"

"No shit."

"Whoa."

"Listen," I said, "would you like to take us there, to Thompson? We'll give you a lift. All you have to do is give us directions."

"No way, José. I'm staying right where I am. Do you know how many weirdos come through those doors on the night shift?" He shook his head. "I'm telling you, between midnight and dawn, it's a freak show." He pointed to a ringed binder sitting next to the cash register. "And I'm getting it all down."

I nodded, forced myself to smile. I felt sorry for the guy. Didn't he realize what it meant to be Ignored? No matter how great his book was—and it wouldn't be great, it would be average—no one was going to read it. No matter what he did, no one was going to pay any attention to him.

"Well, could you tell me how to get there?" I asked.

"It's a suburb of Phoenix. It's near Glendale, just west of Phoenix."

"Can you draw a map or something?"

"It's not on a real map, and I couldn't draw one to save my life. Besides, I don't think the road to it has a name. But don't worry, you'll find it."

James walked into the mini-mart, followed by Jim and Mary.

"Is there a ladies' room here?" Mary asked.

Dan pointed toward the rear of the store. "Through that door by the fountain."

Mary stared. "You heard me!"

The clerk laughed. "We're all Ignored on this bus."

"There's a city," I said. "A city of the Ignored. He's from there. It's called Thompson, and it's just outside of Phoenix."

The others were silent.

"Still want to go home, or do you want to try for it?"

"Let's go back," James said. "Tell the others."

"Yeah," Mary said. "Philipe should know about this."

I considered it for a moment, then nodded reluctantly. "Okay," I said. "We'll tell them. But I'm still going on my own. Once we tell them, I'm out of there. I'm serious. I'm not a terrorist anymore."

"We're with you," James said.

"This is going in my book," Dan said. "This is good stuff." He had opened his binder and was busily scribbling notes.

"I'm going to the bathroom," Mary said, walking toward the rear of the mini-mart.

"Get Don," I told James. "He might as well hear this, too."

"This is great," Dan said, grinning. "This is great."

* * *

Philipe was back to his normal self by the time we returned to the house, as charming and charismatic and persuasive as ever, but I stuck to my guns, and after we'd spelled everything out and given directions on how to get to the Arco station, we were off.

I turned toward Joe before we left. "You still staying?" I asked.

He nodded. "Thompson might be your city, but Desert Palms is my city. This is my home."

"Are you going to carry on the work we started?"

He smiled, nodded. "Ego trip over. I'm working for The Cause."

I clapped a hand on his back. "You're a good man, Joe. I knew it the first time I saw your photo in that newspaper. Whatever happens from here on out, I'm glad we met you. I'm glad I knew you. And I'll never forget you."

"Shit. I'm not dying. I'm just staying."

I smiled. "I know."

It was after midnight by this time, and I was too tired to drive, so I turned the wheel over to Jim. Mary promised to keep him awake, and I moved into the back of the van with the others.

I had never gone to see my parents' graves.

I had not thought about that before, and it occurred to me for the first time as we were traveling on the highway past Indio, heading toward the Arizona border. After all the trouble I'd gone through to find out where my mom and dad were buried, I had not even made the effort to go the cemetery and see where they were interred.

Now it was too late.

I felt bad about that, or part of me did, but I reasoned that even if there was an afterlife, the spirits of my parents had probably forgotten all about me and had not even noticed that I'd never gone to visit their graves.

We would probably be as ignored by the dead as we were by the living.

Would we be ignored by God?

That was a question, and I almost brought it up, almost said it aloud, but Philipe was not here, and he was the only one who would have given it any serious thought, so I said nothing.

I glanced out the back window of the van. How would we find Thompson once we got to Phoenix? If the city was not on any map, if it really was as invisible to the world at large as we ourselves were, how could we hope to find it? Sympathetic vibrations?

I half wished that we had waited for Philipe and the others.

I stared out at the dark desert. Thompson was a suburb of Phoenix, that much we knew. But was it on one of the main roads, was it off one of the highways on a small dirt road? If the same streets that cut through Phoenix passed through this city, how could people not notice it? Surely ordinary drivers stopped there for gas or cold drinks or cigarettes. Surely cars sometimes broke down within the city limits. If there were streets in the city, money had to be provided for their maintenance by the federal and state governments. The real world could not completely bypass an entire city, no matter who its residents were.

Now I was getting off on tangents, bringing in things that did not really have anything to do with anything.

I closed my eyes, intending to rest them for a few moments.

I was awakened at dawn.

"We're there," James said.

PART THREE

Nowhere Land

ONE

We were parked on the side of an otherwise deserted two-lane road. Behind us were warehouses and railroad tracks, vacant lots filled with cacti and growing weeds and the detritus of old construction crews. Before us, shimmering in the clear sunlight of dawn, looking like the Emerald City to our tired desperate eyes, was Thompson.

I blinked, pulled apart my sticking eyelashes. "Are you sure that's it?" I asked. "Are you sure that's Thompson?" I knew the answer, but I had to ask anyway.

James nodded. "Check it out." He pointed out the side window of the van at a green sign I had not noticed before.

THOMPSON, the sign said. 5 MILES.

"We're home," Mary said, and there was awe in her voice.

"What are we waiting for?" I asked. "Let's move out."

Jim put the car into gear, and we drove toward the shining vision before us.

I would have expected us to be wildly excited, enthusiastically talking nonstop, but instead we were quiet as we drove down the deserted road. It was like we were in the last act of a movie, when the heroes, having accomplished their goal, are heading home and will soon part to go their separate ways. The feeling in the van was like that. There was an air of sadness and melancholy, and though none of us knew why, we were all rather subdued. We should have been happy to finally find the city, but I suppose we all realized, at least subconsciously, that this meant that our current lifestyle was coming to an end, and that depressed us.

I stared through the front windshield as we drew closer. I was glad to finally find a society in which I would fit, in which I would belong. And I would not miss a lot of the morally questionable things we'd done with the terrorists. But I would miss the closeness, the camaraderie. For despite what we would say to each other, despite what we would promise ourselves and want to believe, that closeness would not be maintained. We would drift apart. It was inevitable. The intensity of our life would be dissipated as we were assimilated into the day-to-day life of Thompson. We would meet, for the first time in our lives, hundreds, perhaps thousands of others like ourselves, and we'd find new people we liked better than the old. We'd make new friends, and our old friends would gradually move to the periphery of our lives.

Another sign came up on the right, a city limits sign. Over it, we saw as we drove closer, someone had placed a poster: the white background and blue bar code of generic plain-wrap products. In place of the name THOMPSON was CITY, written in block computer letters.

At least someone here had a sense of humor.

"Is this going to be heaven or hell?" James asked quietly.

None of us answered.

We drove past two gas stations and a minimall and found ourselves in downtown Thompson.

The view from afar had been deceiving. Up close, this was without a doubt the most depressing city I had ever seen. It was not shabby, squalid, or run-down, it was not gaudy or in bad taste, it was just . . . average. Completely and totally average in every way. The houses were not alike, though they possessed the blocky sameness of suburbs everywhere. Attempts had obviously been made to decorate each house individually, but the sight was just pathetic. It was as though, knowing they were Ignored, each homeowner had tried desperately to be different. One house was painted shocking pink, another red, white, and blue. Still another was festooned with Christmas lights and Halloween decorations. But sadly, though the houses were different from one another, they were all equally nondescript, all equally forgettable.

And I knew that if I could tell, everyone else could, too.

That was really depressing.

Downtown looked neither tastefully planned nor eclectically jumbled but somehow put together in the most bland and inoffensive way possible. It had no character whatsoever.

We drove up and down the streets of the city. It was still early, and we saw very few people. A couple of cars were at a gas station, their owners tanking up, and here and there people were walking or driving to work, but for the most part the streets were empty.

We drove past a park, a public swimming pool, and there, in front of a square two-story building identified by a freestanding sign as THOMPSON CITY HALL, we saw a middle-aged man standing on the curb, waving us over. He was tall and somewhat heavyset, with a thick walrus mustache, and was smoking a pipe. "Here!" he called, pointing to the marked parking spot directly in front of him. "Park here!"

Jim looked at me, I shrugged, and he pulled into the space. We opened up the van doors and got out, stretching, our bodies cramped and tired after spending so much time in the vehicle. I walked up to the man, not sure of what to say.

He took the pipe out of his mouth, smiled at me. "You must be Bob," he said.

I nodded.

"Dan called. Told me you'd be coming. I'm Ralph Johnson, mayor here." He held out a thick hand, which

I shook. "I'm also the welcoming committee and the adjustment coordinator, which means that it's my responsibility to show you around, answer your questions, find you a place to live, and find you jobs if you intend to live here."

"Questions, huh?" Don shook his head. "We have a lot of those."

"Everyone always does." He looked us over, each of us, nodding to himself as he did so and puffing on his pipe. "Dan said he was very impressed with you guys. And gal," he added, nodding toward Mary. "He must have been. That's the first time he's called home since he left."

"Really?" I said, surprised.

"I guess it was because you were all together. As you've probably noticed, people who are Ignored don't tend to travel in packs. They don't organize. But you guys . . ." He shook his head. "You guys are really something."

"Philipe," I said. "That would be Philipe." I wanted to give credit where credit was due. "He's the one who started the terrorists, got us all together."

"The terrorists?"

"Terrorists for the Common Man. It was Philipe's idea. He thought we'd been Ignored long enough. He thought we should act as terrorists on behalf of all the people who were Ignored, who couldn't or wouldn't stand up for themselves."

Ralph shook his head admiringly. "This Philipe must be quite a man. Where is he now?"

"He'll be coming in the next day or so, with another group of us." James looked over at me questioningly. I knew he was wondering if he should bring up what had happened. I shook my head.

"I'll be looking forward to it," Ralph said. "In the meantime, I guess we should start on your orientation. Why don't you begin by telling me your names and where you're from. Introduce yourselves."

We gave our names and hometowns, brief bios.

The mayor took his pipe from his mouth when we were through, looked at us thoughtfully. "I don't know quite how to put this," he said. "There's no way to say it except to just say it. Have you all, uh,—"

"Killed our bosses?" I asked.

He smiled, nodded, relieved. "Yes."

"Yeah," I told him. "We have."

"Then welcome to Thompson." He started walking slowly up the cement path toward the blocky building. "We'll get you signed in and signed up and then we'll be all ready to go."

The mayor's office, on the first floor of city hall, looked disconcertingly like a larger version of my office at Automated Interface. There was only one window—a small glass square overlooking the side parking lot. The rest of the room was blank, the walls bare, the desk covered with bureaucratic papers, no trace of personalization anywhere. We were given forms to fill out, generic questionnaires that looked like job applications but were supposedly "residency declarations."

After a few minutes, Jim looked up from his form. "You guys have stores here, homes, a city hall. How come this place isn't on any map?"

"Because this is not a real town. Not technically. It's owned by Thompson Industries. They test-market their products here. If we don't like them, then they figure the average American won't like them. We get all the free products we want: food, clothes, electronic equipment, household appliances. We get it all."

I felt a sudden hollowness in my gut. "You mean this city wasn't founded by the Ignored for the Ignored?"

"Hell, no."

"It's not a real Ignored city then."

"Sure it is. To a certain extent. I mean, we're left alone here, we're completely autonomous. It's just that—"

"Just that Thompson owns the land and the

buildings, and you work for the company instead of yourselves." James put down his pen.

Ralph laughed heartily. "It's not as bad as all that. I admit, the concept may take some getting used to, but after a while, you don't even think about it. For all intents and purposes, this is *our* city."

A thought occurred to me. "If you're a subsidiary of Thompson here, if the corporation bankrolls you and supports you, that means you're not Ignored. Thompson notices you. Thompson knows you exist."

That seemed important to me somehow.

He shrugged. "Not really. The statisticians record the number of units of each product we consume, report the figures to their superiors, who forward them to the company's analysts, who report their findings to their superiors, who relay the information to their superiors, until the data finally reaches someone who can make a decision. No one really knows who we are. The big cheeses at the company probably don't even know this town exists."

We were silent.

"We used to be owned solely by Thompson," the mayor continued. "Well, we still are, but we're not *used* solely by Thompson. Other companies pay Thompson for our use. Kind of an interbusiness partnership. A whole host of corporations now provide us with their products. So we get everything free. We get free cable TV, all the movie channels, because they want to know what people want to watch. All of our food is free because they want to find out what people eat. Our stores are stocked with the latest fashions because they want to know what clothes people will buy. The Gallup people have a permanent office here. The random polls you hear about? They're all conducted here, in Thompson."

"*Everything's* free?" Don said.

"Everything. You can take whatever you need. We like to joke that we have the only communist system that actually works. Of course, it's bankrolled by money-grubbing, multi-billion-dollar capitalist corporations."

"Does the government know about this place?"

Ralph sucked on his pipe. He leaned back in his chair. "I don't think they do. You know, I've thought about that long and hard, and I don't believe they're aware of our existence. Otherwise, we probably would've been studied to death. Some military use probably would've been found for us in the Cold War days. No, I think we're one of those corporate secrets that private enterprise keeps under wraps."

"The reason Don asked," I said, "is because men have been after us. Official government-looking guys."

The mayor's face clouded over. "National Research Associates. They're hired by a consortium of companies who're in with Thompson."

"Why?"

"They don't want any of us outside the city, don't want us infiltrating the general population. Figure it'll throw off their outside polls. Right now, see, they run parallel polls, question us, question the general population. We're a big expense. Other companies have to pay through the nose for our services. Some of them don't like it. They keep trying to trip us up, prove we're out of sync."

"And they'd kill us for that?"

He shrugged. "What are we to them? Nothing. Who would notice if we were gone? Who would care?" He smiled slightly. "Thing is, we screw 'em up every time. Either they can't find us or they forget about us. We're almost impossible to catch. Even people specifically looking for us don't notice us."

"They caught one of our guys," I said. "Killed him. In Familyland."

Ralph looked grave. "I'm sorry," he said. "I didn't know that." He was silent for a moment, then he looked up at the clock above his office door. "Look, it's getting late. It's almost nine. Places are starting to open. Finish those forms, and I'll take you around. We've got a lot to go over today."

We finished filling out the questionnaires, handed them back to him. He placed them in a folder on his desk, and stood. "Let's take a walk."

I had not noticed it before, but Thompson was modeled after all those Hollywood movie small towns. The park and the city hall/police station/fire station complex were at the center, the hub of the wheel, and everything spread out from that. The surrounding blocks contained businesses—grocery stores, offices, gas stations, department stores, auto dealerships, banks, movie theaters—and beyond that were homes and schools.

We walked through the business district, Ralph acting as tour guide. Nearly all of the stores were chains—Sears, Target, Montgomery Ward, Von's, Safeway, Radio Shack, Circuit City—and even those that weren't had display windows filled with brand-name items. I felt comfortable walking here. I was aware, intellectually, of the city's complete and utter mediocrity, but I could not help but enjoy a pleasurably gratifying feeling of familiarity as I walked with the others down the sidewalk. It was as though the city and everything in it had been designed specifically with me in mind.

No, I told myself. My wants and needs and desires were not that common. I was not that generic.

But I was.

"Is everyone here Ignored?" I asked Ralph. "Aren't there normal wives or husbands of Ignored people?"

"There were. Still are, sometimes. But if those marriages don't break up, the couples leave." He smiled. "Love really is blind. Turns out we're not Ignored to those who love us. Somehow, though, on a practical level, on a day-to-day basis, those kinds of mixed relationships seem to work better in the normal world than our world. And before you ask, yes, all of our children are Ignored. It is passed on. By those of us who can *have* children. A lot of us seem to be sterile."

"Has anyone made any attempt to find out what we are? Why we're like this?"

"Sort of. I mean, we're always being asked to fill out questionnaires and take telephone polls. And once a year we're all required to take a physical exam that's totally unlike any physical I've ever had. But, no, probably not to the extent you mean. The corporations don't care about us as people; they only care that we do what they want us to do. We do—and I think that's good enough for them. They don't want to look a gift horse in the mouth."

"How long has this place been here?" Mary asked.

"The town was founded in 1963, although it was called Oates then and was owned by Oates Manufacturing. Thompson Industries took it over in 1979, changed the name."

"But has the city always corresponded with the mood of the country?"

"Of course. Why else would it exist? In the late sixties we even had riots here. You should've seen it. Young people said they were tired of being Ignored and wanted recognition. I don't think, at that time, they fully realized what we were. They thought it was imposed on us or something, like we were a legitimate minority and were being oppressed by the system. There were protests at the Oates headquarters, and when that went nowhere there were riots here." He stopped walking, looked around to make sure we were alone, lowered his voice. "Oates sent in troops to quell the unrest. Private troops. A hundred and ten people were shot and killed. No one ever saw it on the news— no one would've remembered it if they *had* seen it— but the troops came in and stood in formation and started taking out citizens. Didn't matter who they were or what they were doing. The troops didn't care. They just opened fire." Again, he looked around to make sure we were alone. "Keep that under your hat, though. That's not something that's talked about around here."

I nodded.

"We gained more autonomy after that, but that was because we'd been cowed into submission. We knew we were expendable. The company could exterminate us all and no one would notice. No one would care." He shook his head. "Then times changed and we changed with them. We said no to Salty Surfers and yes to nacho-flavored Doritos." He shrugged. "And here we are."

We continued walking, no one saying anything for a while. We came to a Mrs. Fields cookie counter, sandwiched in a hole in the wall between Standard Brands Paints and Standard Shoes. Ralph stopped walking. "Oh, you have to try one of these cookies. They're the best in the world."

We stood in front of the window, looking in at tray after tray of fresh cookies. I could smell the scent of baking, a full, sugary, chocolaty delicious odor.

The counter was not yet open, but Ralph rapped loudly on the glass, and an elderly woman in a red-and-white uniform slid the window aside, peeking out. "Yes?"

"We have some new recruits here, Glenda. Think you could spare a few?"

The woman looked at us, smiled hello, then turned back to the mayor. "Sure," she said. "For them. *You* have to wait until regular business hours."

"Oh, Glenda—"

"Don't 'Oh, Glenda' me. You know very well that the only reason you wanted them to try my cookies is because you wanted one, too."

"I can't help it. I love your—"

"Oh, here. Take one and shut up."

She handed Ralph an oversized cookie, passed others out to us as we stepped up to the window.

I bit into the cookie. I wanted to hate it, to prove to myself, if no one else, that I was not typical, not ordinary, not average, not exactly the same as Ralph in my likes and dislikes. But I loved the cookie. The taste was wonderful, a blend of chocolate and peanut butter that was like a concoction out of my dreams. The taste was so perfect that it seemed as though it had been created especially for me.

That was frightening.

Especially since I knew everyone else in town felt exactly the same way.

We stood there eating, making stupid small talk about how good the cookies were, and I looked around me. I'd thought Thompson would be a real town, a real community, not a corporate testing ground, and part of me wished I were back in Desert Palms. Part of me wished I were back in my apartment in Brea.

Part of me loved it here.

We continued walking, ending up back at city hall around lunchtime. Other people were in the building now—secretaries, clerks—and Ralph grabbed the file folder from his desk and took it and us upstairs, handing the folder to a woman standing behind a counter marked HOUSING AND COMMUNITY DEVELOPMENT.

"Denise, here, will assist you in finding housing," Ralph said. "She'll assign someone to take you around until you find a place that's suitable. I assume you'll all need furnished places?"

We nodded.

"No problem." He turned toward me. "I'd like you to come with me, if you don't mind. I'll help you find a place to live."

I nodded. "All right." I turned toward the others. "See you guys later."

"Later," James said.

"Bye." Mary smiled at me. "I think we're all going to be very happy here." Her hand found Jim's and held it.

"I hope so," I said.

I nodded good-bye to Don and followed Ralph back downstairs.

In the lobby, the mayor turned to face me. "I like you," he said. "I trust you. I have a good feeling about you. That's why I want you to tell me about this Philipe."

"What about him?" I wasn't sure what he was after.

"Something's been bothering me all morning. I couldn't figure out what it was. I mean, he's supposed to be your leader, he's this brilliant guy, and he's coming in sometime in the next few days, and you guys act like he doesn't exist. Did you have some type of falling out?"

"Yeah," I admitted.

"Is there . . . something wrong with Philipe? Something I should know before he gets here?"

I hesitated. "I don't know what you mean," I said.

"How can I put this? Certain people who are Ignored are . . . shall we say, disturbed. Something happened to them. Some short circuit in their brain. I've seen it before. We had one guy here who was a pyromaniac. Seemed like a perfectly normal guy, but he felt compelled to burn houses because he said giant spiders lived in them. There was another guy who thought he was communicating with an alien race that expected him to repopulate the world by impregnating dogs. We caught him mounting an Irish Setter. These people are few and far between, but they cause us a lot of problems."

I tried to keep my voice light, noncommittal. "What makes you think Philipe's like that?"

"I don't know. Something about the way you guys seem all hush-hush about him. I might add that those other men were also very charismatic men. Leaders. One was a popular high school teacher. The other was my predecessor, the former mayor."

"Which one was he?"

"The alien dog-fucker."

"Philipe's not like that," I said.

He looked at me for a moment, studying my face,

then nodded, satisfied. He clapped a hand on my back. "Okay, then. Let's get you settled."

I followed Ralph outside. Why hadn't I told him about Philipe? About seeing him kill those two girls? About his "hunches" and his mood swings and his spells? Was it because I was more loyal to Philipe than to my conscience? Or was it because . . .

Was it because somewhere down in my superstitious heart of hearts I believed that Philipe was right, that if he had not killed those girls something would have happened to one of us?

No. That was stupid.

But Philipe's "hunches" had always been right, hadn't they?

Ralph was walking across the parking lot, toward a white city vehicle. "We have plenty of jobs for you if you want them," he was saying. "Recessions never affect us here."

I nodded, pretended as though I'd been listening.

"Take a few days off if you need to. Get adjusted. Then come and see me if you want to work."

We got into the car, and he started talking about the furnished condo that was going to be mine. He broke off in midsentence as we turned onto a street festooned with banners.

"What's all this?" I asked.

"The Andy Warhol Day parade. It's coming up this weekend."

I noticed that the banners hanging from the streetlights and telephone poles were celebrity portraits, the Warhol photo-paintings of Marilyn Monroe and Jane Fonda and James Dean and Elizabeth Taylor.

"Andy Warhol?" I said.

"It's one of our most important holidays."

"Important?"

"To be famous for fifteen minutes," Ralph said. "To be *noticed* for fifteen minutes. That's what we pray for. That's all we ask."

I was about to say something else, something

sarcastic, but I stopped myself. What was I doing? Why was I putting down these people for desiring recognition, these people who had never in their lives been noticed by anyone? We had had our day in the sun. We had had our fifteen minutes of fame. Even if the Terrorists for the Common Man had never been recognized, our deeds were taken note of. We had the newspaper clippings and the videotaped newscasts to prove it. I recalled my own rage, my own desperation before I teamed up with Philipe, and I could not find it in my heart to condemn these pathetic souls for wanting the same thing I had wanted, the same thing all of us had wanted.

I found myself looking up at a giant poster of Warhol hanging from a temporary grandstand set up on the side of the street. "Hasn't anyone Ignored ever been famous?" I asked.

"In 1970, we had a rock group from here that had a top ten hit. The Peppertree Conspiracy. 'Sunshine World.' "

"I have that record!" I said. "I loved it! It was the first record my parents ever bought for me!"

He smiled sadly. "We all have it. We all loved it. Everybody loved it for a week. Now I don't think you could find anyone who isn't Ignored who has a copy. There may be a few forty-fives buried in boxes in garages here and there, but most of the records that were bought were probably tossed or given to the Goodwill or Salvation Army. I bet you couldn't find anyone who even remembers the song now."

"What happened to the group?"

"Teddy Howard's our minister."

"What about the rest of them?"

"Roger died of a drug overdose in 1973; Paul's our local morning shock jock on the radio." He paused. "And I was the drummer."

"Wow." I was impressed, really impressed, and I looked at him with renewed respect. I remembered sitting on my bed when I was little, two pencils in my hands, pretending to drum with the record, imagining myself on stage in front of thousands of screaming girls. I wanted to tell him this, but the funny/sad/ nostalgic look on the mayor's face told me that that might best be left for another time.

He turned down another street. "Come on," he said. "It's getting late. Let's go see your condo."

TWO

I found a job in the planning department of city hall, processing building permit applications. It was a boring job, but I was boring and I was surrounded by other boring people, so I guess, theoretically, I should have enjoyed it.

I did not.

That surprised me. My likes and dislikes, moods and rhythms had always been so perfectly in sync with those of Philipe and the other terrorists that I'd automatically assumed that life in Thompson would be relaxed and fun, that I'd be happy.

That was not the case.

It was not the fault of my coworkers, who welcomed me with open arms and even invited me out for happy hour at a Mexican restaurant at the end of my first day of work. It was my fault. Maybe I'd been expecting too much, had had my hopes up too high, but I was disappointed. The magic simply wasn't there. I guess I'd thought that once I came to Thompson everything would be perfect, everything would fall into place—but it hadn't happened. I was surrounded by a city of people exactly like myself, and I felt as alone and out of it as I always had.

My condo was nice, I had to admit. Ralph had set me up in a furnished two-bedroom split-level in a community called The Lakes, and I was next to a winding man-made waterway bordered by a fifteen-foot greenbelt. I had no complaints there. But somehow having so much room completely to myself seemed awkward, strange, and a little unsettling after spending so much time living in such close proximity to the other terrorists.

The other terrorists.

As I'd feared, as I'd known, we saw very little of each other after that first week. I invited James and Don and Jim and Mary to see my condo, and I went over to visit their new homes, but, intentionally or unintentionally, we were placed far away from each other, at opposite ends of the city, and none of us found jobs in the same area.

I had the feeling that this was planned, that it was done on purpose, but I could think of no reason why that would be the case. We were here among our own people. Why would we be purposely separated? It didn't make any sense.

After all that time with the terrorists, I was probably just paranoid.

Whatever the reason, though, it was inconvenient for us to see each other.

And we started spending more time with our new coworkers and less time with each other.

I heard, third-hand, that Philipe and the others had arrived a few days after we ourselves had and, like us, had settled into the Thompson lifestyle, but I saw none of them and did not make any effort to look them up.

The Thompson lifestyle *was* different. As Ralph had said, everything was free. As far as I could tell, no money ever exchanged hands within the city. I saw no coins or dollar bills. If I wanted something, I simply walked into a store and took it. A shelf inventory was later taken, I suppose, and the results forwarded to the corporation.

Taking things from shelves was not new to me, but being seen was. I was used to walking through stores unnoticed, and it took me a while to get reacquainted with the fact that people could see me. I felt self-conscious in the midst of so much visibility, and it was several weeks before I felt at ease in public.

In addition to movies, videotapes, and cable TV, there was a museum in Thompson, filled with the most mundane art imaginable. There were also pop concerts each Friday in the convention center. And community theater productions of *The Fantastiks* and *Annie*.

I loved it all.

Everyone did.

But something was wrong. I was provided with everything I needed, surrounded by all the things that should have made me happy. Yet something was missing. I knew what that something was, but I didn't want to admit it, didn't want to think about it.

There was a rumor in Thompson that there *was* a real town somewhere in Iowa, a city founded *by* Ignored people *for* Ignored people, and I told myself that if I could find that place I would be happy.

I told myself that.

And every so often I could almost make myself believe it.

THREE

It was the first Sunday in June. June 5, to be exact. During the past month, I'd invited James over for a barbecue and he'd canceled, and he'd invited me to meet him for drinks one Friday and I'd canceled, so I figured it was my turn again, and I went to Von's to pick up some steaks. I thought I'd ask again if James wanted to come over for grill and grog. If not, I planned to ask Susan, this girl from the office who seemed to be showing a little interest in me.

I was pushing my cart through the supermarket, heading toward the meat counter at the rear of the store. I'd just dropped three boxes of Rice-A-Roni into the basket and I turned the corner at the end of the aisle.

And there she was.

Jane.

My first reaction was to hide, to duck quickly back down my aisle, pulling the cart with me, like a hermit crab retreating into its shell. My heart was pounding crazily, and I couldn't seem to catch my breath. I was thrown totally off balance. I had imagined variations of this scenario hundreds of times in my dreams, in my fantasies, and I should have known what to do, how to react, but the sight was such a shock that I was at a complete loss, and I stood there, at the head of the aisle, holding too tightly to my shopping cart, staring. I'd thought I'd forgotten the way she looked, the specifics of her face. I'd thought time and memory had blurred her into the generic. But I had not forgotten, not deep down, not where it counts, and it was painful to look upon her. That face, those eyes, those lips, they brought back a rush of memory. All the time we'd spent together returned in a flood of sensory overload. The good times, the bad times, everything.

She was wearing tight new jeans and a T-shirt, her hair was pulled into a ponytail, and she looked achingly beautiful to me. I was suddenly conscious of the fact that I was wearing the same ratty clothes I'd worn while washing the car this morning. She started to turn her head in my direction, and without thinking I backed behind a display stack of Tide boxes. My heart was thumping, my hands shaking. I was afraid. Afraid she still didn't want to see me, afraid she would hate me, afraid she would be indifferent.

Afraid she was changed.

That was the big fear, that she was not the same Jane I had known. It had been nearly three years since we'd last seen each other, and a lifetime of experience had occurred during that period. We were different people than we had been, both of us, and maybe we weren't compatible anymore.

Maybe she had met someone else.

That was the other big fear, the one I didn't want to acknowledge.

I peeked around the boxes, inched my cart forward. Part of me wanted to run away and leave her to memory, convinced that meeting again would only shatter my long-held illusions. Nothing could possibly ever be as it was before.

But part of me wanted to talk to her, touch her, be with her again.

I watched her sort through packages of chicken breasts. I hadn't thought I'd remembered her this clearly, but I had. I remembered everything about her: the way she blinked her eyes, the way she picked up meat, the way she pursed her lips. It was all there, in my mind and in the flesh, and at that moment I realized how much I truly loved her.

As if responding to some signal or vibration, she suddenly looked up, looked in my direction.

And saw me.

We both stood there dumbly, staring at each other, unmoving. I watched her put the package of chicken breasts she'd been holding into her cart. Her hands were shaking as badly as mine were. She licked her lips, hesitantly opened her mouth as if to say something, closed it.

"Hi," she finally said.

That voice. I hadn't heard it in three years, but I remembered it perfectly and it was like music to me. There was a lump in my throat. My eyes were suddenly moist, and I wiped them with my fingers so the moisture wouldn't turn to tears.

"Hi," I said.

And then I was crying, and she was crying, and she was holding me, hugging me, kissing my wet cheeks.

"I missed you so much," she said through her sobs. "I missed you so much."

I held her tightly. "I missed you, too."

After several moments, I pulled back, grasped her by the shoulders, and for the first time looked at her closely. She truly was prettier than ever. Whatever she had gone through during the past few years, whatever had happened to her, it had left her even more radiantly beautiful than ever.

I realized that I had not really thought of her as beautiful before, when we'd been living together. I'd been attracted to her, of course, but I had not seen in her this exquisite objective loveliness. She was beautiful now, though.

She was also Ignored.

That had not really sunk in yet. I knew it, recognized it, but somehow it didn't quite register.

It also didn't matter at this moment.

I looked closely at her face, at her mouth, at her lips. I looked into her eyes. I didn't know what to say, didn't know how to bring up what I was thinking, what

I was feeling. What were we now? Just friends? Old close friends who had met again after a long absence? Or was she feeling the same thing I was feeling? Did she want to jump back into a relationship, take up where we'd left off? There was so much to go over, so much to talk about. Yet as close as we were at that moment, as close as I felt to her, there was still a barrier between us. We'd been apart for a long time, almost as long as we'd been together, and we couldn't read each other the way we once could.

Then I looked into her eyes, and I knew how to cut through it all. I said what I wanted to say, what I felt: "I love you."

And she answered the way I wanted her to, the way I hoped she would: "I love you, too."

And all that uncertainty was gone. We knew where we stood now. We knew what the other one was feeling, what the other one was thinking.

The words flowed freely from us then, bubbling out and over each other, colliding, overlapping, weaving an interconnected tapestry of two unconnected stories. She said she'd regretted walking out but had been too stubborn to come back and apologize. I told her I'd been willing to crawl but had been too afraid to approach her. I told her I quit Automated Interface, and I told her about meeting Philipe and the Terrorists for the Common Man, but I left out my murder of Stewart and the acts the terrorists had later performed. She told me she'd discovered on her own that she was Ignored, and while working as a waitress had met another woman who was Ignored, an older woman, and had come with her here to Thompson.

Both of us expressed our amazement that we had found each other again. And here of all places.

"We were meant to be together," Jane said, and there was only a hint of playfulness in her voice.

"Maybe we were," I said.

We got our groceries and went to her house, a one-story tract home near Main Street. I was surprised to see a lot of her old furniture, the furniture she'd taken from our apartment, arranged in the spacious living room. She'd obviously felt no need to prove anything to anybody. There'd been no attempt to make the room look unique or outrageous; there were only the furnishings she liked arranged in the way she liked them. I felt comfortable here, instantly at ease, and though I now recognized intellectually the anonymous homogeneity of Jane's taste, it still pleased me. It felt right.

How could I not have noticed that she was Ignored?

Why hadn't I figured it out before this?

Stupidity, I guess.

She made dinner—baked chicken and Rice-A-Roni—and it was just like the old days. I lay on our couch and watched TV while she worked in the kitchen, and we ate in the living room while *Jeopardy!* was on, and it was like we were married and had never been apart. The rhythms were there, our habits and speech patterns and little personal traits all unchanged, and we kept the conversation current, superficial, and I could not remember when I'd ever been this happy.

After dinner, I helped with the dishes. I grew quiet as Jane scrubbed the last of the silverware, and she must have noticed because she looked up. "What is it?"

"What?"

"Why are you so quiet?"

I looked at her, nervously licked my dry lips. "Are we going to—"

"—make love?" she finished for me.

"—have sex?" I said.

We both laughed.

She looked up at me, and her lips looked red and full and infinitely sensuous. "Yes," she told me. She put her soapy hands on my cheeks and stood on her tiptoes and kissed me.

We needed no foreplay that night. By the time our clothes were off, I was hard and she was wet, and I got on top of her and she spread her legs and guided me in.

I fell asleep afterward, a blissful sleep, free of

dreams, and sometime in the middle of the night she woke me up and we did it again.

I called in sick the next morning, talking to Marge Lang, the personnel assistant, and I could almost hear her smile over the phone as she spoke. "We figured you'd be calling in today."

Big Brother was watching me.

I kept my voice nonchalant. "Really?"

"It's okay. You haven't seen each other for a long time."

Such intimate knowledge of my movements and motives and private life should have offended me, but somehow it did not, and I found myself smiling into the phone. "Thank you, Marge," I said. "See you tomorrow."

"Bye."

I glanced through the sheer curtains of the living room and saw outside the bright blue Arizona sky, and I knew that nothing could ruin this day.

I crawled back into bed, where Jane was waiting.

FOUR

I moved into her house the next weekend.

I took only the clothes and personal belongings I'd brought with me to Thompson. Everything else stayed with the condo for the next inhabitant.

Unpacking my box on the floor of the living room, I came across the pair of Jane's panties I'd taken with me when I'd left the apartment. I presented them to her, and she turned them over in her hands. "I can't believe you kept these," she said. She grinned. "What did you do? Sniff them?"

"No," I admitted. "I just . . . carried them with me. I just kept them."

"To remind you of me?"

I nodded. "To remind me of you."

"Wait here a minute." She went into the bedroom, was gone a few moments, and returned with an old T-shirt of mine, a promotional José Cuervo T-shirt I'd gotten free at UC Brea and that I used to wear while washing my car. "I stole it," she said. "I wanted something to remember you by."

"I didn't even notice it was gone."

"You wouldn't." She sat down next to me, put her head on my shoulder. "I never stopped thinking about you."

Then why did you leave me? I wanted to ask.

But I said nothing, only bent down, lifted her chin, kissed her.

I was happy, truly, and honestly happy. What Jane and I had together was average, I suppose—how could it be otherwise?—the same feeling millions of people across America, across the world, had every day—but to me, it felt wonderful and unique, and I was filled with a deep contentment.

We got along better now than we had before. The wall that had existed between us prior to our separation was gone. We communicated intimately and openly—without the miscommunications, misinterpretations, and misunderstandings that had once marred our relationship.

Our sex life was more active than it had ever been. Morning, night, and on weekends, noon, we made love. Some of the old fears and anxieties, however, had not gone away, and even as I enjoyed the pleasures of our newly energized love life, I found myself wondering if Jane was really as blindly and uncritically satisfied as I myself was. One Sunday morning, as I lay on the couch reading the newspaper, Jane pulled open my robe and gave my penis a squeeze and a quick kiss. I put down the paper, looked at her, decided to voice what I was thinking. "Is it big enough for you?" I said.

She looked up at me. "That again?"

"That again."

She shook her head, smiled, but there was no sign of the old impatience or annoyance on her features. "It's perfect," she said. "It's like *Goldilocks and the Three Bears*. You know, one bowl of porridge was too hot, one was too cold, and one was just right? Well, some are too big, some are too small—and yours is just right."

I put down the paper, pulled her up and on top of me. We did it there on the couch.

I wondered sometimes about the other aspects of Jane's life, her friends, her family, everything else she had left behind when she'd come to Thompson. I asked her once, out of curiosity, "How's your mom?"

She shrugged.

"How's your dad?"

"I don't know."

I was surprised. "You don't keep in contact with them?"

She shook her head and looked away, far away, into the distance. She blinked her eyes rapidly, held them open wide, and I could tell she was about to cry. "They ignore me. They can't see me anymore. I'm invisible to them."

"But you were always so close."

"*Were.* I don't think they even remember who I am."

And she did cry. I put my arms around her, held her close, held her tight. "Of course they do," I said. But I was not so sure. I wanted to know what had happened, how they had drifted apart, what it had been like, but I sensed that this was not the time to ask, and I kept quiet and held her and let her sob.

FIVE

The days flowed into weeks, the weeks into months. Spring drifted past, became summer, became fall. A year went by. Each day was like another, and though the routine was established and unchanging, I didn't mind. Truth to tell, I liked it. We worked and played and shopped and slept, made friends, made love. Lived. I rose in the hierarchy of city hall according to the Peter Principle, and Jane became a supervisor at the day care center where she worked. At night, we stayed home and watched TV. Television shows I liked were moved to different time slots, then canceled, but it didn't really matter because others took their places and I liked them, too.

Time passed.

I had a good life. It was boring and mundane, but I was content with it.

That was the weirdest thing about Thompson. The weirdest and most horrifying thing. Intellectually, I could see how pathetic everything was, how desperately ineffectual were the attempts at distinction and originality: the sad efforts to dress and behave outrageously, the endeavors to be different that only ended up drab and gray. I could see the strings; I could see the man behind the curtain. But emotionally, I loved the place. The city was perfect. I had never been happier, and I fit right in.

This was my kind of town.

The range of occupational skills here was staggering. We had not only accountants and office workers—

the most prevalent occupations—but scientists and garbagemen and lawyers and plumbers and dentists and teachers and carpenters. People who were either unable to distinguish themselves at their work or who lacked the ability to hype themselves in their jobs. Many were more than competent—bright men, intelligent women—they had simply been outclassed in their chosen fields.

At first, I'd thought it was our jobs that made us faceless, then I'd thought it was our personalities, then I'd wondered if it had something to do with our genetic makeup. Now I had no idea. We were not all bureaucrats—though a disproportionate number of us were—nor were we all possessed of the same bland character. Here in Thompson I found that, once again, citizens were separating into gradations of visibility.

I wondered if perhaps there were people who would fade into the background here as well, if there were the ignored of the Ignored.

That idea frightened me.

Did I miss the old days? Did I miss the Terrorists for the Common Man? Did I miss the adventures, the camaraderie—

—*the rapes, the murders?*

I can't say that I did. I thought about it now and then, but it seemed so long ago that it was as though it had happened to someone else. Already those days seemed like ancient history, and when my thoughts turned in that direction I felt like an old man looking back on his rebellious youth.

I wondered what Jane would think if she knew about what I'd done with Mary, if she knew about the woman I'd almost raped.

If she knew I'd killed a man.

Men.

I never asked about her missing years, about what she'd done between the time she dumped me and the time I found her again.

I didn't want to know.

Exactly a year and a month from the day we had met again in the supermarket, Jane and I were married in a short civil ceremony at city hall. James was there, and Don, and Jim and Mary, and Ralph, and Jane's friends from work and my friends from work. Afterward we had a reception at the community center in the park.

I had invited only the terrorists who had come with me to Thompson in the van, but as we danced and partied, I felt guilty that I had not sent invitations to Philipe and the others. Somehow, despite all that had happened, I still felt closer to them than I did to many of the people here, and in spite of our rift, I found myself wishing that they were here to share this moment with me. They were my family, or the closest thing to it, and I regretted not sending them invitations.

It was too late now, though. There was nothing I could do about it.

I pushed the thought out of my mind, poured Jane some more champagne, and the celebration continued.

We spent our honeymoon in Scottsdale, staying for a week at the resorts. I used my old terrorist tricks to get us poolside suites at La Posada and Mountain Shadows and the Camelback Inn.

That first night, our wedding night, I snagged the keys to La Posada's honeymoon suite, and I opened the door to our room, then picked up Jane and carried her across the threshhold. She was laughing, and I was laughing, and I struggled not to drop her, finally throwing her, screaming, onto the bed. Her dress flipped up over her head, exposing her white panties and gartered legs, and though we were both still laughing, I became immediately aroused. We'd been planning to wait, have a long bath, a sensuous massage, work our way up to the lovemaking, but I wanted to take her now, and I asked her if she was really sure that she wanted to slowly build up to it.

In answer, she grinned, pulled down her panties, spread her legs, opened her arms for me.

Afterward, lying there, I rubbed my hand between

her legs, feeling our mingled wet stickiness. "Don't you think we should do something different?" I asked. "Don't you think we should try some new positions?"

"Why?"

"Because we always do it in the missionary position."

"So what? You like it that way, don't you? I do. It's my favorite. Why should we force ourselves to meet other people's expectations? Why should we conform to other people's ideas about sex?"

"We *are* conforming," I told her. "We're average."

"It's not average to me," she said. "It's great."

She was right, I realized. It was great for me, too. Why *did* we have to vary our lovemaking just because other people did, just because other people said we were supposed to?

We didn't.

We spent the week swimming in the resort pools, eating at Scottsdale's most expensive restaurants, and having the kind of ordinary, straight, traditional sex we loved so well.

We returned to Thompson tanned and happy, our minds rested and our crotches sore. But something had changed. The city was the same, the people were the same, it was just that . . . I was not. I had been back in the real world, and I found that I missed that world. Instead of returning home after a vacation, it felt to me as though we were returning to prison after a weeklong furlough.

I went back to work and Jane went back to work, and after a few days we became reacclimatized, readjusted. Only . . .

Only that sense of being stifled did not entirely go away. I felt it, in the back of everything, a presence even in my happiest moments, and it made me uneasy. I thought about discussing it with Jane, thought I *should* discuss it with Jane—I didn't want our old communication problems to start again—but she seemed so happy, so blissfully unaware of this malaise that I was feeling, that I was reluctant to drag her into this.

Maybe it was just me. Postnuptial depression or something. It wasn't fair to burden her with my paranoid craziness.

I forced myself to push aside all feelings of dissatisfaction. What was wrong with me? I'd gotten everything I'd wanted. I was with Jane again. And we were living in a city, a society where we were not ignored but noticed, where we were not oppressed minorities but members of the ruling class.

Life was good, I told myself.

And I made myself believe it.

SIX

City hall and the police department had separate personnel departments but shared databases, and I was reading the joint lists of new hirees that was sent monthly to each division when I came across Steve's name. He had been hired as a police recruit, and an asterisk by his name indicated that he had previous law enforcement experience and was on an accelerated promotional track.

Steve? Previous law enforcement experience?

He'd been a file clerk.

When he was with the terrorists, he'd been a rapist.

But it was not my place to bring this up, not my job to question the hiring practices of the police department, and I said nothing. Maybe Steve had changed. Maybe he'd mellowed out, turned over a new leaf.

I posted the list on our bulletin board.

Although I worked at city hall and lived in Thompson and was therefore personally affected by the actions of the city council, I had little or no interest in local politics. Council meetings were held on the first Monday of each month and were televised live on our local community access cable station, but I neither went to them nor watched them.

Ordinarily.

But on the last day of August, Ralph suggested to me that I might want to catch September's meeting.

We were eating lunch at KFC, and I tossed the bones of my drumstick into the box, wiping my hands on a napkin. "Why?" I asked.

He looked at me. "Your old friend Philipe is going to come before the council with a request." ·

Philipe.

I had not heard from him or seen him since coming to Thompson over a year ago. I had half wondered if he had left, gone back to Palm Springs, gone across the country to recruit new terrorists. It wasn't like him to be so quiet, to maintain such a low profile. He liked power, liked being the center of attention. He craved the spotlight, and I could not see him settling down into anonymity. Not even here in Thompson.

I tried to appear disinterested. "Really?"

The mayor nodded. "I think you'll find it interesting. You might even want to come down, attend the proceedings."

"I don't think so," I said.

But I was curious as to what was going on, what Philipe was up to, and one night I turned the TV to the Thompson channel.

The camera was stationary, and was trained directly on the mayor and the council at the front of the chambers. I could not see anybody in the audience, and I watched for a half hour, waiting through discussions of old business and protocol, before the mayor tabled the discussion and moved on to new business.

"The first item on the agenda," he said, "is a request by Philipe Anderson."

Susan Lee, our only female council member, adjusted her glasses. "Request for what?"

"We'll let the requestor explain that himself. Mr. Anderson?"

I recognized him even from the back as he passed before the camera and took his place in front of the podium. He stood straight and tall and confident, his charisma obvious against the blandness of the laid back mayor and lackluster council, and I saw what had attracted the terrorists to him in the first place. I saw—

—*Philipe, covered with blood, hacking at the two unmoving children.*

"That's Philipe?" Jane asked.

I nodded.

"He's more average-looking than I imagined."

"He's Ignored. What did you expect?"

On TV, Philipe cleared his throat. "Mayor. Ladies and gentlemen of the council. The proposal I wish to make is one that will benefit all of Thompson and is in the best interests of not just the community but of all Ignored everywhere. I have here a detailed list of requirements that I will pass out to each of you. It provides an item-by-item accounting of all proposed requisitions, and you can look at it at your leisure and we can discuss it more fully at the next meeting."

He looked down at the paper on the podium in front of him. "The broad outline of my plan is this: Thompson needs its own military, its own militia. We are, for all intents and purposes, a nation unto ourselves. We have a police force to take care of disturbances within our borders, but I believe that we need an armed force to protect our sovereignty and our interests."

Two of the council members were whispering to each other. I could hear excited discussion from the audience.

Jane looked at me, shook her head. "Militarization of the city?" she said. "I don't like it."

"Let's settle down here," the mayor said. He faced Philipe. "What makes you think we need a militia? This sounds like a major expense: uniforms, weapons, training. We have never been threatened; we have never been attacked. I don't see any real justification for this."

Philipe chuckled. "Expense? It's all free. Thompson picks up the tab. All we have to do is request it."

"But it is the responsibility of this council to determine whether such requests are reasonable or unreasonable."

"And this is a reasonable request. You say we've never been attacked, but Oates sent troops in here in 1970 and killed a hundred and ten people."

"That was in 1970."

"It could happen again." He paused. "Besides, in my proposal I suggest that our militia have offensive as well as defensive capabilities."

The mayor frowned. "Offensive?"

"We, the Ignored, have been abused and exploited for our entire history. We have been at the mercy of the noticed, the powerful. And we have been unable to fight back. Well, I suggest that it is time to fight back. It is time to retaliate for all the injustices that have been perpetrated upon us.

"I am offering to train a crack fighting force of our best and most capable men and mount a frontal assault on the White House."

The room broke out in shouts and arguments. Philipe stood there grinning. This was his milieu. This was what he loved, what he lived for, and I could see the happiness on his face. Against my better judgment, I felt happy for him, too.

The mayor, by this time, had lost all control of the meeting. Members of the audience were cheering Philipe, arguing among themselves, yelling at individual council people.

"They've had it their way for far too long!" Philipe shouted. "We can attack, and they'll never see us. Not until it's too late! We'll be in control of the White House! We'll stage the first successful coup in U.S. history! The country will be ours!"

I could see the way this was going. Even if the mayor and the council turned Philipe down, the public was behind him. If Ralph and the rest of them wanted to keep their jobs, they'd have to go along with his proposals.

I turned off the TV.

Jane placed her head on my shoulder, held my hand. "What do you think's going to happen?" she asked.

I shrugged. "I don't know," I said. "I don't know."

For the next several months, the Thompson channel was the preferred source of news for everyone in the city. It must have really thrown off the Nielson ratings.

Our local cable newscaster, Glen Johnstone, provided nightly updates on the training and equipment procurement of the militia. Because of our unique status in relation to America's top industries, all Philipe and his followers had to do was fill out special order forms for the guns and vehicles they wanted and wait for them to arrive. Someone, somewhere, keeping tabs on orders, probably noted an increase in the demand for military supplies, and someone somewhere probably ordered production increased. New jobs were probably created.

I wondered, at first, why there was no crackdown, why no one from Thompson or National Research Associates or one of the other corporations put a stop to this, why no one from the FBI or the ATF conducted an investigation. On television, Philipe made clear his intent, refusing to tone down his rhetoric. "We will bring down the power elite!" he declared. "We will establish a new government in this country!" I realized, though, that our broadcasts were probably as ignored as everything else about us. The reason no one put a stop to Philipe was because no one knew what he had planned—even though he came right out and stated it over the airwaves.

I thought, for the first time, that his plan might actually work.

Two hundred men initially signed up for the military. There turned out to be an unexpectedly high number of former army, air force, and marine officers in Thompson, and these men were recruited by Philipe to train the initiates. Philipe took fifty of the recruits himself and trained them as terrorists. These were to be the advance guard, the ones who would infiltrate the White House and pave the way for the others.

Two tanks were shipped to Thompson on the back of a semi truck.

Army jeeps arrived at the Jeep dealer.

Crates of automatic weapons were delivered.

Finally, after what seemed like forever, Philipe announced in a prime-time meeting/rally in the city council chambers that the militia was ready to start on its mission to Washington, D.C.

I had never seen such war fever, and it made me more than a little uneasy. Jane felt the same way. So did most of our friends. So did James, Don, Ralph, Mary, and Jim.

But the city was ready for this fight, ready to take on the known world, and there was a big parade on Saturday to see our army off. Flags and banners were waving; confetti was thrown; the high school marching band played. I stood on the sidewalk with Jane, waiting for Philipe. What he had done had not been erased from my mind—

swinging the knife, "My name is not David! It's Philipe!"

—but it had been superceded by his unwavering dedication the past few months, by his obvious commitment to what he perceived to be the betterment of Thompson and the plight of the Ignored. I differed with Jane here. She saw this as grandstanding; I saw it as an extension of the terrorists, proof of Philipe's belief in his cause.

The militia came marching down the street, in step, and I had to admit they looked good, looked professional. Foot soldiers were preceded by jeeps and trucks and the buses that would later carry them across country. Finally, at the tail end of the parade, riding in an open tank, waving to the adults, throwing candy to the kids, was Philipe.

I moved forward until I was standing on the curb. This was the Philipe I had first met. This was the Philipe who had led us. Standing tall and proud as the convoy rolled through the center of town, he glanced from one side of the street to the other. As I'd expected, as I'd half hoped, he saw me, caught my eye. He gave me a slight smile, then saluted. I nodded back. I felt a lump in my throat, shivers on my arms as I watched them pull away. If this was a movie, I thought, there would be stirring music and a sunset in the background. This was dramatic stuff. This was heroic.

The parade continued to the edge of the city limits. The bands and the marchers fell by the wayside. And the militia continued on.

They hit the White House Thursday night.

The Thompson channel had sent correspondents and cameramen along with the soldiers to cover the event, and on Thursday evening every TV in the city was turned to the station.

We saw our tanks and jeeps rolling down the capital's streets, framed dramatically in front of familiar landmarks, and though I still did not support the war effort, I could not help feeling a surge of pride and something close to patriotism as I realized that our men were successfully invading Washington, D.C.

But while our people were Ignored, invisibility did not extend to their equipment, and we should have known that such a blatant full-frontal assault would not go unnoticed. Our military vehicles stood out in the civilian traffic like Godzilla at a tea party, and as they turned a street corner, heading toward the White House, they were halted by a blockaded street and a cadre of U.S. soldiers.

The tanks and jeeps braked, rolled back a few feet, stopped. A standoff. No one shouted, no one spoke; the two sides might have been communicating by radio, but there were no bullhorns and the street was silent. The minutes dragged on. Four. Five. Ten. There was no sound, no movement, and the correspondent covering the event got on camera, admitted that he didn't know what was happening but would let us know as soon as he did.

The coverage shifted to the White House, where another reporter was following Philipe's advance force. They had successfully hopped the fence and were dashing across the White House lawn, crouching black shapes against the moonlit grass.

Suddenly, the station switched back to the street, where U.S. troops were now firing on our men.

Our reporter was screaming incoherently, trying to explain what was happening but doing a poor job of it.

We could see what was happening ourselves, though.

Our militia was being routed.

Even with all of their weapons, even with the training, our forces were barely adequate, and going up against the best soldiers in the world, they didn't stand a chance.

Our tanks fired once each, hitting nothing, then blew up.

The men in the jeeps, now spread out across the street, fired at the U.S. soldiers and their vehicles, but did not seem able to hit anyone or anything. They began dropping like flies, picked off and taken down by military sharpshooters, and then they abandoned their weapons and turned tail and ran.

The reporter and his cameraman beat feet as well.

The screen was black for several seconds.

Then we were back at the White House where Secret Service agents—the only humans as bland and faceless as ourselves—were chasing Philipe and his advance men back across the lawn. Security lights were on, trained on the area in front of the building, and the Thompson correspondent explained even as he retreated to the park across the street that one of Philipe's men had set off an alarm, alerting the President's security forces to their presence.

One of our men was shot trying to climb the fence and escape.

Please, God, I thought, don't let it be Philipe.

Then I saw Philipe running. I recognized his gait, his build, the movement of his arms. He leaped, grabbed the bars of the fence, swung himself over. There was the sound of gunfire, but if it was aimed at Philipe it missed him, and he was running across the street, toward the camera.

Again the screen went blank.

"We've lost our feed," Glen Johnstone, anchoring in Thompson, announced.

I quickly switched channels, expecting to see special bulletins on the network stations, thinking that of course they'd break into regular programming for an assault on the White House, an obvious attempt on the President's life, but there were only the usual sitcoms and police shows.

I turned to CNN, watched for an hour. Nothing. I waited until the eleven o'clock news that night, flipped back and forth between ABC, CBS, and NBC.

The attack made the ABC news. Thirty-second footage right before a commercial: a shot of the White House from a vantage point across the street, Philipe and a handful of men running away, being chased by other men in suits. The anchor allotted them one line: "In other news today, the Secret Service repelled a small group of individuals attempting to break into the White House grounds."

Then they cut to a douche ad.

I sat there next to Jane in silence, staring at the commercial. That was it? After all that preparation, after all the training, that was it? Over two hundred men had left Thompson on Saturday, a trained militia, with tanks and trucks and jeeps, in order to stage a coup.

And all they rated was one line on one newscast.

I turned off the television, crawled into bed. I realized, perhaps for the first time, how truly pathetic we were. Philipe had organized a fighting force, had come up with a workable plan, and it had all been for nothing.

Less than nothing.

I wondered how many members of our militia had been killed. I wondered if they had been jailed.

Philipe returned to Thompson a week later, chastened and humiliated, surrounded by the tattered remnants of his army.

The government had not even considered them enough of a threat to jail. No charges had been pressed.

A hundred and fifty-three were dead.

We were more than willing to treat Philipe as a hero, but in his own mind he was a failure, his grand schemes laughable, and from that point on, he shunned the public eye and retreated into obscurity.

Glen Johnstone attempted to do a follow-up show, to interview Philipe about what had happened, but for the first time in his life, Philipe turned down free publicity.

I never saw him on television again.

SEVEN

The new year came. And went. Jane and I decided that we wanted a child, and she threw away her pills and we tried for it. No luck. She wanted to consult a doctor, but I said no, let's just keep trying. I had a feeling it was my fault, but I didn't want to know for sure.

When I'd graduated from college, when I'd first gotten the job at Automated Interface, it seemed like I had just been starting out, like I had my whole life ahead of me. Now time was speeding by. Soon I'd be thirty. Then forty. Then old. Then dead. The cliché was right: life *was* short.

And what was I doing with my life? What was the point of it? Would the world be any different for my having lived? Or was the point that there was no point, that we existed now and one day we wouldn't and we might as well try to have fun while we were here?

I didn't know, and I realized I would probably never know.

James came over after work one day, and Jane invited him to stay for dinner. Afterward, James and I retired to the back porch and reminisced about the old days. I reminded him of the first time I'd gone out with the terrorists, to the courthouse, and we both started laughing.

"I'll never forget the judge's face when you said, 'Get a dick!' "

I was laughing so hard I was crying, and I wiped the tears from my eyes. "Remember Buster? He just kept yelling, 'Pussy!' "

We continued to laugh, but there was a sadness in it now, and I thought of Buster. I remembered the way he'd looked, there in Old Town in Familyland, when the suits had shot him down.

We grew quiet and stared up at the stars. It was an Arizona night sky, all of the major constellations visible against the clouded backdrop of the Milky Way.

"Are you guys awake?" Jane called from the kitchen. "It's so quiet out there."

"Just thinking," I said.

James leaned back in his chair. "Are you happy here?" he asked.

I shrugged.

"I've heard there's a land somewhere," he said. "A country of Ignored."

I snorted. "Atlantis or Mu?"

"I'm serious." His voice grew wistful. "We could be free there. Really free. Not just slaves for Thompson. Sometimes I feel like we're pets now, like trained animals, just doing what we've been told to do, over and over again."

I was silent. I knew what he was feeling.

"I heard it was a town," I said. "In Iowa."

"I heard it was a country. Somewhere in the Pacific, between Hawaii and Australia."

Inside, I heard the rattle of dishes.

"I'm thinking of leaving," James said. "There's nothing for me here. I feel like I'm just putting in time. I'm thinking of looking for that other country." He paused. "I was wondering if maybe you wanted to come along with me."

Part of me wanted to. Part of me missed the excitement and adventure of being on the road. Part of me also felt stifled here in Thompson. But Jane loved it here. And I loved Jane. And I would never again do anything to jeopardize our relationship.

And part of me loved it here, too.

I tried to turn it into a joke. "You just haven't found any poon here," I said.

James nodded solemnly. "That's part of it."

I shook my head slowly. "I can't go," I said. "This is where I live now. This is my home."

He nodded, as if this was the answer he'd been expecting.

"Have you asked any of the other terrorists?"

"No. But I will."

"You like it here, though, don't you?" I looked at him. "I know what you think of this place. But you still like it here, don't you?"

"Yeah," he admitted.

"What the fuck are we? We're like robots. Push the right buttons and you'll get the response you want."

"We're Ignored."

I looked up at the sky. "But what does that mean? What is that? Even being Ignored isn't consistent. It's not an absolute. There was a guy at the place I worked, a friend of mine, who could see me, who noticed me when no one else did. And what about Joe?"

"Magic has no laws," James said. "Science has laws. You keep trying to think of this in scientific terms. It's not genetics; it's not physics; it doesn't conform to any set of rules. It just is. Alchemists tried to codify magic and they came up with science, but magic just exists. There's no rational reason for it, no cause and effect."

I shook my head. "Magic."

"I've done a lot of reading on the subject. It's the only thing that makes sense to me."

"Magic?"

"Maybe that's the wrong word." He leaned forward, the front legs of his chair coming down on the porch. "All I know is that whatever makes us this way cannot be measured or quantified or explained. It's not physics, it's metaphysics."

"Maybe we're crystals that have been astral-projected into human form."

He stood, laughed. "Maybe." He looked at his watch. "Look, it's getting late; I gotta go. I have to work tomorrow."

"Me, too. For no pay."

"It's a weird world."

We walked through the house, he said good-bye to Jane, and I accompanied him out the front door to his car. "Are you really leaving?" I asked.

"I don't know. Probably."

"Let me know when you decide."

"Of course."

I watched him pull away, watched his taillights disappear around the corner. I was not tired, and I didn't feel like staying inside and watching TV. Neither did Jane, and when she finished washing the dishes, we went for a walk. We ended up in my old neighborhood, standing on a small dock to which was anchored a child's sailboat.

We looked out over the small man-made lake that wound between the condos. Jane put an arm around me, leaned against my shoulder. "Remember when we used to go out to the pier at Newport?"

"And eat at Ruby's?"

"Cheeseburger and onion rings," she said, smiling. "That sounds good right now."

"Clam chowder at the Crab Cooker sounds better."

We were silent for a moment.

"I guess we'll never live in Laguna Beach," she said quietly.

A mosquito buzzed by my head, and I slapped at it. The condos across the water looked cheap to me all of a sudden, the lake pathetic. I thought of the deep darkness of the ocean night, the clusters of lights that marked the beach towns visible from the pier, and I felt unaccountably sad. I felt almost like crying. More than anything else, I wished things were different, wished we were back in our old life in our old apartment and none of this had ever happened.

I wished we weren't Ignored.

I turned, pulled her with me back toward the sidewalk. "Come on," I said. "It's getting late. Let's go home.

EIGHT

The murderer came into the office in the middle of the morning, getting off the elevator and walking calmly over to the front desk.

I caught him out of the corner of my eye, a brightly colored blur, and I glanced up to see a short, heavyset man in a clown suit and mime makeup open the small swinging gate that separated the public waiting area from our work area.

My stomach lurched; my mouth suddenly went dry. Even before I saw the knife in the clown's hands, I knew why he was here. My first thought was that someone had been allowed into Thompson who hadn't yet killed his boss and that that person was going to kill whoever was his boss here. But I didn't recognize the clown, and I knew he didn't work on this floor.

And then I noticed that no one was looking at him.

No one saw him.

All this I thought in the space of a few seconds, the time it took the clown to walk up to Ray Lang's desk. put a hand over Ray's mouth, and draw the knife across his throat.

I lurched to my feet, knocking over my chair, trying to scream but unable to get out any sound at all.

He drew the knife slowly, expertly. The blood did not shoot, did not squirt, but oozed and flowed from the thin opening, spreading down over Ray's white shirt in a continuous wave. Hand still holding Ray's mouth shut, the man quickly shoved his knife first in one of Ray's eyes, then the other. The blade emerged with pieces of white and green goo stuck to the otherwise red steel.

The man wiped the blade off on Ray's hair before taking his hand from the planning inspector's mouth. The noise that issued from Ray's bloody throat was more a gurgle than a scream, but by now he was flailing around wildly enough that he had gotten the attention of everyone in the office.

The clown grinned at me, did a little jig. I looked into his eyes, and I knew that he was insane. Even beneath the clown makeup, I could see the craziness. This was not the temporary insanity of Philipe. This was the real thing. And it scared the shit out of me.

"There he is!" I cried, pointing, finally able to move, to act, to speak. People were running over to where Ray was slipping bloodily out of his chair, but no one heard me, no one paid any attention to me.

And no one saw the murderer.

"You're almost there," the man said, and his voice was a crazed raspy whisper. He laughed, a sound like fingernails grating on a chalkboard. "Oh, the things you'll see. . . ."

And then he was gone. Vanished. Where he had been there was nothing, only clear space.

The air felt heavy, filled with the burnt-rubber smell of drilled teeth.

I looked around wildly, ran to the elevator, waited for it to open, all the while scanning the room. But there was nothing. And when the elevator door did not open, when it was obvious that the murderer had not simply turned invisible and made for the exit but had actually disappeared, I hurried back behind the counter to where Ray lay dying.

Paramedics arrived, performed emergency lifesaving procedures, rushed Ray to the hospital, but he was dead even before he left the floor, and they were unable to revive him.

After Ray's departure, I became the center of attention. The police were there, photographing the chair, taking down statements, and a crowd gathered as I gave my story. The same people who had been ignoring me as I screamed and pointed at the murderer were now all ears as I related what I'd seen, what had happened. I recalled what the clown had said to me: "You're almost there."

What did that mean?

But I knew what that meant.

I was becoming Ignored here in Thompson.

Like he was.

The Ignored of the Ignored.

I remembered as a child going on a ride at Disneyland called Adventures Through Inner Space. On the ride, you were supposed to feel as though you had been shrunk by the Mighty Microscope and were entering the invisible world of the atom. I wondered now if I was in just such an invisible world, a world that most people couldn't see, that existed concurrently with the visible universe.

Maybe the murderer was a ghost.

I wondered about that, too. People throughout the years, throughout the centuries, who claimed to have seen ghosts? Maybe they'd just seen an Ignored Ignored. A man like that would be two steps removed from normal human life. Perhaps there were no ghosts. Perhaps there was no afterlife. Maybe we just ceased to exist when we died. Maybe the whole concept of life after death had originated with a misinterpretation of Ignored sightings.

I wished there was a history of our people, a history of the Ignored.

Ralph got off the elevator and hurried immediately over to where I was talking to the police. "I was at the bank when I heard. What happened?" he demanded.

The cop questioning me gave him a brief overview of what had occurred.

Ralph looked at me. "You're the only one who saw anything?"

"I guess so."

"We need you," the mayor said. "For whatever reason, you can see this guy. You can help us track him."

For whatever reason.

I knew the reason, and I was frightened. It was getting worse. Like some progressive disease. At one time, I had had normal friends, participated in normal society. But I had faded into the ranks of the Ignored. Now I seemed to be fading even more. At the moment, I appeared able to bridge the gap between the regular Ignored and this guy—whoever, *what*ever he was. But would I eventually become like him, invisible to everybody? Would James and Jane and everyone else I knew stop thinking about me, stop noticing me, and one day look around and find that I was not there, that they could no longer see me?

No, I told myself. It didn't work that way. I wouldn't become invisible. I wouldn't *let* myself become invisible.

"He's crazy," I said. "He's insane."

"Don't worry. You won't be in any danger. Someone will always be with you. You don't have to hunt him down, just track him. Like a bloodhound."

"That's not what I'm worried about."

"We'll take him out," the cop said. "He won't kill again."

"That's not what I'm worried about," I said.

"Then what are you worried about?"

I looked away from them, unable or unwilling to share with them my true fears. "I don't know," I lied.

NINE

He struck again, an hour later, killing Teddy Howard in the church and leaving the reverend's slit-open body to flop around on the altar like a gutted fish until unmerciful death arrived.

TEN

The mood of the city changed overnight. Instantly, everyone became tense, nervous, on edge. It was like the Night Stalker days back in Southern California. Thompson had never had serial killings before. There was a crime rate, of course—with rape and domestic violence statistically on a par with the national average. But there had never been anything like this, and when the police composite based on my description was printed in the paper and shown on the Thompson channel, the fear factor jumped up considerably. The clown costume struck a chord in everyone, and the fact that there was an Ignored out there who was ignored even by us, who was trapped in that boss-killing initiation mode, scared everyone. Gun sales shot through the roof. Even Jane started sleeping with a baseball bat next to the bed.

And yet . . .

And yet I could not get as worked up about the killer as everyone else. I had seen him, I knew how dangerously deranged he was, but it was not the fact that he was a murderer that disturbed me.

It was the fact that no one but me had seen him.

You're almost there.

I had been Ignored at Automated Interface, at UC Brea, perhaps for my entire life. I could deal with that. I had accepted the fact that I was different from normal people. But I could not accept the idea that I was different from the other Ignored.

That I was getting worse.

I went to work the next day, and I noticed for the first time that the nods and smiles I had once gotten from my coworkers at city hall were no longer forthcoming. How long had this been going on? Had I been fading away for a while now and just not noticed it?

I tried to think about what I discussed with my coworkers and friends. Was it any more boring than the conversational topics of others? Was I that forgettable even here? Again, my thoughts on being Ignored were swinging back again. Maybe I wasn't average because I was Ignored. Maybe I was Ignored because I was average. Maybe I had brought this on myself. Maybe there was something I could do, some way I could change my behavior or personality, that would reverse the process.

I was temporarily transferred from the planning department to the police department. Here I was not ignored. I was an important detecting device in the eyes of the mayor and the chief, and I was treated as though I were Hercule Poirot.

The only problem was that there was really nothing to go on, nothing that could be done to facilitate the capture of this lunatic. I could only walk around town, followed by two detectives, and see if I could spot him anywhere. For an entire week, I spent my days walking through offices and stores and shopping centers, my eyes peeled for the clown or for someone who looked like he could be the clown. I rode with patrolmen up and down neighborhoods. I looked through books of mug shots.

Nothing.

And I became more and more uneasy. Even while walking, I noticed that I was not noticed, and the feeling was eerily reminiscent of those early days when I'd first discovered that I was Ignored. I thought of Paul and the way we'd found him at Yosemite, naked and crazy and yelling obscenities into crowds of people at the top of his lungs. Was that what had happened to the clown? Had he just snapped under the pressure of such unremitting isolation?

Was that what would happen to me?

You're almost there.

I said nothing of my fears to Jane. I knew that was wrong. I knew I was falling into the same pattern as last time. I should be sharing everything with her. We should be facing all problems together. But for some reason I could not bring myself to confide in her. She would probably be even more frantic than I was. And I didn't want her to go through the hell I was going through.

But at the same time, I did want to talk to her. Desperately.

I didn't know what was the matter with me.

I told her I had witnessed the murder and had been the only one to see the murderer. But I did not tell her why. I did not tell her what had really happened.

The creepiest thing that week was my meeting with Steve. He was a full-fledged lieutenant now, and the chief had put him in charge of coordinating security at city hall. On the off chance that the murderer might strike again at the scene of his original crime, the chief was asking for a maximum ten-second response time to a disturbance anywhere in the building. This way he figured the murderer could be caught in the act.

Steve was asked to implement this policy, and he met with me in order to more accurately determine how quickly the murderer had moved from the elevator to Ray's desk, how distracted he had been by the other people in the office, how quickly he had disappeared after being spotted. He gave me a no-nonsense official phone call on Thursday asking me to meet him in the planning department before lunch, and after spending the morning on neighborhood patrol, I arrived on the second floor at eleven-thirty. Steve was already there.

And he didn't recognize me.

I knew it instantly, although it took a few moments of by-the-book Q&A for the fact to really sink in.

He did not know who I was.

We had spent all that time together as terrorists, as colleagues, friends, brothers, and now he did not even remember me. He thought he was meeting me for the first time, that I was simply a faceless bureaucrat from city hall, and it was unnerving to speak to him, to know him so intimately when he obviously didn't know me at all. I was tempted to tell him, to remind him, to prod his memory, but I did not, and he left without realizing who I was.

There were no more murders, no assaults, no sightings, and gradually the police began to lose interest in me. I was transferred back to city hall, told to keep my eyes open and report anything suspicious, and was promptly forgotten about. In the planning department, my return was not noticed or remarked upon.

I had completed my first week of work since returning when I saw the mayor coming toward me across the first-floor lobby on my way out. I waved to him. "How's the search going?" I asked. "Any leads?"

He said nothing, looked at me, past me, through me, and continued walking.

ELEVEN

When I awoke the next morning, there was a new tree outside our bedroom window.

I stood in front of the window, staring, a clenched, tight feeling in my chest. The tree was not a small sapling or a potted palm that someone had placed in our front yard. It was a full-sized sycamore, taller than our house, growing, deep-rooted, in the center of the lawn.

It had purple leaves.

I didn't know what it was or what it meant, I only knew that it frightened me to the bone. I stood there, unable to take my eyes off the sight, and as I stared I saw the front door of the house open and Jane walk across the lawn to get the newspaper from the front sidewalk.

She walked through the tree, as if it weren't there.

The clenched feeling grew, spreading within me, and I realized that I was holding my breath. I forced myself to breathe. Jane picked up the paper, walked back through the tree and into the house.

Was it an optical illusion? No, the tree was too clear and definite, too *there*, for it to be a mere image.

Was I crazy? Maybe. But I didn't think so.

Oh, the things you'll see. . . .

I quickly pulled on a pair of jeans and hurried outside. The tree was still there, big as life and twice as colorful, and I walked up to it, reached out to touch it.

And my hand passed through the bark.

I felt nothing, no warmness, no coldness, no displacement of air. It was as if the tree weren't there at all. I gathered my courage, walked through it. It looked solid, not transparent or translucent, and while walking through I saw only blackness. Like I really was inside a tree. But I felt nothing.

What the hell was it?

I stood there, staring up at the purple leaves.

"What are you doing?" Jane called from the kitchen.

I looked back at her. She was watching me through the open window with a puzzled expression, as though I was behaving incredibly stupidly, which I suppose to her I was. I walked around the tree, then across the grass to the front door. I went into the kitchen, where she was mixing batter for blueberry muffins.

"What were you doing out there?"

"Looking at something."

"What?"

I shook my head. "Nothing."

She stopped stirring, glanced at me. "You've been behaving strangely ever since that murder. Are you sure you're all right?"

I nodded. "I'm fine."

"You know, a lot of people who witness violent acts, even policemen, go to counseling to work through what they're feeling."

"I'm fine," I said.

"Don't get so worked up. I'm just worried about you."

"I'm fine."

"I—"

"I'm fine."

She looked at me, looked away, went back to mixing the batter.

The tree was still there after breakfast, still there after I took my shower. Jane wanted to go to the store and pick up some groceries for dinner, and I happily volunteered to go for her. She said fine, she had a lot of work to do around the house anyway, and I took the list she gave me and drove off.

I'd been acting as if nothing out of the ordinary had occurred, but I saw other purple trees in the park, red and black bushes growing in the center of Main Street, a silver stream passing through the Montgomery Ward's parking lot, and it was obvious that overnight something really bizarre had happened.

Had happened to me.

No one else in town seemed to see these manifestations.

Jane had asked me to go to the IGA—she liked their produce better than Von's or Safeway—and while inside the supermarket I saw another tree, identical to the one in my yard, growing out of the meat counter, its branches passing through the ceiling.

I stood there staring at the tree as other shoppers passed around me. There was no way I could live with this day in and day out, no way I could pretend to live a normal life while fantasy forests were popping up around me in the midst of my ordinary surroundings.

Was this what had happened to the murderer?

I quickly got what I came for and hurried home. I found Jane mopping the kitchen floor, and I put the sack of groceries on the table and came right out and said it: "Something *is* wrong."

She looked up, not surprised. "I was hoping you'd tell me what it was."

I licked my lips. "I . . . see things," I said. I looked into her eyes, hoping to see a hint of recognition, but there was nothing. "Do you know what I mean?"

She shook her head slowly.

"There. Outside." I pointed through the window. "Do you see that tree? The one with the purple leaves?"

Again she shook her head. "No," she said softly. "I don't."

Did she think I was crazy?

"Come here." I led her into the front yard, stopped at the base of the tree. "You don't see anything there?"

"No."

I took her hand, pulled her through the tree. "Still nothing?"

She shook her head.

I took a deep breath. "I'm fading away," I said.

I told her everything. About the clown, the police, Steve, Ralph, the people at work who no longer saw me. About the trees and bushes and streams I'd seen on my way to the store today. She was silent when I was through, and I saw tears in her eyes.

"I'm not going crazy," I told her.

"I don't think you are."

"Then why—?"

"I don't want to lose you."

I put my arms around her and held her tightly, and she cried into my shoulder. My own eyes were overflowing. Oh, God. Was I going to be separated from her again? Was I destined to be parted from her once more?

I pulled back from her, tilted her chin up until she was looking in my eyes. "Do you still see me?" I asked.

"Yes." Her nose was running, and she wiped it with the back of her hand.

"Am I . . . different at all? Do you think about me less often? Do you forget I live here?"

She shook her head, began to cry again.

I hugged her. That was something. But it was only a temporary respite, I knew. She loved me. I was important to her. No wonder I would linger longer in her consciousness. But eventually, inevitably, I would fade from her sight, too. I would move in and out of focus. Maybe one day I'd be home and she wouldn't know it. I'd be sitting on the couch and she'd pass right by me, calling my name, and I'd answer and she wouldn't hear me.

I'd kill myself if that happened.

She grasped my hand firmly. "We'll find someone," she said. "A doctor. Someone who'll be able to reverse it."

I turned on her. "How?" I demanded. "Don't you

think if there was a way to do that it would've been done already? You think everyone likes living here? You think they all wouldn't want to be normal if they could, if there was a way to do it? Christ!"

"Don't yell at me. I just thought—"

"No, you didn't. You didn't think."

"I didn't mean they could actually reverse the process, but I thought they could slow it, stop it from progressing. I thought—" She burst into tears and ran away from me, across the grass, into the house.

I followed her, caught up to her in the kitchen. "I'm sorry," I said, holding her, kissing the top of her head. "I don't know what got into me. I'm sorry. I didn't mean to get mad at you."

She hugged me back. "I love you," she said.

"I love you, too."

We stood like that for a long time, not moving, saying nothing, just holding tightly to each other as if that embrace could keep me anchored so I wouldn't fade away.

I called James that night. I wanted to talk to him, wanted to tell him what was happening. The more people I brought into this, the more people who knew, the more heads we had working on the problem, the more likely it was that something could be done about it.

He answered on the fourth ring. "Hello?"

"James!" I said. "It's me!"

"Hello?"

"James?"

"Who's there?"

He couldn't hear me.

"James!"

"Hello?" He was becoming annoyed. "Who is this?"

I hung up the phone.

I had not seen Philipe since the day of his departure for the White House assault, had not heard a word about him since his return. But I wanted to talk to him. I needed to talk to him. If anybody could understand what had happened to me, if anybody could do something about it, it was Philipe. He might be psychotic, but he was also the most competent, ambitious, and farsighted person I knew, and though I had a lot of reservations about contacting him again, I had to do it.

I just hoped he could see me.

I tracked him down through city hall's computer. I found him living in a small one-bedroom apartment in the run-down west side of town. Here, amidst the less well tended residences of the city, the attempts to individualize houses, duplexes, and apartments were not as visible, not as obvious, and the entire area seemed especially nondescript. It took three passes for me to even find his apartment building.

Once I did locate where he lived, I parked on the street and sat for a few moments in my car, trying to gather up enough courage to knock on the door. Jane had wanted to come, but I'd vetoed that idea, telling her that Philipe and I had not parted on the best of terms and that it was probably better if I went alone. Now I wished that she had come with me. Or at least that I'd called Philipe ahead of time to let him know that I wanted to see him.

I got out of the car, walked up to apartment 176. I knew if I waited any longer, I would probably talk myself out of doing it, so I just forced myself to go up to his door and ring the bell.

My heart was pounding as the door opened, my mouth suddenly drained of saliva. I took an involuntary step backward.

And there stood Philipe.

My fear disappeared, replaced by a strange, heartrending sense of loss. The Philipe who stood in the doorway before me was not the Philipe I had known, not the boundlessly forward-looking man who had recruited me into the terrorists, not the take-charge leader who had led us through our adventures, not the

crazed delusional psycho of the sandstorm night, not
even the defeated would-be hero who had returned
from Washington, D.C. The Philipe who stood before
me was a pathetically average man. No more, no less.
The seeker and searcher who had once seemed so bold
and charismatic now looked gray and nondescript. The
brightness was gone from his eyes, the spark that had
once animated his features apparently extinguished. He
looked exhausted, and much older than he had the last
time I'd seen him. He was a nobody here in Thompson,
and I could see how that weighed on him.

I tried not to let the shock show on my face. "Hey,
Philipe," I said. "Long time no see."

"David," he said tiredly. "My real name's David. I
just called myself Philipe."

My name is not David! It's Philipe!

"Oh." I nodded, as if agreeing with him, but there
was nothing for me to agree with. We looked at each
other, studied each other. He saw me, I realized. He
noticed me. I was not ignored by him. But that was
small consolation. I wished I had not come.

He remained in the doorway, not inviting me in.
"What do you want?" he asked. "Why are you here?"

I didn't want to just jump right in, but I didn't know
what to say to him. I cleared my throat nervously. "I
got married. Remember me telling you about Jane? I
found her here. She's Ignored, too."

"So?"

I looked at him, took a deep breath. "Something's
happening," I said. "Something's gone wrong. I need
your help."

His eyes held mine for a moment, and it was as if he
was searching within me to see if I was telling the
truth, as though he was somehow testing me. I must
have passed the test, because he nodded slowly. He
moved away from the door, back into the apartment.
"Come on in," he said. "We'll talk."

The inside of his apartment had the same stultifying
old-lady look his house had had, and it felt a little

creepy to walk into the small living room and sit down on the tan flowered couch underneath the cheap oil painting of a mountain lake.

"You want anything to drink?" he asked.

I shook my head, but he went into the kitchen and got two beers anyway, putting one open can in front of me. I thanked him.

I still didn't know what to say, still didn't know how to bring up what I'd come here to talk with him about. "Do you still see any of the terrorists?" I asked.

He shook his head.

"What about Joe? Do you ever hear from him?"

"I think he's crossed over. I don't think he's Ignored anymore."

Not Ignored anymore.

Was that possible? Sure it was. I thought of myself, of my own situation, and I felt chilled.

"It's not a static situation," he said. "You can move one way or the other." He took a long, loud sip of his beer. "We're moving the other way."

I looked sharply over at him.

"Yeah. I know why you're here. I can see what's going on. I know what's happening."

I leaned forward on the couch. "What *is* happening?"

"We're fading away."

The fear I felt was tempered with relief. I felt the same way I had when I'd found out that there were other Ignored: scared, but grateful that I would not have to face the situation alone. Once again, Philipe had come through for me.

"No one sees me anymore," I said.

He smiled wryly. "Tell me about it."

I looked at him, at his pallid complexion, his ordinary clothes, and I started to laugh. He began laughing, too, and all of a sudden it was like the old days, like Mary had never happened, like Familyland had never happened, like Desert Palms had never happened, like we were in my old apartment, hanging out, friends, brothers forever.

The ice was broken between us, and we started talking. He told me about his quick fade into obscurity after the White House fiasco, about the long months of living here, in this apartment all alone. I told him about my life with Jane, and then about the murderer and about my discovery that I was becoming as Ignored here as I had been in the outside world.

I took a swig of beer. "I also . . . see things," I said.

"See things?"

"There," I said, pointing out the window. "I see a meadow with red grass. There's a black tree at the far end that looks kind of like a cactus with leaves and branches."

"I see it," Philipe said.

"You do?"

He nodded sadly. "I wasn't going to say anything. I didn't want to alarm you. I wasn't sure you'd progressed as far as I had."

"What is it?" I asked. "What's happening? Why are we seeing these things?"

He shook his head. "I don't know. I have some theories. But that's all they are. Theories."

I looked at him. "Do you think it's reversible, our condition? Or do you think we'll just keep fading away forever?"

He stared out the window, at the red meadow, at the black cactus tree. "I don't think it's reversible," he said softly. "And I don't think there's anything we can do about it."

TWELVE

The murderer struck again on Thursday.

I don't know why I continued to go to work, but I did. I could have done what I'd done at Automated Interface, just stopped showing up. I could have, and probably should have, spent my remaining time with Jane. But I kept setting that alarm each morning, kept going in to city hall each day.

And on Thursday the murderer returned to the scene of his crime.

He was not wearing a clown suit this time, so I did not recognize him. I was not really working, but was sitting at my desk, staring distractedly at the fluorescent pink rock formation that had grown through the window since yesterday, thinking for the millionth time of what I would do when I became invisible to Jane, when the elevator door opened and he stepped onto the floor.

I took no notice of him until it was almost too late. Out of the corner of my eye, I saw him walk across the lobby toward the front desk, and there was something familiar about the way he moved, but it didn't really register in my brain.

Suddenly the air felt heavy, smelled of drilled teeth.

I stood, instantly on the alert, my mind putting together the guy getting off the elevator, the familiar way he moved, the clown.

He jumped me from behind.

I was grabbed around the neck, and I saw for a brief second a flash of knife metal. Instantly, instinctively, before my conscious mind even realized what I was doing or why I was doing it, I twisted to the side and simultaneously threw myself to the ground, missing the attempted stab and landing on top of the murderer. He hit the ground with a muffled *oomph*, lost his grip around my neck, and I rolled away, climbing to my knees and then my feet, grabbing a pair of scissors from the top of my desk.

He was as crazy as he had been before, and I saw the look of disconnected dementia on his face as he grinned at me, knife held forward. "I know you've been looking for me, fucker. I saw you out there."

I backed slowly around the edge of my desk, putting it between us. I did not like the way he looked. He was bald and middle-aged, with a bulbous, naturally clownish nose, and there was a disturbing shifting quality to the cast of his features that somehow made him seem saner with the makeup on.

"I don't want you here," he said. "You can't come in." He stopped on a low blue bush that was growing up from the floor, and his foot disturbed the leaves, knocking a few of them off.

He could touch these manifestations.

With a sudden flying leap, he flung himself at me, lunging over the desk, knife arm outstretched. He was off balance and missed my stomach by a wide margin, but he was already righting himself and I jumped to the side and slashed at him with the scissors. I hit him across the face, one scissor blade puncturing his cheek. He let out a primal cry of rage and pain that distorted his already distorted features, and I pulled the scissors out and stabbed lower, embedding the twin halves into his chest. I felt the blades hit bone, felt a rush of hot blood spill over my hand, and again I pulled the scissors out, shoved them hard into his stomach.

I backed away.

No longer screaming, making only a low pitiful strangled crying sound, he staggered off the side of the desk and onto the floor. His blood spattered both the city hall tile and the blades of orange grass growing up from it. He was losing a lot of blood, and his skin looked gray and pale, as though he was dying.

I prayed to God that he was.

The entire encounter had passed unnoticed in front of the eyes of my coworkers and the two contractors applying for permits at the counter. Around us, the normal office routine of the planning department continued on as usual.

A secretary carrying blueprints to Xerox stepped into a puddle of blood, did not see it, did not leave footprints.

The murderer looked at me, glassy-eyed. "You . . ." he began, then trailed off. He lurched to his left, past another desk—

—and through the wall.

I blinked. I could see the wall behind the desk, but suddenly I could see a meadow behind the wall, sloping ground leading away from the hill atop which I was standing. I rushed forward, tried to follow him, tried to chase after him, but though I could see the path on which the murderer was running, it was not there for me. I did not go into the meadow. I ran into hard stucco, hitting my head.

I staggered back, staring through the transparent wall as, wounded, bleeding, crying piteously, the murderer limped off, down the sloped meadow, across the orange grass, into the purple trees.

THIRTEEN

The nightmare was over, but no one knew it.

I had single-handedly saved Thompson from what would have probably been an unending string of serial murders.

And Jane was the only one who was aware of it.

I tried telling Ralph, tried telling the police chief, but neither one of them could see me. I even wrote an anonymous letter, sending copies to the mayor, the chief, the paper, anyone I could think of who might be able to get the word out, but no one paid any attention, and the official search for the murderer continued blindly along.

I spent the next week in the bedroom with the shades drawn, coming out only to eat and go to the bathroom. It wasn't the lack of recognition that was bothering me. It was not even the fact that I had killed another man.

It was the intrusion of this . . . other world.

For that was what it was. Another world. I knew that now. More and more often, I saw unfamiliar horizons, alien plant life and geologic formations, color schemes not of this earth. I did not know if they were part of another dimension that shared the same space as our own or if there was some other explanation, all I knew was that this other world was intruding on my space with greater frequency and greater intensity. Even locking myself in the bedroom did no good, because more often than not these days, the rug wasn't the rug but was a carpet of orange grass, the walls weren't solid white but were transparent windows on strange landscapes, the ceiling a skylight through which I could watch brown clouds float across a gold sky.

I could have withdrawn entirely into myself, pulled away from Jane, but I did not. I tried to fight these visions or manifestations or whatever they were, but I did not push Jane away from me as I probably would have done in the past. Instead, I kept her close, told her everything I saw, everything I felt, and it seemed that when I was with her, when we were together, that other world faded a little and I was more fully in Thompson.

I saw the creature on Sunday.

Until now, my glimpses into this alternate universe had been limited to landscapes, to plant life and rocks. I had seen nothing animate, nothing alive. But on Sunday morning I awoke, opened the bedroom drapes, looked outside, and saw the creature. It was staring at me from across an orange meadow. I watched it move sideways across the tall grass. It was like a spider, only it was as big as a horse, and there was in its face, visible even from this distance, a look of sly knowledge that chilled me to the bone. I saw its hairy mouth open, heard a loud sibilant whisper, and I quickly let the drapes drop, stepping back and away from them. I did not know what the creature had said and I did not want to know, but something told me that if I continued staring at it, watching it, I would be able to make out what it was saying.

I crawled back into bed, pulled the covers over my head.

Later that day, I went again to see Philipe. Jane wanted to come, but I told her she couldn't. I said Philipe would be spooked, that he would not want her with us, and though she didn't like that at all, she believed it. It wasn't true—I'm sure Philipe would have loved to meet her—but for some reason I did not want her to meet Philipe, and I did not feel bad lying to her about it.

He opened the door to his apartment before I was halfway up the walk, and I was shocked by the change in him. It had been less than two weeks since I'd seen him last, but in that time he had deteriorated badly. It was nothing specific, nothing I could put my finger on. He wasn't thinner than he had been, he hadn't lost all his hair, he had just . . . faded. Whatever had set Philipe apart from everyone else, whatever had made him unique, an individual, seemed to have gone, and the person standing before me was as bland and unremarkable as a department store mannequin.

Had the same thing happened to me?

Then he spoke, called my name, and some of his old self was back. I recognized the voice, heard in it the intelligence and drive that had once drawn me to him, and I followed him into his apartment. The floor was covered with dirt and beer bottles and uprooted alien plants, and I looked at him. "You can . . . touch those things?" I asked.

He nodded.

I reached for a blue branch lying on his coffee table, and my hand passed through it. I was filled with an overwhelming sense of relief.

"You'll be there soon," he said sadly.

You're almost there.

I nodded. I looked around at the damage, at the destroyed plants and shrubs. I cleared my throat. "Do you still have those, uh . . . ?" I trailed off.

He knew what I was getting at. "Not since that last time. Not since the terrorists broke up."

"You haven't . . . killed anyone?"

He smiled slightly. "Not that I'm aware of."

There was a question that had been bugging me since that night of the sandstorm, since I'd followed him into that house, and I figured that now was the time to ask it. "You were talking to someone," I said. "That night. Answering questions. Who were you talking to?"

"God, I thought."

"You thought?"

"It was the same voice that had named me Philipe. I'd heard it a long time ago. In my dreams. Even before

I knew I was Ignored. It told me to call myself Philipe, told me to put together the terrorists. It told me . . . other things, too."

"Your hunches?"

He nodded. "I thought I saw it once, in one of those dreams, hiding in the shadows in a forest, and even though it scared me, it impressed me." He paused, looked far away. "No, that's not exactly true. It didn't just impress me. It filled me with awe. I know it sounds crazy, but I thought it was God."

"And now?"

"Now? Now I think it was someone—some*thing*— from the other side."

The other side.

I looked through the window at the purple forest across the street, and a chill passed through me.

His voice grew quiet. "I thought I saw it the other day. Outside."

I didn't want to hear what he'd seen or what he thought he'd seen, but I knew he was going to tell me anyway.

"It was hiding in the background, in the trees, and there were a lot of spider things in front of it, spider things the size of camels. But I could see its eyes, its eyebrows, its teeth. I saw hair, fur, and hooves. And it knew me. It recognized me."

The goose bumps were all over my body. I was afraid to even look in the direction of the window.

"I used to think we were God's chosen," Philipe said. "I thought we were closer to God than everyone else because we were so obviously average. I believed in the Golden Mean, and I thought that mediocrity was perfection. This was what God meant man to be. Man had the potential to go farther or fall shorter, but it was this perfection of the median that would bring us into God's graces.

"Now—" he looked out the window. "Now I just think we're more receptive to the vibrations, the messages, the . . . whatever it is that's coming from that place." He turned toward me. "Have you ever read a story called 'The Great God Pan'?"

I shook my head.

"It talks about 'lifting the veil,' about contacting a world that sounds like the one we've been seeing." He walked across the room to an end table piled with library books and picked one out, handing it to me. "Here. Read it."

I looked at the cover. *Great Tales of Terror and the Supernatural.* One of the pages was marked, and I opened it to that spot. " 'The Great God Pan' by Arthur Machen."

"Read it," he said again.

I looked at him. "Now?"

"You have something better to do? It'll only take you a half hour or so. I'll watch TV while you read."

"I can't—"

"Why did you come here today?"

I blinked. "What?"

"Why did you come here?"

"To . . . talk to you."

"About what?"

"About—"

"About what you've seen. You've seen the thing I've described, haven't you?"

I shook my head.

"Then you've seen the spider things."

I looked at him, nodded slowly.

"Read."

I sat down on his couch. I didn't know what bearing he thought a fictional horror story could have on the situation we faced, but I found out almost immediately. Indeed, the situation in the work was eerily similar to what I had experienced with the murderer, uncomfortably close to what Philipe had described. A mad scientist finds a way to breach the gap between this world and "the other world." He sends a woman through, and she returns completely and utterly mad. She has seen the awesome, godlike power of a creature the ancients inadequately referred to as the great god Pan. She has also been impregnated there, and when her daughter grows up, the daughter possesses the ability to pass between the two worlds at will. In this world, our world, the daughter is a murderer, courting men, then letting them see her true face and driving them to suicide. She is finally discovered and killed.

Throughout the story, Philipe had underlined several passages. One in which the daughter is walking through a meadow and suddenly disappears. One noting the strange, heavy feeling left in the air after she passes between the two worlds. One describing the "secret forces," the unspeakable, unnameable, unimaginable forces that lay at the heart of existence and are far too powerful for human comprehension. And the final line of the story, stating that the daughter, the creature, was now permanently in that other world and with her true companions.

It was this last that sent a chill through me. I thought of the murderer, mortally wounded, running toward the safety of the purple trees.

Philipe was looking at me as I closed the book. "Sound familiar?"

"It's a story," I said.

"But it's truer than people think. Truer, maybe, than the author knew. We've seen that world, you and I." He paused. "I have heard the voice of the great god Pan."

I looked at him. I didn't believe him, but I didn't disbelieve him, either.

"What we are," he said, "are transmitters to that world. We can see it; we can hear it; we can carry messages from it. That's our purpose. That's why we're here. That's why we were put on this earth. It even explains the gradations of Ignored. You and I can communicate with the powers there. We can tell it to the other Ignored. They can tell it to the half-and-halfs like Joe. Joe and his kind can tell the rest of the world."

"But the other Ignored don't hear us anymore," I pointed out. "And I thought you said Joe was no longer Ignored."

He waved away my objection.

"Besides, that can't be all we are, transmitters. That wouldn't make us average; that has nothing to do with being ordinary—"

"No one is only one thing. A black man is not just black. He's also a man. A son. Maybe a brother, a husband, a father. He might like rap or rock or classical music. He might be an athlete or a scholar. There are different facets to everyone. No one is so one-dimensional that they can be described by a single word." He paused. "Not even us."

I did not know whether I believed him. I did not know whether I wanted to believe him. It would be nice to think that being Ignored was not the sole attribute of my existence, that it was not the defining feature of my being. But for my purpose in life to be entirely unrelated to that, to have nothing whatsoever to do with my individual talents or collective identity . . . I couldn't buy that. I didn't want to buy it.

Philipe leaned forward. "Maybe this is where the human race is going; maybe this is where it's all been heading. Maybe we're the goal, the ultimate by-products of this Ignored evolution. Maybe one day everyone will be able to pass back and forth between worlds. Maybe we are Helen's companions," he said, pointing to the book.

I thought of the murderer, of his obvious insanity, and though it did remind me of the daughter in the story, I shook my head. "No," I said.

"Why not?"

"We're not evolving into higher beings who can move at will between worlds or dimensions or whatever the hell this is. We're fading out of this world and into that other one. We're being sucked into it. And then we'll be gone. That's the purpose of evolution? For people to be dragged away from their loved ones to live with monster spiders? I don't think so."

"You're looking at it from a short-sighted—"

"No, I'm not." I shook my head. "Besides, I don't care. I don't want to go there. I don't even want to be able to see it. I want to stay right here with Jane. If you spent as much time thinking about how we can stop this process as you've spent thinking about what it is, we could probably survive."

"No, we couldn't," he said.

No, we couldn't.

I stared at Philipe. I had not realized until that moment how much I had been counting on him to get me out of this mess, to save me, and his flat negation of hope was like a stake through my heart. All of a sudden, I saw that his elaborate theories, his weaving of our facts into Machen's fiction, were merely attempts to deal with the certain knowledge that we were not going to be able to come back, that we were doomed. Philipe, I saw, was just as frightened of the unknown as I was.

"What are we going to do about it? I asked.

"Nothing. There's nothing we can do."

"Bullshit!" I slammed my hand down on the coffee table. "We can't just fade away without a fight."

Philipe looked at me. No, David looked at me. Philipe was gone, and in his place was a tired, resigned, and defeated man. "We can," he said. "And we will."

I stood up angrily and walked without speaking out of his apartment. He said something behind me, but I could not hear what it was and I did not care. Tears of anger burned my eyes, and I strode through the purple trees to my car. Philipe could not help me, I knew now. No one could help me. I wanted to believe that a miracle would occur, that something would stop this inevitable progression before it claimed me entirely, but I could not.

I drove away, through Thompson and through that other world.

I did not look back.

FOURTEEN

Magic.

I clung to James's idea, wanting desperately to believe that what afflicted me was not irreversible, was not the inevitable result of a logical progression but could disappear overnight with the wave of a wand or the application of some as yet undiscovered power.

Hadn't Philipe been hinting about that? Magic?

I tried to sustain my belief in the days that followed. But even if it had been the vagaries of magic that had made me this way and not the deliberate building blocks of genetics, the fact remained that I was getting worse. In the mirror, when I looked at myself, I saw someone older-looking than me, someone duller. Around the house, Thompson was disappearing, being taken over by orange grass and silver streams and pink rocks and purple trees and hissing spiders the size of horses.

I began praying to God to make that other world disappear, to make me normal, but He—or She—ignored my pleas.

Were we ignored by God?

The only time I felt all right was when I was with Jane. Even the imposition of that other world faded somewhat in her presence, the inside of the house, at least, remaining free from its influence, and I kept Jane with me as much as possible. I did not know if it was my imagination or if Jane really did protect me from those alien views, but I believed in her, believed that she was my talisman, my amulet, and I took advantage of what she could give me.

We tried to figure out why she might have this power—if it was a power—and what we could do to harness it, amplify it, but neither of us could think of anything, and the only thing we knew to do was stay with each other and hope that would stave everything off.

It didn't, though.

She quit her job to stay home with me. It didn't really matter—everything in Thompson was free, anyway, and she could just go to the store and pick up what we needed when we needed it.

I don't want to make it sound like we just sat around waiting for the end, feeling sorry for ourselves. We didn't. But neither did we pretend that nothing was wrong. We faced the truth—and tried to make the best of things under the circumstances.

We talked a lot.

We made love several times a day.

We'd been living for the most part off our usual junk food staples—hot dogs, hamburgers, tacos, macaroni and cheese—but Jane decided that we might as well take advantage of the time we had left together in an epicurean way as well, and she went to the store to get steaks and lobsters, crabs and caviar. None of these things were to our taste, or at least to my taste, but the idea of living it up at the end definitely appealed to Jane, and I didn't want to rain on her parade.

Time was too short to waste it arguing.

I was sitting in the living room watching a rerun of *Gilligan's Island* when she returned from the store, carrying two huge sacks of food in her arms. I stood to help her. She looked around the room. "Bob?" she said.

My heart lurched in my chest.

She didn't see me.

"I'm here!" I screamed.

She jumped at the sound of my voice, dropping one of the sacks, and I ran over to her. I took the other sack

from her arms, put it down on the floor, and threw my
arms around her, hugging her tightly, squeezing her. I
pressed my face into her hair and let the tears come. "I
thought it was over," I said. "I thought you couldn't
see me anymore."

"I see you. I can see you." She held on to me as hard
as I held on to her, as though I were perched at the edge
of a crumbling cliff and she was trying to keep me
from slipping away. There was fear in her voice, and I
knew that for those first few seconds before I'd
screamed, when she was scanning the living room, she
hadn't been able to see me.

I was going to lose her.

Milk was draining onto the carpet from a split and
overturned carton, but we didn't care. We held on to
each other, not letting go, not saying anything, not
needing to, as the afternoon shadows lengthened on the
orange grass outside.

I was awakened in the middle of the night by a voice
calling my name. It was not a low voice, a hushed
voice, a whispered voice, as those sorts of voices
always are in movies. Rather it was shouted but
muffled by distance, like someone yelling to me from
across a field.

"Bob!"

I sat up in bed. Next to me, Jane was still asleep,
oblivious.

"Bob!"

I pushed off the covers and got out of bed. I pulled
open the drapes and looked outside.

Thompson was gone.

I was staring out at an orange field. At the opposite
end grew a forest of purple trees. Beyond that, in the
haze of distance, were pink mountains. A dark black
sun hung lightlessly in an illuminated gold sky.

"Bob!"

The voice seemed to be coming from within the
trees. I looked in that direction and saw, moving within

the forest, hints of blackness that looked like the spider things. Beyond that, darker and more indistinct, was a larger unmoving object that I somehow knew was alive. This was where the voice was coming from.

How did it know my name?

"Bob!"

"What?" I called back.

"Join us!"

I was not scared, although I knew I should have been. That dark shape in the forest should have terrified the hell out of me. But the voice was warm and comforting, and something about the fact that this had finally happened, that the waiting was over, made me feel relieved.

"Come!" the voice called. "We're waiting for you!"

Before me, the window and wall dissolved. As though in a dream, as though hypnotized, I walked through what had been the wall and felt different breezes blowing my hair, different air in my lungs. Even the temperature felt not the same. It was not hotter or colder, it was just . . . different.

I was in another world.

I was filled with a strange sense of well-being, a lethargic sort of contentment that persisted despite legitimate warnings and concerns that were being brought up intellectually by my mind.

I moved forward.

"No!"

Jane's voice, shrill and desperate, filled with a hopeless, helpless, agonized despair, cut through the warm fuzziness of my feelings, and I snapped my head around to look at her. For a brief fraction of a second, I was standing in the front yard of our house and she was screaming at me through the window, then I was again in the field and she was yelling at me from a wall-less room that looked like it had been plunked down in Oz by a tornado from Kansas.

"Bob!" that other voice called. It was no longer so warm and comforting. In fact, it seemed nearly as threatening as its origin, that huge black shape in the trees, and I tried to walk back toward Jane, toward our bedroom, but my feet would not move in that direction.

"Bob!" Jane screamed.

The scene flickered again. I saw the yard, the house.

"Jane!" I called.

"I see you!" she cried. "I notice you! I love you!"

I don't know what made her yell that, what made her think of that, what led her to believe that those words would do any good, but they elicited a deep rumble of rage from the shape in the trees, and I was suddenly able to move again. I turned and ran toward her, and that other world, that strange world, began to recede, fading slowly from sight until it was entirely gone. I ended up naked, outside, on the grass, pressing my hands and face against the bedroom window as, on the other side of the glass, Jane did the same. I did not know what had just happened or how, but I knew that she had pulled me back from the brink. She had saved me.

I ran around to the kitchen door and waited until Jane unlocked it, and then we were in each others' arms.

"I heard you yell something and then I saw you outside and you were . . . fading!" Jane sobbed. "You were disappearing!"

"Shhh," I said, holding her. "It's all right."

And it was. There was no gold sky, no orange grass, no purple trees. There was only our house and Thompson and the Arizona night sky. If this were a movie, it would have been her love for me that brought me back, that saved me from disappearing into that other world, but somehow I knew that that was not what had done it. It was a part of it, but only a part. It was also the fact that she saw me. That she did not ignore me.

And that she said those words. In that order.

"I see you—I notice you—I love you."

Magic.

"I love you," she said again.

We're not Ignored to those who love us.

I clutched her tightly. "I love you, too," I said. "And I see you. And I notice you. And I will never stop noticing you. Never."

FIFTEEN

I went out the next day and I was invisible. Completely invisible. No one saw me, no one heard me. I was not just ignored. I did not exist.

I'd thought it was over. I'd thought I could go back to work, that my condition had reversed itself, that everything would be back to normal, but as I got out of the car and walked up the steps of city hall, I noticed that no one looked at me. I went inside, walked past the mayor's secretary, and she did not see me. I stood in the doorway of Ralph's office. He looked right through me.

"Ralph!" I said.

No response.

I considered playing with him, fucking with his mind, picking up objects and moving them around the room. But what was the point? I turned around, left. I realized for the first time that even if I had been able to do so, I would not have wanted to go back to work.

I no longer wanted to be here.

I no longer wanted to live in Thompson.

I got into my car, drove back home.

I thought about what I was, about who I was, about what I wanted as I drove. Test-marketing products? Being a human guinea pig? Was there any meaning in that? Was that a legitimate reason for existence? Perhaps. As Ralph had told me once, "Someone's gotta do it."

But that someone was not me.

Maybe living and working in Thompson did give

some of the Ignored a sense of purpose. Maybe products did get made because they went over well in
Thompson, and maybe people were then hired to make
those products, creating jobs, and maybe the people
who bought those products were made happy by them,
and maybe part of the responsibility for that did go to
the Ignored of Thompson.

But that wasn't enough for me.

Thompson was Automated Interface all over again. I
was a nobody here. I was nothing.

And I wanted to be somebody. I wanted to be
something.

I pulled up in front of the house, and I sat there for a
moment. I watched Jane through the front window,
watched her vacuum the living room.

It had all turned to shit. All of it. Everything. The
road I had taken had come to a dead end. The Terrorists for the Common Man had disintegrated in an orgy
of blood, and in a city of my own people I had turned
into what I had tried to escape.

What could I do next? Where was I to go?

What about Jane?

I sat there for a few moments more, then I went
inside and told Jane everything. I had her call her
friends.

None of them could hear her.

We went downtown, walked through the mall. No
one saw us. Either of us. We were invisible. Jane had
pulled me back, but I had pulled her forward, and now
both of us were trapped in this no-man's-land, ignored
by the Ignored.

Jane grew quieter and quieter as it became increasingly obvious what had happened.

"I don't see any of those weird things," she told me
in Nordstrom.

"Neither do I," I said. "Anymore. I think that part of
it's over."

"So we're just stuck here. This way."

I nodded.

She dropped her purse and ripped open her blouse.

"What are you doing?" I said.

She unfastened her bra, kicked off her shoes, unzipped and pulled down her pants.

"Knock it off!" I was starting to get scared.

"Why? No one can see me."

She pulled down her panties.

"Jane!"

She ran up to an older couple, took the man's right hand and put it on her breasts. "Feel my tits!"

The old man looked shocked, pulled away, but though he obviously could feel her, he could not see her, he could not hear her.

"Jane!"

"Eat me! Eat my hot pussy!"

She stood naked in the center of the store, screaming obscenities, but no one looked at her, no one paid any attention at all, and I took a bathrobe from the lingerie department and put it around her shoulders and led her out of the mall and back to the car.

I drove her home.

SIXTEEN

Jane spent the next two days in bed. I was worried at first that she would not snap out of it. I had not expected her to react this way, and it scared me.

But on the third morning she awoke before I did, and by the time I got up she was already making breakfast.

"Temporary insanity," she said sheepishly as I walked into the kitchen.

I sat down at the table, poured myself a glass of orange juice, pretending that nothing out of the ordinary had occurred. "Is that what happened when you first found out you were Ignored?"

"No. Just this time. Delayed stress syndrome, I suppose. I guess I stored it all up."

"But you're okay now?"

"I'm okay."

I looked at her. "So what are we going to do?"

"What do you want to do?"

I realized that there was nothing tying us down, nothing holding us here. We had no responsibilities or obligations anywhere. We were free to do anything we chose. "I don't know," I admitted.

She walked over to the table, frying pan in hand, and slid two eggs onto my plate. "I don't want to stay here," she said. "That's for sure."

"I don't either." I looked at her. "Do you have any idea where you would like to go?"

She smiled shyly. "The beach?"

I nodded, grinned. "The beach it is."

* * *

I called Philipe that afternoon while Jane was packing. I wasn't sure if he was still here or if he had passed over to the other side. I wasn't sure if he would be able to hear me or see me. But he was here, and he could hear me, and he promised to come over immediately. I gave him directions to our house.

He arrived in fifteen minutes, looking even more pale and washed-out than he had the last time, if that was possible. But I could still see him, and Jane could see him, and despite all that had happened, I felt warm and good as I finally introduced my friend and my wife to each other.

Philipe spent the night with us.

During dinner, I explained exactly what had happened, exactly what I had seen, exactly what Jane had done.

He nodded. "So you think it's recognition by others that keeps us anchored here, huh?"

"It's possible."

"Then why am I still here?"

"Because I know you." I took a deep breath. "Because I see you. I notice you. I love you."

He grinned. "Worth a try, huh?"

"Can't hurt."

"What about when you're gone?"

I was silent.

He laughed. "Don't worry. I'm not bucking for an invitation."

"It's not that—" I hastened to explain.

"I know," he said. "I know."

As a matter of fact, I had been thinking of asking him to accompany us. But I'd wanted to talk it over with Jane first.

"Why don't you come with us?" Jane asked. I met her eyes, nodded my thanks.

He shook his head. "This is where I belong. These are my people."

"But—"

"No buts. I think I have enough faith and belief in

myself to fight off any onslaught. No one's going to tell me I don't exist."

I smiled, nodded, but I was worried.

In the morning, Philipe helped me pack the car. Jane finished cleaning the house. She did not want to leave a mess for the next tenants.

"Are you sure you don't want to bring your furniture?" I asked her. "We could always get a U-Haul truck."

She shook her head. "No."

Then we were ready to go.

Jane got into the car, buckled her seat belt. I turned to Philipe. Despite our differences, despite our disagreements, despite everything that had happened, I felt sad to be saying good-bye. We had been through a lot together, good and bad, and those experiences had created a bond between us that could never be broken. I looked at him, and his once-sharp eyes that were now not so sharp were wet at the edges.

"Come with us," I said.

He shook his head. "I'm not fading anymore. I'm coming back. In a few weeks I'll be stronger than ever. Don't worry about me."

I looked into his eyes, and I knew he knew that it was not true. An understanding passed between us.

"So where're you going to go?" he asked. "Back to Palm Springs? You might be able to recruit some new terrorists."

"That isn't me," I said. I gestured around me, at Thompson. "And this isn't me, either. I don't know what *is* me. That's what I need to find out. But you stay here. You start up the terrorists again. You fight the fights for our people. You keep the faith."

"I will," he said, and his voice was soft. "Take care."

I wanted to cry, and a tear did escape down my cheek before I could wipe it off. I looked at Philipe, and on impulse I gave him a quick hug. "*You* take care," I said.

"Yeah."

I got into the car.

"Good-bye," he said to Jane. "I haven't spent much time with you, but I feel like I know you anyway. Bob did nothing but talk about you the whole time we were traveling together. He loves you very much."

She smiled. "I know."

They shook hands.

I started the car, backed out of the driveway. I looked toward Philipe. He waved, smiled.

I waved back.

"Good-bye," I said.

He ran after us as we pulled away, and he jogged behind us as we pulled onto the road out of the city. He stood there, in the middle of the street, waving, as we left Thompson.

I honked back at him.

And we continued east until Philipe was lost to sight and Thompson was only a tiny irregular speck in the distance.

SEVENTEEN

We lived in motels while we looked for a home.

There was no property available in Laguna Beach, no uninhabited houses for sale, so we moved up the coast to Corona del Mar.

I suggested that, since we were invisible, we should just pick the house we liked and live there. We shouldn't worry about finding a place all to ourselves. There was no reason we couldn't find some big house and co-exist with the owners. We'd be like ghosts. It would be fun.

So we lived for a time with a rich couple, in a too-large mansion on a bluff overlooking the ocean. We took the guest room and the guest bathroom; we used the kitchen when the owners were gone or asleep.

But it was unsettling to live that close and that intimately with others, to be privy to their privacies. I felt uncomfortable seeing people when they thought they were alone, watching them scratch themselves and mutter to themselves and let their true feelings show on their faces, and we moved up the coast, to Pacific Palisades, finally finding a white elephant belonging to a has-been entertainer no longer able to keep up with the payments. It had been on the market for the past two years.

We moved in.

The days flowed from one to the next. We'd get up late, spend most of the day on the beach, read and watch TV at night. It was pleasant, I suppose, but I had to wonder: what was the point of it all? I had never really bought into Philipe's idea that we had a specific destiny, that fate had some plan in mind for us, but I had thought that my life would eventually lead somewhere, that it would have a purpose, that it would mean something.

And it didn't.

There was no point. We lived, we died, we tried to make the best of things in between. That was it. Period. No pattern had emerged from the series of disjointed events that were my existence because there was no pattern. It had made no difference to anyone that I had been born.

And then Jane announced that she was pregnant.

Overnight, *everything* changed.

This was the point, I thought. Maybe I would make a mark upon the world and maybe I wouldn't. But I would leave behind a child, and how that child turned out would depend on me and Jane. And maybe that child would make a significant mark upon the world. And maybe not. But maybe his or her child would. And whatever happened, however far down the line it might be, it would be because of me. I was a link in that chain.

I had a purpose.

I remembered Ralph telling me that the children of Ignored people were always Ignored themselves, and I told Jane, but she didn't care and neither did I. She said that she didn't like the lifestyle in Pacific Palisades, that she wanted our son or daughter to grow up in a different environment, and once again we moved up the coast, settling in a beachfront house in Carmel.

The first trimester passed, and Jane was showing, and both of us were happier than we'd ever been in our lives. We tried contacting her parents, but they could neither see us nor hear us, and though it was expected, that was a disappointment. But it didn't last long. There were too many other things to do, too many other things to be grateful for. We pored through books of names. We read manuals on parenting. We stole baby food and furniture and clothes.

We had been taking long daily walks along the beach, but when Jane began to get bigger and to tire more quickly and easily, she switched her allegiance to indoor exercise equipment. She told me to keep up the walks, however, and though I protested at first, I soon agreed. She said she didn't want me to balloon up to her size. And, she admitted, she wanted to have some time alone, without me always hovering around.

I understood.

I even grew to like my solitary walks along the beach.

And then it happened.

I had walked a mile or so down the sand and was on my way back when I saw a strange disturbance in the air some ways ahead. I jogged forward, squinting.

Flickering across the sand was the faint outline of a purple forest.

My heart leaped in my chest. I was cold all over, and I could not seem to catch my breath. Terrified, I ran back toward the house. I reached it, bolted up the steps.

Jane shrieked my name.

I had never heard her scream that way before, had never heard the sound of pure abject terror in her voice, but I heard it now and it caused my insides to squeeze painfully in a viselike cramp of fear. I doubled over, barely able to move for the pain, but I forced myself to keep running.

"Bob!!" she cried.

I dashed down the hall into the bedroom.

And there was the murderer.

He was on our bed. He had ripped off all of Jane's clothes and was straddling her, holding a knife to her neck. He had survived somehow. He was alive and had come back and had tracked us down.

He saw me out of the corner of his eye, and he turned to face me.

His zipper was down, his penis out.

He had an erection.

"Oh, here you are." He grinned. "I was wondering when you'd show up. I wanted you to watch your wife blow me." He reached next to him, picked up her torn panties, held them delicately to his nose, sniffing loudly. "Mmmmmm," he said. "Nice and fresh."

I took an angry step forward, and he pressed the knife against her skin, drawing blood. She screamed in pain.

"Don't try anything," he said. "Or I'll slit her fucking throat."

I stood in the doorway, paralyzed, not knowing what to do. In some hopeful, overly imaginative part of my brain, I thought that maybe Philipe had faded into that other world by now and that he would pop out of nowhere and save us and drag this guy back where he had come from.

But that didn't happen.

The murderer leaned forward. His erect penis pressed against Jane's closed lips. "Open your fucking mouth," he ordered. "Or I'm going to cut that baby out of your stomach."

She opened her mouth.

And he pushed his penis in.

Instinct took over. If I had thought about it, I would not have done what I did. I would have been afraid for the life of both Jane and our unborn child, and I would have done nothing. But I did not think. I saw his erection slide into Jane's mouth, and I reacted instantly, crazily. I lunged forward, leaped, and landed against his back, my hands on his head. He probably would have shoved the knife into Jane's throat, but at that second she bit down, hard, and he screamed in agony, temporarily losing control. I yanked back on his head, pulling him off Jane, and grabbed for the knife. It sliced through my palm, and I can't say that I didn't feel the pain, but I did not stop, and I twisted his neck as far as I could to the right until I heard it crack. His screams were silenced and he went limp, but he was still holding on to the knife, and Jane pulled it out of his hand and shoved it through his crotch. A wash of blood poured over her distended stomach, cascading onto the sheets.

She pulled it out and shoved it through his chest.

I rolled over, still twisting his neck, and both of us fell off the bed onto the floor.

I jumped to my feet, waiting for him to get up again, but this time he was dead.

Really dead.

I looked around, saw no orange grass, no purple trees, nothing from that other place.

Jane was still holding the knife, and she was shaking like a leaf, sobbing uncontrollably, looking down in horror at the blood that covered her body. She kept spitting, and a line of saliva dribbled from her lower lip.

I could feel the knife cut on my palm now, and my own blood was pouring around the side of my hand and dripping onto the floor, but I ignored the pain and walked over to her, gently removing the knife from her hand and lifting her to her feet, taking her into another bedroom.

"Are they sending people after us?" Jane cried. "Are they after us because I wouldn't let them take you?"

"No," I said, stroking her hair and helping her down onto the bed. "That's it. It's over. It was just that one guy. And he was after me. Not you."

"Maybe they'll send more of them."

"No," I said. "That's it."

I didn't know how I knew that that was true, but I did. One of Philipe's "hunches," maybe.

"It's all over," I said.

And for once I was right.

It was.

EIGHTEEN

I buried the body that afternoon.

I chopped it into pieces first.

The next day, we packed up what we owned and moved up to Mendocino.

NINETEEN

Four months later, Jane gave birth to a nine-pound boy.
We named him Philipe.

TWENTY

I think, sometimes, that I have been lucky. That I am fortunate to be Ignored. I may be average in my makeup, but I have not been average in my experiences. I have seen things normal men have never seen. I have done things normal men have never done. I have lived a good life.

It is a wonderful world in which we live. I have come to realize that. A world that is truly filled with miracles. And though my nature may preclude me from fully appreciating those miracles, at least I know that they exist.

And I try to teach that to my son.

I cannot be forgiven for the evil I have done in my life. For I have been evil. I believe that now. I know that now. Murder is an inherently evil act, no matter what the circumstances, no matter how convincing the rationalizations. Murder is evil no matter who does it or for what reason.

If there is a God, only He or She will be able to forgive me for what I have done.

The one thing I can say for myself is that I have learned from my mistakes. All that I have experienced and gone through has not been for nothing. The person I am now is not the person I once was.

So maybe there was a point to all of my journeys and side trips, to the meandering series of disconnected events that has been my life.

I still wonder what we are. Descendants of aliens? Genetic mutations? Government experiments? I

wonder, but I am not obsessed by the question the way
I once was. It is not the focus of my existence.

My son is.

Philipe is.

I don't know if I believe in God or the devil or
heaven or hell, but I can't help thinking that there is a
reason why we are the way we are. I do believe that we
were put on this earth for a purpose. I don't think that
purpose is merely to exist. I don't think that purpose is
to be noticed like everyone else. I don't think that purpose is test-marketing products for the mass consump-
tion of middle America.

But I don't know what the purpose might be.

Maybe I will find out someday.

Maybe my son will find out.

And what about that world that I glimpsed, that I
almost entered? I think about it often. What was it?
Heaven? Hell? Nirvana? Was it the place mystics and
gurus see when they meditate for so long that they supposedly lose all sense of individual self? Or was it
another dimension, existing concurrently with our
own? I have read and reread "The Great God Pan," and
somehow I can't buy that interpretation.

But I can't offer an alternate theory.

Whatever it is, whether its origin is mystical or scientific, the existence of that glimpsed world somehow
set to rest any anxieties I might have had about death
and the afterlife. I don't know that I was ever really
bothered or worried about what might happen after
death, but I must have been concerned at some level
because I feel lighter now, more at ease. I don't know
if there is something after death—no one can know for
certain—but I'm pretty sure there is, and it does not
frighten me.

We still live here in Mendocino, by the ocean. In the
mornings I write, while Jane watches Philipe and
works in her garden.

We spend the afternoons together.

It is a good life, and we are happy, but I sense even

now that we may eventually want more. I think some-times of what James told me in Thompson, about there being a country of the Ignored, a land across the sea, an island or a peninsula where people like us live free and peacefully in a sovereign nation of our own.

And I think that it would be nice to raise children there.

And I stare at the water and I think to myself that someday, perhaps, I will learn to sail.

DON'T MISS THESE
OTHER TALES OF UNSPEAKABLE
HORROR BY BENTLEY LITTLE
AVAILABLE FROM SIGNET. . . .

A New Class of Terror

UNIVERSITY

Jim Parker, editor of UC Brea's newspaper, did not want to come back to school this semester. And Faith Pullen was wary of taking the job at the library. They were right. Because Something Evil has invaded the California campus once praised for its high honors. Now violent death is crowding out pep rallies for space on the front page, leaving streaks of bloody ink in its wake. And one terrifying question remains in the minds of all: Who in hell can stop it?

**"Absolutely the best . . . A master
of the macabre."
—Stephen King**

Old Friends, New Horrors . . .

DOMINION

Dion Semele is a teenager trying to make friends in a new school and meet the girl of his dreams. But something is happening inside him: a powerful force is struggling to escape. His sleep is disturbed by dreams of a past world that seeks to control him. And Penelope Daneam is smart and pretty and trying to be normal, despite her unusual family. Since birth she has been cared for by a sisterhood of women who own a local Napa winery. It is here that Dion and Penelope will meet their true fate. Not as lovers, but as catalysts for a reign of incredible terror.

"Bentley Little does an electrifying job of keeping the reader in suspense."
—*West Coast Review of Books*